Novels by
MacDonald Harris

ᔑ

Private Demons

Mortal Leap

Trepleff

Bull Fire

The Balloonist

Yukiko

Pandora's Galley

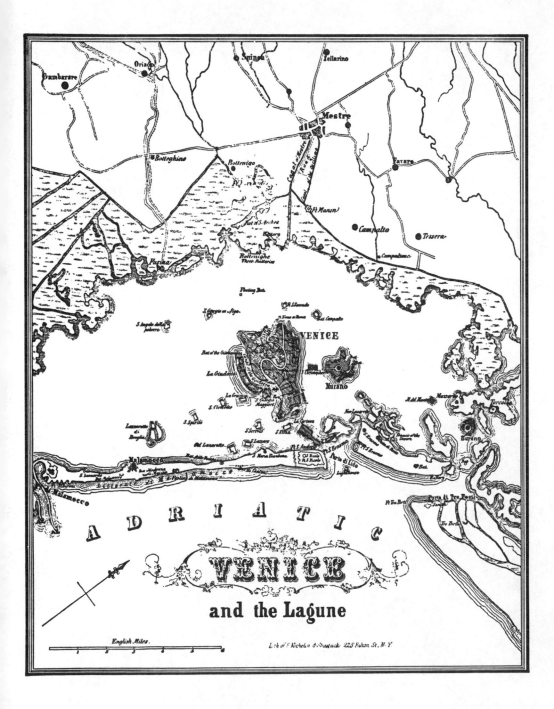

VENICE
and the Lagune

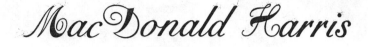

MacDonald Harris

Pandora's
Galley

Harcourt Brace Jovanovich
New York and London

Requests for permission to make copies
of any part of the work should be mailed to:
Permissions, Harcourt Brace Jovanovich, Inc.
757 Third Avenue, New York, N.Y. 10017

Translations from Homer in the text are adapted
from Albert Cook, translator,
Homer: The Odyssey. A New Verse Translation.
New York: W. W. Norton & Co., 1967.

Printed in the United States of America

Library of Congress Cataloging in Publication Data

Heiney, Donald W   1921–
Pandora's galley.

I. Title.
PZ4.H4687Pan [PS3558.E458]   813'.5'4   78–22254
ISBN 0–15–170802–9

First edition

B C D E

For Sergio and Alberta

I veri amici xe pochi

Saecula ni pereant, decisaque cesset origo,
Et repetat primum massa soluta chaos,
Ad genios fetura duos concessit et olim
Commissum geminis fratribus illud opus
Cum morte invicti pugnant genialibus armis,
Naturam reparant, perpetuantque genus.
Non mortale mori, non quod cadit esse caducum,
Non a stirpe hominem deperiisse sinunt.
Militat adversus Lachesin sollersque renodat
Mentula Parcarum fila resecta manu.

Lest earthly life pass away and the process of generation be cut off, and material existence dissolved, returned to primordial chaos, propagation was made the charge of twin genii, and the act itself assigned to twin brothers. They fight unconquered against death with their life-giving weapons, renew our nature and perpetuate our kind. They will not allow what is perishable to perish, nor what dies to be wholly owed to death, nor mankind to wither utterly at the root. The phallus wars against Lachesis and carefully rejoins the vital threads severed by the hands of the Fates.

—Bernardus Silvestris, *Cosmographia* 2.14

Pandora's Galley

AT THE TIME WHEN THE

At the time when the French invaded Venice, or tried to, there were a good many foreigners serving in the Navy of the Serenissima. One of these was an American, so-called, named Malcolm Langrish. I first came across his name in a document I was reading in the Museo Correr, in July of 1975. It appeared that he had taken a certain part in the events of 1797 which I had come to Venice to study, and, although he was a minor figure, it seemed that he had served in a curious way as a sort of pivot around which the others had turned. There were some suggestions, also, that he differed a little in his character from the ordinary sea-captain of his time, and might be a person of greater interest than he seemed at first. It struck me only that he was a colorful figure who might be worth investigating, some time later, if I had the opportunity. I made a note on a scrap of paper, I believe; but if I did I've lost it.

The text I was examining was a rare volume: the *Raccolta di documenti inediti della Rivoluzione e Caduta della Repubblica di Venezia*, published anonymously in Florence in 1800 but actually, as I knew, the work of Cristoforo Tentori. The reference to Langrish was contained in a report from the Inquisitors of State to the Senate on the events of April 20 and the days following. It indicated him simply as the captain of the *Pandora,* the vessel involved in the engagement at the Lido, and was somewhat am-

1

biguous as to whether his behavior on this occasion was to be commended or not. Probably the Inquisitors had not quite made up their minds on this point. I suspected the name was misspelled; probably it was really Langridge or Langritch. But by some miracle the document had it right.

Whether or not I saved the scrap of paper, the name stuck in my mind, and soon I began to run across other references to it. From these I gradually pieced together a notion of who Langrish was. Not much is known about his early years. He came from the town of Fairhaven, just across the Acushnet River from New Bedford in Massachusetts. I have not been able to find out very much about his family. His ancestors seem to have emigrated from St. Mary's Isle in Kirkcudbright Bay, in southwestern Scotland; the very place where John Paul Jones, by coincidence, later carried off a celebrated raid, or act of piracy, as you prefer. (He landed and robbed the manor house of its silver.)

Our Captain Langrish was not so celebrated as this, or so patriotic. During the War of Independence, in fact, the Langrish family got into trouble with the local citizenry, for some reason, and found itself accused of harboring Tory sentiments. I suspect that this suspicion was not justified, or at least that the truth was more complicated. Malcolm's father, a gentleman farmer of somewhat eccentric tendencies, was an amateur scholar and a reader of Locke and Montesquieu. By nature he was thoroughly rational. These readings, which led others to revolutionary principles, led him to a skepticism of everything, including revolution. When the momentous events of 1775 began, therefore, he was prevented by his temperament from making any conspicuous exhibition of the strained enthusiasm then current. This probably aroused the ire of the less fortunate in the countryside, all the more so because most of them owed him money. At any rate, chased off his farm by the Sons of Liberty, who set fire to his barn, barbecued his milch-cow, and violated the maid-servant, he removed with his family to Boston. With the fall of Boston to the rebels (March 17, 1776) the family moved again, to Nova Scotia, a part of America that remained loyal to the Crown in those tumultuous times. In Halifax the family disappears from history, and the story henceforth is that of the son Malcolm.

Malcolm, the younger of two sons (the other was called Sholto), was born in 1757 and therefore a youth of eighteen when the war broke out. He had a reasonably good education, as far as I could gather, having been taught Greek and Latin by a certain Father Dottle, the vicar of the church down the lane, an Anglican gone wrong and hopelessly lost in the Lotus-Land of Hellenism. He also learned to sail at an early age, in a skiff on Buzzards Bay. At the age of fourteen he made his first voyage to the Caribbean, in a sloop in the charge of his older brother. They went to Havana for sugar, and to Jamaica for coffee and rum. He made several more of these summer voyages in the family sloop, the last, when he was seventeen, under his own command. When the family removed to Halifax he took service as a midshipman on a British frigate; not out of any particular political sentiment, evidently, but simply because going to sea was a trade he understood. He served in the Royal Navy until 1785, rising to the rank of sailing-master. He was passed over for higher promotion because of his colonial origins and his lack of gentle blood. He resigned his commission and took French service briefly, at one point commanding a mortar-brig in the action at the Scheldt. The next time he turns up, in 1788, he is in Russia, commanding a small frigate, the *Skoryi,* in the Battle of the Liman against the Turks. In this he distinguished himself well enough to receive a George's Cross of the second order from the Empress. With the end of the Black Sea campaign, he seems to have passed briefly through Turkey, then went to Candia, the Morea, Corfu, and finally Venice, where he took service with the Navy of the Serenissima in 1790. The *Pandora* was the last of the several small vessels he commanded in the seven years that followed. She is described in various documents as a galeotta or a chebeck, that is, a small lateen-rigged vessel for work in the shallow water of the lagoon, designed to be propelled either by oars or by sail. These details interested me because, among other things, I am an amateur naval historian and an amateur sailor. I am afraid I am an amateur at everything, including story-telling, so I can only proceed in this business as best I know how.

But the real event, in my somewhat haphazard investigation of these matters, was my discovery of Langrish's diaries. These I found, quite unexpectedly, in the archives of the Massachusetts State Historical Society in Boston, in the late fall or early winter of 1975. They consisted of six octavo volumes bound in calfskin, along with some loose papers which the Society had preserved in folders, without any particular attention to chronology or sequence. In an hour or two of reading I quickly grasped two things: first of all that the diaries, while curious and in some respects almost unreadable, were of undoubted importance; and second that it was impossible to deal with their intricacies while sitting at the uncomfortable table in the reading room of the Society. I arranged to have the diaries photocopied, and went away with about seventeen pounds of facsimiles on whitish glossy paper.

There followed a month or more of reading the diaries. These materials gave me an entirely new picture of the man. I saw now what the Inquisitors had meant by hinting at his eccentricity. The diaries contained very few concrete references to incidents or personalities, and many of these were inscrutable. There were financial accounts, notes on navigation, observations on the probable nature of the Deity and the opinions thereon of the Congregational Church, the Church of England, the Swedenborgians, and the Sufi mystics of the eleventh century, and inscriptions in an indecipherable cursive that I identified, after some difficulty, as classic Greek. The most personal entries in the diaries might be described as ontological soul-searchings. Langrish seems to have had serious doubts, from time to time, whether he existed. He also had a considerable interest in philology. Entire pages of the diaries were covered with such things as conjugations of irregular verbs, in languages that ranged from French and Venetian to Hebrew. On another page he had signed his name forty-three times, all in different styles.

Decidedly he was not an ordinary sea-captain of the eighteenth century. I returned to Europe in early 1976, and spent a week or two in Paris. There I found a single reference to Langrish in the Bibliothèque Nationale: a letter from Villetard, the secretary of the French Legation in Paris, in which "Langriche" (the French could not spell so well as the Inquisitors) was described as "a dubious and dangerous personage, perhaps an agent of the English." Since it was not convenient to have the document reproduced, I merely copied the reference. I ought to have copied the whole letter, and wished later that I had. But the name of Villetard—this was the first time I had encountered it—was a valuable hint, and one that proved useful to me later.

In February I was back in Venice with Ann, in my old quarters in Ca' Muti Baglioni, near Campo San Cassan. I still had the vague idea of writing a naval history of the Republic, ending in 1797. This sent me to the Museo Storico Navale, near the Arsenal, and to the Archivio di Stato at the Frari. In the Archives, on a typical gray and gloomy Venetian day in March, I happened to encounter the obscure but ubiquitous name again. I was reading a letter of memorandum delivered to the Venetian Senate by Junot, a special envoy from the Army of Italy commanded by General Bonaparte, and dated 8 Germinal An V, that is, April 28, 1797. The gist of it was that the General in Chief of the Army of Italy, enraged at the atrocities committed against his troops on Venetian soil, and against peaceable vessels of French flag in Venetian waters, demanded an indemnity of six million francs, the release of all political prisoners, the surrender of the funds of French émigrés held in Venetian banks, the removal of the Senator and Procurator Francesco Pesaro from office, and the arrest of a long list of persons, beginning with the three Inquisitors of State and continuing through Pizzamano, the commander of the Castel Sant'Andrea which secured the entrance to the port, and a number of lesser military figures. The last of these was "l'infâme et sanguinaire renégat et mercenaire Langriche, Américain, capitaine du malfamée frégate Pandore." Infamous and bloodthirsty—these adjectives, finally, decided me to write the story of Malcolm Langrish.

IMAGINE, THEN, THE <u>PANDORA</u>

Imagine, then, the *Pandora,* a small trim vessel eighty feet or so on deck, lying on the flat surface of the lagoon, her sails hanging limply. Astern and a little on the larboard quarter the town of Chioggia lies as though floating on the water. The houses in their various colors—pink, light blue, yellow, dark brownish-red— seem to shimmer a little at the lower edges where they balance on their own reflections. A campanile sticks up out of the houses, not quite straight. In 1797 everything looks much as it does now. The sun is already warming the lagoon a little. It is nine o'clock.

Ahead, over the bow, the long sand-spit of the Lido runs away as far as the eye can see, separating the lagoon from the Adriatic Sea. There is a channel hugging close along the Lido on the lagoon side, marked with a crooked row of stakes stuck in the mud every so often. Beyond the stakes the water is marshy and shallow for six miles or more away to the Terraferma, which can be seen as a hazy line on the horizon. A few creeks and inlets meander through these shoals, but they are shallow and unmarked, and for the most part only the local fishermen can find their way through them. In the channel ahead is a beacon: a cluster of pilings bound with chains at the top, and surmounted with a lantern and an image of the Virgin. The beacon approaches only very slowly; the *Pandora* is barely moving in the faint breeze from the north. This Tramon-

tana is the last of the night wind. It will soon die away completely
as the sun warms the plain behind the lagoon. Then the Scirocco
will come up, and by afternoon freshen into a stiff hot breeze with
the smell of Africa to it. In between, however, there will be
calm—Pacienza, as the Venetians say.

The Lido at this point is only a few yards wide. Along its
seaward side, protecting the lagoon from the winter storms, is a
wall of white Istrian stone, the so-called Murazzi, completed only
a few years earlier in 1782. It is the last great public work of the
Republic, and in fact nothing of any importance is to be built in
Venice after it, unless you count the railway station. The quarter-
deck of the *Pandora* where Malcolm is standing is only a little
lower than this wall, and over it he can catch glimpses of the upper
works of a brig. It is a mile or so out to sea, working its way along
parallel to the Lido under full sail except for a clewed-up course.
From the foremast a pennant hangs straight down in the almost
windless air, and at the main gaff is another patch of limp colored
cloth. Yet, although there is no more wind in the open sea than
there is in the lagoon, in some way the brig is making progress. A
half an hour ago she was a little astern of the *Pandora*. Now she is
abeam, or even a little on the bow. This annoys Malcolm, because
the *Pandora* with her fine lines and lateen rig ought to be the faster
vessel, above all in light air; or in no wind at all, which is irrational.
He stares out from under his hat-brim at the foot of the mainsail,
as though trying to decide whether a slight trembling that appears
there from time to time might be fixed by tightening a bolt-rope.
He does not think that it would. In fact, the more he stares, the
less he is able to convince himself that the mainsail itself is more
than a slightly exasperating phantom, or a film on the eyes. From
his readings in the philosophers of antiquity he has learned to
doubt all—even to doubt that he himself exists. Is not this deck on
which he stands a dream—the yellowish and slightly oily lagoon a
dream—his philosophy itself a dream? What difference can it
make to the Eternal Plan whether the wind blows at a lesser or a
greater velocity, or whether this vessel moves over the water or
not? If all is not a dream—assuming that the universe is
purposeful—then there must be some use for it all. But he will be
Dangled if he can see any use of it. He can not see why it should
not be a dream. If there were any use for it—if there was a
probability of it all tending toward anything—then he might believe. But—

The crew of Schiavoni—mercenaries like Malcolm himself, Istrians and Dalmatians from the Venetian provinces across the Adriatic—lie in the shade under the bulwarks, examining themselves for fleas, playing number-games with their fingers, dozing, telling indecent stories. They are a spooky-looking bunch. In spite of their individual peculiarities they all look alike in some way; they are lean greenish-colored men with faces like pug-dogs, and no hips. Fioravanti, the mate, paces nervously back and forth on the quarter-deck. And there is someone else, Malcolm knows without turning around. By his shoulder and slightly behind him is a large shadow, smelling faintly of something like cloves and musk—a person who in some way gives the impression of an absence rather than a presence, until he speaks. The voice is a rich full-chested basso, with rumbles at the bottom.

Mark Anthony: "Dat Frenchmon he moving well, Copn."

Malcolm: "Yeaop."

Mark Anthony: "He keep on like dat, he going to beat us to de pass."

Malcolm doesn't bother to reply. He is familiar with these elliptical forms of denigration, since he has known Mark Anthony for most of his life. This large outline, looking something like a rain-cloud, simply appeared on the dock in Kingston Town and climbed aboard as though the sloop belonged to him, throwing his sea-bag down the scuttle into the cabin. "I a sailor, Mon," he rumbled to Sholto. "You need a good sailor, to work dis pretty sloop of yours." Whereupon he turned to and began seizing a loose rope-end, with an old needle he extracted somewhere from his person. Malcolm's brother he called Mon to the end, although Malcolm himself, out of some inverted and slightly ironic respect, he began calling Copn from the time he was seventeen and old enough to take charge of the sloop himself. One would think that, since they have wandered around the world together for a quarter of a century, Mark Anthony might be some sort of companion to Malcolm. But Mark Anthony is not sociably inclined. He is sufficient unto himself. He has his own ideas about things. He is frequently arrogant, sometimes sulky, and very few things meet completely with his approval, including Malcolm himself. To make a good story, he is probably descended from some African king or other.

Well, Mark Anthony observes that the captain is impassive. He is not going to do anything. If anybody is going to do anything, it is up to Mark Anthony himself. He seizes the main shroud, pulls himself up, and begins climbing with surprising agility for a man of fifty. There are no ratlines; this is impossible because there is only one shroud. But the shroud has a turk's-head braided around it every three feet or so for a handhold, and with the aid of these Mark Anthony goes up as swiftly and easily as though it were a stairway, using his feet as well as his hands; for he is barefoot. When he reaches the masthead he perches for a moment on the yard, looking out over the sea-wall. Then, wrapping his leg around the shroud, he comes sliding back down and drops to the deck like a dancer.

Mark Anthony: "Copn, dat Frenchmon, he putting out sweeps."

Malcolm: "I expect."

Mark Anthony: "He anxious to get to de pass before nightfall. He go on like he is, he going to be dere before us."

Malcolm: "The Scirocco will come up in a while."

Mark Anthony: "By de time Scirocco come up, he be so far ahead we never cotch him."

Malcolm: "I'm familiar with the wind in these parts. Who do you think is running this vessel? Will you tell me that? Are you running it or is somebody else?"

Mark Anthony: "You running it, Copn, and to tell de truf you not running it very well. You better instruct dese Slabs to get out dere oars and row, or you never going to see dat Frenchmon again."

But the Captain is apparently deaf and also paralyzed, or turned into a stone. He stares out at the line of stakes ahead, his hat jammed over his eyes and his mouth clamped shut like a molested bivalve.

Mark Anthony turns to the Greek cook, who pretends at least to understand a little English. "I knowed him since he fifteen years old and he always dat way. He very decisive. Once he decide to do de wrong ting, he never change his mind. Before he use dem sweeps, he prefer to be cut up in little bits. He a sailing mon, see. He vain bout his sailing bility. He full of vanity. He tink he cotch anyting by sailing."

Malcolm: "Full of vanity, am I?"

Mark Anthony: "You full of vanity like a young girl."

Malcolm: "Oh, you know about young girls too, do you? It

seems there are no limits to your vast erudition. You're a regular walking encyclopedia, I can see that."

The basso subsides to a series of little insect-like clicks, almost inaudible. "You magine I don't know what a cyclopedia is, Copn. But cyclopedia, he some kind of book. What good books do you, I ask you dat? You run a book up dis mast, see if he make dis *Pandora* go faster."

Well, Malcolm should put out sweeps. That is exactly what they are on board for, stowed away in their place under the bulwarks, to move the vessel in the light and capricious winds of the lagoon. If he doesn't use them it is for two reasons. The first is that calm weather puts him in a foul mood. The second is exactly that cited by Mark Anthony, that he is vain about his ability to make the galeotta move under sail alone. He is a deep-water man—a New Englander. He scorns oars and sweeps, which are for mud-sailors. If he can not make the *Pandora* move under sail he will not make her move at all. So, after glancing out to seaward at the brig, and muttering to himself a few more times, he goes down into the tweendecks, gets into his berth, and reads Homer to quiet his nerves,

> "Ανδρα μοι ἔννεπε, Μοῦσα, πολύτροπον, ὃς μάλα πολλὰ
> πλάγχθη, ἐπεὶ Τροίης ἱερὸν πτολίεθρον ἔπερσε·
> πολλῶν δ' ἀνθρώπων ἴδεν ἄστεα καὶ νόον ἔγνω,
> πολλὰ δ' ὅ γ' ἐν πόντῳ πάθεν ἄλγεα ὃν κατὰ θυμόν,
> ἀρνύμενος ἥν τε ψυχὴν καὶ νόστον ἑταίρων.
> ἀλλ' οὐδ' ὣς ἑτάρους ἐρρύσατο, ἱέμενός περ·
> αὐτῶν γὰρ σφετέρῃσιν ἀτασθαλίῃσιν ὄλοντο."

"Tell me, Muse, about the man of many wiles, who wandered off afar when he had sacked Troy's holy citadel; he saw the cities of many men, and he knew their thought; on the ocean he suffered many pains within his heart, striving for his life and his companions' return. But he did not save his companions, though he wanted to: they lost their own lives because of their recklessness."

In short, an unsatisfactory hero. We may wish him to be a hero, but it is difficult for Malcolm to do this because he can not conform to a pattern or standard which has never come into his head. Even if this were possible, he doesn't have the requisite qualities. First of all he is too old for the role. A hero of this kind of yarn ought to be, ideally, about twenty-three. Then the ladies will take an interest in the matter. Malcolm is forty. He is tall and rectangular, giving the impression of being built out of square corners, like a barn door. He has a broad sun-burned face, with a look—not puzzled exactly but preoccupied—as though he were trying to untangle some knot inside, about an inch behind his brow. His hands are large and gnarled. All this is in his favor. But there are numerous scars on his body, including a saber cut on the bridge of his nose and tapering away across the cheek. This scar gives him a ruffianly air that, although quite inconsistent with his character, has proved useful at times. Still it is not really pretty.

Furthermore he disdains to take any care at all with his physical person. He ties his hair with an old piece of spun-yarn in the back; he doesn't like wigs and almost never wears one. His usual garb is an old blue coat, a battered tricorne, a pair of faded and stained buff breeches, white stockings (no stockings at all at sea), and boots of Russian leather. His cuffs and collar are sometimes not very clean. His fingernails even less, and some of them usually broken. And there are certain other habits. For example he blows his nose with thumb and forefinger; something no hero would ever do, no Achilles, no Hamlet, not even Satan in the council of Fallen Angels. Useless to argue that everyone did in the eighteenth century, except for fops who wore lavender-scented handkerchiefs hanging gracefully from their sleeves—or that practical seamen and men of action have something other to do than bother with the tender sensibilities of readers in another age— Malcolm blows his nose with his fingers. This behavior will never do.

Then there are his Politicks. A hero can have Politicks or not have them, but if he has them they have to be of the right sort. Malcolm, having been chased out of his country and deprived of his birthright by a revolution, has a deep dislike of disorder, even in the name of progress. To the objection that it is impossible to make an omelet without breaking eggs, he would reply that it is even harder to make eggs out of an omelet. He accepts the injustice of the Venetian Republic because it is at least an orderly injustice. Out of expediency, because the sea is his trade, he served in the Royal Navy at a time when Britain was at war with his own country. And so on. All this can hardly endear him to a patriotic readership. Still, if it hadn't been for these circumstances, he would not be wandering around the world like a lost soul, taking service with the Russians, with the Bey of Tunis, with the Venetian Republic, with anybody else who could make use of him, instead of staying home in Fairhaven, Massachusetts, and tending to his business. So if his Politicks had been correct there wouldn't have been any story. But what will you? History is a refractory substance to deal with, hard and yet brittle, like glass. It is transparent: anyone can see right through it by opening a history-book. Glass can magnify things, or illuminate them, but it can only do it by bending light. It is a very difficult thing, bending light. Try doing it with your fingers.

When Malcolm comes out on deck again it is about noon. The Scirocco has come up now and the *Pandora* is moving along well. The water slips by under the rail with a yeasty foaming sound. He puts on his hat, in a characteristic way—first setting it on his head and then slapping it down in front to the level of his eyebrows. The hat ends up cocked forward at an angle, shading his eyes and giving him a truculent and slightly bellicose air, since he is obliged to turn up his chin in order to be able to see. He stares out ahead over the bowsprit. Along the channel ahead are various objects: clumps of trees, a ruined church, a sand-bar with some mysterious erection on it, perhaps an abandoned beacon. All these things shimmer, fracture, and leak sideways through the effect of the sun on the water. There is a smell, not of the sea, but of mud and rotten vegetation. A few yards astern something that might be a piece of white paper follows along juddering in the lucid air, the air in which colors are magnified and objects seem suspended as in a liquid, the air of Canaletto's paintings. The butterfly, wavering off now to one side and now to the other, follows the small vessel as an albatross might follow a ship in the real sea. Everything is miniature: the ship is miniature, the sea is only thirty miles long, the city in the distance is miniature compared to Rome or Paris. At any place along the channel a man, with a little effort, could pitch a stone over onto the Murazzi. The *Pandora* is steered with a tiller, like a small boat.

Malcolm: "Watch where you're going there, you Bulgarian."

The helmsman comes alert, pushes at the long beam of the tiller, and veers away from the edge of the channel where the *Pandora* is beginning to stir up a line of greenish mud. He gets her going down the channel again, between the sand-spit on one side and the line of stakes on the other.

Some huts and clumps of houses come into view along the sand-spit. San Pietro in Volta passes by to starboard. For a while the brig offshore is hidden behind the town: a cluster of pastel house-fronts, a dusty piazza, a brick church with arches in white Istrian stone. Then the houses straggle away, the sand-spit comes to an end, and the Malamocco pass opens out slowly to the right. The brig comes out from behind the sand-spit and is fully visible for the first time. Malcolm gets out his glass and steadies it against the mizzen-shroud. The brig's topsails are filled now; the pennant at the forepeak turns and snakes lazily. The flag at the gaff can clearly be made out as the tricolor. Her bottom is foul; he can see grass at the water-line as she rolls. There are several patches in her foresail. The gun-ports are closed and it is hard to make them out. There is no sign that the brig has noticed the small lateen-rigged vessel following along parallel to her behind the sand-spit. She seems to be sailing along in her sleep. Malcolm shuts the glass with a clap.

Fioravanti waits for him to say something. But the captain is silent. This makes Fioravanti bite his lip and pace around on the quarter-deck. It is not for him to speak first! Yet he is slightly offended in his amour-propre. He is the mate after all, and the captain might discuss things with him a little, if only to demonstrate to the crew that he, Fioravanti, is taken into confidence. Still he is too proud to show the slightest sign of this breach of courtesy. He is a Venetian after all—the only Venetian on board in these times when the Republic prefers to hire foreigners to man its navy. And that counts for something. The blood of an ancient sea-people flows in his veins, a race that for half a millennium ruled the Levant. His skin is the color of pale sherry, with a translucence to it that makes it seem lighter than it is. There is a slightly sleepy air about him, a trace of the Byzantine; indolent, and yet nervous and alert. His eye-sockets are hollow, with the eyes set in the mottled shadows that are a Venetian characteristic even in children, suggesting a touch of depravity or knowing vice. As a matter of fact, if Fioravanti has a secret it is that he is a devout Catholic, which is not fashionable among Venetian men, and might expose him to ridicule if made public. Malcolm knows this but does not reveal it, neither has he told Fioravanti that he knows. Fioravanti is morose and distant. He is a man of gentle reserve. He dresses neatly. He is sensitive and easily offended, but friendly if he thinks the other person is friendly. He knows Italian well, a little French, and believes that he speaks English. But he prefers to speak Venetian, softer and more subtle than the flamboyant and assertive, rather operatic Italian. Finally he can no longer contain himself.

Fioravanti: "Cossa ga, Sior Capitàn?"

Malcolm: "Twelve nines. And what looks like a swivel-gun on the foc's'le."

Fioravanti: "Maladeto."

Mark Anthony: "Dey twelves, Copn. French brig of dat class, she have a dozen twelve-pounders."

Malcolm: "You know all about it, do you?"

He is cheerful. He feels better now that the wind has come up. He doesn't really care whether they are nine-pounders or twelves. Let them be eighteens! As long as the wind holds. It is only ten miles now to the Lido pass, and the *Pandora* is slipping along with white water boiling under her stern.

Fioravanti agrees with Mark Anthony. They are probably twelves. Big guns for such a small ship. His eye roves pessimistically over the six-pounders on the *Pandora*'s main-deck and the long nines on the bow. He paces the quarter-deck.

The argument, leaking off the quarter-deck and down the ladder, passes down to the Schiavoni on the main-deck. They begin debating whether the Frenchman has twelve-pounders or nines. Some think one, some the other. One offers the opinion that the guns would not be in pounds at all, since the French have changed the system of weights and measurements since the Revolution. It would be in kilograms. Another doesn't know what a kilogram is. A kilogram is a pound, you blockhead, only that's what the French call it.

From this they pass to Revolutions in general, and then to the subject of La Mèrega, where the captain came from. The Schiavoni are not strong on geography. La Mèrega, that's far away, they are sure of that. It is farther than Milan. Farther than Genoa. It is an island in the sea. One says it is an island in the sea, another that it is the same as the Azores. One that it is another name for England.

Another: "Cogione, no sai gnente de gnente. La Mèrega is

across the Western Ocean. It's bigger than Rome, bigger than all of Italy."

This one is on the right track. It was discovered by a Genoese, he adds.

This provokes the first intervention of Viscovich, an old seaman with a large broken nose that gives him a certain air of authority.

Viscovich: "Bah. The Genoese are nothing. We beat them right here at Chioggia, in the time of Pisani." (This was back in the fourteenth century.) "There was a captain, Pisani. They had him in prison, you know. The Signoria locked him up because they didn't like the look of his face. But they had to let him out to fight the Genoese. He beat their asses for them. Son merda, i Genoesi. The Genoese are shits."

Still, the other points out, it was a Genoese who discovered La Mèrega.

The Scirocco is blowing smartly now, raising a few whitecaps on the lagoon. The *Pandora* is charging along like a young horse, tossing her head slightly. She needs a careful hand on the tiller. She is shallow and light, a thing not meant for heavy weather. If it starts to blow a little she will quickly put her rail down in the water, and then her deck; and then, perhaps, her masts. Malcolm whips his head around at the helmsman now and then, to try to catch him napping. But the fellow is gripping the tiller with a great seriousness, no doubt feigned. Malcolm goes back to looking out at the glaring water ahead from under his hat, as though from under a porch. On the bow are two small islands, San Servolo and San Lazzaro. They approach rapidly. First they are only two clumps of trees and some roof-tops wavering on the horizon ahead. Then the low sea-walls with some spidery docks come up out of the water and slide past. A curious monk on San Lazzaro, standing by the sea-wall and absent-mindedly scratching his groin through his robe, gazes out at the passing galeotta.

San Lazzaro slips by, and the city gradually comes into view from behind the island. It is only two miles or so away under the lee rail, shimmering slightly on the water. San Marco is directly abeam. The many cupolas of the Basilica are like inverted chalices, complexly worked and chased in gold, slightly in need of cleaning. Near it the Campanile rears up, with the angel at the top catching the sun. Sticking out of the water nearby are the lesser churches:

San Zaccaria, the Pietà, San Giorgio Maggiore with its steeple in imitation of the Campanile but wearing a green dunce-cap to show it is not so important. At this time of day, the hour of the Siesta, the wide basin before San Marco is almost empty. A few gondolas crawl by like black insects. There is a barge with a reddish sail.

Helmsman: "Eh. Venecia."

He yawns, scratches himself, and stares at the city with a furtive lasciviousness, as though it were a beautiful woman. It is hot. He lets the tiller go for an instant, stands on one foot and then the other to take off his breeches, and sends them sailing across the deck. Since he was previously barefoot, and naked to the waist, he stands grinning at the city in nothing but his drawers and an old hat with an undulating brim. The *Pandora,* left to herself, begins to slide off a little toward the line of stakes on the left.

Malcolm: "Hey, look sharp. Look where the hell you're going. You Sheepherder. You Bulgarian. You Stivalone."

All these are synonyms, implying that he satisfies his amorous impulses by putting the sheep's hind legs in his boots.

Malcolm: "Are you on a sight-seeing tour or are you a helmsman? Steady as you go. Nothing to leeward."

Helmsman: "Gnente a sotovento."

Like the other Schiavoni he is an odd-looking fellow—a long neck, a lean and hipless lower body, and a greenish cast to his skin like mother-of-pearl. The wavy hat casts a shadow over his face. He attempts a scowl, but it is too pleasant in the warm sunshine. It ends by his showing his teeth, quite harmlessly, as though he wants to demonstrate how white they are.

GOING BY TO STARBOARD

Going by to starboard is the last of the Lido villages, San Nicolò. Beyond it the sand-spit widens into a broad island dotted with clumps of trees. There is a small pine-forest, then some scattered oaks, then a cluster of cypresses marking the Hebrew cemetery. Because of the trees the brig will be invisible now until she comes into view in the pass.

Malcolm needs to know what the God-dangled tide is doing. He stares at one of the stakes going by at the edge of the channel. From the ripples he sees that the slack water has passed and the tide is beginning to flood. This will slow him, but he still doesn't want to get to the pass too soon.

Malcolm: "Slack all."

Mark Anthony: "What you doing, Copn?"

Malcolm: "Running this Flaming vessel. Smartly, you baboons!"

Padding about in their bare feet, the Schiavoni let the sheets run and belay them again on the pins. The three big lateens belly out and crinkle, fluttering at the edges. With sheets slacked the *Pandora* barely makes headway against the tide. She goes slowly on down the channel, toward the pass and the open sea. The Schiavoni gaze out over the bow and swing their arms impatiently. For some reason, perhaps sheer animal spirits, one of them emits a brassy yell, a kind of a yip.

Across the channel from San Nicolò is the Castel Sant'Andrea, the only defense of the port in these days when the military establishment of the Republic has been allowed to fall into decline. A flag turns lazily on a staff, but there is no other sign of life. The fort is manned by Militia under the command of Domenico Pizzamano, a patrician general from an ancient and prominent family. The Militia were called up only a few weeks before, when it became apparent that these French, heady with the wine of Revolution and setting everything at odd's ends, were headed in the direction of Venice. So far they—the Militia—have had no opportunity to distinguish themselves.

Fioravanti: "Ah. Maladeto. There she is."

Around the trees at the end of the Lido appears a bowsprit with a pair of narrow jibs; then the foremast and bow of the brig; then the entire vessel. She has turned and is running directly into the lagoon before the wind. She rolls slowly in the long swell from the sea. The ports on the larboard side are open now and the guns are visible. Mark Anthony was right; they are twelve-pounders.

At the sight of the brig only a mile away the Schiavoni seem to be unable to contain themselves. They begin emitting sharp cries, barks, and Dionysian yelps. An old waistcoat comes off, and a tarboosh sort of a hat, and both go overboard. More clothes fly in the air. The Schiavoni run back and forth on the deck, barking and yelling. One of them stops to stare with a corpse-like fixity at the brig, and snaps his teeth at it.

Malcolm: "Ready about. Wake up, you Paphlagonians. Stand by sheets."

The *Pandora* tacks slowly in the channel. The brig, with both courses clewed up now and foretopsail backed, has made a broad turn to the west and stopped almost dead in the water, a quarter of a mile to seaward of the Castel Sant'Andrea.

On top of the fort is the crimson banner of Saint Mark with its winged lion, flying in the Venetian manner from a stave so that it hangs down like a window-curtain. On a flagstaff next to it, rather lazily and by fits and jerks, two flags go up, a black over a white: a signal that the port is closed.

The three flags lift slowly in the afternoon breeze and are clearly visible now. In any case both Malcolm and Pizzamano, and presumably the Frenchman, know that a decree of the Signoria of April 17, three days ago, forbade "the entry into the ports of the

Estuary, including those of Chioggia, Malamocco, and San Nicolò, to foreign vessels of any nature armed for war." So the black and white flags are redundant; a rhetorical flourish of Pizzamano, so to speak, to precede the more important dialogue of fire and iron that is about to begin. The brig, declining to enter into this contest of flags, still shows only her tricolor.

Malcolm is not paying very much attention to the brig. He is watching the fort. It is a formidable affair, a kind of anthology of military architecture which has accreted at various periods since the sixteenth century. There is a low wall of white stone projecting out into the lagoon, and on top of it various buildings and structures of red brick. At one end is the massive blockhouse, a cube as big as a church, surmounted by a cupola-shaped watchtower. There are two light culverins on top of the blockhouse. The main batteries are in low arches or ports along the water, sighted to fire directly across the channel to the Lido.

Some kind of activity is visible now on top of the fort. There are black spots moving, and a cluster around one of the culverins. After some delay there is a white spark, and a puff of yellowish cotton that spreads out slowly in the wind. A plume of water sprouts on the lagoon, a good two hundred yards short of the brig.

Fioravanti gazes gloomily at the small patch of foam on the water.

Mark Anthony: "Militia, Copn."

Malcolm: "A warning shot."

Mark Anthony: "Have to get a good deal closer to de Frenchmon dan dat, to warn him properly."

In the tweendecks the Greek cook is passing out muskets and cutlasses. He has an old forage cap on his head, and a ragged greatcoat he has borrowed from somebody. His face is yellow and sickly. He has, however, a kind of fanfaronading air, and his eyes are sharp and brilliant. He takes a musket for himself, fingering it with nervous grimaces, and checks to be sure there is dry powder in the pan. The Schiavoni crouch under the bulwarks with the various weapons of their choice, muskets or cutlasses, sticking up their heads to look at the brig which is now startlingly near and seems to have grown in size. They gabble among themselves. Viscovich makes his cutlass hiss in a circle. Then he stops it and tries the edge with his thumb.

The brig has braced her topsail now and is coming on slowly. The gun-ports are still open but her guns are not run out. Malcolm glances around him: at the fort, at the brig, at the sand-bar of the Lido under his bow. He pushes his hat down with a slap. His metaphysical doubts are forgotten now. He is practicing his trade and doing something that he knows how to do. A joy comes over him, the keen white excitement of one who knows he is about to slaughter someone in a manly and skillful way.

Malcolm: "Helm up. Slack all. Stand by to jibe."

The *Pandora* falls off the wind and comes back in a long curve toward the fort. She jibes, then, still curving around, she comes up into the wind with sheets slacked. The big lateens belly and flap lazily. The *Pandora* waits under the fort, barely drifting.

Fioravanti: "What's he waiting for, Pizzamano? Why doesn't he fire his battery?"

Malcolm: "Pacienza." He has been told this by Venetians so often that it is a pleasure to hand it back to them.

Fioravanti: "Maladeto."

Malcolm: "You up forward, leave those Goddam sheets slack. I want just bare steerageway."

With her courses still clewed up the brig skirts along the edge of the shallow water toward the fortress. She begins to turn slowly. Her starboard bow comes into view, then the topsides with the six open gun-ports. The guns are run out now.

The lower-works of the brig disappear in a large puff of smoke. The six reports come across the water almost but not quite at the same instant: dull thuds as though someone has dropped a half-dozen bowling balls. *Bump bump bump. Bump. Bump bump.*

Malcolm: "Now, you clowns! Trim sheets! Let's get moving. Helm up. Steady as you go. Keep a little to the left of the brig. Fioravanti, man the forward nines."

Fioravanti: "No broadside?"

Malcolm: "I'll tell you if I want a broadside. Get a move on, you freaks up there. Trim, trim!"

The nacreous arms and legs of the Schiavoni flash in the sunshine. They bend to the sheets, briskly enough but in a dithyrambic and stylized way, as though it were a ballet. A few more garments sail into the air. Finally, they throw off all their clothes and begin emitting barbaric whoops—yelps, barks, yips, cries of

"Evoi!" and "Viva San Marco!"—and other sounds like ducks or strange birds.

The three lateens are trimmed in. The *Pandora* digs in her flank and begins to move again. The water hisses under the rail. They go by under the main battery of the fortress, the black muzzles of the twenty-fours staring out at them one by one as they pass. The brig is turning slowly to bring her still unused larboard battery to bear. Malcolm can clearly make out the faces of the French; he catches the gleam of a button on a coat.

At this moment Pizzamano finally makes up his mind to fire his twenty-fours. There are a dozen or more sharp bumps like thunderclaps, and the fort disappears in a rising curtain of smoke. A tower of water the size of an elm-tree springs up just off the *Pandora*'s bow. Another ball flashes across the channel, only a foot or two above the water, and raises a shower of sand on the Lido shore. The brig is unscathed. The nearest round has struck the water a hundred yards or so from her.

Malcolm is enraged. He takes off his hat and puts it back again. He stares at the fort, his mouth set like a vise.

Malcolm: "The God-dangled Farmers. Fling them to Tophet. They damn near hit us."

Mark Anthony: "Militia, Copn. Dey no danger dey hitting you, less dey shooting at someting else."

Malcolm turns his back on the fort. Where is the Flaming brig? There she comes, swinging around to point her larboard battery at him. He glances behind him at the row of stakes marking the channel.

Malcolm: "Up helm. Slack sheets."

Fioravanti: "Shallow water in there!"

Malcolm doesn't bother to answer. He veers directly off through the line of stakes and across the shoal. A little mud boils up in the wake; the *Pandora* leaves a stain of brown behind her on the lighter green. Malcolm looks around at the brig. As he hoped, she is following him into the shallow water. She curves over against the edge of the channel and immediately goes aground. Her masts lurch sharply to the side, then slowly come upright. He can hear yells in French.

Fioravanti (pointing at something just ahead): "Seca."

Malcolm: "I know it. Just hold your pee. Hard alee!"

The *Pandora* comes quickly around, missing the sand-bar by a few feet. The yards bang over. The brig is two hundred yards away, hard aground, with her bow pointed at the *Pandora*. Everything is clearly outlined in the brilliant sunshine. It is curious that there are no spectators to the scene; only the fort and the men in the two vessels seem to notice what is going on. The Lido shore is deserted. A single figure moves along the sandy beach toward San Nicolò, perhaps a boy going home from fishing. The roof-tops and cupolas of the city gleam golden and imperturbable as usual in the distance, as though asleep in the sunshine.

Up on the bow the gunners are busying themselves around the two long nines, which are loaded with canister, or what passes for canister in the Venetian navy: canvas bags crammed full of scraps of iron, musket-balls, links of chain, a rusty pair of scissors, or whatever comes to hand. A dart of fire springs from a touch-hole, and the gun lurches back. When the smoke clears the Schiavoni are already sighting the other gun. There is a flash and a snarl from the touch-hole. The second gun springs back with a bang that jars the timbers of the deck. Out ahead the bag from the canister floats in the air like a dead bird. The Schiavoni cheer wildly.

The *Pandora* has fallen off and is filling on the other tack. Malcolm squints through the shreds of smoke at the brig. The first round has evidently gone high and done nothing much except break her fore-yard. But the other has had a spectacular success. It smashed through the bulwark and went on down the deck, leaving a path of broken timber and splinters behind it. He catches sight of a patch of blood on a man sitting, as though resting, by the foremast.

There are yells and shouts. The *Pandora* is making directly for the brig; only a ship-length separates them now. Small orange flowers blossom here and there on the brig. From the mizzen-mast near Malcolm's head a splinter flies out and falls to the deck. The Schiavoni, crouched down to avoid these whizzing flies, move about like cats picking up muskets and cutlasses.

Somebody or other: "Stand by to board! Where is the fucking hook?"

The Schiavoni: "Evoi! Ah-eee! San Marco!"

Fioravanti: "Ave Maria, gratia plena, benedicta tu in mulieribus."

Malcolm: "Get down, you Flaming idiots."

Schiavoni: "San Marco! Tweeg! Quack quack!"

Fioravanti: "Ave Maria, gratia plena."

The Greek cook comes out of the tweendecks with a musket in hand, stands upright to look at the brig, and slumps instantly to the deck crumpled over the musket. Under his head a pool of crimson appears and widens; an enamel-like surface crinkling slightly at the edges. Malcolm runs forward, skirting the pool of blood. He has forgotten to take out his saber and now he struggles rather clumsily to free it from the flapping scabbard. The grappling-hook sails through the air with a line snaking behind it.

The two vessels strike heavily, with a grate of wood and splinters. The greenish-white bodies of the Schiavoni, like so many frogs, swarm over the bow. Malcolm, Fioravanti, and Mark Anthony follow after. There is a good deal of confusion. The brig's bulwarks are higher than those of the *Pandora,* and there is not room on the narrow bow for more than a pair of men at a time. Malcolm pulls himself up with some difficulty and tumbles over. Through the smoke he catches a glimpse of a French sailor, begrimed and white-eyed, with a pike poised ready to thrust. At the same instant the man bends double, and the pike bounces on the deck. It is slightly uncanny. Malcolm hears no musket-shot, there is no cutlass anywhere near the Frenchman; he simply bends in the middle and falls. Malcolm is not conscious of any sound at all, although the air is full of musket-smoke and he can see mouths open in yells and cries. The wounded man by the foremast, blood covering his face and soaking down into his shirt, sits on the deck with his hands resting on his knees.

Another man comes at Malcolm with a pike. He slips to one side and slashes violently with his saber. The blade strikes something—he feels the shock in his wrist—but whether it is the pike-staff or solid bone he has no time to tell. He skirts the mainmast and makes his way up the ladder to the quarter-deck, clambering over a man who is sliding down it head-first. The young French captain is standing by the companionway, just forward of the wheel. He holds a brace of pistols at the level of his chest, pointed at Viscovich who is dancing up the ladder on the other side. He pulls both triggers. One pistol flashes, the other misses fire.

The young captain drops the pistols and cries, "Je me rends!" Viscovich rushes at him on tiptoes, still as though he were dancing. The captain turns away, and at the same instant the cutlass flashes in the air. The hat spins from the head, and the young captain falls with an odd twist in his body. The head is almost severed: it rests on the deck at right angles to the body. Bright arterial blood spurts from the opening and springs out in jerky rhythm.

It is over. Malcolm himself has harmed no one, with the possible exception of the pikeman he slashed at sideways without seeing him very clearly. In addition to the captain there are four other French dead. The surviving Frenchmen are clustered on the main-deck, surrounded by the Schiavoni who caper and gabble at them. The French are a tattered and hungry-looking lot; they look emaciated and their hands and faces are stained with black from the guns. The French captain's pistol-shot has just grazed the top of Viscovich's head. A rivulet of blood runs down into his eye and across the cheek. He shakes his head, as one might dislodge a fly, to clear the eye. Then his tongue emerges to lick at the blood on the cheek. He has a contemptuous expression.

Where is Fioravanti? He is lying under the rail of the quarter-deck, almost hidden by the hanging coils of main-braces, as though he has crawled into that sheltered place to be alone. There is a deep saber-cut under his ribs and he has lost much blood. Malcolm pulls up the main-brace to look at him. The eyes are wide open, staring at the coil of rope, but the irises are dry and a filmy look has come over them. One hand is bent, with a finger pointing to the chest, as if to indicate the heart. The hand is frozen, claw-like, in the act of making a sign of the cross.

Malcolm turns away and finds Mark Anthony at his elbow. He seems too large for the small brig; he has to bend to avoid hitting his head on the boom. He points, in a solemn and Shakespearean gesture, at the fort. The black and white banners on the flagstaff are gone. In their place is a recall pennant with a vessillo or naval ensign below it: a signal to break off the action and retire.

Mark Anthony: "Fort commonder, he cross at us. It makes a mon vexed, to have dose big twenty-fours and not hit anyting wit dem."

Malcolm: "He almost hit something. Thunder take him. He almost hit us."

Mark Anthony: "Militia, Copn."

The sun is low in the sky and reddening. It is five o'clock.

Viscovich, squatting on his hunkers, is ripping up a bandage from a dead Frenchman's shirt. Mark Anthony too has a picturesque cloth tied around his head, with a blood-spot on it, like a hero in a painting. It is only now that Malcolm notices the name of the brig, carved in gilded letters over the companionway-hatch, the carving a little shabby and the gilt beginning to wear off the letters: *Libérateur d'Italie*.

THE BRIG IS STILL AGROUND BUT

The brig is still aground but the flood-tide will soon set her free. A heavy peota, manned by a dozen or more oarsmen, is putting out from Sant'Andrea toward the two vessels locked together at the edge of the channel. The Schiavoni have pulled down the tricolor and are dumping buckets of water on the decks to wash away the worst of the gore. Tarpaulins are pulled over the corpses. Malcolm notices a French midshipman standing at the quarter-rail who has not joined the other prisoners up forward; a gangling figure with a long equine face and a lock of hair fallen over the brow. He has a rather wild look. One hand is on the rail, the other pressed to his waist just at the top of the breeches as though he has a stomach-ache.

Malcolm is in the act of approaching this person to ask if he is second in command. The midshipman watches him in alarm until he is five feet or so away. Then he turns and scrambles onto the rail, balances for a moment, and falls outward. An instant later there is a dull splash from under the quarter.

Malcolm: "Oh, Crucks. Man a boat, somebody. Lively, lively."

The Schiavoni run for the gig stowed upside down on the cabin scuttle. It is splintered a little from the *Pandora*'s second nine-pounder but still looks serviceable. Somebody comes up with a musket and levels it at the thrashing shape in the water. Malcolm pushes the musket-barrel down.

The midshipman, under water most of the time and coming to the surface only now and then, is struggling to divest himself of the heavy blue coat that prevents him from swimming. He manages to get it off except for one sleeve which clings to the wet arm, and begins swimming with the coat dragging. He goes under again. He has not taken off his boots. He is not going to be able to stay afloat much longer.

Malcolm takes off his own boots and hat, then his coat and his saber, and steps off the stern into the air. He feels the bone-chilling shock that comes when you have failed to prepare your mind against even relatively warm water. Cursing inside, he claws his way back to the surface. The midshipman is farther away than he expected. He is not making very much progress swimming, but the flood-tide is slowly carrying him away from the brig. Malcolm strikes out rather heavily, impeded by his own tight breeches and his lack of practice. The current by this time has carried both of them under the bow of the brig. The midshipman seems almost exhausted and Malcolm thinks how he can best support him in the water until the Schiavoni manage to get the gig launched. To his surprise, as he approaches, the midshipman manages to wrench himself over on his back, one knee comes out of the water, and a boot strikes Malcolm sharply, catching him just between the shoulder and the chin.

At this Malcolm almost loses his temper. He launches himself at the figure in the water, overwhelming it with his greater weight and driving it down under the surface. He is on top and the midshipman underneath. This makes it easier for him, Malcolm, to float and may also have some effect on the attitude of the midshipman. Then he becomes aware of a third and unexpected effect. The midshipman is entirely under water. The four legs are tangled and Malcolm's hand is pressed down on the struggling chest. He feels a very strange sensation, a kind of wild warmth or urging to do something he can't quite specify. The water no longer seems cold and he has no desire to get out of it or even come to the surface. Without being able to say quite when he became conscious of it, he finds himself lying face down on a young woman with his knee between her legs and one hand on her breast.

He lets go as though he has touched something hot. They both come to the surface.

She: "Tried to. Drown . . . me. You. Stupid brute."

Malcolm doesn't bother to enter into a debate on the rules of polite warfare, kicking people unexpectedly, et cetera. He gets carefully around behind her and begins towing her by the shirt-collar, which removes him from the range of the flailing hands and feet and also has the advantage of choking her enough to keep her from talking. Over his shoulder he sees that the Schiavoni have the gig hooked into the falls and are lowering it efficiently. It occurs to him only now that she has spoken English, in a thin, nervous, but rather savage voice. He loosens his grip on the shirt.

Malcolm: "If you'll stop kicking maybe you won't drown. You don't seem to be much of a swimmer."

She: "Pig. Stu— . . . Stupid brute."

It is clear that his efforts at life-saving are not appreciated. Another person less humanitarian might simply swim off and let the Schiavoni have a shot at her with the musket. At least miss her narrowly. Instead he lets go of the shirt and tries for another grip around the chest, abandoning this for a reason that leaves him in a state of electric tingling. After this he hangs onto the waist, simply trying to keep the two of them afloat. The gig is in the water now and in a few strokes of the oars it is alongside them. The narrow waist under Malcolm's grip is, in some way, soft and muscular at the same time. In the middle of the stomach, to his bafflement, there is a hard squarish place. The Schiavoni, baying like fox-hounds, pull the two of them over the gunwale and into the gig.

The gig is leaking badly and the Schiavoni thrash away at the oars to get it back to the brig before it sinks. Someone throws a jacob's-ladder over the rail. The rescued prisoner goes up first, followed by several mother-of-pearl frogs. The one below pushes her bottom to encourage her, and gets kicked on the head for his pains.

Schiavone: "Agh! What the Devil! I'll cut your tripes out, you whelp."

Malcolm manages to get them up the ladder without further kicks from the one and threats from the other. The Schiavone who was kicked is still feeling the sting. Clearly he would like to inflict something on this odd-looking creature, whatever it is, to make his head feel a little better. On the deck of the brig he pushes up to her and squeezes the arm.

Malcolm: "Leave off that."

The Schiavone looks at Malcolm. He bares his teeth. Then he drops the arm.

Malcolm: "Now then. You've got something stuck in your breeches there. Give it to me."

No reply. The white face covered with drops of water is defiant. The sodden hair clings to the head in tangles, and a hand comes up and brushes it away from the face.

Malcolm: "Just as you like. In that case—"

He approaches to grab the thing, whatever it is, that she has tucked into her waist. The hand that has brushed away the hair comes up with remarkable alacrity and strikes him on the ear, stinging sharply. After this she backs away, kicks at him ineffectively, gets in another blow with her fist, and stands waiting with teeth clenched like some small fierce animal. Malcolm makes no effort to defend himself. He stands an arm's-length away, out of reach of the fist, waiting.

The Schiavoni: "Hey, Captain!" "Bravo!" "Swat him one now. Why do you let a man hit you?"

Malcolm: "Because it isn't a man."

And in fact, with the shirt and breeches soaking wet and the chest heaving in anger, anyone can see that this is so.

Schiavoni: "Hey, look at that. The Franzesi have women in their navy. It's the Revolution. Hurrah!"

By this time practically all of them have gathered around the scene, except for the half-dozen guarding the French prisoners on the main-deck. This is a rare treat. It is better than the puppet-show in the Piazza, in which Pulcinella hits the Constable. The costumes are better too.

Malcolm: "Clear away, all of you. Down to the main-deck. I'll handle this by myself."

They go slowly off down the ladder, looking back with weak grins. Finally they are all gone but Mark Anthony.

Malcolm: "You too."

Mark Anthony: "Copn, in my opinion, dis person—"

Malcolm: "I don't require your opinion just now. A little later I may ask for it."

Mark Anthony gives him a long stare, with dignity. He adjusts the bandage on his head. Then, taking his time, he goes down the ladder to the main-deck with the others.

Malcolm: "Now see here. You've got something concealed in your clothing. I'm going to have it. I'd advise you to hand it over freely. If you give it freely then you won't be harmed. But if not I'll just come and take it."

Whatever effect this speech has on her, it has its effect on Malcolm himself. He feels the blood coming to his face, and the same kind of warm and unspecified urging that trickled through his limbs in the water. And she is not even pretty. At least not soaking wet. Probably not even dry. Her face is too long, and her chin large. Her figure is not of the kind fancied by most sailors. She looks like somebody's younger brother, perhaps, who is trying to carry a couple of buns in his shirt. Still that itching warmness. Tarnation!

She stares at him palely. Her mouth works. She seems reluctant to speak at all to this person who has treated her so rudely in the water. But perhaps speaking is better than the alternative implied in not speaking.

She: "You are English?"

Malcolm: "I speak English."

She: "At least you're an officer. So you must understand that it is not proper to make *inquiries*—even—about a woman's person."

Malcolm: "You don't hit like a woman. Most women slap. You hit with a closed fist. Besides you're in military uniform. I recommend you hand over whatever it is you've got there. If I'm not strong enough to take it from you, those fellows down there can help."

This in fact must be a disturbing suggestion to her. The Schiavoni are weaving in and out from various hiding-places on the main-deck. A white shoulder, or a part of a head with a single eye, appears now and then from behind the mast.

She: "At least you will leave me alone in the cabin for a few moments. Then I will give you what you want."

Malcolm: "Nope."

A moisture of anger is forming in her eyes. She looks as though she is about to hit him. Except that this was not very effective the first time. Or to go overboard again; but evidently she has had enough of swimming.

She: "Then turn your back, please."

Malcolm: "Nope."

For a moment they stand facing each other, in the two pools of water that drip from them and soak into the deck. Her eyes moist but gritting her teeth in anger at him, at herself, she turns away. She is fumbling with the shirt and unbuttoning the square fall of the breeches. When the breeches are buttoned again and everything in order she turns to him with a small oblong packet wrapped in oiled cloth. Her face has colored during this process but her mouth is still firmly set.

Malcolm in the meantime has put his own coat, hat, and boots back on. He slips the packet into his coat. He beckons for Mark Anthony to come up from the main-deck. The heads of the Schiavoni appear from behind hatches and deck-works, like sprouting flowers.

To cover his own slight confusion—which is inexplicable, since he has behaved with absolute correctness in the whole matter—he begins discussing matters of seamanship with Mark Anthony. The tide will free the brig in half an hour. She will be difficult to handle, however, with the fore-yard hanging down like a broken wing.

Malcolm: "Better send down the fore-yard before it falls down. The peota will tow you. Take her to the Arsenal. Watch those Frenchies. They're tricky devils. I'll come around to the Arsenal later."

Mark Anthony: "Where you going, Copn? You in charge of bote of dese vessels now. You had better stay here and mind dis brig."

Malcolm: "Mind your own Tarnished business."

Mark Anthony: "You bout to do someting foolish, Copn. I can tell."

Malcolm gives him a stare made out of New England granite. Then he beckons to the English girl, who is still standing by the rail. After a moment's hesitation she follows him without a word. On the main-deck he waves for a quartet of the Schiavoni to follow. He clambers over the rail and drops down to the *Pandora,* which is a good deal lower in the water than the brig. It is a little awkward. As the girl climbs down he offers her his hand, feeling rather foolish. The four Schiavoni leap down lightly after, as though they were on springs.

The Greek is still crumpled in a heap on the deck, with the musket sticking out from under him.

Malcolm: "First, cover that up. Then cast off. Recover the grappling-hook. Get out a couple of sweeps and push free. Presto, presto."

The Schiavoni retrieve various garments lying around on the deck—an old hat here, a waistcoat there—and put them on. They push off with the sweeps, and one takes the tiller. The apple-bowed peota, with its oars working like the legs of some cumbrous insect, has almost reached the two vessels locked together at the edge of the channel. Malcolm prefers to leave before it arrives. He has begun to realize now that the action he is taking in this affair—although he has believed at each step to be conducting himself in an impeccable and orthodox military manner—might seem curious to anyone not in possession of all the facts.

As he expects, the Militia officer in charge of the peota is somewhat puzzled to see the two vessels separate and the galeotta move away up the channel with her big lateens swelling in the breeze. The peota is still a hundred yards or so away, too far to hail effectively. It stops in the water, the oars dripping. The officer in charge stares in his direction. But the *Pandora* is moving too briskly to overtake under oars anyhow. The peota pulls on toward the brig.

The *Pandora* slips rapidly up the channel toward the city. There is a mumbling and crashing from the water breaking under the bow. One Schiavone is at the helm; the other three have all they can do to handle the sheets as the *Pandora* goes up the twisting channel between the two rows of stakes. The English girl stands under the break of the quarter-deck, sheltered from the wind.

She: "I'm cold."

Malcolm: "Of course you are. You're soaking wet and it's still early in the year. You shouldn't have gone in the water if you didn't want to be wet. I'm wet too."

She: "Don't be cross with me."

Malcolm: "Why in Tophet shouldn't I be cross with you? There's a cloak in the tweendecks, hanging on a hook. On the larboard side, if you know what that is."

Thé cloak is Fioravanti's, but Malcolm hardly thinks of that. She goes into the tweendecks and comes out wrapped in a musty black garment that comes down to her knees, with brass buttons in front. It is a little large for her but not too much. A hand comes out to push the wet lock away from her brow, then it disappears into the cloak again.

She: "I'm still cold."

He ignores her and addresses himself to the helmsman. He has other things to think about. San Marco and the Molo are coming up fast.

Malcolm: "Helm down a little. Luff. Steady that. I want to round up to the Molo and back the foresail to stop her, understand?"

Helmsman: "Sì, Sior Capitàn."

The pink block of the Ducal Palace goes by. Then the Piazzetta gradually opens out so that they are looking, as it were, down the great throat of the city: the Campanile, the two free-standing columns by the Molo, the clock-tower with its Moors, the broad Piazza beyond. Luckily the Molo is almost deserted. There are a few gondolas and a small trading-vessel from Cyprus. He selects an empty stretch of quay and angles in toward it.

Malcolm: "Steady now. Hard alee—let go sheets—back the foresail up there—smartly, you apes!"

The *Pandora* rounds up, comes slowly to a stop with foresail aback and main and mizzen snapping, and hesitates. Then her bow falls downwind, and she drifts sideways almost exactly into the space on the Molo that Malcolm has marked out. The helmsman drops the tiller, gets out a sweep, and fends off the small Cyprian ship.

It is a neat bit of ship-handling. But the English girl doesn't seem to notice. She is gazing quite blankly past him at the city. Her arms are folded inside the cloak hugging herself. Her long chin tremors a little with the cold, but otherwise she shows no expression.

Malcolm pushes his hat down in front. She is really a prize Ninny. He growls at her in monosyllables.

Malcolm: "Come on."

She: "Where?"

Malcolm: "Never mind. Just come."

He climbs over onto the quay and sets off across the Piazzetta. She follows at his elbow, without a word. The sun is setting behind the Giudecca but it is still light. Once in the Piazzetta he realizes that he has no idea what to do with her now. It is the most crowded and conspicuous part of the city. People stare at the girl with her stringy hair in the military cloak. A boy grins, and an old gentleman in a wig and black toga gets out a lorgnette to examine her. An Egyptian Plague on these Venetians and their curiosity. Malcolm stops to reconnoiter the situation. He is uncertain whether to go back to the Molo or plunge off into the thick of city. Then he pushes the girl behind him. Moving through the crowd a hundred yards or so away is a purple blotch—rather shapeless—as though Canaletto had accidentally dropped a blob of paint on his well-known view of the Molo. There is no mistaking the outline. It leans slightly and is characterized by a large nose which precedes it in the direction of its motion, like the figurehead of a ship.

Malcolm: "Oh, Blast. That Crocodile."

She: "What?"

Malcolm: "Cristoforo. The Missier Grande."

She: "Who? I don't understand."

Malcolm: "The Constable of the Inquisitors of State. Ever hear of the Pozzi? That's the dungeons down in the bottom of the Prisons. Half full of water, with rats swimming around. That's where they throw people who are accused of Politicks."

The purple toga, in the glimpse that Malcolm has caught of it, is drifting in an aimless way in the direction of the *Pandora* moored alongside the Molo.

She: "But what's he doing?"

Malcolm: "Looking for you, probably."

She: "How would he know I'm here?"

Malcolm: "He sniffs things out. With that nose of his."

She: "But I haven't done anything wrong."

Malcolm: "Keep the cloak wrapped around you."

He rather unceremoniously takes her arm and tows her away in the other direction, a little faster than she would have wanted to go. They are both still soaking wet. Their clothing has stopped dripping, but they leave a track of wet marks across the Piazzetta. Malcolm keeps moving until he is under the porch of Sansovino's library with its great gloomy arches of marble. Here he stops and turns, with the girl at his elbow. It is almost dark under the portico, but the square outside is still filled with a rusty pink light.

There is no sign of Cristoforo. Perhaps he has gone on board the *Pandora,* or perhaps he has simply melted into the evening shadows. Malcolm is about to take the girl and make off down under the portico, with the idea perhaps of finding some inn or locanda to put her in. But at that moment he becomes aware that someone has approached from behind and is standing at his elbow.

He turns, and the man hands him a folded slip of paper. It is a piece of note-paper from the Caffè Quadri, across the way on the Piazza. There are only three words written on it. *Villa Baraoni, Brenta.*

He examines the man. There is nothing unusual about him. He is an ordinary waiter from Quadri's, in a striped waistcoat and shirt-sleeves.

Malcolm: "Who gave you this?"

The waiter says nothing. But Malcolm sees now that at the far end of the portico is another person who is unmistakably interested in what is going on: a small black-clad man with a narrow face. One arm is withered and hangs down, as narrow as a broomstick, with a baby-like hand at the end of it. The man appears not to be watching, but his very indifference, the intentness of his looking in some other direction, gives him away.

Waiter: "A gondola, Captain?"

Malcolm nods.

The young Englishwoman is watching with her large gray eyes. The damp lock has fallen onto her brow again. She shows no signs of uneasiness. She is simply interested.

She: "What is it?"

He starts to take her arm, and then changes his mind. He *waves* her with his hand, not quite touching her; as you might guide some rare animal, a llama or a fragile gazelle, across a lawn. They go off following the waiter in his striped waistcoat.

IN SPITE OF THE COLD AND

In spite of the cold and her wetness, in spite of the uncertainty of her situation and her ignorance of the intentions of this officer or captain whose sword clanks in a most disagreeable manner whenever he moves, Winifred finds something secure or even cozy about the small black cabin of the gondola. She is seated in a kind of reclining armchair or sofa at the rear of the little cabin. The opening behind her is partly covered by a kind of black velvet robe. On either side of the cabin are shutters with little vanes that can be opened or closed. The whole interior of the cabin is finished in black: black lacquered wood, black leather, black velvet cushions, black carvings of an ornate and allegorical sort. All this ought to produce a funereal effect, but for some reason it doesn't. It simply enhances the dim half-darkness that shuts out the hugger-mugger and buzzing world outside and makes one feel snug and protected. Even under circumstances that are at best ambiguous and at worst, perhaps, perilous to the point of the desperate. Who exactly, for example, is this officer who has taken the pains to pull her out of the water at the expense of getting himself wet and now, without a word of explanation, is conducting her to an unknown place for an equally unknown purpose? He seems to be a person of a certain dignity; although this is perhaps only contempt. He sits bolt upright at the other end of the cabin, on a small wooden chair without upholstery, still wearing his hat, even though in a sense the cabin constitutes a kind of indoors, and gentlemen customarily remove their hats indoors in the presence of ladies. In the gloom she can make out his dark-blue coat with shabby epaulets, the soaked breeches clinging to his knees, and the saber stuck awkwardly along his leg in the confined space. When their eyes happen to meet he glances in some other direction, usually about three inches to the left of her head. He has a square blunt look about him and seems to be not a young man at all, rather old in fact; perhaps forty. She is obliged to admit that so far he has done her no harm, even if he treated her rather roughly when they were in the water together. What then does he want of her? The most plausible explanation of all these events, she has begun to decide now, is that the small Venetian vessel attacked the *Libérateur d'Italie* for the express purpose of taking her into custody, on account of the packet. But the packet is now safely in the pocket of the officer's coat. Why then is he taking the trouble to conduct her off somewhere in this gondola? He is perhaps no better than a pirate. Men are—one knows what men are. Winifred begins to feel a slightly giddy emptiness inside her, just below the place where her ribs end; and decides not to pursue this chain of thought any longer.

She turns to look out through the half-draped opening behind her. First she can see the gondolier's legs, then the narrow swan-necked stern of the gondola, then a stretch of the Grand Canal with the last of the sunset glowing on the palazzi. From the quay near the Ducal Palace another gondola detaches itself and moves slowly out onto the molten-gold surface of the water. A window-pane catches the setting sun and flashes bright orange for an instant, then dims. She turns back to the officer, who is still sitting in his stiff uncomfortable way with his hands on his knees.

Winifred: "What is your name, please?"
Malcolm: "Langrish."
Winifred: "It sounds Scottish."
Malcolm: "It is."
Winifred: "Then you're Scottish?"
Malcolm: "I'm American."
Winifred: "Oh."
She reflects at this. Then she presses him crisply.
Winifred: "But why don't you serve in the American navy?"

Malcolm: "I picked the wrong side in the War of Independence."

Winifred: "Oh. Which side *was* the wrong side?"

Malcolm: "The wrong side in any war is the one that loses."

Winifred: "I see."

Another pause for thought.

Winifred: "Then that should make you friendly to the English."

At this he mutters something inaudible. He seems now not exactly hostile or contemptuous, only indifferent. This makes her situation seem, if not a little brighter, at least a little less desperately mysterious. More conversation could hardly do any harm, although she will have to be careful not to touch on subjects that seem to irritate him, like the American War. Still there might be dozens of such subjects, and she has no idea of what the others are.

Winifred: "I'm Winifred Hervey."

He barely inclines his head, leaving his hat on and not removing his hands from his knees.

This is not very encouraging. She continues the attack, brushing a still damp lock of hair away from her forehead.

Winifred: "If it's not impolite, might I inquire where it is we're going?"

Malcolm: "You might inquire."

Winifred: "And where *are* we going?"

A slight note of exasperation begins to creep into her voice; the tone in which one might speak to a sulky child who refuses to answer.

Malcolm: "Villa Baraoni. On the Brenta."

Winifred: "And where is that?"

Malcolm: "It isn't far."

Winifred: "Ah."

She arranges herself into a prim, even light manner for the next question, almost as though it were a matter of idle curiosity, even a jest.

Winifred: "Am I a prisoner of war?"

Malcolm: "There isn't any war taking place just now far as I know, except one between the French and Austrians."

Now it is her turn to be silent, deciding that it might be better not to ask what the alternatives are to one's being a prisoner of war.

After a while, by some miracle, he clears his throat and actually addresses a remark to her. It is the first time he has spoken except to answer her questions, rather grudgingly.

Malcolm: "Besides, how can you be a prisoner of war if you're a civilian?"

Winifred: "Why am I a civilian?"

Malcolm: "All women are civilians."

Winifred: "Ah."

They are both silent for a few moments while Winifred thinks about this. The implications seem favorable to her circumstances, but she can't be sure. To cover up the awkwardness she turns in the armchair again and glances out past the gondolier's legs. The palazzi behind are rotating rapidly. The gondola is just in the act of turning from the Grand Canal and entering a small waterway lined with crumbling and rather decrepit houses on either side. The water has a sewery smell, of fish, of rotten vegetables, and of other more unspeakable things. The sunset is fading now and the pastel façades of the palazzi are gradually losing their colors. The shape behind has detached itself from the wall and is curving out into the Canal, like a lean rat stealing out across the water.

There is no sound but the plashing of water along the hull and the slight grating of the oar, at even intervals, as the gondolier bends his weight against it.

Winifred: "I believe there may be another gondola following us."

He glances past her through the opening at the rear of the cabin, says nothing for a moment, and then speaks to the gondolier in Venetian.

Gondolier: "Sì, Paròn."

They go on for a short distance between the rows of houses that cut off the light on either side. Then the gondola swings abruptly to the right and enters an even smaller canal. On one side it scrapes along a wall covered with a blackish moss; on the other side there is hardly room for the oar to ply. Then it glides into a kind of concavity in the unbroken wall of houses: a water-doorway at the entrance of a palazzo. It is almost dark now. In the cabin she can barely see Captain Langrish's eyes under the brim of the hat, and the occasional gleam of his saber.

Winifred: "Where are we?"

Malcolm: "Rio Ognissanti."

Winifred: "Why are we stopping here?"

Malcolm: "It seems to be a good idea."

The gondolier is looking back down the rio. The black shape appears and goes by the opening at the end. The gondolier waits for a few minutes longer, then he gets out his oar, uses it to push the gondola out of the doorway, and sets it against the curiously shaped thole pin and begins rowing again. Instead of turning back the way they have come the gondola continues on down the rio, scraping now and then against the walls. There is a sharp turn to the left: the gondolier is skillful and can turn his long narrow craft on the point of a needle. After a time it comes out of the rio into the open water. It is totally dark now and Winifred has no idea where she is; whether they are headed back toward the city or away from it. Through the shutters at her side she sees dim yellowish lights passing by. Then these disappear behind and there is nothing but darkness on all sides, no houses or islands. Only a small flickering light is visible now and then in the far distance.

A half an hour or more goes by in this manner. Neither of them speaks. There is the even plash of the oar and the soft slow lurch of the gondola with each stroke.

She becomes aware of something that has been evident before but has not really struck her: the sofa or broad armchair she is occupying, almost in the middle of the gondola, is meant for two persons. It is richly upholstered in leather, with velvet arm-rests and tassels, and two could easily sit on it with six inches of space between them. Instead Captain Langrish has chosen to occupy the small chair at the other end of the cabin, which looks hard and uncomfortable. His silhouette against the starlight is still bolt upright. She has still not decided what to make of him. Her curiosity is provoked by his way of speaking, in a colonial twang very different from the well-bred London drawl she is used to. "Yeaop." "Naop." He closes his mouth abruptly at the end of each short sentence, so that everything sounds as though it ends with a p: "It isn't farp." A curiosity strikes her to know the color of his eyes, but unfortunately it is too dark to see them. She is very much interested in the colors of people's eyes, which she regards as an index of character. She tries to remember them from earlier in the afternoon and decides they were a deep gray-green, the color of the sea after a storm. She is rather intimidated by the large scar on his cheek. The wound has just missed the eye, and this makes one's own eye feel odd if one looks at it. Fortunately it is too dark to see it now. Fortunately, unfortunately; it strikes her that her reasoning is circular, or rather helical. A helix rotates, but it ascends to new levels with each turning. She has been trained to a degree in logic and even in mathematics, although she does not always care to apply these rigors to her practical thinking. For logic may stray, or tell lies, whereas the heart—this leads her into a realm of thought, or of reverie, which she quickly abandons.

She certainly does not intend to invite him to share her broad armchair (a sofa for two persons is called in England a love-seat, she remembers irrelevantly) but it could hardly do any harm to try to engage him in conversation again. He even seemed to unbend a little, before, when she persuaded him to answer a question or two.

Winifred: "Aren't you cold?"

This is the wrong way to begin. He says nothing, only makes a kind of contemptuous exhalation through his nose, a sort of audible shrug. Perhaps he shrugs with his shoulders too, although it is too dark to see.

Winifred: "I'm very cold. If I don't change these things soon I'm going to catch something."

He ignores this personal reference too, only remarking that once clothes are wet in salt water they won't dry.

The conversation seems to have taken a turn in which she is asking for his sympathy, the last thing in the world she desires. She backs away and launches off in another direction.

Winifred: "Who was the man who gave you the note?"

Malcolm: "A waiter."

Winifred: "No. The one with the funny arm."

Malcolm (shortly): "The note was from Villetard."

Winifred: "Who?"

Malcolm: "You don't know Villetard?"

Winifred: "No."

Malcolm: "The secretary of the French Legation."

Winifred: "Oh."

She meditates this for a few minutes.

Winifred: "What does he have to do with the matter?"

Malcolm: "I might ask you that."

Winifred: "You might, except you never say anything unless you're spoken to. You only sit there like a lump in that uncomfortable chair."

This, she realizes as soon as she has said it, may be a little risky. If he is the unprincipled pirate that he may very well be, he is capable of moving and coming to sit beside her. A slight fluttery feeling arises in her throat and then gradually subsides. He goes on sitting where he is. Instead, with the slight premeditative clearing of his throat that she begins to recognize as one of his habits, he speaks.

Malcolm: "You say you're English."

Winifred: "It isn't that I *say* I'm English. I *am* English."

This piece of petulance throws him into a silence again. Perhaps he may not recover? No, after a few seconds he goes on.

Malcolm: "Then why were you on a French ship?"

A pause. He makes the small sound in his throat again as though he were getting over a cold.

Malcolm: "And in a . . . uniform."

The significant hesitation before the word suggests that for a civilian to wear a uniform (all women are civilians) violates some serious article of the conventions of warfare, and may have mysterious and unspecified consequences. And also, perhaps, that the breeches and shirt, especially when wet (Winifred herself is conscious of this) are . . . immodest. Winifred has worn breeches when she followed the hunt in the Kentish countryside, but her father and uncles didn't approve of this either. She draws the boat-cloak around her, covering her knees.

Winifred: "I came to rejoin my fiancé in Venice. He's French. Venice is cut off from the mainland by the war, as you know. So I had to go to Rome and take the ship at . . ."

Here she realizes she is divulging military information, and stops abruptly.

Malcolm: "Ancona."

Winifred: "Ah, you know that?"

Malcolm: "We know a great deal. You may have noticed that my vessel was able to meet yours exactly when it appeared off Chioggia."

Winifred: "I didn't notice anything, and I don't even know where Chioggia is."

Malcolm: "You haven't explained about the uniform."

Winifred: "Well, you see. The *Libérateur d'Italie* was not exactly a passenger vessel. It was a warship. And sailors are—you know—all kinds of people . . ."

Perhaps she has said the wrong thing again. He might take this as a slight on his profession, or on his own moral character. But he only waits for her to go on.

Winifred: "So it seemed better for me to—dress as I did."

Malcolm: "And you expect me to believe that? That everyone on the brig took you for a man?"

Winifred (with composure, even a little primly): "I *hoped* you would believe it."

The preliminary growl in the throat again. He embarks on a new subject.

Malcolm: "This fiancé of yours. This French fiancé. What's he doing exactly in Venice?"

Winifred: "He is studying music."

Malcolm: "And you're coming to join him?"

Winifred: "Why not?"

Malcolm: "It seems like an odd time."

Winifred: "An odd time for what?"

Malcolm: "For him to be studying music. And for you to come to join him."

Winifred: "For rejoining one's fiancé there is no special time. One does it as soon as possible. There is a great Silver Cord pulling people together under such circumstances."

Malcolm: "I know nothing about all that."

The silhouette in the starlight shifts its position a little. The shoulders rise and then come down. Probably he is slipping his hands into his coat-pockets to warm them a little.

This reminds Winifred of the packet, which she has almost forgotten. The fluttery feeling comes back into her throat again, and this time it doesn't go away. The thought occurs to her that it was foolish to try to conceal the packet inside her clothing. If she had simply thrust it into her own coat-pocket, as Captain Langrish did, it would have sunk to the bottom of the lagoon along with the coat. But this sort of thing could not be anticipated. Still she has made a botch of the whole business. She realizes now that she will have to explain it in some way to Jean-Marie.

Winifred: "Captain Langrish."

The silhouette remains absolutely motionless.

Winifred: "You are an English gentleman. That is, you are not exactly English, but you speak English and you are an officer. I am sure you are aware that there are matters ladies must keep private and which it is not proper for a gentleman to inquire into."

No response. He waits for her to go on.

Winifred: "As I explained, I came to Venice to rejoin my fiancé. Now there is the matter of the small packet of papers which you took from me, in a rather rude way I must say. It would be awkward if anyone else were to see them. They concern only myself and my fiancé. You must understand that between two persons—"

He interrupts her rather bluntly. "I've spent most of my life at sea. I don't know very much about what goes on between two persons."

Winifred: "Then the packet?"

Malcolm: "I'll keep it for a while."

Winifred: "Still, as a gentleman . . ."

Malcolm: "I've already told you. I don't know much about these matters. Still, it seems to me that when young women go around in military uniforms, kick people in the head, strike with their fists closed instead of slapping in the proper way—"

Winifred: "I see. They lose their prerogatives as ladies. Is that it—?"

Silence.

Winifred: "In that case, why don't you open the packet immediately and delve into my most intimate secrets. Tell them to the gondolier too if you like."

Malcolm: "It's too dark to read, for one thing."

Winifred: "Perhaps the gondolier has a light."

She says this rather snappishly, since this is how she feels. With difficulty she subdues the increased rate of her breathing. If she became angry he might become angry too and she doesn't know—it suddenly occurs to her that there might be a peril in his becoming angry. He says nothing. Then in the dark she hears him making the small preliminary rustle in his throat again.

Malcolm: "I can promise not to delve into your most intimate secrets. If that'll satisfy you."

She feels a warmth mounting to her face. What on earth *did* she mean, anyhow? It is obvious that there are no intimate secrets—of hers—in the packet. And her lie, her outburst, was . . . immodest. The two words themselves—*intimate secrets*—have opened up a door of possible communication between them that ought to remain shut. She is unable to make the hotness of her face go away.

For a long time neither of them says anything. There are no more lights now on the lagoon, even in the distance. Captain Langrish is a dim shape in the chair, his saber jangling whenever he shifts his position slightly. But it is not really totally dark. The darkness outside is not quite as dark as the darkness in the cabin, and even in the cabin, after a time, shapes become visible. She can see where his face is under the hat, and the white gleam of his eyes now and then, when he turns his head so that the dim light from the shutters catches them. She remembers his scar, a rather frightful thing, and tries to make it out now, but there isn't light enough. The face is only a blur, swimming a little in the darkness, without features. Perhaps he is not an English officer at all but some kind of a brigand or . . . what? A buccaneer. This is the word she has been groping for. When he moves there is a creak of leather, from his boots or perhaps from his belt. The creak of leather, she reflects, is a thoroughly masculine sound. She is tired. She closes her eyes for a while, then opens them again. The figure in the chair stirs. In spite of herself her attention is fixed by the dim oblong of the face. It seems to grow larger, not only the face but the whole figure; the arms, the torso, the outstretched legs. There is a clank from the saber. Is he rising from the chair?

Her throat feels tight. Something cold, quite definitely cold but at the same time warm, passes from her shoulders into her breasts and then makes its way lower down into her body. The figure in the darkness floats weightlessly and grows larger. There is a smell of leather and mud. And another rankish musky odor, from her own body or from another. She tries to move her limbs, to raise her arms, and can not. The muffled figure floats down toward her, over her. The dim light is cut off. Something wet and warm descends on her face. She turns her head but the prickling warm thing is still there. Her knees under the cloak are pressed tightly together. But now something insinuates its way under the cloak and she feels it touching her. It is cold, damp, and curving. It progresses slowly across her limbs. It clanks: it is attached to the floating figure with a chain. She is determined that the saber shall not slip up any higher on her body. Her knees are watery and there is no more strength in them. Her shoulders are pressed back tightly against the sofa. She emits a small half-suppressed cry, a kind of yelp. Then she opens her eyes.

Captain Langrish is still sitting in the chair. He stares at her curiously but says nothing about the sound she has made. She forces herself to stay awake. She wishes to rub her eyes, to clear the fuzziness from them; but feels it is better not to move. Ahead of the gondola, past Captain Langrish's shoulder, she can see more lights now, and something that is possibly a slightly darker line of land against the water. The lights draw nearer and become brighter, expanding apart as they approach. There are huts with lighted windows scattered at intervals along the muddy shore. Then a cluster of houses, and a rather large building with a tower on one side. They have passed into the mouth of a river or large canal. When she speaks to him it is in a normal tone, a tone with a cultivated show of indifference.

Winifred: "Where are we now?"
Malcolm: "Fusina."
Winifred: "And where is that?"
Malcolm: "Entrance to the Brenta."

She is uncertain whether he is still angry over their quarrel—if that is what it was—or whether these brusque phrases are only his ordinary way of speaking. She wonders if she ought to bring up the matter of the packet again. No, better not to. If only the thing were at the bottom of the lagoon! Winifred begins thinking rapidly, first about the packet and then about other matters. When she asked Captain Langrish about the note he said it was from Villetard, the secretary of the French Legation. Then he asked her if she knew Villetard, and even seemed (perhaps) mildly surprised that she didn't. In this case perhaps she is not in Captain Langrish's custody at all, but (in some mysterious and labyrinthine way) in Villetard's, and Captain Langrish is only acting for Villetard, or carrying out his orders. But how could this be, when only this afternoon it was Captain Langrish who led the boarding of the *Libérateur d'Italie* and inflicted a frightful carnage on her crew, including poor Captain Laugier? The more she thinks about this the less sense it makes; and perhaps it is not meant to make sense,

perhaps it is only a deliberate plan to confuse her. But if you begin
to think that everyone around you is conspiring, speaking about
you and making plans behind your back, then you are mad. This
she knows. Unless, that is, people really *are* making plans about
you behind your back. Then you are only shrewd to notice it. Is
she shrewd, or mad? Probably neither. It is a presumption on her
part to imagine, on the one hand that she is singular enough to be
mad, on the other hand that her affairs are important enough that
the whole city of Venice and environs (the gondola now seems to
have carried them a good distance from the city itself) is conspiring to interfere in them. A powerful wish arises in her and domi-
nates her thoughts: that Jean-Marie were with her to advise her
and protect her in all this, or at least to explain what in Heaven's
name is going on.

There are only a few dim lights floating by now, rather far away,
across the fields from the canal. The gondola passes under a
bridge. There is a plashing of wavelets from the muddy bank.
Then a village goes by; a lighted doorway, a woman framed in it
for an instant to stare at the gondola moving past up the canal.
Darkness again. To the right, visible in fragments through the
shutters, some shadows of tall narrow trees, perhaps poplars or
cypresses. Now and then one of the crooked stakes that seem to
be stuck in the mud all about in this part of the world. Then the
rhythmically grating sound of the oar ceases. The gondola drifts.

She hears the liquid murmur of the oar again. The gondola slips
through the water with a faint rustle as soft as the tearing of silk.
Then it bumps against some stakes and stops. The dirty white
stone of a water-stair is visible. Beyond that only darkness.

The gondolier speaks from behind, in the soft and flowing lilt of
the dialect.

"Èccoci, Paròn."

THE GONDOLIER LEADS THE WAY

The gondolier leads the way up a path overgrown with weeds. There are some indistinct shapes in the starlight that are probably trees. Winifred makes out ahead a large rectangle of darker gray, cutting off part of the sky. As they approach this becomes a good-sized country-house in the Palladian manner. They ascend some stone stairs that grit with dust or sand underfoot. Under the porch the starlight is gone and it is totally dark again.

Somehow the gondolier finds not only the door but a bell-pull. There is a dull tinkle of the bell inside, barely audible.

Nothing happens. Winifred hears a cricket in the darkness, and the faint rustle of wind in the trees. The gondolier rings again.

There is the creak of a window above them, although nothing can be seen.

Voice: "Chi xe?"

Gondolier: "Amici."

The window closes. After a long interval a kind of spectral cry rises from inside the villa, as though someone were calling or asking a question. There are footsteps on the marble behind the locked door. The sound of ironwork being manipulated is heard. The heavy door opens a hand's-breadth, and is stopped by a short chain. Someone is behind it with a lamp. A slit of yellow light appears along the door-edge, silhouetting the gondolier in his faded purple jacket.

The gondolier, without a word, produces an envelope from his trousers and passes it through the door. Winifred is able to see him clearly for the first time. He is very young, hardly more than a boy.

The odd bird-cry echoes again from inside the house.

"Luciana. Cossa gh'è? Xe tarda, sai."

The door remains ajar on its chain but the lamp disappears. They are obliged to wait again for a time, evidently while someone inside opens and reads the letter.

The lamp slowly approaches the door again. There is a final clank as the chain is removed. The door swings open. A woman in peasant dress holds the lamp and stands aside for them to enter. Captain Langrish, who follows last, hesitates at the doorstep, but she motions for him to enter too.

The entry-hall is a broad corridor with a high ceiling, extending through the villa to the rear where it ends in a stairway. It is illuminated only by a pair of tapers set in tall bronze candlesticks, one on either side of the stairway at the end. By the stairway stands the mistress of the house: a lean woman, no longer young, with a dark sun-burned face and a rather stringy neck. She is clad in an Indian dressing-gown that ends just below the knees, white stockings and slippers, and a turban. There is something aviary about her whole person. She has a bird-beak, a crane-like angle of the shoulders, a bird-like way of standing with one foot turned out.

Bird-Woman: "I am Elisabetta D'Artigny Baraoni. You are Mademoiselle Hervey?"

Winifred, rather flustered, nods. The Bird-Woman speaks French with a heavy accent, rolling the r's and lilting the syllables in a characteristic Italianate way. She barely inclines her head to Captain Langrish, who is standing some distance to the rear. Taking this for a sign, he makes a small bow himself, turns on his heel, and leaves through the door which is still standing open. He has not said a word. The gondolier follows him. The serving-woman goes immediately to the door, pushes it shut, and chains and bolts it.

As uneasy as she has occasionally felt in the presence of Captain Langrish, Winifred finds herself a little disconcerted at his abrupt departure. On the one hand the departure itself has removed any possibility that he might represent a menace to her; on the other hand it has left her in the company of this bizarre creature whose own character, and intentions toward her, are uncertain.

Mme. D'Artigny: "What is that odd garment you are wearing? It is certainly not yours. It doesn't fit you very well."

She speaks to the servant in dialect. The woman comes forward and helps Winifred off with the cloak. She stands revealed in the midshipman's breeches and shirt, which are still damp and cling to various parts of her person.

Mme. D'Artigny: "Mais ça c'est honteux, Mademoiselle. It's a disgrace."

Around her neck on a cord hangs a curious lorgnette in sculptured gold. It has a pivot where the two arms join, so it can be adjusted to eye-width. The two arms are in the form of allegorical figures with outspread wings holding the round circles of glass. She raises this instrument and examines Winifred more carefully through it.

Mme. D'Artigny: "Is it the officer who dressed you in that way? Besides, you seem to be wet. Did he treat you in a rude manner? Est-ce qu'il t'a rudoyée?"

Winifred speaks for the first time, in her own French which is at least as good as that of Mme. D'Artigny Baraoni.

Winifred: "Absolument pas. On the contrary, it was he who rescued me from the water when I fell in."

Mme. D'Artigny: "Ah. In any case all that must come off immediately. Luciana!"

Servant: "Siora, sì."

In spite of the ferocious events of the day Winifred sleeps soundly. The fact of the matter is that there were so many events in the day, and they were forced onto her consciousness with such an unremitting velocity and richness, that she hardly recalls all of them distinctly, not even the sight of poor Captain Laugier lying in a pool of blood with that terrible wound in his neck. The room is cold but it is warm in the bed, which has a feather comforter on it. She is not in the least distracted by the strange bed and the rather odd nature of her surroundings, not to mention her hostess. She has slept in many beds in her young life and has traveled about the world by herself to a degree not considered conventional—or even proper—for young ladies of good breeding and family.

She sleeps—sound and safe. At least so she feels, and that is the important thing. In the heaviness of sleep is borne away the oddness of her situation—delivered by an enemy of the French into the house of a Frenchwoman, or at least an odd creature who is half French, and into the protection of Villetard, the secretary of the French Legation. And Captain Langrish departed, with the packetful of secrets she has been enjoined most strictly to guard with her life—the packet, she was told, should be destroyed rather than fall into Venetian hands. But she does not think of that either, for the moment. It is all submerged in a delicious black oblivion. Even the sounds are the sounds of sleep: a faint wind in the cypresses. A dog barking far off across the countryside.

And while she sleeps, who is Winifred exactly? In many respects she is a typical free-thinking young woman of her century, one who has read Locke, Hume, Montesquieu, and Burke. And yet to call her a bluestocking would hardly do justice to the impetuous and often imprudent physical side of her existence, a life at least as full of activity as that of the average well-bred young man. At sixteen she rode to the hunt like a boy, disdaining side-saddles, and was marked by the Master with the blood of her own fox. The French finishing school in Passy that followed, operated by some rather worldly Carmelite Sisters, added to her grace perhaps but did little to diminish her restlessness, or her dissatisfaction with the restrictions usually placed on the activities and movements of her sex. (The Sisters allowed her to ride in the Bois, accompanied by three other girls and a riding-master, and she retains an affection for them for this if for nothing else.)

The violent events of 1792 obliged her to leave Paris and come back to the estate in the Kentish countryside. There she was, twenty. She was bored and had nothing to do. Her widowed father, in spite of his quite conventional gestures of affection for her, really cared only for the hunt and the bottle of port he put away every evening before going to bed. The family was well-to-do and possessed, in addition to the property in Kent, a town house in St. James Square occupied by her two bachelor uncles. Edmund and Monty, deprived of any useful activity by the rule of primogeniture, had nothing much to do with themselves but read free-thinking literature as she did. Winifred preferred living with them rather than with her father, even though their ideas about what was proper for a young lady were not very much more liberal. (Their Politicks were confined to the social order and which men should command which others; not what a young lady ought to wear while riding in Hyde Park, or which side of the horse her legs should be on.)

She had no suitors, and didn't want any. She wasn't even pretty, as Malcolm was so quick to observe. It was true she was *passing through* an age when all young female animals are attractive to the opposite sex. She had a good complexion, and large gray eyes that she knew somehow (she certainly hadn't learned it from the Sisters) to use to advantage. But the long face, the large chin and eyes—her resemblance to a horse was unmistakable. Winifred was "coltish" (so said her uncles). But she was grown to a long-legged young horse now, feeling her adulthood, able to kick harder and wanting to range farther, out of the home pasture, over the hill to distant meadows. And yet there was something about her: she would never be a mare. The colt would always be there. Even as an old woman—it was impossible to imagine her as an old woman.

She rather baffled her uncles. They had no objection to bluestockings but were dubious about tomboys. Still they did nothing about it. What could they do? Life in St. James Square was the equal, almost, of that in Paris, and certainly preferable to the dull estate in Kent. The brothers ran a kind of joint-company male salon, if such a thing can be imagined. On Sunday evenings especially, but also on other nights of the week, persons of both sexes and various nationalities met to discuss the current state of the world and its well-known maladjustments, with general sympathy for the recent events in France. Once the shaggy and ill-kempt Charles Fox himself even appeared, fresh from his spectacular debates with Pitt in Parliament, arguing stoutly—not only that the Revolution was just—but that its justice justified its errors and even its crimes. That was a bit thick for Edmund and Monty, but they followed Voltaire in disagreeing with a fellow's opinions but being ready to defend them—if not to the death—at least to a reasonable degree. French visitors came as well, and a few Polish patriots exiled by the partition of their homeland.

* * *

It was on one of these Sunday evenings that Winifred first heard the words of that Swiss watchmaker's son and vagabond who had set Europe on fire: "Man is born free and everywhere he is in chains. We think ourselves the master of others, and we remain greater slaves than they. How did this change come about? I do not know. What can make it legitimate? That question I think I can answer."

The reader was a young Frenchman all in black satin: black coat, black knee-breeches, black waistcoat, stockings, and shoes. A black cravat, newly fashionable, in place of the lace still worn by younger men. A placid narrow olive face with drooping eyelids, and in spite of this a vivacious and even slightly excited manner. Jean-Marie de Fontenay (the noble particle, she discovered later, was at least partly spurious and derived from his mother's side of the family) was twenty-three, only a little older than she was. He read distinctly and with an elegant Parisian grasseyement, glancing at his audience now and then from under his bird-like lashes.

"To renounce liberty is to renounce being a man, to surrender the rights of humanity and even its duties. For him who renounces everything no indemnity is possible. Such a renunciation is incompatible with man's nature; to remove all liberty from his will is to remove all morality from his acts. Finally, it is an empty and contradictory convention that sets up, on the one side, absolute authority, and on the other, unlimited obedience. Is it not clear that we can be under no obligation to a person from whom we have the right to exact everything?"

Jean-Marie no doubt had his own interpretation of these significant words, Edmund and Monty referred them to the parliamentary struggle between Fox and Pitt, and to Winifred they meant quite something else. They spoke to something in her womanly nature that she had hardly recognized, herself, to this moment. For she, like any healthy young woman, was strongly inclined to—what her nature called her to. Yet to marry (and any other expression of this impetus was unthinkable) was to submit one's self to the absolute tyranny—one backed by the force of law—of a person who might reveal himself as a brute, or simply an indifferent fox-hunter and port-drinker like her father. But if Politicks could rest on a Social Contract, could not also marriage? Could not one imagine a union of souls, of intellects, and of—

other things (Winifred had been raised on a country estate and was familiar with how colts were made) as equal as that which governed the relations of men in America, or in Revolutionary France? Jean-Marie would no doubt agree; he would have to agree; he was bound by his principles and by the ideals of Rousseau which he declaimed so fervently. His waistcoat, she discerned by examining it more closely, was embroidered with a fine scrollwork of black on black. Later in the evening, seating himself quite spontaneously at the pianoforte (bought by the uncles in a sporadic and isolated effort to convert Winifred into a marriageable young lady), he played a sonata or two of the younger Scarlatti, effortlessly and with a certain grace, if not with a very great force. His fingernails, unlike those of Mr. Charles Fox, were immaculate. Winifred became a Rousseauist on the spot.

She read *Julie, ou la Nouvelle Héloïse*, obtainable only with difficulty from a bookseller in Soho and certainly not in her uncles' library of Politickal tracts and boring tomes from the previous century. Even though it concerned a relationship that was in some respects not quite proper, it confirmed her notions—they were not notions, they were firmly held principles—of ideal marriage. For Julie, in spite of her touching affection for Saint-Preux, remained true to her unloved husband Wolmar, the three of them living in amicable and happy terms in the same house. And for Julie (in the book) everything revolved around this matter of being True. If husband and wife were equally True to each other, then there could be no dominance of one over the other. The trouble with matters in the present age was that wives were obliged to be True, whereas other rules applied to husbands. The principle, transferred back again from the Home to the Body Politick, might even be held to justify the excesses of the Revolution—as Mr. Fox had pointed out—although he hadn't put it quite in those words. Louix XVI had not been True to his people, so they, quite properly, cut off his head. And when M. Robespierre (a person she did not care very much for, to tell the truth) had not been True to the Revolution, they had done the same for him. These things were all very unfortunate, but they were the affairs of men. If they wished to cut off each other's heads, it was important at least that it be done according to the proper principles.

The relations of men and women were quite something else. No husband had ever proposed to cut off his wife's head, except perhaps someone like the Marquis de Sade. (Winifred had heard of him, although even the bookseller in Soho didn't have books of *this* sort.) Because, in the relations of men and women, love (amour was not quite the same thing, and M. Rousseau had difficulty with the matter because he was obliged to write in French) entered into the matter of being True. And no matter how true you were to a principle, you would never harm anybody on account of that principle when love was involved.

Winifred had discovered something. If others had discovered it before, or were discovering it simultaneously in this same city, it made no matter. If men and women were True (and they would surely be, as soon as they listened even for a moment to Rousseau or read *La Nouvelle Héloïse*) then love would be transformed, and along with it marriage, the family, and finally all society. For society was only a large family, one that quarreled frequently and suffered from a lack of consideration, often, of other members' feelings. Once Winifred conceived this principle, although she confided it to no one, she remained True to it permanently and irrevocably; it was as much a part of her as her complexion or the timbre of her voice.

By 1796 events on the Continent were not looking quite so frightful. The more moderate Directoire had succeeded to the excesses of the Jacobins; the guillotine was dismantled and a structure something like a constitutional government erected in its place. Winifred began to be concerned about the fate of the Carmelite Sisters, with whom she had passed four happy years in Passy, and from whom nothing had been heard since the suppression of religious orders in '93. Since she was twenty-five now she was mistress of the inheritance left her by her mother, and she made up her mind quickly what needed to be done. She put on a waterproof mantle and a traveling-hat, packed an old green portmanteau that belonged to her uncles, and embarked for Paris via Folkestone, Ostend, Ghent, and Lille. This was not easy, since France and England were still ostensibly at war; although Lord Malmsbury was in Paris at the time treating for peace. Winifred used her gray eyes to advantage and surrendered a certain number of her mother's gold sovereigns to dishonest officials. She arrived in Paris in November, just as it was evident that Lord Malmsbury's efforts were coming to nothing. What was the reaction of the uncles? They shrugged. They were helpless. They had been unable to prevent her from riding in Hyde Park in breeches, and now they were unable to prevent her from traveling alone and unescorted in a country with which Britain was technically in a state of war.

She did not find the Sisters. They had been dispersed to the countryside and were said to be living near Nogent. Without very much difficulty, however, she found Jean-Marie. He had dropped the particle from his name and found a minor post in the Directoire, in the Ministry of Foreign Affairs. His post was highly confidential, but actually it had to do with communications with the Army of Italy under General Bonaparte, since he spoke a passable Italian. (He had learned it to study the cantatas of Galuppi and Vivaldi, although he didn't explain this to his superiors when he applied for the position.) He had useful connections: an aunt of his was a cousin of Letourneur and he had once been introduced to Barras. He seemed to be delighted by Winifred's unexpected arrival, although in a young Frenchman it was hard to tell delight from courtesy, and he found her lodgings in rue des Francs-Bourgeois, not far from the Hôtel Carnavalet. Winifred was soon introduced into intellectual circles that accorded with her enthusiasm for Rousseau, Helvétius, and the Philosophes. She saw Jean-Marie frequently, although, because of the confidentiality of his position at the Ministry, most of their conversation was about music. He was an accomplished violist as well as a pianist and harpsichordist, and Winifred, fumbling to recall her own girlish pianoforte lessons, managed to accompany him in a sonata or two of Boccherini. She much preferred to talk about Rousseau, on which subject Jean-Marie had a curious attitude which might be described as a combination of the enthusiastic and the languid.

Both Rousseau and music were dangerous potions for young persons of the opposite sex. Bliss it was in that dawn to be alive, as a poet accurately noted, and to be young was very heaven! Winifred began to feel that, if it were her destiny to be True to something, it might quite possibly be Jean-Marie. He made her feel strange in parts of her that heretofore had been dark and obscure, and were now filled with a premonition of indeterminate bliss, as though some thing in her that had previously been inert was now warming and flowing. For his part he embraced her once in a fiacre and smiled at her frequently—when no one was noticing—with his warm and well-bred charm. Little further in the way of intimacy was possible, since he lived with his aunt, who was a rather severe old lady with ideas dating from the Ancien Régime; and she, Winifred, lived alone in lodgings so that her position was—ambiguous.

Pseudonyms of a pastoral sort were fashionable, and in Jean-Marie's set she became known as Clélia. This was his private name for her in their more affectionate moments, or playfully when others were present. He found the name Winifred terribly stiff and Protestant—English in the worst sense—and preferred to think of her (as she was in part) as a shepherdess in a novel on the order of Honoré D'Urfé's *Astrée*: "Ah Clélia, comme tu es charmante, avec ta longue figure anglaise, ton calme nébuleux et Ossianique." It was impossible to insert "Winifred" into a sentence like this. It began with that serpentine consonant which no French tongue could wrap itself around, and besides . . . well, in short: "Ah Clélia, comme tu es charmante." It was a double misunderstanding; she took him, perhaps, for a hero out of *Werther,* or even of *La Nouvelle Héloïse* itself: but which? the dull husband Wolmar? the charming but illicit lover Saint-Preux?

In January he was unexpectedly posted to Italy, on a mission so confidential that he could not even explain to Winifred where she was to write him. Before he left—they had only two or three days—they were engaged. The declaration took place in the presence of the aunt, which, Winifred felt, conferred upon it at least some measure of authenticity. It all seemed quite casual, not to say haphazard. Things were done differently on the Continent, or perhaps it was only the effect of the Revolution. The aunt, although she lived in a town house in Place des Victoires and had a half-dozen or more servants, was called Citizeness Lablanchière. Winifred called her Ma Tante and she called Winifred Ma Pauvre Fille; perhaps because she was separated from her fiancé, or perhaps because she was not as wealthy as she, the aunt, was. This latter, Winifred felt, was a curious sentiment for a Citizeness.

For three months nothing was heard from Jean-Marie. Winifred had a miniature of him on the dressing-table in her tiny room in the Marais. She was deeply in love. She thought about little else. She was angry with herself, even, for this intrusion of the sentimental and personal into her previous devotion to philosophical thought. Worst of all, she found herself longing for Jean-Marie not only with her head and her heart but in baser regions she had preferred to pretend were common only to farm animals. That embrace in the fiacre had been a folly! In a single instant it had taught her the urgency and grace of a man's body, the odor of musk and leather, the hard and yet tender pressure of fingers at one's waist. And Paris was full of young men at least as attractive, as well placed, and as accessible as Jean-Marie. Their eyes fixed on hers and refused to turn away whenever she entered a room. But Winifred remained True.

JEAN-MARIE IS WITH A CORPSE

Jean-Marie is with a corpse, watching it, looking at it. Perhaps it is his father. The room is light, with a grayish illumination from a large window, but even so it is hard to tell where he is exactly or what the room is. The details of the furniture, the window, and the walls are vague. The corpse is lying on its back on top of the bed. There is a fly on the cheek, walking toward the eye. Is the eye open or closed? He is not sure, and doesn't care to look at the eye to see. The fly will reach it in a few seconds. Frightening. But angering too: he is frightened of the corpse and angered at the fly. He tries to wave it away. To no avail. Several times he waves, his hand moving closer and closer. The fly ignores him. Finally he brushes too close; the fly flies off but his hand strikes the face just at the curve of the cheek. He is terrified. A sensation as of meat: there is meat inside there, cold meat. But enclosed in a disgusting white opaque resilient membrane, like the skin that forms on boiled milk that is allowed to cool. Yielding to the touch, leaving a slight concave depression that only gradually fills in again. He tries to make a sound but is unable to. He is paralyzed. A feeling like a cold fire runs through him instantly, from head to toe. This wakes him up.

You should never sleep on your back. Imagine someone sleeping on his back. Sound asleep, unaware of what is going on in the room. Ça fait peur. It's scary. Anything could come and seize him by the throat, penetrate his nostrils, coil softly around his genitals like a snake and gradually enclose them. The soft vulnerable part of him is unprotected. Now imagine him sleeping on his side; curled up with bent knees, the blanket snug on his neck. It is snug, safe, secure. It feels good to think about it. It is sleeping on his back, he is sure, that causes dreams. But even though he is always careful to go to sleep on his side—the left side, left arm under his head, left knee bent slightly and the other knee drawn up over it—he often awakens in the middle of the night or in the morning, as he does now, on his back. He is covered with a cold moisture: his sleeping-shirt is soaked. He turns onto his side and raises himself, throws back the covers, and puts his feet over onto the cold floor. These Venetians insist on having marble floors, and they also have a quaint custom of removing the rugs at Easter and laying them back down again only in November. He raises his bare feet and props them on the edge of the bed.

"Massimo!"

There is no answer. The apartments are large and the walls thick; still Massimo ought to be listening because he knows that it is late in the morning and that he will wake up soon. Jean-Marie focuses his eyes across the room to the mantel-clock by Le Noir, with allegorical figures in gilt and bronze representing the Rape of Europa. It is stopped. Massimo has not wound it. It is probably about eleven. Massimo, even though he is only seventeen or eighteen, gives himself certain airs and imagines himself a little gentleman, a petit-maître. Borrowing Jean-Marie's waistcoats without permission, parading in the Piazza with a perfumed hand-kerchief in his sleeve, taking the air in the evening in the gondola when Jean-Marie isn't using it. Sometimes, to bring him down from his high-horse a little, Jean-Marie calls him Minimo. He doesn't care for this, and sometimes it pricks him into good manners. At other times it just makes him sulk.

"Minimo!"

While waiting, Jean-Marie passes the time looking for his slippers, casting his eyes around those parts of the room he can see from his position on the bed. He locates one of them under a kind of Renaissance commode with bowed legs on the opposite side of the room. The other one is invisible.

Jean-Marie (more loudly, this time with a note of impatience in his voice): "Massimo!"

The door to the bed-chamber is ajar. After a considerable wait he hears Massimo's voice in the distance, at least two rooms away.

Massimo: "Cossa voleu?"

Jean-Marie: "Que voulez-vous, Monsieur?"

Massimo: "Che voulé vou, Moussou?"

Jean-Marie: "I want you to come here, of course."

Massimo appears in the doorway, bland, his thin handsome face with its Venetian eyes-set-in-shadows as innocent as a child.

Massimo: "Sì, Paròn."

Jean-Marie: "Oui, Monsieur."

Massimo: "Oui, Moussou."

Jean-Marie: "What do you think I want? I want coffee."

Massimo: "Sùbito, Moussou."

Jean-Marie sighs and does not bother to explain that sùbito is tout de suite. Ordinarily Massimo speaks in dialect and Jean-Marie in Italian. But Massimo is attempting to learn French so he can become a waiter at Florian's or Quadri's. This is a difficult task, because Massimo has no skill in languages. He has not even learned Italian properly, and he is trying to master French.

Jean-Marie: "Wait, Massimo. Come back."

Massimo: "Oui, Moussou."

Jean-Marie: "First find my slippers."

He finds the slippers and brings them to the bed, then goes off to make the coffee. Jean-Marie goes into the dressing-room, washes his hands and face in a basin, and dries them with a towel. Then he removes the sleeping-shirt and dresses in a shirt, a pair of aubergine-colored breeches, and white stockings, sitting down on a chair before he takes off the slippers in order not to touch the cold floor. Since the Revolution most young Frenchmen, and a good many Venetians, have abandoned knee-breeches in favor of pantaloons. But he continues to wear breeches, for two reasons, one personal and one Politickal. First, he has a well-shaped leg and sees no reason to conceal it; and second, the breeches are old-fashioned and suggest perhaps that he is an émigré or at least conservative in his opinions, exactly what is required for his purposes. In concession to the times, however, he wears no wig and brushes his hair in the style called en oreilles de chien: cut straight across the brow at the level of the eyebrows and left long at the sides to cover the ears. Massimo comes in with the coffee and sets it on the small round mosaic table by the chair.

While he is drinking the coffee Massimo brings him the rest of his clothes. The shoes (Jean-Marie prefers soft Florentine pumps to boots), an embroidered waistcoat in dark red to go with the breeches, and the cravat. Nobody but a hopeless reactionary wears lace anymore. The cravat is from Bond Street. With his narrow musician's fingers he ties it skillfully in a knot under his chin.

Massimo: "A coat, Moussou?"

Jean-Marie: "The English spencer."

This too Jean-Marie has bought in London. It is a kind of short riding-coat, snugly cut to show off the figure if yours is as good as Jean-Marie's, and ending just below the waist. (It is called a pet-en-l'air in French, but Jean-Marie ignores this vulgarity.) Finally he selects a soft black hat with a flat top and a short, slightly curled brim, also fashionable. Then, finishing the coffee, he puts on the hat and takes his gloves from the table.

Massimo: "Gondola, Moussou?"

Jean-Marie: "No. I'm going to the Piazza."

He crosses into the corridor and goes down the stairs, followed by Massimo carrying a large old-fashioned key with an iron sphere, like a small cannon-ball, attached to it with a chain. Jean-Marie has forgotten the dream and is in a better humor now after his coffee. At the bottom of the stairs is an atrium surrounded by graceful Corinthian columns. The Ca' Pogi was built in the previous century by a Senator who was found guilty of some indiscretion by the Council of Ten and banished from Venice in disgrace. It is not on the Grand Canal, but it is not far from it and the quarter is quiet, which is an advantage if you take music seriously as Jean-Marie does. There are marble cherubs along the staircase and a pair of small sculptured lions at the bottom. In the atrium, if you turn right, you come to a massive portal of wrought-iron in elaborate fretwork. This opens onto the water-stairs on Rio Ca' Foscari, where the gondola is kept. The street door, across the atrium on the other side, is of heavy carved oak; it is almost as elegant as the water-door but not quite. Massimo unlocks this door with the key and lets him out. Jean-Marie is now in the small lane that leads off in a crooked fashion around the church of San Pantalon. It is so narrow that by raising his arms he can touch the walls on either side. And he knows that in a niche a short way down the street, where a few straggly vines sprout from the stones, he will have to deal with the cats.

The cats by all evidence belong to Ca' Pogi; they were there before he came. Perhaps they are the genii loci of the place; if they are not demons at least they are the familiars of demons. Curiously enough, they offer no resistance when he comes home to the palazzo, but contest the way furiously whenever he tries to leave.

And these are no ordinary cats. The cats of Venice are wild as Hell. They are twice as large as ordinary cats. They stalk the calli at will, and are not interfered with. They communicate over houses. At night their phallic yawps, echoing over the roof-tops, sound like eerie human cries, or infants being tortured. If a corpse is found in the rio, and no human culprit immediately visible, the folk of the quarter will say, Xe la zata del gato, it's the cat's paw that has done this.

There are probably three or four of them in the niche at the end of the calle, but they slink around and over each other so that it is hard to count them. Jean-Marie crosses to the far side, but the calle is narrow. When he comes opposite the niche there is a brindle flash and one of the beasts scrambles up the vines ready to spring; and then another.

He should have brought his stick, he thinks. But it is not etiquette to carry a stick in the daytime.

Cat: "Hsssss!"

Jean-Marie: "You Devil. Retrovade Satana!"

They decide to allow him to pass, this time. One of them is missing an eye. He stares at Jean-Marie redly out of the other.

Because of his success with the cats, Jean-Marie is in an even better mood. Still the day is young yet. There is no telling what will happen. He makes his way through a Chinese puzzle of streets—which, since it is in his quarter, he has mastered like a Venetian—crosses a rio on a bridge, and comes out on the Grand Canal near San Tomà. Here he takes a tragheto or ferry-gondola across to the San Marco quarter of the city.

The tragheto is a plebeian means of transport. It only costs a brass coin, and you share the gondola with all kinds of people. The Venetians of the common class prefer these tragheti to bridges, because you don't have to climb up and down on them, which is bad for the heart; and also because there is a certain grandeur attached to riding in a gondola, even if you have to share it and it only costs a soldo. The Rialto bridge, in fact, is called the Tragheto dei Cani, because it is the only place that dogs can cross the Grand Canal. Dogs are not allowed in a tragheto. But anybody else is.

Jean-Marie often makes use of the tragheto; first because of his republican principles, and second because people always talk in the tragheto and he can listen to what they are saying. This morning, in addition to Jean-Marie, there are five passengers in the tragheto: two merchants, a pair of stone-masons, and an old woman with a shopping-basket. The old woman says nothing and the two merchants are talking about some linen they propose to buy, whether it has been illegally imported and if so whether it would be wise to get involved in buying it. The younger one is in favor of taking the risk, the older one counsels caution.

The other conversation is more interesting. The two masons are talking about Bonaparte, or Buonaparte. The one says that the name sounds almost like an Italian, one of us.

The other: "Eh, of course, tricks. It's a name to win us over to their side."

The one: "Or the scoundrel chose it so that no one would know his real name—a name in bad repute."

The other: "And Napoleone—one of those names people are taking these days, names out of books—like Brutus, Alcibiades, Scipio—none of them Christian names. They'll bring bad luck to those that bear them. Not a name anyone has heard of, like Zorzo, or Marco, or Bepi, or Todaro, or Carlo."

It is decided that General Bonaparte is probably non-existent, an imaginary being, a name made up to hide some dishonored old captain who has disgraced himself, or invented by the French to flatter Italian ears. Jean-Marie concludes that the lower classes are anti-French, but mainly on grounds of ignorance. The tragheto bumps in between the stakes and the narrow plank pier, and Jean-Marie and the others get out.

Jean-Marie is almost as familiar with this part of the city as he is with his own San Pantalon quarter. By way of Campo Sant'Angelo, the Ponte de la Malvasia Vechia (that is, Old Malmsey Bridge), and Campo San Fantìn he arrives in five minutes in the Frezzeria. This narrow street bent in the middle at a right angle—once the quarter of arrowsmiths, as its name indicates—is now relegated to

ridotti, houses of ill repute, and privately employed ladies who
stand in doorways. At another time Jean-Marie might be interested in these activities. But nothing much is going on in the
Frezzeria at this hour in the broad daylight; it comes to life only at
ten in the evening. There is that stale and dingy air that always
hangs over places of vice in the daytime. He goes on past the
church of San Geminiano, through the archway, and out into the
Piazza just as the great bronze voice of the Marangona, the bell in
the Campanile, booms out the noon. The pigeons scatter and then
settle down again.

On either side of the Piazza are the long arched façades of the
Procuratie Vechie and the Procuratie Nove, occupied by various
offices of the Signoria, and under the respective porticos are the
two cafés, facing each other across the vast empty square. Quadri's
is the more recent, having been founded only in 1775, and is
patronized mainly by foreigners; Venetians, especially those of the
patrician class, prefer to go to Florian's. Jean-Marie, crossing the
Piazza at an angle, directs himself toward the latter.

Florian's is already crowded. Although the day is cool, Jean-
Marie selects a table outside under the porch. From this point he
can see in both directions, and also the tables are closer together
and people talk louder, because of the noise from other tables and
the general openness under the portico. Inside, in the small rooms
upholstered in red velvet, the air is more intimate and people keep
their voices lower, especially if there is someone else in the room.
Jean-Marie takes down a Gazette from the rack and sits at a table
pretending to read it. The news is rather stale because of the
blockade, and perhaps Jean-Marie has read it before, but it doesn't
matter. He fixes his eyes onto the columns of type with an expression of great curiosity and intelligence.

On his left is a table of patricians who have evidently just come
out of the Procuratie after a morning's work. One, who seems
more animated than the rest, is a plump and florid young man in a
wine-colored coat, breeches to match, white stockings, and low
shoes. The others are dressed more simply, in black or dark blue.
On the far side of the table is a small old man with an irascible
manner, supporting his chin on a silver-headed cane. He is covered down to the ankles in a toga that seems too large for him. In
addition to this he wears a flowing cap and an old-fashioned lace
neck-cloth, neither of them very clean. He says nothing and only

looks morosely from one to the other, out of his deep-set eyes, as the younger men talk.

The table on the other side is occupied by a pair of officers who seem to be from the Arsenal, to judge from their talk, and from what little Jean-Marie knows about uniforms. Jean-Marie listens to both conversations at once and at the same time tries to read his Gazette. This is not easy, because of the general din, clink of crockery, voices from farther tables, people passing by under the portico, and so on. From the table of patricians he catches: ". . . advanced over his superiors by Barras . . . disreputable . . . reward, so they say, for marrying Barras' discarded mistress."

Jean-Marie pricks up his ears. It is not clear who is disreputable, Barras or Bonaparte. And he didn't know that Mme. Beauharnais, the present wife of the General, had been Barras' mistress. If it is true; perhaps it is not. Meanwhile the conversation from the other table is also interesting. He catches the name *Libérateur,* a word that interests him very much.

Waiter: "Signore?"

Jean-Marie: "Sherbet. And a glass of water."

Waiter: "Sùbito."

This damnable interruption has made him miss something important, probably.

The florid young man is telling an anecdote about Bonaparte's wedding night. The General, it seems, encountered virile opposition from the bride's pet dog, Fortuné. This gentleman was in possession of Madame's bed. . . . The General wanted him to leave, but to no avail. He was told to share the bed with Fortuné or sleep somewhere else. He had to take it or leave it. At the worst possible moment Fortuné bit the General on the leg.

There is laughter. Jean-Marie now recognizes two of the patricians. The old gentleman in the toga is Paternian, a Senator and a member of one of the oldest and most respected families in Venice. Next to him is his nephew Alvise Contìn, a taciturn young man with a frowning expression. He is twenty-six, barely old enough to vote in the Maggior Consiglio. When the others laugh he only smiles, in a slightly reserved manner.

The patricians glance at Jean-Marie, take him for French or English, and go on talking in dialect as they have from the beginning.

The florid young man has information that Joséphine wears no drawers. She has formed this habit in her childhood, for reasons connected with hygiene, ventilation, and the tropical climate of her native Martinique.

Florid young man: "She is said to have excellent genital hygiene."

Another: "Who says so?"

Florid young man: "Many people."

One of those in a position to know, apparently, is the young Captain Charles, the hussars officer with whom she was infatuated at the time of her visit to Milan last year. There are several other tales of this sort. Jean-Marie reflects that Bonaparte shares the misfortune of the Bourbon monarchs: that all his most personal and private affairs become public overnight, chiefly through the indiscretions of women. His sherbet comes and he sips it slowly from the spoon. He still has one ear cocked toward the patricians, but he is now listening almost exclusively to the two officers on the other side, one a captain and the other a lieutenant. They too speak Venetian.

Captain: "The Frenchman was hove to under the fort it seems. Requesting permission to enter. Perfectly proper."

Lieutenant: "Not at all. He fired first. No question about that."

Jean-Marie has difficulty hearing. That Infernal waiter banging his dishes!

Captain: " . . . Sant'Andrea. According to Pizzamano's own report . . ."

Lieutenant: ". . . only a warning shot. The *Libérateur* fired a broadside at the fort, I tell you. Then the *Pandora* came up on her bow, fired, and boarded . . ."

The officers too now glance in his direction. He is deep in his Gazette and obviously a foreigner. Still they lower their tone. After that he can make out only fragments.

They soon get up from the table, clap on their tricornes, and leave in opposite directions, one going off to the Boca de Piazza, the other toward the Arsenal. Jean-Marie turns his attention to the other table, where the patricians are now talking about Politicks. The florid young man is referring to certain principles. The Rights of Man are mentioned. But his high talk is mocked by a middle-aged man in a short wig.

"Bah. Do you know what they come to, your fine principles? The principle of all Revolution—get down from there, I want what you've got."

Florid young man: "That's not what Montesquieu says."

Short wig: "Montesquieu's not in charge in Paris just now."

Florid young man: "Still, the French only want everybody to be equal."

Short wig: "Only! That's a large only, Zuane. Who's equal? Am I equal to my gondolier? Are you equal to the Doge?"

There is laughter and somebody calls the florid young man a Jacobin. He himself evidently doesn't take what he is saying entirely seriously. His face becomes even redder; he lifts his shoulders and laughs with the rest. He is excited, but in a jocular tone. He persists.

"But! Really. If the Senate voted a constitution, and some other reforms, it still might be possible to—"

Short wig: "To what? Give up, eh? Kiss their foot."

Florid young man: "No, no. To make an alliance with the French. After all our real enemies are the Austrians. The General"—(he carefully avoids the word Bonaparte, which the foreigner at the next table might understand)—"has already driven them clean out of the Terraferma for us. If we could come to terms—after all, both France and Venice are republics."

Short wig: "You're naive, Zuane, if you trust the French any more than the Austrians."

The florid young man looks around the table. But he finds no allies. The others are skeptical. He sighs.

"Then we'll have to fight."

Jean-Marie would very much like to have Paternian's opinion on this point. But the Senator is not very loquacious. And anyhow, just at this moment, two old gentlemen dressed in black, with black tricornes and black silk stockings, come down under the portico and stop at the table. Paternian erects himself, rather painfully, with the aid of his cane. The three patricians exchange greetings in the old-fashioned manner, taking off their caps with the left hand while the right hand goes grandly to the heart.

"Cari vechi . . ."

"Lustrissimo . . ."

The others rise too. There is a chorus of Lustrissimos. With Venetian indolence, the mouth hardly open, this soon becomes

Strissimo, Tissimo, Issimo, and finally an inaudible whisper. Likewise with Ecelenza, which starts with Celenza and dies away to Zenza, Senza—this last with faint malice, since it also means "without," and the old gentlemen are penniless Barnaboti, so-called because they reside in the San Barnaba quarter of the city in houses provided by the state.

The whispers die away and the Barnaboti totter off under the portico. The others sit down again. The conversation turns to recent events on the Terraferma, and they begin discussing the Pasque Veronesi, as it is already coming to be called. It seems that on Easter Monday, only a few days ago, the inhabitants of Verona rose up against the French with pikes and kitchen-knives, where-upon the French brought in troops and put down the revolt with much bloodshed. Contìn is of the opinion that this uprising was deliberately provoked by the French, whereas the florid young man blames Austrian agitators. Nobody blames the Veronese, who are Venetian subjects. There is nothing new in all this and Jean-Marie hardly pays attention. He finishes his sherbet, takes a sip of water now and then, and for a moment forgets himself and begins following with interest an account in the Gazette of the visit of a Turkish potentate to Paris. The entertainment was sumptuous. He feels a twinge of regret for Paris. *After a collation at the Luxembourg, His Excellence was accompanied . . .*

He breaks off, not because of what the patricians at the next table are saying, but because he realizes that in the few moments he has been reading the paragraph about the Turkish visitor someone has set something on the small table in front of him. The man is already working his way off through the crowd under the portico: a square figure in a shapeless gray coat and a tricorne. Jean-Marie sighs and opens the note with his fingernail.

Ponte Marcello. Deux heures précises. Ne manquez pas.

He glances at the clock-tower across the Piazza. It is a little after one-thirty. He has plenty of time. But the conversation at the next table is dull, about Politicks again, although he hoped they would go back to more anecdotes about Joséphine and Barras. Jean-Marie sets a lira on the table, puts the Gazette away on the rack, and leaves.

AFTER MAKING HIS WAY THROUGH THE

After making his way through the usual series of connected streets shaped like dogs' hind legs, Jean-Marie comes out in Campo Santa Maria Formosa, an open rectangle with a large baroque church filling one end of it. From here the Ponte Marcello is only five minutes' walk. It is a remote and quiet part of the city. He slows his pace and glances at the clock in Campo Santa Marina, pretending to stop for a few moments and look into a shop-window full of crucifixes and religious vestments. It is important not to arrive too early and loaf conspicuously at the meeting-place, which in some respects is worse than being too late. It is important also not to pull out his watch, which would be a clearly visible signal that he is awaiting a rendezvous. He idles slowly along the calle, turns to the left, and arrives at the rio and the bridge just as the church of Santa Marina peals out the hour.

The gondola is exactly on time. It is creeping along the rio only a short distance away. It bumps against the quay. He steps lightly onto it, opens the door of the felze, and slips in.

He sits down on the small black chair, which might have been made for a child. It is so low that his knees pitch upward in an undignified way. Villetard is reclining on the sofa at the other end of the felze. It is some time before Jean-Marie's eyes adjust to the gloom. Finally he makes out the pupils of Villetard's eyes, which examine him for some time in silence. The face, with its high pale brow and its thin mouth almost without lips, is hardly visible in the shadow under the hat. Villetard slouches on the sofa, his right arm over the cushion behind him and the withered left arm in his lap. The baby-hand resting on the breeches is even paler than the face. The tiny nails, Jean-Marie observes, are immaculately groomed.

Villetard: "No one followed you?"

Jean-Marie has not looked to see, but nobody ever follows him. He is only a harmless music-student and not even Massimo takes him seriously, let alone the Inquisitors or the Council of Ten.

Jean-Marie: "No."

Villetard: "What have you been up to this morning?"

Jean-Marie (crisply): "Contacts with plebeians. Research on the reactions of the working class."

Villetard: "These are the persons to whom you are dispensing the informant funds?"

How to answer this question without precisely answering it? Jean-Marie maintains an air of dignified nonchalance.

Jean-Marie: "A pair of stone-masons, in the San Tomà parish."

Villetard: "And what did they provide?"

Jean-Marie: "Some opinion of General Bonaparte. There is a good deal of misinformation about him. Some people believe him to be Italian. Others, that he doesn't exist."

Villetard: "And then?"

Jean-Marie: "At Florian's."

Villetard: "So?"

Jean-Marie: "Some patricians including Paternian, a Senator. They were talking about the possibility of constitutional reforms, along with an alliance with France. The alternative would be a declaration of war."

Villetard has nothing to say to this. He doesn't seem very interested. Probably he knows about opinion in the Senate and is not impressed with Jean-Marie's show of information. He is silent for another period. So it is Jean-Marie himself who has to launch into the next subject.

Jean-Marie: "Yesterday the *Libérateur d'Italie* entered the lagoon, or attempted to."

Villetard: "And?"

This is another annoying habit of the man. If you tell him something he will just look at you blandly, with an air that is not so much skeptical as indifferent, and after a time he will say: Eh bien? Or sometimes: Et après? It implies that what you have related is of no importance, or didn't tell him anything he didn't already know, and that he is still waiting for something of value, or something of insight and intelligence, to issue from you.

Jean-Marie: "It seems there was an engagement and the *Libérateur* was captured. It's not clear who fired first. Pizzamano, the commander of the fort, has made a report."

Villetard: "How do you know this?"

Jean-Marie: "Sources among the officers at the Arsenal."

Villetard allows this too to pass without comment. Perhaps he has an idea what the sources amount to. Jean-Marie's eyes are accustomed to the gloom now and he can make out the face under the hat more clearly. One of its qualities is that the thin lipless mouth, although usually without expression, is very flexible. At least the ends are; the middle part remains fixed as though drawn with a pencil. The ends can move up or down at will. Now they curve up slightly; and then straighten out again.

Villetard: "Your fiancée is unharmed. You didn't ask about her."

Jean-Marie realizes that he has made a serious blunder. He ought to have asked immediately about Winifred. Villetard can only regard this as a curious omission on his part. He *is*, of course, interested in Winifred. It was on this account that he listened so intently to the conversation of the two officers at Florian's, and not for any military reason. If he has neglected to ask about her, it is because it has slipped his mind for a moment. And also because of Villetard's annoying way of assuming that it is he, Jean-Marie, who is to provide all the information, while Villetard simply slouches there with his arm over the sofa, looking at him as though he were a zoo specimen, without even blinking. Still, his failure to ask about her has left the suggestion in the air that he is not interested in Winifred, and therefore that there is something vaguely spurious or inauthentic about his behavior—for instance, that he is perhaps more interested in music than he is in either Winifred or the affairs of the Legation. Naturally Villetard himself offers none of these conjectures. He only contemplates Jean-Marie out of his small eyes that (Jean-Marie notices now for the first time) are set slightly too close together on either side of the narrow nose, which accounts for his alert and beady look in spite of the general expressionlessness of his face.

Well, it is necessary to consult one's wits and embark in another direction.

Jean-Marie: "And the dispatches?"

Here at least he has said the right thing. In order to convince Villetard that his reactions are correct and that he is responding to events in a manner consistent with his ostensible role in the matter, he ought to have inquired first about Winifred, then about the dispatches, then about the welfare of the French crew of the brig. This would have demonstrated that his concerns were first of all the very natural one of a young man in love, second the interest of a professional agent in the only really important part of the matter, and third a humanitarian sentiment that is less important than the other two but would round off the picture, so to speak, by completing the authenticity of his personality. And at the same time, of course, a humanitarianism that would lose nothing by the fact that it is also an expression of patriotism. As it happens, Jean-Marie does not have a chance to deliver this symmetrical triad, because the other voice bursts out coldly into the middle of his thoughts.

Villetard: "It was a mistake to entrust this matter to a woman. It was Carnot's idea. He always was a fool."

He has a certain kind of intellectual courage or audacity, no question about that. In the first place, what he has just said is a kind of oblique slur on Winifred, and in Jean-Marie's presence. More important, he has without any obliquity at all called a Minister of War and a member of the Directoire a fool. The fact is (Jean-Marie keenly observes) that Villetard is angry. He agrees with his government that Venice is eventually to fall to France, but he has his own ideas on how this is to be done. As a specialist in subversive activity he believes it can be done from within the city, with little or no violence, and for months he has worked to this end. Now those fools in Paris, along with the boy-general who has his own political ambitions, are about to wreck everything with their amateurish cloak-and-dagger antics.

Villetard: "The *Libérateur* was sent deliberately to the Lido as a provocation. This is Bonaparte's doing. He's trying to provoke a war, so that he can distinguish himself as he has done so brilliantly in the past. It was a blunder on Carnot's part to send the dispatches on a vessel that was certain to be captured. The notion that Mlle. Hervey could pass herself off as an Englishwoman who accidentally happened to be on board on private business is idiotic."

He hardly glances at Jean-Marie, who of course is the private business referred to. Jean-Marie is used to these manners by now.

Villetard: "In addition she was foolish enough to wear male dress on board, and a French uniform at that."

This stupefies Jean-Marie. He finally brings himself, at last, to inquire about Winifred, more out of curiosity now than the tender concern of a bridegroom for his fiancée.

Jean-Marie: "And so . . . she . . ."

Villetard: "She narrowly escaped being treated as a prisoner of war. The others are in the dungeon at San Giorgio. Who is Captain Langrish?"

Jean-Marie: "I don't know."

Villetard: "Well, you should know. You should find out."

If he notices that Jean-Marie too is growing angry, or at least annoyed, he shows no sign. Probably it is a matter of indifference to him.

Villetard: "He's the captain of the *Pandora,* the vessel that attacked the *Libérateur.* At least you should know that from your sources in the Arsenal."

This last slightly sarcastic. It occurs to Jean-Marie for the first time that, while he is following stone-masons and geriatric patricians around the city, Villetard is perhaps having *him* followed.

Villetard: "An English, or American. A mercenary in Venetian service. He may be an agent of that fool Carnot. In any case he seems to be playing a double game. For some reason he slipped Mlle. Hervey away from the others and brought her to the Molo. I was able to get a word to him, and she was taken . . ."

He is almost on the point of telling Jean-Marie where she was taken, then he changes his mind.

"She was removed to a safe place. The Venetians may know she was on board, because that reptile of a Cristoforo was sniffing around on the Molo and barely missed her. But no one knows where she was taken. No one, that is, but Captain Langrish."

There is a silence. Jean-Marie adjusts his cravat. What is he supposed to say? He had already asked about Winifred.

Jean-Marie: "So the dispatches are also—in a safe place?"

Villetard: "We don't know that. Langrish's role is unclear. If he is our agent then perhaps he has the dispatches. In this case Paris ought to have kept us informed. If he is not, then Mlle. Hervey would hardly give them to him. Unless she is somebody else's agent too."

Villetard definitely has a suspicious nature. Probably it is necessary in his profession. It does not endear him to Jean-Marie, however.

Villetard: "See here, my young friend. I've been working for weeks—for months—to carry off a certain rather difficult trick. If I am successful, matters will arrange themselves—Venice will fall into our hands like a ripe fruit, without the least harm to anyone. But for this to happen, it is necessary for me to be in possession of a certain list of persons in that packet. Without it I will be greatly hampered. But that isn't the most important point. If the packet should fall into Venetian hands, things will be very bad for us and our friends. People will get hurt. *Certain people* will get hurt, M. Fontenay." The small eyes boring in Jean-Marie's direction suggest strongly who the certain people are. *"I must have that packet"*—(here his voice rises to a kind of animal growl from between his clenched teeth)—"no matter what the cost—no matter if Venice and all its fine palazzi sink into the sea. Or failing that, I must have the absolute certainty that it has been destroyed unopened."

Jean-Marie is a little shaken by this vehemence. He has not thought Villetard capable of feeling so strongly about anything. He straightens his cravat, and with some difficulty meets the beady glance at the other end of the felze. Villetard calms down a little.

Villetard: "I have two tasks for you. First, seek out Langrish on some pretext. Perhaps he's interested in music."

(A faint irony here.)

Villetard: "He lodges with an old woman in Rio Ognissanti, in the San Trovaso parish. Your English is excellent. It shouldn't be difficult. I want to know why he protected Mlle. Hervey. There are three possibilities. He may be Carnot's agent. He may be an agent of the Inquisitors. Or he may have acted as he did simply for some personal reason."

He does not make points on his fingers as other people do. His right arm remains behind him on the sofa, the left in his lap. He has it all in his head.

Jean-Marie: "Should I tell him that—Mlle. Hervey is my fiancée?"

Villetard: "You might as well. He'll find it out anyhow, if he doesn't already know it. When you have the information, put nothing in writing. Leave a message for me at the Caffè de la Nave. You'll receive instructions and I'll meet you again."

He stops here, and Jean-Marie rises to open the door of the felze. But he has forgotten that Villetard has two things to tell him.

Villetard: "Second. Mlle. Hervey has been told to go to the English Residency when she arrives. You were to leave your address with the Resident. Have you done it?"

He would not ask unless he knew that Jean-Marie has *not* done it. He meant to do it, and then in some way the twentieth went by, the day when Winifred was supposed to arrive, and he hadn't done it. He says nothing.

Villetard: "If she goes to the Resident and finds he doesn't have the address, she's capable of doing something foolish, like coming to the Legation. Take care of it. You know where the English Residency is?"

Jean-Marie: "Campo Santi Apostoli."

Villetard: "And do you remember by any chance how the gentleman is called?"

Jean-Marie: "Mr. Birdsell."

The mouth-ends curve up again, then down. He raises his voice only slightly to speak to the gondolier.

"Nando."

"Paròn, sì."

A few minutes of silence. Then a slight lurch as the gondola rasps against the wall at the side of the rio. Villetard makes a sign, without removing his arm from the sofa. Jean-Marie opens the small door and goes out, holding his hat by the brim. He steps onto the quay, the door of the felze shuts, and the gondola glides away. The man at the oar does not even turn his head to look at him.

At first he is not sure where he is. Then he sees a bell-tower over the house-tops and recognizes it as Santa Sofia. It is only a few steps to Santi Apostoli. In the campo he is about to ask someone where the Residency is, but at that moment, directly ahead of him, he catches sight of a doorway with a kind of Wedgwood medallion set in a niche next to it, a white lion and unicorn on a blue background. The two beasts, although rampant, look relatively harmless. He pulls the wooden handle at the end of the wire, and somewhere inside the bell jangles.

The shutters open over his head.

Voice: "Chi xe?"

Jean-Marie: "Amici."

He realizes almost immediately that he should have spoken in English. The servant lowers a basket for his card. He starts to take out a card to write a message on it, then puts the card away.

Jean-Marie (in his faultless English): "I want to speak to the Resident."

Voice: "No ghe ne xe."

Jean-Marie: "When will he be back? I must speak to him, do you understand?"

He is perplexed. The horns of the dilemma press him. On the one hand, now that he has pretended he knows only English he is unable to communicate with the servant. On the other hand, Villetard has often cautioned him against putting anything in writing. Still, the situation is different here. If he simply left a card in English with the address—

While he hesitates the servant grows impatient. She tells him once more the Resident is not in, then pulls up the basket. The shutter closes.

Jean-Marie opens his mouth to speak again, but in the end only sighs. He leaves the campo and goes off through the narrow streets in the direction of the Rialto. An old man eating grapes, in a doorway, stares curiously at his English coat.

BY THE TIME HE GETS BACK TO

By the time he gets back to Ca' Pogi, by way of the Rialto bridge and Campo San Polo, it is almost four. Jean-Marie prefers not to carry a key to the palazzo with him, because the old-fashioned key with its iron ball makes an unsightly bulge in his pocket. He rings for Massimo. The bell needs mending and only makes a kind of metallic clunk. Still Massimo can surely hear it, and Jean-Marie obstinately refuses to ring a second time. Finally, after five minutes or more (perhaps it is not quite so long), Massimo comes down and opens the door.

Jean-Marie ascends the broad and elegant marble staircase to his apartments. He feels a sense of luxury, of privilege. This is how one should always live, in a palace with the water lapping below! With a few good friends, music, a glass of wine, and now and then, for diversion in the evening, the perfume of a frock. Now, however, it is still broad daylight. He is expecting persons about five, and it is only a little after four. There is no hurry. Jean-Marie does not like to be hurried. He moves in a leisurely manner around the chamber, taking off his hat and coat and setting them on a chair. Massimo comes with chocolate and puts away the hat and coat. Sipping the chocolate, Jean-Marie sets about changing his clothes. He goes into the dressing-room, takes off his waistcoat, shirt, and breeches, and washes his face and hands in a basin of warm water.

He dislikes cold water and Massimo keeps a kettle constantly boiling in the pantry, to pour into the wash-basin to bring it to exactly the right temperature. Then he pours eau-de-cologne onto his hands, rubs them together, and applies it to his face. Finally he dresses again in a pair of loose comfortable breeches in the Turkish fashion, a waistcoat, and a soft flannel smoking-jacket.

Jean-Marie: "Massimo."

Massimo: "Paròn, sì."

Jean-Marie: "Oui, Monsieur."

Massimo: "Oui, Moussou."

Jean-Marie: "Go to the pantry and see if the cakes and coffee are ready."

Massimo: "They are, Moussou."

Jean-Marie: "Go and see again."

In reality, as both of them know, he only wants to get Massimo out of the room so he can do something private. And Massimo, he is sure, knows what the thing is too. Still it doesn't matter. One trusts servants or doesn't trust them but it amounts to the same thing in the end. They always know everything. In any case Jean-Marie is unable to lock up things properly because he doesn't like to carry keys about his person. So Massimo, knowing where the keys are kept (his is left alone in the house all day), can do whatever he pleases. He drinks the wine, Jean-Marie is sure of that; and probably also the Armagnac. He has all the instincts of a flunky; that is, a person who derives his importance not from his own qualities but from the importance of his master, and yet at the same time does not respect the master. The fact is that the Revolution has not come to Venice yet. He is not sure how Massimo would take to the idea of the Equality of Man. Perhaps it would make him worse.

Jean-Marie takes a key out of the bedside table and uses it to open the tall narrow decorated cabinet (it is called in Venetian an armereto) against the wall opposite the bed. In the drawer of the armereto is another and larger key. He inserts this into the heavy ebony casket on the floor nearby and opens it. In the casket is a strong-box, the key to which is also kept in the armereto. Inside the strong-box is the money provided him by the Legation for a certain confidential business.

Jean-Marie is meticulously scrupulous about the handling of financial matters. His household expenses and personal allowance, both generous, are paid him in draughts from Paris through an ordinary banker. He never mingles these funds with the money in the strong-box, which comes from Villetard and is for quite another purpose. It is to find its way into the hands of certain Venetians—those of a certain sympathy or Politickal conviction, of whom there are a good number in the city—who might provide information interesting or useful to the Legation. Naturally it is impossible for the Legation itself to have any connection with such persons: their usefulness would be destroyed. And so the strong-box. No receipts pass between Jean-Marie and the Legation and no questions are asked. Jean-Marie mentally counts the number of visitors for this afternoon—there will be four—and takes out four silver scudi from the leather bag in the box. Then he closes the box and casket and locks them, puts away the keys in the ar-mereto, and locks the armereto and replaces its key in the bedside table. Massimo may take a scudo from the strong-box now and then, but the matter of the keys will at least keep him busy.

A final glance in the looking glass. He adjusts the cravat: the knot is not quite right but it will do. The smoking-jacket is a splendid idea. It is an English jacket and excellently cut. His guests will probably not notice but it gives him satisfaction anyhow. He leaves the chamber in excellent spirits, shutting the door behind him. As he goes along the corridor he glances into the pantry. The cakes are on a tray and Massimo is tasting the icing on one with his finger. The silver coffee-pot is set out. All well. He passes into the salon and beyond it into the music-room. Except for the salon this is the largest room in the apartments. The walls are hung with Flemish tapestry, and the figured ceiling of stucco, with its gilt amorini, is excellent in its acoustic properties. The two broad windows facing the rio are open now, since the late afternoon air is mild. The room contains two palms in majolica urns, a divan, a Florentine table inlaid in ivory and ebony, a half-dozen chairs, music-stands, a large candelabrum with three tapers, and a Silber-man pianoforte which Jean-Marie has imported from Germany.

He places the four coins into a saucer on the table. Then he goes to the window and glances out onto the rio, rubs his hands lightly together, and sits down at the pianoforte. He selects the second book of Couperin's *Pièces de Clavecin* and begins playing with his long, elegant, supple, and quick fingers, hardly glancing at the music, which he knows almost by heart. His guests are late as Venetians usually are. He has played two pieces of the Couperin and is in the middle of the third before he hears the imperfect clunk of the bell from the pantry.

It is Marangoni with his viola da gamba, panting a little from carrying the large instrument up the staircase. He smiles. Neither of them says a word. Jean-Marie gets up from the pianoforte, goes to his viola in its case by the table, and takes it out. They sit down. While they are opening their music Zuccato and Angelìn, the two violinists, arrive together. Again no one says anything. Zuccato and Angelìn take out their instruments, sit down, and begin tuning them. Marangoni, who is already tuned, provides an A from the pianoforte. Finally Luca arrives with his viola d'amore, silent like the others but lifting his shoulders in apology for being last.

Jean-Marie's viola da braccio is a fine Cremona, a six-stringed instrument with an excellent tone. It hardly needs tuning from day to day. He makes a fine adjustment to a string or two, nods to the others, and they embark onto Boccherini's quintets. Boccherini has written a hundred and thirteen of these, and in a half-dozen afternoons they have gone through only a third of them. There are still many more to go. For an hour they play on in perfect contentment. Angelìn, the first violinist, is an excellent musician and concert-master at the Fenice. The second violinist Zuccato is younger and not so skilled, but still competent. Jean-Marie himself is of course only an amateur, although (as he flatters himself) he might easily make a living as a violist if it were necessary and if he applied himself more. There is never time enough to do all the things one wants. The graceful, reiterative, precisely balanced sounds of the quintet float out through the windows and over the rio. Jean-Marie has noticed that music is improved somehow when it is reflected from water. The heavier throaty contralto of Marangoni's viola da gamba marches along under the other voices, as though supporting them and sustaining them from below. The two violins, it seems to Jean-Marie, are feminine. His own viola da braccio is tenor; the heavier viola d'amore with its seven strings is baritone. The two male voices pass around and through the voices of the violins, Jean-Marie sometimes joining with or pursuing Angelìn for a few bars while the viola d'amore concerns itself with the other violin; then the four may switch partners so that Jean-Marie finds himself paired for a while with the lighter strains of

Zuccato's violin. In all this the contralto of the viola da gamba is a kind of admonishing voice: a duenna that accompanies the four to be sure that nothing untoward takes place, but might wink at the embrace of two notes, now and then, at the end of a phrase. Five, Jean-Marie thinks, is an excellent number: two, and two, and one left over. It is a pity there are so few quintets. Luckily Boccherini has written a good number.

It is impossible for Jean-Marie to play such elaborate music by himself; except on the pianoforte, where the effort of concentration interferes with one's pleasure. Polyphony is dear to the nature of Jean-Marie. His mind is polyphonic; his intelligence is polyphonic. If intelligence (as has been claimed) is the ability to maintain two opposing ideas in the mind at once without going mad, then Jean-Marie is intelligent. He is also androgynous; another evidence of his polyphony. He understands women well and can associate himself with their mental states. Not that there is anything lacking in his masculinity. On the contrary. His androgyny is an ambivalence of the spirit, of the finer understanding, only. But it is precisely in this realm—the realm of music, shall we say—that the understanding and the spirit are not corrupted by the gross imperfection of bodies, their violent animal hungers, their crudities. Like the Rousseau who is his avatar, Jean-Marie is a sensualist, but a sensualist who is also a musician and an idealist. For is not music a matchless, a unique example of what the pure communication of souls might be? In music two personalities—say those of Jean-Marie and Angelìn, or rather those of his own viola da braccio and Angelìn's violin—may mingle and know each other in their full and intricate complexity, yet as lightly as a butterfly sipping at a flower. Music is superior to life. This Jean-Marie knows; yet he is still somewhat puzzled over the relation between the two. For life is necessary in order for music to be. Without fingers filled with blood no sound can issue from the viola da braccio. Jean-Marie gazes at his own fingers on the throat of the instrument. They are pale and bloodless. They might be of alabaster.

They finish a book of the quintets and close the music. Somebody, perhaps Angelìn, says *ah*. It is really only a kind of sigh of satisfaction. It is almost twilight outside now and the high rectangles of the windows are turning gray. Massimo comes in silently, closes the windows, and lights the tapers in the large standing candelabrum behind the chairs. Jean-Marie goes to the table, gets the parts of his opera *Armide et Zoë,* and passes them out. He himself sits down at the pianoforte. His abandoned viola he leaves leaning against the chair. He has written the opera in London and Paris; and now in Venice, with nothing to do in the long afternoons, he has amused himself by transcribing it for pianoforte and strings. With a nod and a chord he begins.

The overture is light, symmetrical, and blithe, with a faint nuance of the triste: something like Boccherini, in fact. It is in C major, since Jean-Marie is not as skilled in other keys and things are easier if there are not too many black notes. They finish it, turn the page, and launch into the first act. The others are sight-reading, since he has promised them the opera but not shown it to them before. Jean-Marie glances now and then at Angelìn, the most experienced of the four and the one with the most authority in matters of composition. As he has hoped, Angelìn nods and smiles when they reach Armide's aria with its fine bit of duet at the end. Rinaldo's entrance in the second act is not so well done, and Jean-Marie is not quite satisfied with it yet. But the second duet, between Armide and Zoë, goes well in string arrangement. The two violins complain and exhort, reproach each other, contend for the favor of Rinaldo who is represented by the deeper viola d'amore. The duet turns into a trio, then a quartet. The act ends in a kind of flourish with codas which Jean-Marie has borrowed from Lully; although he hopes Angelìn won't notice. Angelìn makes no sign that the codas are familiar to him. The last act is a success too. On the whole Jean-Marie is pleased with this first tentative sight-reading, in spite of the usual halts and maladjustments of such performances. He stands up at the pianoforte. Angelìn indicates admiration with a smile and a kind of sideways wagging of his head. The others smile. The opera is good. Jean-Marie attempts, successfully as he believes, to control his expression of satisfaction.

Massimo, summoned by the end of the music, comes in with the coffee and the cakes. He sets the tray on the table and leaves. The cakes too are excellent; they come from a pastry-shop in Campo Santa Margherita which Jean-Marie has only recently discovered. Angelìn makes the same sound he made at the end of the Boccherini: *ah.* But since his mouth is full it comes out *mm.* The others stand about rather awkwardly, trying to balance the coffee in one hand and the cake in the other. It is not what they are used to; they are musicians and not drawing-room elegants. But the cakes are good. The coffee Massimo makes with the same boiling water he keeps in the pantry to warm Jean-Marie's wash-basin. Neither Massimo nor Jean-Marie is an expert at making coffee. But the others seem to find it excellent: they drain their cups, smile, and set the cups on the table.

It is time for them to leave. Jean-Marie tactfully indicates the saucer at the end of the table. Carrying their instruments, they pass by the saucer, each taking a scudo and slipping it as though absent-mindedly into a waistcoat pocket. Angelìn, at the head of the staircase, turns and shakes hands. Jean-Marie raises his hand to the others in a sign of farewell. Except for Angelìn's small sounds of satisfaction, no one has spoken from the time they arrived.

JEAN-MARIE TAKES HIS

Jean-Marie takes his evening meal alone, in a corner of the salon set off by a screen from the rest of the room. There is no dining-room. The food is brought in from the trattoria in the nearby campo. There is a small sole in butter, then cutlets, green peas, and a morsel of excellent cheese to conclude. With this, a bottle of Verona wine, only half full since Jean-Marie has drunk the rest of it the previous evening. He is generally abstemious in his habits and eats lightly. In this way he is as slender at twenty-seven as he was at fifteen.

Dinner over, he goes to his chamber and dresses again: a clean shirt, pale salmon-colored breeches, a waistcoat in ocher with gold brocade, and a rich umber tail-coat with gold cuffs and facings. A hat—what would go with the brown coat? He selects a chestnut-colored tricorne with a gilded brim. Then he takes his gloves and stick from the table, glances at himself once more in the slightly tarnished Murano glass, and goes out.

The gondola slips away from the water-stairs and glides without a sound, as if by magic, down Rio Ca' Foscari. Jean-Marie leaves the small door of the felze open, and the vanes of the black shutters adjusted so that he can see out the sides. The heavy black robe that covers the rear opening is also removed, so that by turning his head he can see Iseppo's legs and the long oar working in the thole-pin. Iseppo is a middle-aged man, taciturn and occasionally surly. But he is tireless at the oar, and patient at waiting for hours in remote parts of the city, which he is often called upon to do when he serves Jean-Marie.

The gondola emerges from the rio and describes a broad turn into the Grand Canal. The weather has changed and the sky is overcast. The water, silvery-gray in the dim fragments of starlight that pierce through the clouds, is almost deserted at this time of the evening. This noble curve from Ca' Foscari to San Marco is the most distinguished part of the Canal. The ornate palazzi that go by in the darkness—marble and white Istrian stone stained with patches of soot, slightly crumbling—bear the names of the leading families of the city: Ca' Nani, Ca' Rezzonico, Palazzo Grassi, Ca' Paternian. The church of San Samuele—with its odd and dwarf-like little portico of the thirteenth century clutched in the grip, as it were, of its baroque façade—slips by through the half-opened shutters.

The Canal widens and begins to open into the broad basin before San Marco. But, a little beyond San Samuele, the gondola turns off to the right and begins working its way into the dangling peninsula of Dorsoduro, which is not quite so aristocratic. The rio is a narrow and dank-smelling affair with the walls of houses close on either side. Iseppo keeps to the left to allow room for his long oar to work. Ahead another small rio branches off to the left. As he approaches it Iseppo emits the gondolier's odd cry of warning, like the call of some tropical bird.

Ah-o-é.

There is no answer. In absolute silence except for the light plashing of the oar, the gondola curves into the new rio. The houses on either side cut off the starlight. Only now and then a lamp, or a tiny lantern before a shrine, illuminates a patch of yellow wall. Jean-Marie senses with his body that the gondola has made another turn to the left. The oar gurgles as Iseppo sets it in the water. The gondola scrapes against the quay, slows, and stops.

Iseppo: "Rio Ognissanti, Paròn."

Jean-Marie: "Wait here."

Iseppo doesn't bother to reply. Jean-Marie steps out, with care not to soil his clothes on the slimy stone. He sets off down the quay, keeping in the dark under the walls of the houses as best he can. A man stands in an open doorway, his face visible in the red glow as he draws now and then at his pipe. Jean-Marie almost speaks to him, then changes his mind. He overtakes a little girl carrying a milk-can, but decides she won't do for his purposes either. A little farther along he finds what he is hoping for: a trattoria with an open door and lights inside.

There is only one customer, an old man eating liver and polenta. There is a boy to serve him, and a woman standing at the stove in the single room of the place.

Jean-Marie (in English, in a clipped and aristocratic accent): "D'you know where Captain Langrish lives, if you please?"

The boy simply stares at him. The woman turns her face from the stove, without hostility but also silent to indicate that she doesn't understand.

Jean-Marie, as he has planned, shifts to Italian with an English accent. With his musician's ear, his fine sense of tone, this delicately balanced exercise in phonetics is not difficult. It is perhaps even too well done. It is wasted on the audience.

Jean-Marie: "Captain Langrish. English or American. He lives nearby. Lodges with an old woman."

Old man: "Ma. Xe el Meregano."

He gets up from the table and points with his fork, out the door and down the quay. The others agree. It is the American that the gentleman wants. This is easy. He lodges with Siora Bettina. It is very near. Just at the end of the rio.

Old man: "Tuto dreto. Just follow your nose. Go to the end of the quay. Then turn and come back to the first door. A red house with a black door."

Jean-Marie thanks them and leaves. He goes down the quay in the dark until it ends at Rio San Trovaso. Then, as the old man has advised, he retraces his steps back to the first door. The house may once have been red; now it is the brownish rust-color of half the houses in Venice. The door is possibly black. It is certainly very dark in there under the wall of the house. He glances into the doorway, locates the bell-pull, then moves off a little way down the quay to examine the situation. The trouble is that, immediately under the wall of the house as he is, it is impossible to see upward to the windows to get a notion of where the captain's room might be.

There is a bridge across the rio only a few houses down. Glancing about him, Jean-Marie reluctantly leaves the shelter of the wall and crosses the bridge, with a flash of oily water visible under it in the starlight. On the other side he finds a relatively shadowy door to stand in, although unfortunately there is a lamp on the bridge that throws a dim yellowish light. He makes himself as inconspicuous in the doorway as he can. He is conscious of the glow from the lamp catching the gold brocade of his coat.

The rust-colored house opposite is a narrow one. There are three stories, with two windows to each. On the ground floor there is only one window and the door. The house is shaped like a guillotine, and the dark doorway at the bottom is the hole where you put your head. Supposing he pulled the bell-pull and Siora Bettina answered. He could say he was looking for a lodging. In fact he could even *take* a lodging. It is a masterful idea. With entry to the house he could soon find out which is Langrish's room, try to get the best of the landlady in some way, and search the room to see if the dispatches are there. It has the merit of audacity and it might work. But suppose the captain himself came to the door. He would hardly do that, a lodger in the house. Still, even if he did, he, Jean-Marie, could say he was looking for a lodging. Or, another party might come to the door. Some servant. No telling who might come to the door. Another lodger even. The trouble is that after his several months in Venice Jean-Marie is fairly well known and might be recognized as the young Frenchman who is (supposedly) studying music and lives in Ca' Pogi near San Pantalon. Not likely in this humble neighborhood. Still it is a risk.

While he is turning over all these possibilities in his mind Jean-Marie is startled to see a crack of light appear in the doorway across the rio. The door opens and a man in military uniform appears silhouetted in the light from behind. He is carrying his hat, a tricorne like Jean-Marie's except that it is black and has a larger brim. This person glances indifferently out across the rio for a moment. Then he sets his hat on his head and jams it down in front with his hand. He turns, looks about as if undecided which way to go, and sets off to the right.

At Campo San Trovaso the figure is visible traversing the square patch of starlight. Then it disappears again beyond the boatyard (the squero it is called in Venetian) where gondolas are built and repaired. Jean-Marie waits for a moment, then crosses the bridge and follows. He has been able to see the man clearly for only an instant, after he closed the door behind him and before he put on his hat. The captain looked tall, squarely built, and ready for anything. His coat is black or blue, his breeches white. The end of a saber gleams under his coat on the left.

Jean-Marie steals on across the campo, past the church and the squero, and along the quay of Rio San Trovaso. The black blur ahead crosses a bridge to the other side of the rio. It continues down the quay, then turns to the right and disappears into a cleft between the houses. Jean-Marie can guess now where the captain is headed. He is going to Campo de la Carità on the Grand Canal, where he will take the tragheto across to the San Marco quarter.

Jean-Marie follows on into the dark labyrinth of houses, at a leisurely pace, since it is no longer important to keep the captain in sight. Again he is uncertain what to do. To get into the same tragheto with the man, and confront him in some way on the chance that he is carrying the dispatches on his person, is impossible. There was that gleam of the saber—Jean-Marie himself has only his stick. It might have been better not to follow the man at all—instead to stay behind at the house, with the certainty that he was gone, and try the other plan of pretending to rent a room in order to gain entry into the house. But who goes about renting rooms at this hour of the night, when everyone's door is locked? Besides there is his conspicuous clothing. He ought to find some more unobtrusive way of dressing himself. Perhaps Massimo could buy him some Venetian clothing. But then he couldn't pretend to be an English who speaks Italian with an accent. What to do? The thing is very complex. And yet—a sort of keen acuteness flows through Jean-Marie—the sense of his polyphonic intelligence—which enables him to balance all these alternatives in his mind at once and examine them clearly.

The black shape ahead has reached the Carità. Jean-Marie stops at the end of the street, reluctant to enter the campo. The tragheto, he sees, is on the other side of the water discharging its passengers. It will be five minutes or so before it returns. Langrish crosses the campo, then goes under the vine-covered pergola of the tragheto-landing where he is not very visible. Jean-Marie slips cautiously out into the campo, staying as well as he can under the dark wall of the church. From this point he can see the figure in the pergola a little more clearly. The captain doesn't pace about or fidget as most people do when they are waiting for something. He stands motionless with his hands under his coat-tails, looking out at the water. Across the Canal at San Vidal is the stonecutter's workshop—a ramshackle shed, and some immense blocks of marble standing about in the open field, gleaming in the starlight.

It occurs to Jean-Marie that if he hurried back to Iseppo he might cross the Canal in his own gondola, lurk about among the blocks of marble, pick up the captain's trail again when he lands, and follow him to find out where he is going. But he doesn't hurry back. For one thing he would be too visible in the stoneyard—the blocks of marble would perhaps reflect the starlight, focus it so to speak, as in a painting by Caravaggio—he is uncertain about the effect of chiaroscuro. For another thing it is starting to rain. A few drops are beginning to patter down, bringing a smell of wet dust. To continue would mean getting his clothes wet. He should have brought a cloak—for example the gentleman's riding-cape, light but waterproof, which he bought in London. This would also extinguish those plaguey gleams of braid on his coat. Still there is his hat. . . .

Motionless, a spectator, keenly aware of every aspect of the scene, he watches as the tragheto comes back across the water, with three or four shadows standing erect in it like souls passing to the Land of the Dead. He hears the bump as it pushes its way into the stakes. The passengers get out, two of them conversing in low tones. In the street behind Jean-Marie there is the sound of steps and a man appears, half-walking and half-running toward the landing, a stocky Venetian in a frock-coat and tricorne. He is in a hurry and anxious to catch the tragheto.

Stocky man: "Ao! Aspeta!"

The captain is just stepping into the boat. The ferryman waits an instant or two for the stocky man, who hurries down the narrow pier and tumbles into the gondola rather clumsily. There are no other passengers. The ferryman pushes away; the tragheto swings its bow around and starts back across the Canal.

Across the campo, where Jean-Marie lurks under the façade, the squeak of the oar against the thole-pin is clearly audible. There is the faint rustle of rain, and a smell of wet stone. Jean-Marie watches for a few moments longer. Then he turns up his coat and retraces his steps back through the narrow streets to San Trovaso, keeping in the shelter of the walls to protect his clothing from the falling drops. In Rio Ognissanti, after a little searching (he has not paid careful attention to where he has left the gondola), he finds Iseppo waiting in the shadows like a surly statue, motionless.

Jean-Marie ducks into the felze and out of the rain.

"To the Frezzeria."

A RIDOTTO, THAT PROMINENT FEATURE

A ridotto, that prominent feature of Venetian life in the eighteenth century, is a kind of public-house or place of resort, devoted to the seven games that one can play with cards: faraone (or faro), biribisso, picheto, panfilo, bassetta, sette e mezzo, and maccà. Ridotti are described in some detail in Molmenti's massive compendium of Venetian private life, *La storia di Venezia nella vita privata* (3 vols., Bergamo, 1927–29; a rare book, but a set may still be found now and then in the second-hand bookshops in Calle de la Mandola). The best-known ridotto, founded by Marco Dandolo in 1628, occupied a magnificent set of rooms in a palazzo in the parish of San Moisè. Detailed views of the interiors of such establishments may be seen in the canvases of Longhi and Guardi in the Museo Correr, and the paintings accord exactly with the descriptions in Molmenti. At each table is a patrician in toga and wig, with various piles of sequins and ducats before him, prepared to serve as banker in the game for anyone who presents himself. It is impossible to verify whether the other guests are patricians, and in any case many of them wear masks. In Guardi's *La sala del Ridotto* there is a lady in a domino who does not seem to be paying very much attention to the gaming. She seems to be in the act of leaving the room, but she is stopping to look over her shoulder at an elegantly clad gentleman who is making a low bow to her in the

Venetian manner, with his hand over his heart. Her dress is rather revealing, even by eighteenth-century standards. For some reason she has black ribbons about her wrists. She is accompanied by a dwarf, black as ink, who clutches at her skirts. Perhaps she is not even a lady.

In short, interesting relationships both male and female may be contracted in a ridotto, and any acquaintance you make in a ridotto will be confined to the ridotto; if you happen to meet such a person outside in the city he will behave as though he has never met you. Not only do people wear masks, but they often use pseudonyms. It is extremely democratic. You might speak to a lady and not know—who she is. The wife of a Senator or perhaps nobody at all, a person of quite ambiguous status. In this way the ridotto provides exactly that Liberty, Equality, and Fraternity heralded by the Revolution but which, to tell the truth, has not quite been achieved in some respects in France itself by 1797.

Unfortunately—perhaps for these very reasons—Dandolo's was closed by a decree of the Signoria in 1774, no doubt at the instigation of the Inquisitors, who are for the most part senile old men with rather rigid ideas on the subject of moral conduct. The power of the Inquisitors is such, in fact, that many patricians who privately attend the ridotti publicly condemn them as corrupting to the youth and a menace to civic morality.

But anyone can open a ridotto. A ridotto is simply a set of private apartments, rented by a gentleman for the entertainment of his friends. A gentleman may prefer not to entertain his friends in his house, which would interfere with the privacy of his family, and so maintains the ridotto for this purpose. A number of such ridotti appear after Dandolo's is closed. How can the Inquisitors keep track of them all? They spring up like mushrooms, which grow in the dark, and are succulent and expensive. One such is Crespi's in the Frezzeria. The address is not quite so respectable as San Moisè, but neither is it so conspicuous. What the English call hypocrisy, the Venetians call discretion. A ridotto is of course open only to friends of the proprietor, but anyone can go there, provided he is well dressed and has someone to introduce him. If he doesn't know anyone to introduce him, he can simply walk in and hand his hat and gloves to the servant as though he is a familiar of the place.

* * *

Jean-Marie, in fact, has been introduced into Crespi's by a friend, a Francophile patrician he met at a musical soirée. He is thoroughly familiar with the place and the servants are acquainted with him. He pushes open the unlocked door in the Frezzeria, goes down a narrow corridor to the rear of the house, and comes out in an anteroom where he gives the footman his hat, gloves, and stick. Then he passes on into the room beyond; not very large but richly decorated, with damasked walls and a gilded stucco ceiling. The tables are covered in green baize. At them a dozen or so people are playing faro or basset. Some of them are masked, some not. In addition to the gaming-tables there are divans, armchairs, and small round tables with lace cloths, all of great elegance, in the Louis Quinze style of a generation before. From the next room comes the sound of a lute and a not very skillful feminine voice singing an aria of Scarlatti.

Jean-Marie briefly catches the eye of an abbé, in polished shoes with bright red heels and silver buckles, who is seated with a lady in a black mask, which covers her eyes but exposes a mole in her pale and perfect cheek. They are evidently not seeking company. He finds a place at another table and sits down. The game is faro. To his right is his friend Balbi, the Francophile patrician, who is serving as banker. Beyond Balbi is a lady of the kind called in Venice, with only slight irony, a zentildonna: not a patrician but not a commoner either, probably the wife of a wealthy merchant with a palazzo on the Grand Canal. She wears a papier-mâché mask that makes her look like a kind of white beaked eagle, a small three-cornered hat, and a shawl of fine Levantine silk, the importation of which is forbidden by law. Since it would not be proper for her to go about the city alone, she is accompanied by her cavaliere servente or official admirer, a gentleman who is charged with picking up her gloves and handing her into gondolas, and is probably on excellent terms with her husband. The others at the table are a pair of graceful young men who seem to be together, one in domino and the other unmasked. There is a pleasant buzz in the room, a click of shuffled cards, a scent of perfume. There is never any talk of Politicks or any other serious conversation in such places. The talk consists of badinage, polite flirtation (one of the young men is evidently pleased by Jean-Marie's elegant dress, and perhaps even his person), or technical comments on the game. No names are exchanged. The language is

Italian and not dialect. Occasionally Balbi makes a remark to Jean-Marie in French.

Jean-Marie plays for an hour or so. He feels lazy and cat-like, content, in the elegantly appointed room with its muted sounds. He wins about twelve scudi, loses them again, and takes a gold sequin from his pocket and sets it on the table. He usually loses, but very little, only a few scudi. Tonight he runs finally into a streak of luck and plays the sequin into a small pile of gold, which he leaves negligently on the green cloth by his elbow.

Balbi smiles. "Vous avez de la veine ce soir, mon ami."

Masked young man: "What did he say?"

Unmasked: "That the gentleman has good luck."

Masked young man: "That's true. And also he has fair eyes."

This with a glance and a coy smile. Jean-Marie is not offended, although he has never felt the slightest inclination toward his own sex. In any case the flirting is only playful, since the graceful young men are together and the other—the unmasked one—shows no signs of jealousy. The game breaks up. Jean-Marie has won thirty sequins, over six hundred lire, the wages of a workman for a year. The young man in the domino, inspired by the voice from the next room which has stopped now, calls for a lute and embarks into a sentimental song in high falsetto, accompanying himself. The voice is almost a perfect soprano; only on the higher notes does it crack a little to indicate that it is simulated by a male larynx.

Unmasked young man: "You sing as beautifully as the Sirens, and you are just as naughty, I think."

Masked: "Oh. And who has made me naughty?"

Balbi leaves the room. Perhaps he doesn't approve. Jean-Marie is hungry and raises his hand to the servant. After only a moment the man returns with a slice of cold veal between two pieces of bread; a dish or confection invented by that Fourth Earl of Sandwich, well known in London at the time when Jean-Marie visited there, who was so fond of gaming that he was unwilling to leave his table to eat. Along with this a glass of wine. The graceful young men have disappeared, also the lady in the white beak. Jean-Marie sits alone at the table for a few minutes eating and drinking, the pile of sequins still untouched by his elbow. Outside it is raining steadily now. There is a patter of drops on the rio, and a gurgle of water running through a drain somewhere inside a wall.

The room, he sees, has filled while he was playing. He catches sight of Zulietta at a nearby table otherwise occupied entirely by men. As a connoisseur he can only admire the spectacle, and who could not? She has the translucent pale-sherry complexion of well-bred Venetians—dark eyes set in shadows—hair of a rich auburn with traces of a lighter gold or bronze. She wears the hair long, fastened with a simple ribbon at the back, and her gown is cut so low that as she turns it reveals, occasionally, the dark buds at the centers of her breasts. She is the only woman in the room who is unmasked.

She seems to be in bad spirits—not to say exasperated— although perhaps it is only in play. She cries out something in annoyance, flings her cards down, and then smiles in spite of herself as the men at the table laugh.

Zulietta: "It's impossible. Somebody's cheating."

Middle-aged man: "You never cheat, Zulietta."

Zulietta: "Not at cards."

She catches Jean-Marie's eye briefly and then glances away. She goes on remonstrating with her fellow players. Watching the lips and half-catching the sounds, Jean-Marie follows the conversation without much difficulty.

Zulietta: "Won't somebody lend me something? Only a sequin."

Middle-aged man: "I'm too old to lend you a sequin, Zulietta. Besides I have a wife at home."

Zulietta: "If you lent me a sequin I would make you forget your wife."

Middle-aged man: "Only a sequin? You're too modest."

Zulietta: "Well, say five sequins."

Middle-aged man: "Your charming self at the table is so pleasant, Zulietta, who would want more?"

On the other side is a young man in an indigo jacket and a short wig. She turns to him. "You, Carlo."

Carlo (laughing; turning out his pocket to show it is empty): "As you see, Zulietta, I've lost this evening like you."

Zulietta: "Bah. All of you."

She gets up, exasperated but still with her smile of natural good humor. With her hand on her hip she gives the impression of surveying the room. But when she begins to walk, slowly and deliberately, she comes directly to Jean-Marie's table and sits down.

Zulietta: "Ciao, caro. You've won."

Jean-Marie: "Comme ça."
Zulietta: "What does that mean?"
Jean-Marie: "Poco poco."
Zulietta: "It's not so poco."

She counts the pile of sequins playfully and abstracts one for herself. He takes it away from her after a small tussle. His glance dropping, he finds himself gazing at the two pale amber hemispheres almost entirely revealed in the low gown.

Zulietta: "Don't be so cruel. You have plenty. At least buy me a chocolate."

Even in grappling for the coin she has lost none of her dignity. She has a prim, faintly ironic smile, which she makes more effective by raising her chin a little. She is almost aristocratic. Or more precisely, she is an ingeniously perfect simulacrum of the aristocratic, except that one can see it is a simulacrum.

He orders the chocolate, and it comes. She sips it with grace; her manners are perfect. It is not necessary for her to use the napkin which the servant sets tactfully by her elbow. She touches a single finger to the edge of her lips, once, and licks it neatly. She finds a crumb of sandwich on Jean-Marie's plate and tastes it. Then she gets up and pulls him by the elbow.

"Lend me your luck, Zanetto."

For the rest of the evening she takes possession of him completely. She gives him her gloves to take care of, her shawl, her fan, and obliges him to follow her to a table where a group of ladies and gentlemen are playing basset. He lends her a sequin, then another. She loses them both, then turns to him with another sample of the prim little smile, raising her chin.

He shakes his head.

Zulietta: "Another scudo, then that's all."
Jean-Marie: "I don't have any more."
Zulietta: "Oh Zanetto, don't be tiresome. Your pocket is full of sequins. You can hardly drag yourself about, your coat is so heavy."

He himself loses a little too, not much. A little after midnight the table breaks up. Zulietta arises languorously, takes her gloves from him, and slaps them lightly on his cheek.

Zulietta: "Come."
Jean-Marie: "Your fan too."
Zulietta: "You carry it."

He follows her into the next room, which is almost empty. A single party is still playing at one table. They pass out a door into the corridor. The corridor extends along the rear of the house, with small barred windows opening on the rio. There is a rather bad odor here, either from the rio or from something in the house itself. Zulietta seems not to notice. Still holding her head high, she lights a candle from the low-burning lamp in the corridor and goes up the stairway. Jean-Marie follows, carrying the fan.

At the top of the stairs she enters a room, waits for him to come in, and closes the door behind him. She sets the candle down and pushes the heavy bar to lock the door.

Jean-Marie crosses the room and looks out. Below under the window is the rio, invisible in the darkness. He can only sense from the smell and the faint sound of water that it is there. The storm has passed and only a few drops of water are falling now. But the rain has intensified everything; the odors, the sounds, even the keenness of the air. The houses across the rio are dimly visible: spectral presences with black rectangular eyes.

She comes to him and stretches her arms around both sides of his body. But instead of embracing him she reaches beyond to close the heavy wooden shutters. Then she turns away again, playfully, and crosses the room.

The candle, which is guttering, leaks only a dim light. Her fingers reach for the fastening of her gown. She still wears the little smile with chin slightly raised.

Zulietta: "Listen, Zanetto. I want to be loved in the French fashion."

WHEN WINIFRED FINALLY WAKES UP

When Winifred finally wakes up, the morning—unlike those mornings in stories in which one awakens with sunlight flooding into the room—is gray, with a thin mist clinging to the marsh around the villa. Lina brings up her breakfast, such as breakfast is on the Continent: a rusk and a tiny cup of bitter black coffee. Luciana, the woman of the night before, is the housekeeper. She speaks only Venetian, or at least pretends not to understand French. Lina speaks both Italian and a little French, and is also somewhat more amiable. She was raised in Padova and is bored in the country. She is happy to have a visitor of her own age, one to whom she can chatter away to her heart's content and even make oblique and vaguely disrespectful comments about the Contessa, as she calls Mme. D'Artigny Baraoni. Perhaps she really is a countess. Anyone on the Continent who has a vaguely noble male relative is a countess. On the Continent Winifred herself might be considered a countess. In any case Mme. D'Artigny Baraoni is not called the Contessa because she is married to a count, since she would rather be burned at the stake with bands playing than marry anybody. (So says Lina.) The Contessa is a consecrated, not to say ferocious, spinster. Men are not even allowed in the house. There is a gardener-cum-coachman called Annibale but he has never even set foot inside the door. Lina explains all this before Winifred has even got out of bed.

Lina: "Mademoiselle likes the coffee?"

Winifred: "It's horrible. Isn't there something else? Some bacon and eggs?"

Lina: "For breakfast? One could scour the countryside. Everything is in short supply because of the war, you understand. The peasants hide everything. I'll go now and find you some clothes."

While Lina is gone Winifred discovers why she felt so wretched even before she was properly woken up: she had caught cold from her ducking the day before followed by five hours in wet clothing. Her throat is scratchy, her nose already feels swollen, and she has a headache. She resolves to say nothing about this to the Contessa, suspecting even from her slight acquaintance that the Contessa would find some way to reproach her for this malady, or turn the blame on her. Probably it was not wearing wet clothes that caused colds, it was wearing breeches. If she had only fallen into the lagoon in a dress. . . .

Lina returns almost hidden under an armload of dresses, stockings, drawers, petticoats, and slippers. She lays all these things on the foot of the bed and begins displaying them with the dexterity of a shop-clerk.

Lina: "Mademoiselle is about the same size as the Contessa. The Contessa has no figure at all, you know. As straight as a pine board. Mademoiselle is made charmingly, like a boy. That is very chic, fashionable just now. In Paris the ladies bind their chests so as to look like boys."

Lina does not possess the tact, or the prudery, to leave the room while Winifred disrobes. Instead she stares at everything, with the cheerful curiosity of a spectator at the theatre who has paid for her ticket and intends to enjoy the show. Winifred finds this inspection is making her slightly vexed, perhaps only because she has a cold. She has always been self-conscious about her small bosom and flat hips. Still it is courteous (or shrewd) on Lina's part, observing that the Contessa's body and Winifred's are the same, to compare one to a board and the other to the latest fashions in Paris. Winifred only reluctantly slips off the nightgown lent her the night before, sits down on the bed, and reaches for a linen undergarment.

Lina: "Ah, English ladies have no hair under their arms. How nice. It is probably the climate. Things grow more slowly when it's cold."

Winifred (rather shortly): "We remove it."

Lina: "Perhaps, but English ladies—to judge from Mademoiselle, I can't say that I have known very many—have less hair in general than we do. The legs—Mademoiselle's are so smooth. And *there,* too. Now Mademoiselle has only a pretty little tuft. But we others—here where it is warm everything grows more. Ah! the Contessa. You should see! She has a bush like an old Jew's beard."

Winifred feels the blood mounting to her face. She pulls the drawers over her legs, stands up abruptly, selects a muslin gown with a high waist and a pair of yellow slippers, and banishes Lina from the room.

Winifred: "I don't care to discuss such things. I have a cold. Bring me some tea. And an egg. Boiled. For exactly three minutes. We will dispense with the bacon, if it is true that the peasants have hidden it all. And don't stand there staring at me."

Lina: "Ah! English ladies don't care to discuss—such things when they have a cold?"

Winifred: "Go!"

Later in the morning Winifred attempts to go for a walk, but a chill mist hangs over the marshes and a peacock blocks her way on the narrow path. He hisses and spreads his tail at her, threateningly or perhaps amorously; Winifred can not tell which would displease her the more. She retreats, leaving him master of the path. She tries several other paths, but they only lead to the muddy canal or end in a tangle of undergrowth. When she comes back to the villa it is after eleven. It is now, about the time that the sun dispels these miasmas, that the Contessa customarily arises. She and Winifred take their colazione together in an enormous dining-room with a domed ceiling, decorated with frescoes that are perhaps genuine Tiepolos. A risotto, cheese, bread, a blade or two of asparagus, a sour Verona wine to which the Contessa adds water both for herself and for Winifred.

Contessa: "We live simply. I'm not rich, you know. Besides the times are bad and the peasants have hidden everything. Out of sheer churlishness. Because they don't want the French to have it. Foolishness. There's plenty for everybody. The countryside is deserted; there's no one here. All the landowners have gone off to the Dominante." (Which is the way those on the Terraferma refer to Venice.)

Winifred: "Why have they gone off?"

Contessa: "Because they're afraid of the French."

Winifred: "Then why haven't you gone off?"

Contessa: "You ask a great many questions, don't you? Because I'm not afraid of the French. The French are a civilized people. What has happened in France in these years is a breath of fresh air in this stupid old Europe. I have many French friends, and I am not afraid of a word like Revolution. Why has General Bonaparte come to Italy? I will tell you, Mademoiselle Hervey. To liberate us. To liberate us from ourselves, from our stupid old ways, from all the cobwebs in our heads, from all the idiocies we go on doing only because our grandfathers did them. These patricians, these landowners of the Terraferma, Mademoiselle Hervey, are afraid of words like liberty and equality. They quake if you mention them. They are afraid someone is going to take their villas away from them. But the French, Mademoiselle Hervey, are not going to take their villas away from anyone. They are only going to liberate us from six hundred old men in the Ducal Palace who swagger about in long robes and tell us what we must do. We want to be governed by reason, Mademoiselle, and not by six hundred stupid old men. Reason. Do you know what General Bonaparte is? He is Montesquieu on horseback."

After this Winifred finds that she and the Contessa get along better. As they linger over their wine and cheese they talk about Montesquieu, Voltaire, Diderot, and Helvétius. (The Contessa is not quite so enthusiastic about Rousseau.) The Contessa contends, and develops the idea at great length, that France is essentially a feminine nation and Italy a masculine. This in spite of the brilliant and fulminating (éclatant is the word she uses) success of the French armies. She means the idea in a more subtle and profound sense, a sense of national temperament and intelligence. The Italian mind is capable of great deviousness and complexity, but not of intelligence. Because intelligence (Mademoiselle Hervey) is not a matter of fixing broken carriages or inventing guns but of seeing into the heart of things, such as the human soul, and understanding their workings. She herself derives her intelligence (although she doesn't put it quite this way) from her French mother, a certain Mme. D'Artigny who was from Grenoble and perhaps (Winifred thinks) was the originary of the possibly authentic title. Why the mother abandoned Grenoble to marry an unprosperous landowner of the Terraferma is unclear. Perhaps it was for the villa, which is said to have been designed by Palladio. At any rate the father succumbed, probably, to the miasmas of the marsh and died very soon, while the Contessa was still an infant. (That is *very* hard to imagine.) Baraoni, says the Contessa, she will give to the six hundred old men and they can stick it (foutre, not a very nice word) in their togas. For herself, she is D'Artigny.

Winifred feels that the Contessa comes at her something like the peacock, barring her way on the path of conversation and then spreading feathers that she, Winifred, can not hope to match. Yet, in spite of her jabbing words and the bird-like, insistent little motions of her nose and chin that accompany them, she is a person with a sort—her own special sort—of winsomeness, one feels after a while. And she is generous! She gives freely of her bed and board, such as she is able to afford, and she offers Winifred a great heap of clothes of all kinds, by no means old; in fact some of them appear never to have been worn. They agree perfectly on books and their authors (except for Rousseau), and Winifred has her own reasons for sharing the Contessa's predilection for French culture. The subject of Jean-Marie, however, does not come up, at least not directly. They come the closest to it, perhaps, in touching on Winifred's rather disastrous arrival in Venice, and her reasons for wanting to come there.

Contessa: "I myself won't inquire, Mademoiselle. It is not for me to meddle in these grand affairs of the world, the affairs of men. I will only mention that a note has come this morning from M. Villetard, inquiring about a certain envelope or packet of dispatches. M. Villetard seemed to attach great importance to this matter of the dispatches. I have no idea what he is referring to. He asked me to inquire of you, however, where the dispatches are at present, and in any case to see that they are delivered to him as soon as possible."

Winifred has nothing to say to this.

Contessa (gazing at her sideways, like a bird about to peck): "I imagine this is why you were on board the *Libérateur*."

The Contessa seems so well informed that it hardly seems necessary to tell her anything else. Winifred understands now that M. Villetard has arranged to have her sent to the villa and thus avoid the consequences—the consequences to her, and also to M. Villetard—of her arrest by the Venetians. (Captain Langrish was perhaps an accomplice in all this, although his part of the business is still a mystery to Winifred.) So evidently the Contessa is trusted by this official of the French Legation to carry out a confidential and perhaps important favor. Whether she, Winifred, should trust the Contessa to the same extent is not clear. On the one hand there are her panegyrics of salons and Paris life, her grammatical if abominably pronounced French, her spirited and erudite discourses on D'Alembert and Helvétius; all evidences of a genuine Francophilia. On the other hand the Wicked-Grandmother nose and chin, the oblique glance and beady eye that follow Winifred in all her movements in the villa and even, she feels, through the walls when she is in her room. The Contessa already knows a great deal. She knows about the packet, and she knows it was the *Libérateur d'Italie* that brought her to Venice. But Winifred is resolved that the Contessa should not know any more, at least not through her part, whatever she might learn through mysterious means of her own.

For one thing, she has not been told to confide the story of her life to any half-crazy old Venetian lady who seems to be on intimate terms with the French Legation. From the beginning of the affair she has been impressed with the absolute necessity of saying nothing to anybody about anything. She was simply to deliver the packet into the hands of the proper person, without explaining anything even to him, and then go about her private business. Why Winifred was selected for this task—she, a foreigner in a country full of authentic French citizens ready to expire for their nation's cause—was not clear. A carriage was even sent to rue des Francs-Bourgeois for her, to the great marvel of the concierge and the landlady. Of Carnot she knew only that he was one of the five Directors who ruled France and that he occupied himself chiefly with the Ministry of War. He received her in his office in the Luxembourg, and—rather sharply, with a little bark—dismissed the two huissiers armed with muskets who had escorted her through the door.

The office was poorly equipped. There was not even a proper desk. Maps were spread out over the floor, with a long steel rule and a pair of dividers still on them. Carnot was a pallid man with a pessimistic way of looking out at the world from under his tousled hair. He was dressed soberly, in a dark gray jacket, a black waistcoat, and a rather untidy white blouse with a cravat. His hair looked like a mouse's nest, as though he had not had time to brush it, or perhaps had contempt for this cranial excrescence that needed attention every day and was displaced by the slightest wind, and looked forward impatiently to the day when he would be a bald old man writing his mémoires, able to do as he pleased. He did not accord with Winifred's idea of what a Revolutionary general ought to be like.

Carnot: "You are the Citizeness Fontenay?"

Winifred: "Not at all. I am Miss Hervey."

Carnot (annoyed, consulting the notes on his table): "Ah. You are only engaged to the Citizen Fontenay. No matter, it's all the same. I see now that M. Fontenay calls you Clélia."

The revelation of this intimacy made Winifred stiffen.

Carnot: "How charming. You are an admirer of the pastoral novel?" Without allowing her to reply he goes on. "I can assure you that our intelligence is excellent and we know everything about you. You are a British subject, I believe, and possess an English passport."

Winifred: "Yes."

Carnot: "Excellent. I imagine you are sorry to be—separated from M. Fontenay?"

Winifred said nothing. She was not prepared to ask M. Carnot questions about *his* wife, if he had one, and saw no point in this line of interrogation.

Canot: "Very well. I have arranged for you to rejoin him, if you are willing. You husband—excuse me, your fiancé—is in Venice. He is there to study music, but he is also there for other things. He is being handsomely paid. . . ."

He abandoned this sentence and started over.

Carnot: "He is a young man of means and comfortably situated in Venice. It is a charming city. A city made for love."

Bother his impudence! There was dandruff on his coat too.

Winifred bit the inside of her lip to conceal her annoyance and for two pennies would have walked out of the room. M. Carnot didn't seem to notice.

Carnot: "The two of you will be happy there. It is impossible not to be happy in Venice. The Directoire, as I say, has arranged for your transportation. It will be at government expense. You will go by dispatch-coach to Marseille, by ship to Civitavecchia, then to Rome, where you will receive further instructions from the Embassy. I don't know whether it is necessary to give you a lecture on Italian geography. There is the Papal State, which occupies the center of the peninsula including the Marches and the Romagna. In the south is the Kingdom of Naples; to the north is the Cisalpine Republic, consisting of Milan and various territories liberated from tyranny by the French. The only independent state of any consequence remaining is the Venetian Republic."

Winifred: "I am familiar with Italian geography." (Although this was not exactly how it had been taught her by the Sisters.)

Carnot: "Tant mieux. So that to a certain degree you will be passing through, shall we say, hostile territory. The Papal States, first of all. And then Venice."

Winifred: "Venice is hostile?"

Carnot: "In principle Venice is a Republic. In practice it is a most odious tyranny. Liberal ideas are suppressed. The Inquisitors are mad dogs."

Winifred: "Yet you said it was impossible not to be happy in Venice."

Carnot (after a moment's thought): "At that point I was referring to personal life. Now I am referring to Politicks."

She said nothing. After a while he cleared his throat.

Carnot: "Since you are going to Venice anyhow there is a little favor I would like to ask of you. I have a gift to send to M. Fontenay. Un petit rien."

Turning his attention to the objects cluttering the table, he removed, from under a pile of papers, a small flat packet evidently wrapped in waxed cloth and tied with a ribbon.

Carnot: "A little nothing. But a nothing which, between me and M. Fontenay, has a great importance. I will not talk about the Revolution, and what is or is not important to the Revolution. I will only say that if this packet is delivered safely into M. Fontenay's hands it will be very good for him, and if it is not delivered into his hands it will be very bad for him. You are a woman and you will understand this."

Winifred bit the inside of her lip again, felt her expression darkening, and controlled herself only with difficulty. M. Carnot, who was said to be a ladies' man and adept at the arts of the salon, evidently regarded the fair sex as suited for the secrets of love but not those of Politicks. And what was the insufferable man doing now! Without taking his eyes from her he was undoing the ribbons of the packet and unfolding the cloth. It was stuck together with wax, and he used his long fingernail as a letter-opener. Inside, she could see, were papers, and some tiny black balls like pepper-corns. Still keeping his glance fixed on her—perhaps to be sure she was far enough away that she couldn't read the writing—he removed one of the papers and spread it flat. He groped for a pen, found it on the floor, and jabbed it into the inkwell. He *had* to look away from her, at least, while he wrote. It was no more than a word or two dashed across the page. Then he folded everything up again. Went for a candle, and dropped hot wax all around the folds of the cloth. Tied the green ribbons, with a jerk at the end, found a stick of sealing-wax and melted it in the candle, and sealed the ribbon with several large hot globs. He groped for and found the Great Seal of the Directoire, which was almost as large as the packet itself, and squashed the wax flat. A moment of silence. He was still studying her.

Carnot: "I might add that the third eventuality—that of the packet falling into Venetian or other foreign hands—would be even worse. The consequences for M. Fontenay, in that case, would be dire. There is lead shot in it"—he weighed the packet in his hands—"and it will sink if thrown into water. It may also be burned. But neither of these things should happen. Instead it should be concealed on your person, taken to Venice, and handed to M. Fontenay without explanation. And please take note of this. When you come to Venice you will arrive as a private person and an English subject. You should have nothing to do with the French Legation or anyone connected with it. You should present your-self to the English Resident, Mr. Jonathan Birdsell, and inquire as to M. Fontenay's address. The Residency is in Campo Santi Apos-toli, near the Rialto. Can you remember that?"

Winifred only made a kind of sniff. M. Carnot did not seem to notice. He was not paying very much attention to her, only to what he himself was saying.

Carnot: "After the packet is delivered to M. Fontenay your duties will be completed, and you may resume your—"

He started to say something like conjugal bliss, saw the expression on Winifred's face, and altered his course in mid-sentence.

Carnot: "Private affairs. The secretary in the anteroom will provide you with a mandat for the dispatch-coach. Good-day."

As she turned to go he thought of something else.

Carnot: "Time is of importance, by the way. You must be in Venice by the twentieth of April. That is three weeks from now."

And so it all took place, exactly according to M. Carnot's wishes. It annoyed her to be carrying out the will of this person she found not only intellectually arrogant but lacking in the decencies of polite intercourse (the French were correct but not courteous; it wasn't quite the same thing), but she did want to be with Jean-Marie, from whom she had heard nothing for three months. She went back to rue des Francs-Bourgeois and packed her green portmanteau and a hat-box, the dispatch-coach whisked her to Marseille, she was put aboard a fast sloop, and five days later she was in Civitavecchia.

In Rome the Embassy was expecting her. A young clerk, with very few words and no explanations, installed her in a cabriolet drawn by two bays and driven by a coachman who was perhaps deaf and dumb; he said not one word to her for the next four days. Her needs were seen to at each nightly stop: Terni, Foligno, Fabriano, and finally Ancona. She had very little idea where she was going each day, or where she had stopped at night. In Ancona she stopped in an inn where everything was provided but where she asked no questions and no explanations of anything were offered.

Ancona was a dull place, a town on a rocky peninsula with the sea on either side of it, with nothing to do but walk around a weedy piazza in the evening. Winifred possessed a passable Italian taught her by the Sisters in Passy, but she spoke to no one. The Papal Marches were in French hands by this time and there were French soldiers in the streets, but she had nothing to do with them; partly because it would have been improper to have anything to do with soldiers anyhow, and partly because of the seal of confidence charged upon her by M. Carnot. (Winifred was resolved to be True to M. Carnot even if she disliked him; after all she had given him her word, if only by her silence when he had explained all these matters to her.)

The next morning a naval lieutenant called for her and escorted her aboard the *Libérateur d'Italie*, which was lying offshore in the roadstead. Then after all the hurrying there was a period of waiting: two days of it. Winifred's cabin was tiny and uncomfortable, but she displaced two officers from it in order to occupy it; they slept in hammocks swung from the deck-beams. Finally they sailed. They had been waiting for a fair wind, or a political development, or perhaps a conjunction of Venus with the moon; Winifred had no idea and no one explained anything to her. As for the packet, for two weeks she had been carrying it concealed in her clothing, sewn into an undergarment. It would be necessary to wash one's undergarments eventually but the promise to M. Carnot took precedence.

However Winifred conceived another idea. The fancy struck her to dress as a man again, as she had in the Kentish countryside and riding in Hyde Park. Her skirts were impractical on the damp decks in the evenings. The midshipman's uniform fitted her perfectly. There was even a short dirk in a scabbard: she tried its sharpness and cut her thumb, and had to suck off the blood. Clad in this way she would be less conspicuous and more comfortable, and in the event the brig became involved in an action she might even pass herself off, with her short hair and her slim figure, as a boy.

This last, however, was only a subterfuge she invented in order to conceal her real reasons from herself. Her real reason was that she felt better in the naval uniform, more active and less restricted, able to speak her mind as she felt, in short a different person; and yet a different person who was *herself* in a way the person in petticoat and skirts had not been. There were beige breeches, a trim blue coat, and a hat with a tricolor cockade. The packet remained in a kind of pouch she had sewn into her drawers, just under the heavy black belt of the breeches. Winifred felt blithe, imagining herself suddenly appearing before Jean-Marie in this garb. But then of course she wouldn't wear the uniform in Venice. She had forgotten the Politickal aspects of her journey, which she understood perfectly well even though M. Carnot had not deigned to explain them to her. That man! It was maddening that the Revolution produced the same kind of fatuous male donkeys that she had to deal with in England all of her young life.

The brig worked its way slowly up the Adriatic coast, sometimes putting in for the day at ports like Pesaro or Rimini and sailing at night. There was an English squadron offshore, and Austrian warships had also been reported off the Dalmatian coast. Captain Laugier proceeded with caution, and evidently he too had instructions to arrive in Venice exactly on the twentieth. Winifred began to take a certain interest in Captain Laugier. A kind of camaraderie sprang up between them; quite chaste of course. He was a Provencal, stocky and burnt by the sun, taciturn and capable of remaining motionless at the quarter-deck rail for hours, but dexterous when there was something physical to be done. He was hardly more than her own age but he was already an experienced seafarer and captain of a vessel. (The Revolution *did* work, you see, in spite of M. Carnot, and young merit was rewarded.) Winifred found it pleasant to spend the night watches on the quarter-deck with Captain Laugier, wrapped in a greatcoat against the damp. He had no comment to make on her uniform and only seemed faintly amused by it. After a while he took the habit of addressing her, with absolute gravity, as Monsieur l'Aspirant, which was the rather absurd word for midshipman in French.

Laugier: "You see those lights, Monsieur l'Aspirant? That is Ravenna."

Or: "A foul wind tonight, Monsieur l'Aspirant. Dead ahead. A Tramontana, they call it hereabouts."

Or: "Tomorrow or the next day, Venice, Monsieur l'Aspirant. Let's hope the Venetians don't object to our entering. They'll be foolish if they do. Their navy is not in good condition just now."

The compass-light faintly illuminated the face of the man at the wheel. Captain Laugier was a motionless silhouette against the rail. Winifred felt stirring in her, like a dream awakening and slowly acquiring solidity, a thing she had longed for since she was a girl of twelve without quite understanding what it was she wanted: a sense of comradely and taciturn complicity in belonging to the world of men. When Captain Laugier left his post at the rail to glance at the compass his face was outlined in the lamp: square, sturdy, expressionless, the set of the mouth faintly skeptical. He had an odor, when he stood at arm's-length from Winifred at the rail, of damp wool and some very faint but pungent Provençal spice, perhaps oregano. The notion formed at the back of Winifred's thoughts, quite unwillingly and in spite of her efforts to repress it, that it was someone like Captain Laugier she had had in mind in wishing to fall in love at the age of sixteen, not precisely a musician and model of drawing-room elegance like Jean-Marie. Was one's life then inexorably committed to the decisions of a single moment—a moment when one's thoughts might be clouded by—vapors that came from shadowy and unknown, perhaps dubious parts of one's nature? A moment in a fiacre and an odor of leather—

But Winifred remembered: True! All this would be forgotten—only a week she had passed on a vessel with people whose names, in a few years, she would hardly remember. It was important, not only to be True, but not to be a silly girl who changed her mind with every passing fancy. The golden cupolas of Venice drew the brig onward like a magnet. On the nineteenth it was off the mouth of the Po; in the night between the nineteenth and twentieth it crept slowly up on the land-wind past the Adige. Before dawn a mysterious person was taken on board out of a boat; a fisherman, perhaps a pilot. At daylight a town was visible on the larboard bow; a clump of trees, some pastel blotches half-sunk in the water.

The wind was still light and from the west. Captain Laugier was determined to enter the lagoon by nightfall. He ordered sweeps run out. The *Libérateur* moved heavily, reluctantly, through the viscous water that clung to her sides like syrup. To the right was the open sea; on the left the long sand-spit of the Lido ran ahead until it disappeared in the morning haze. There was a low sea-wall along this part of the Lido, and behind it objects could be discerned: spindly posts, a hut on a marshy island, the faint distant outline of the Euganean Hills. For an hour Winifred had been watching something that remained in the same position relative to the brig, exactly abeam through the mizzen-shrouds, while the Lido had slowly slipped by. Finally she called Captain Laugier's attention to the oddly shaped set of triangles moving along behind the sand-spit.

Winifred: "There's a vessel following along with us."

Laugier: "It's nothing, Monsieur l'Aspirant. A fisher. Or a trading vessel, that supplies the towns in the lagoon."

CONTESSA: "I IMAGINE THIS IS WHY

Contessa: "I imagine this is why you were on board the *Libérateur*."

Winifred is determined to turn the conversation away from the packet, even if it involves an indiscretion about her private life.

Winifred: "If you must know, I came to Venice to rejoin my fiancé."

This slight sharpness seems to mollify the Contessa somewhat. She respects people more, perhaps, when they stand up to her a little. She surveys Winifred in her sideways bird-like way, and makes what passes with her for a little smile.

Contessa: "Ah, there is a fiancé. And may one know more about this interesting person?"

Winifred: "What is there to say? He is a . . . young man."

Contessa: "A Venetian possibly?"

Winifred smiles, lifts one shoulder slightly, and stirs her coffee.

Contessa: "Very well, I can see you don't care to say more. It's your business after all. He can be a Turk or a Red Indian for all I care. You're of age and you can marry exactly whom you please. I'm not one to meddle."

And then on she goes, meddling.

Contessa: "And where did you meet your Turk or Red Indian? In Paris, I imagine."

Winifred: "In London."

Contessa: "Ah then, he's English."

Winifred decides to persist in this stiff, formally amiable, slightly distant manner, which seems to entertain the Contessa, and also has the benefit of conveying the absolute minimum of information.

Winifred: "Possibly."

The Contessa smiles again. Her pieces are moving across the board and Winifred will soon be checkmated. To allow the implication to remain in the air that her fiancé is English without denying it is—almost—to tell a lie. The Contessa is playing, quite deliberately, on her English sense of honor. She can not go on saying "possibly" all day. Winifred decides to upset the chessboard. She speaks quite sharply. This is not difficult because she feels sharp.

Winifred: "I'm sorry. These are personal matters. Ce sont mes affaires à moi. In my country, you understand—"

But the Contessa raises her hand to interrupt her. The hand with the finger upraised moves back and forth, denying that Winifred's personal affairs have the slightest interest for her. With her other hand she is sipping coffee and has to swallow it and set the cup down before she speaks.

Contessa: "Quite, quite. D'accord. You English do not confide, you defend the privacy of the soul. For my part you may marry whomever you please. I can only give you my opinion. I would never marry, Mademoiselle Hervey. But if I did marry, I would not marry an English. I would marry a Frenchman. A Frenchman marries and that is that, he goes his own way and his wife is free to do as she pleases."

Winifred stiffens inside, managing a doll-like smile on the outside. The Contessa could hardly conceive how totally in opposition all this is to her own principles.

Contessa: "And even less would I marry a Venetian. The Venetians are even worse. The Venetian will lock you in the house and give you stilts to walk on, so you can't go too far. You don't believe me, do you? The stilts are called zoccoli. Take my advice, Mademoiselle Hervey, don't marry an English, but above all don't marry a Venetian."

Winifred (still a little stiffly): "I don't intend to do either."

And so she has got it out of her.

* * *

Winifred is getting a little exasperated with the Contessa. In spite of her generosity. It is true that Winifred is eating her food and wearing her clothes. And sheltered under her roof. A thousand plagues take her generosity! She is only doing it because M. Villetard has told her to; paid her perhaps, or obliged her through some mysterious power that is a secret between them. It is boring in this damp old villa, even if it is designed by Palladio with frescoes that are perhaps Tiepolos. Winifred has only been here for a day but she has had enough. She is cross, perhaps, because of her cold. Besides she has begun to long for Jean-Marie—for *anyone* to talk to other than the Contessa and Lina—but especially for Jean-Marie. A little cloud of guilt hovers in the back of her thoughts, where she is careful not to examine it too carefully: the packet. If it is so important to M. Carnot, and to M. Villetard, then no doubt it is important. And it is not only a matter of being True to M. Carnot. If the packet didn't get delivered, M. Carnot said, it would be bad for Jean-Marie. Oh, bother! These affairs of men! If only the packet were at the bottom of the sea! Still—if she went to Venice, perhaps, she might find Captain Langrish and by some miracle—if he hasn't disposed of it—

After lunch she goes for another walk. The Contessa perhaps disapproves, but no one has *forbidden* her to leave the villa. The sun has come out now but a thin mist still hangs over the marsh. The peacock is absent, perhaps taking his afternoon nap. A heavy dew clings to everything, soaking her shoes and confining her to the pathway along the canal. There is a village a quarter of a mile or so down the canal. She remembers seeing its lights as she passed in the gondola with Captain Langrish, and there was talk about it in the villa. She has forgotten its name; something that begins with *mal*. As she walks the houses begin to come up out of the mist. The first thing she sees is a church, small and rather dilapidated, set at an angle to the canal, with a broken wall along one side.

History (that intractable and brittle substance that fills the past, so that we can see objects like Winifred through it only slightly distorted) has flowed on like a kind of glassy lava while Winifred and Contessa were quarreling in the villa. The headquarters of the Army of Italy have advanced from Gorizia and are now across the Austrian border in Villach, threatening Vienna itself. La Hoz has occupied Vicenza and Padova on the twentieth. On the twenty-first the troops of General Baraguey d'Hilliers occupy Mestre, the Brenta, and Fusina. Venice itself is impregnable behind its lagoon, but the entire Terraferma is now in French hands. On the church door, which is decrepit and about to fall off its hinges, Winifred finds a freshly pasted handbill. At the top is a female allegorical figure with a Roman fasces in one hand and a standard in the other. Arranged around this, in bold type, is a grandiloquent sort of military frieze or fanfare.

Armée d'Italie

Liberté   (here is the figure)   Egalité

Au Quartier Général de Villach, le 12 Germinal An V

LE GÉNÉRAL EN CHEF

De L'Armée d'Italie

After this follows the hortatory part.

People of Italy, the French army comes to break your chains. It is your independence we bring you. The French people is the friend of all peoples. You may receive them with confidence. Your property, your religion, and your customs will be respected. We have no grudge except against the tyrants who oppress you. Bonaparte.

This is all very fine. It is exactly as the Contessa has said. Still Winifred is not sure she wants to be liberated on this damp pathway, by people she has not even been introduced to. She hears a whinny and a jingle of spurs, not very far away down the path. A troop of chasseurs in green coats has entered the village and stopped while their officer dismounts. She can see them clearly through the trees, the green of the uniforms only slightly blurred and wavery in the watery atmosphere. She turns and goes back to the villa, losing her way once so that she soaks her skirts in the damp grass. At the villa everything is quiet.

She goes upstairs to her room and changes her gown. As she comes back down the broad staircase she hears a jangle of the bell and the sound of Luciana's footsteps hurrying across the marble floor.

Contessa: "Luciana, cossa gh'è?"

Luciana: "Soldadi."

Contessa: "Oh, là là."

She comes herself to see—hurrying, but with great dignity, or to put it more precisely a solemnity.

The officer is standing in the open doorway. Behind him the other chasseurs have dismounted and are standing holding their bridles, or patting the necks of their horses in the way that cavalrymen do. The horses steam in the misty air.

Officer: "Mme. D'Artigny Baraoni?"

The Contessa nods. It is not quite a bow.

Officer: "Lieutenant Longpré, at your service."

At close range he looks more rough-and-ready than he did at a distance. His boots are muddy and he is unshaven. The chasseurs in the dooryard are grimy wretches. They look hungry and their uniforms are ragged. The bridles of their mounts are patched and mended, and one of them wears a red-stained bandage around his head. They are the troops that stormed the bridge at Lodi, defeated Wurmser at Castiglione, captured Mantova after the long siege, passed through the three-day ordeal of Arcola, and charged and routed the larger Austrian army at Rivoli.

Officer: "Your name is known to the Quartier Général, Madame. We have orders to ensure your safety and see to it that no one molests you."

Contessa: "I am not accustomed to being molested."

Officer: "The district is full of brigands and English agents. The contadini are hostile."

Contessa: "I am familiar with the hostility of the contadini. They don't want to pay their rents."

Officer: "Last Monday in Verona the scum of the streets rose up and slaughtered the French."

Contessa: "Surely they didn't harm civilians?"

He doesn't respond directly to this.

Officer: "It was put down only with the greatest difficulty. I would advise you to take precautions, Madame. Close your shutters and keep your doors locked. Allow no one in the house. Who is that?"

He has caught sight of Winifred, behind the Contessa at the bottom of the hall.

Contessa: "My niece."

Officer: "Enchanté, Mademoiselle."

Winifred says nothing. She is mildly astounded to find that the Contessa is capable of lying; and to the French, for whom she professes such an admiration. And further, on behalf of a person for whom—as far as Winifred can tell—her approval is severely limited. It is a mystery.

The Contessa's expression is as usual, bird-like and severe.

Officer: "We are quartered in Fusina. If we can be of any help, send a message."

Contessa: "You are very considerate. Would your men care to take something? A glass of wine, or something to eat?"

Officer: "Ce n'est pas recommandé. If the brigands—that is the contadini—noticed that you were offering us assistance—"

Contessa: "I see. Perhaps you are right."

Officer: "As it is, we have only inspected your house along with the others, to look for brigands and English agents. Au revoir, Madame."

He mounts with a jangle of spurs; the gaunt horse lunges ahead before he has his right foot in the stirrup, and the troop leaves the dooryard at a trot. They are gone.

The Contessa turns away from the door with an odd expression, as though she were suppressing a smile of triumph. Her mouth is tightened into a fine line, and wrinkled slightly at the corners. When she speaks, it is as much for her own benefit as for Winifred's; or rather, it is as though she were addressing an audience.

Contessa: "Heroes."

Still, Winifred can see, she is a little disconcerted to see they are so dirty.

At dinner Winifred broaches the subject.

Winifred: "I think, with all respect, that I should go back to Venice soon. I am terribly grateful for your hospitality, of course. You've been very kind—"

Which is not really true, but then it is: she is sitting right there at the dining-table wearing the Contessa's clothes.

Contessa: "It's not a good idea just now. The Venetians are not friendly to the French. You heard what the officer said."

Winifred: "But I'm not French."

Contessa: "True. But—we would have to wait for word from M. Villetard."

Winifred: "What on earth has he got to do with it?"

Contessa: "He speaks for M. Lallement, the Minister."

Winifred: "But I've just explained to you I'm English."

Contessa: "You are very headstrong, do you know that, Mademoiselle Hervey? You should entrust yourself to those who know more about these matters, and have your best interests at heart."

Winifred: "I think I know my interests better than anyone else."

Contessa: "You're a very wise young lady then."

It rains that night, and the weather changes. Winifred lies in bed listening to the water pattering on the tiles and splashing softly off onto the mud around the villa. There are other sounds: the creak of shutters, the rustle of wind in the cypresses outside the window. Winifred can not sleep. She gets up, puts on a light dressing-gown, and winds a turban around her head like the Contessa's, fashioned out of a scarf. This Oriental habit is suited to the climate, and it also makes it unnecessary to do anything about one's hair until morning. Taking her candle, she opens the door and slips out into the corridor.

In the room across the corridor the Contessa is asleep. Winifred detects a peculiar rhythmic sound from behind the door: a snort, then after a moment a whir like a bird taking flight. The floor is marble and cold to her feet: she has neglected to put on her shoes. The corridor crosses the villa from side to side, and there are four or five rooms opening off it. The room next to her own is evidently a spare bed-chamber. She opens it cautiously and finds a brass bedstead without a mattress, an old armoire, and a good deal of dust. The armoire is empty.

Across the corridor, at the corner on the front of the villa, is another spare chamber, immediately adjoining the Contessa's own room. In fact, opening the door and entering silently, she finds a connecting door into the Contessa's chamber: presumably locked, but it is too risky to try and anyhow there is no reason to do so. The shutters are tightly closed and the air is musty. The candle-light penetrates only dimly into the corners of the room. It is piled with trunks, wardrobes, and old baggage and rubbish of all kinds. Dusty garments hang on hooks around the walls. In the gloom Winifred makes out a bird-cage on a tall stand, a collection of whips and riding-crops, and an ancient fowling-piece of the previous century.

Clothing is precisely what she is looking for. The clothing provided her by the Contessa is elegant if somewhat austere, but none of it is very well suited for travel. Particularly she wants boots, against the dampness of the marsh, and a warm and dry coat. The fact is that she still nourishes the hope of finding her midshipman's uniform somewhere in the villa. It is possible that the Wicked Grandmother has burned it by this time, but she is so parsimonious that it seems unlikely she would destroy anything. From the looks of this room nobody has thrown anything away for several generations.

Closer examination reveals, however, that all the clothes and most of the other things in the room are for feminine use. This means that all the rubbish in this room was generated by the Contessa in the course of a lifetime, or by the mother after the father died. Perhaps everything male was thrown out in a maenadic frenzy at that time. So much the better; she will surely find a pair of boots that will fit her, and a coat. Although it seems less likely, now, that she will find the uniform here. For one thing it could hardly have acquired, in only two days, the thick coat of dust that seems to cover everything in the room.

Winifred, acquiring a good deal of dust on her own clothing and person, searches the room thoroughly. There is nothing much in the clothing on the hooks that interests her, although she finds a kind of redingote in the style of a half-century ago and leaves it on top of the clothing hanging from the hook, lest she should change her mind and want it later. The trunks and wardrobes are more difficult. She opens a trunk and finds it mostly full of old letters. (She really *is* engaged in a breach of hospitality now; she can no longer pretend that she is merely wandering around the villa because she can't sleep.) In closing the trunk she lets the lid slip from her fingers, and it drops with a bang. She stands perfectly quiet in the half-darkness for a time, her heart pounding. From the next room comes a thrashy rustling, perhaps of bed-clothes. A half-muffled little bird-cry penetrates the wall.

Contessa: "Lina?"

There is no answer. From beyond the wall, silence. After a long time Winifred, her heart still beating a little harder than usual, slips out of the room and closes the door with infinite pains. She goes back down the corridor toward her own door. Then she becomes aware that there is one door on the floor, in addition to the Contessa's own, that she has not yet explored. At the end of the corridor, just at the head of the stairs, is a cubicle with marble walls: a small and evil-smelling latrine. This she is familiar with— unwillingly but necessarily. But not the door just before it, one that exactly resembles the other doors to the bed-chambers. Her hand goes to the door-handle and presses it: it is locked.

Now Winifred—she can hardly imagine how she, a well-brought-up young Englishwoman whose father is a country gen-tleman, has been driven to such an extreme—commits a genuine dishonesty, far worse than opening the trunk. Next to the kitchen and immediately adjoining the dining-hall, she knows, is a pantry. And in the pantry are kept all the keys to the house. She knows this because Luciana went to the pantry for the key to her own room, the night when she came here with Captain Langrish. She goes down the broad marble staircase with her candle. The stair-case ends in the central hall, its ceiling painted in blue and gold— rather shabby, the paint peeling here and there to reveal a yel-lowish plaster—and held up by statues along the wall in the shape of male Greek slaves. She goes down the hall, enters the dining-room from the rear, crosses it, and opens the small white-enameled door of the pantry. There is a light under the kitchen door and she can hear small culinary sounds. The keys are in a row hanging from hooks. There are too many; she can't take them all. But at the end is a large mass of keys that looks as though it may serve for everything. Taking this, she slips out of the pantry leaving the door open (she is getting a little reckless now in the excitement of search) and hurries back up the staircase. The sixth or seventh key she tries opens the door.

It is a kind of storeroom. There are cabinets with bed-linen, a row of wash-basins on a shelf, brushes and brooms for cleaning, and a cupboard full of things like brass candlesticks and lanterns, all immaculately polished. The whole room is clean and neatly ordered. Evidently Lina presides here; it is nothing like the room across the corridor filled with the Contessa's rubbish. The room is small, and occupying the narrow end wall is a large armoire, polished and smelling of rubbing-oil. In it there is only a single garment: the salt-stained military cloak, buttoned and hanging neatly from a hook. It is still just the slightest bit damp: as Captain Langrish says, once things are wet in salt water they never really dry out. Winifred restrains the impulse to take it with her now. Instead she closes the armoire and steals out of the room, leaving the door unlocked. She has just hung up the mass of keys on its hook in the pantry when there are footsteps from the kitchen, unexpectedly and without a sound to warn her of their coming.

Luciana: "The Siorina wants something?"

Winifred: "I'm hungry. Can't you fix me an egg?"

IN THE SMALL HOURS BEFORE

In the small hours before daylight—it is perhaps five o'clock in the morning—Lina knocks on the door and then slips in without waiting for Winifred to answer. Winifred is instantly awake, sitting up in bed in the darkness.

Lina has no lamp or candle. The room is totally dark. Winifred identifies her only by her voice.

Lina: "Come to the Contessa, please."

Winifred: "Now? But why?"

Lina: "She asks you to come, please."

Winifred: "In her chamber, you mean?"

Lina: "On est là-bas dans le salon."

The impersonality of French is one of its flaws. One is in the salon, but who? The Contessa? Someone else? If Lina meant only the Contessa she would have said *elle*. And besides, why would the Contessa be in the salon by herself?

Winifred dresses in the dark, putting on a light pelisse over her gown and groping for her slippers. She follows Lina along the dark corridor to the staircase. Here a faint light penetrates from the hall, where the two large candle-stands are burning at the bottom of the staircase. The door to the salon is open and there are voices.

The Contessa, also in her night-clothing and turban with a dressing-gown, is talking to a short pudgy man in a black frock-coat. The man's breeches are muddy and he holds his three-cornered hat in his hand. Someone else is waiting outside in the hall, a coachman.

Contessa: "It is from M. Villetard. You are to come to Venice immediately."

Winifred: "Surely not now. It's the middle of the night."

Contessa: "The instructions are quite clear. I've questioned the man thoroughly."

Winifred examines him. He has a shifty eye, and a habit of wiping his nose with the back of his hand. His hat is greasy too. He is not a savory-looking person. On the other hand the coachman, who is visible through the open door to the hall, is an old fellow who looks quite decent, if a little shaggy and unkempt.

Winifred: "Are there written instructions?"

Contessa: "Written instructions are not necessary. I know this man thoroughly. I have had business with him before. M. Villetard's instructions are particularly explicit about the dispatches. He has sent a message about this before, you will remember. He says now that if the dispatches are not in your possession—"

Winifred: "I understand. I'll go up and dress. Have the man wait."

Contessa: "And the dispatches?"

Winifred: "I won't be long."

She turns abruptly, leaves the salon, and mounts up the broad marble staircase again. It is dark at the top. For some reason no one has seen fit to light so much as a candle on the upper floor. So much the better for her purposes. That precious packet! What a fuss everyone makes about it. Well, she has not got it. She is determined not to let the Legation know she doesn't have it—this might be bad for Jean-Marie, as M. Carnot strongly hinted. And it won't do for Captain Langrish to give it to the Venetians either. She must get it back—hide it from the French so she can give it to the French. In her own sweet time and with great calm, as though she has never lost it. Surely this can't be too difficult. It is only a few scraps of paper. And Captain Langrish is—not a beast. When one knows him a little, he seems—not amiable exactly, but at least human, in his way. The best would be to go straight to Jean-Marie and explain the thing to him. He will know what to do. Between the two of them, they can approach Captain Langrish and . . . Well, Jean-Marie will know what to do.

All these thoughts with the rapidity of lightning. They occupy only a few seconds, as she goes up the stairs. She is keenly awake and alert to everything; the thoughts, and the sensations of things about her, burn in her mind like tiny sparks. In her room she slips off the pelisse and gown and dresses for the second time, with some difficulty in the dark. Drawers, petticoat, and a long linen gown that comes to her ankles and has sleeves for warmth. If only she had her walking-boots! They have disappeared along with the rest of the uniform. She gropes for and finds some slippers of soft Florentine leather with low heels. They will have to do. The sovereigns! She has almost forgotten them. She carried the three gold coins in the pocket of her midshipman's breeches, and kept her head enough to remove them when she undressed that first night. They are in the drawer of the dressing-table, knotted into a handkerchief. She takes the knotted handkerchief with her as she slips out the door. She feels her way along the wall, which is damp and smells unpleasantly of plaster. Somehow she has passed the door of the storeroom and becomes aware, through a vile odor, that she has arrived at the latrine. She retraces her steps and comes, after only a few feet of groping in the darkness, back to the door she is seeking. It is still unlocked, by some miracle. Because of Lina's neatness it is easy to find things. She opens the armoire, which creaks alarmingly, removes the cloak from the hook, and slips it on. It has two large pockets, and into one of these she drops the knotted handkerchief with the three coins in it. Then she steals out, leaving the storeroom door open in order not to make unnecessary noise. She can still hear voices in the salon as she slips out the rear door.

The cloak is tightly buttoned around her neck. Inside it she feels warm and comfortable, secure. The cloak is a little damp, but it is relatively dry compared to the marsh. She keeps her hands thrust into the pockets to keep them warm too. In the right-hand pocket she can feel the knotted handkerchief at the bottom. She goes down the dike in the direction of the village. It is almost daylight now. A thin haze of gray is beginning to appear along the line of poplars that marks the horizon to the east. The rain has stopped but everything is dripping wet: the trees, the grass. After a while she begins to make out house-tops against the grayness. She passes a woman on the dike, probably going out to her cows. The woman gives her a single glance from under her shawl and passes on without speaking.

Winifred skirts around the church and arrives at the first house, a low hut with a tile roof. The whitewash is spattered with mud along the ground. There are no windows and only a single door for an opening. She remembers now the name of the village: it is Malcontenta. There are more huts, then the dike widens into a kind of irregular square or piazza of beaten earth facing the canal.

On the piazza is a rude establishment that seems to be a tavern or osteria: there is a bush over the door to indicate that wine is sold. Outside the door a pair of unpainted wooden tables with chairs. Miracle of miracles, the osteria is open at this time in the morning and there are lights inside.

Inside a woman is down on her hands and knees vigorously scrubbing the floor, which is paved with rough stones.

Winifred pauses at the door and smiles uncertainly, her hands still deep in the pockets of the cloak.

Winifred: "Buongiorno, Signora."

Her Italian is only half comprehended. No one in the osteria speaks anything but Venetian. The woman calls in dialect to someone in the rear of the place.

Winifred (trying out her own dialect): "Bon zorno."

Voice from the rear: "Cossa gh'è?"

A man appears, apparently the woman's husband; and behind him a grandmother, still blinking with sleep.

Winifred: "I'm English. I want to go to Venice."

Wife: "Cosse dise?"

Husband: "Xe inglese, sai."

Somehow the three-sided conversation plunges on, partly in Italian, partly in Winifred's five words of dialect. It seems to be important to them to establish that she is not French. Evidently the man understands this. He repeats it to his wife several times.

Husband: "No, no, xe inglese, te digo, sai."

Once this fact is established everything goes beautifully. She speaks Italian and they Venetian—both in phrases no more than a word or two long—and the gap between is bridged with good will.

Winifred: "I require a boat, you see. To go to Venice."

Husband: "Na barca?"

Winifred: "Sì, sì, una barca. Per andare a Venezia."

Husband: "A Venecia. Sì, sì."

They are sending for someone, perhaps a boatman. The grand-mother goes off and presently the husband follows to see why she is taking so long. The wife insists that Winifred seat herself at a table. She breaks into expressions of dismay and concern, pointing at Winifred's skirt. She is lamenting that her fine gown and slippers have gotten muddy in her way along the sodden path. Winifred tells her it is nothing. The important thing is to arrive in Venice, either clean or muddy, it makes no difference. The woman goes away, still mourning the muddy skirt, to fetch something in the kitchen. Winifred is seated at a table near the back of the osteria, facing the open doorway. She can see the small square of beaten earth in front of the osteria, and beyond it the dike and the canal. There is the rhythmic beat of hooves in the distance, and the grit of wheels running in the mud. The sound grows louder. Winifred finds that her heart is pounding. A light carriage bursts into view and goes by at a trot. It is a kind of landau with a black leather top, spattered with mud. Only a shoddy little buggy, really. One would have thought a Legation could do better. She can't see the occupant through the muddy window, but the coachman is the old man she saw waiting in the hall of the villa. It is gone in an instant. The sound of hooves gradually fades in the distance. Winifred has been holding her breath and now she releases it.

The wife brings up coffee, in an earthenware cup. It is not as bad as the coffee in the villa, probably because they can't afford to make it as strong. And in place of the horrible rusk there is a kind of ring-shaped bun (na buzzola, the woman calls it) which even comes close to appetizing, perhaps because Winifred is hungry from her walk over the marsh. She still has her cold and feels miserable but it doesn't affect her appetite.

The woman apologizes that there is nothing but the buzzola. They took everything, you know.

Who?

The Franzesi. They took everything—they cleaned out the place. The ham. All the wine. And the silver, adds the woman. Only a few spoons. She doesn't want to give the impression that they are rich folk who have silver. They had a few spoons, that is all. Also the cheese. They made off with a whole cheese. She makes a circle with her arms to show how large the cheese was.

And did they pay?

Pay? They paid a fig. Why should they pay? They were soldiers. The woman seems to find this perfectly natural. There is no resentment in her tone. Still, Winifred thinks, it is well she has said she is not French. She wonders if the proclamation is still up on the church-door.

The husband and grandmother appear with the boatman. The husband, Winifred notices now, has a swollen reddish ear with a few pinpoints of blood congealed on it; also he walks with a limp. Probably this happened when the ham and the spoons were liberated. The boatman seems very young; he is a boy.

Husband: "Mio fio."

Winifred: "Ah, it's your son."

The son seems to be about thirteen, although perhaps he is older. The father and mother swear (in Venetian; Winifred guesses this is what they are swearing) that the boy is an excellent boatman and has gone many times to Venice. It is a matter of two hours, perhaps three, no more. They hold up fingers and point to the clock to show how many hours. It suddenly occurs to Winifred, drinking her coffee and eating her buzzola, that these are the poor people her Revolutionary principles are supposed to benefit, not to exploit. She begins trying to explain that she has money and will pay for everything, that they should not be concerned about money. They, likewise, seem to retort that she, Winifred, should not be concerned about money. They expect, perhaps, a lira or two. In her pocket Winifred has only the three gold sovereigns. She recalls that, in the opinion of the French lieutenant, these people are little better than bandits. She hesitates, puts her hand in and out of the cloak pocket several times, and finally produces the handkerchief and unknots it.

Winifred: "I have money, you see. Ho soldi. I would want to pay for everything. Simply tell me the fair price and I will pay."

The four of them—the boy too standing somewhat awkwardly not knowing what to do with his large hands in the presence of the foreign lady—watch as the three golden coins come out of the handkerchief and onto the table.

They all begin shaking their heads—the husband and wife vigorously, the grandmother sadly—and expressing negatives. They would not dream of taking a gold coin for so little. The three sovereigns, Winifred realizes, would probably buy the osteria and everything in it. They refuse. She is their guest. A lady, a young lady, alone on the marsh! It is not to be thought of. The French are abroad, you know. (They give the impression it is the French who are the brigands and not they! Evidently it is a matter of opinion.) No, Bepi will take her to Venice, and safely too. It is a matter of three hours, at the most four. They make signs for her to knot the coins up in the handkerchief again. And to keep them in the pocket and not show them to anyone, you know, because some people . . .

Husband: "Bepi!"

As she leaves, following Bepi, the wife impulsively slips another buzzola into the pocket of her cloak, carefully selecting the left pocket, the one that doesn't have the money in it. There are no farewells. They say nothing. They watch her go down the dike along the canal, a few paces behind Bepi.

The boat is tied to a pair of stakes at the canal-bank. It is unpainted, the grayish color of weathered wood, and there is a good deal of water in it from the rain.

Winifred: "Is it large enough? It's a very small gondola."

Bepi explains that it is not a gondola but a sandolo. A sandolo is not as large as a gondola but it is very quick, because it is light and because there are two oars. He clambers down the muddy bank, leaving Winifred on the dike, and rather embarrassedly begins sponging the water out with a dirty rag that looks as though it might once have been a shirt. A gleam of light appears on the houses in the distance; the edge of an orange sun crawls out on the muddy horizon to the east.

Winifred, using more Italian and her five words of dialect, begins explaining that it doesn't matter if there is water in the boat, that she is in a hurry and wants to get to Venice as soon as possible. The fact is also that she doesn't care to stand so conspicuously on the dike now that the sun is up. Conceivably the stocky man in his landau might come back to see if he has missed her somewhere on the road.

Winifred: "Partiamo sùbito. Never mind the water."

The boy understands. He clambers up the bank again and helps Winifred down, she muddying her skirts and slippers a good deal more in the process.

Winifred is in the sandolo, pulling up her skirts as best she can out of the water and wrapping them around her legs. As for her slippers and stockings, she takes them off and sets them on the thwart beside her. The water is warm or at least tepid on her bare feet.

Bepi is evidently used to seeing ladies take off their stockings, or too young to consider it an important spectacle, and pays no attention whatsoever. She sits in the middle of the boat, and he stands toward the stern and fits the oars into the two knotted thole-pins. The oars are so long that they cross. His right hand is opposite his left shoulder, and the left opposite the right. He is correct that the sandolo is very quick. They slip down the canal as though drawn by magic. The thin morning sun begins to warm Winifred a little through the cloak. She eats the second buzzola from the coat-pocket, with savor, and finds that even after this she is still hungry.

At Fusina, at the mouth of the canal, a thin haze still hangs over the marshes although the sun is beginning to burn it away. A little above the village the canal widens out to the size of a small river. Bepi stays close under the right bank. A few hundred yards from the village he stops rowing and allows the oars to trail. He seems to be looking intently at something ahead and a little to the left, on the other bank of the canal. Winifred, who is sitting facing the stern, turns to see what it is. Beyond the village, on the stone mole by the Customs-House, she makes out a pair of figures. Although they are only gray silhouettes in the mist she can see the thin upright lines of the muskets slung over their shoulders.

Bepi: "Tegna basso."

He motions for her to lie down in the boat. She stretches out in the half-inch of water on the planks, with her head cushioned on the thwart. Bepi begins to row again, slowly, keeping close to the mud and reeds along the bank. His eyes are still fixed on the other bank of the canal. After a while Winifred's curiosity overcomes her and she raises her head, enough to see over the low gunwale. The figures are clearer now and have assumed color. They are a pair of gendarmes in red coats, black boots, and black hats. Farther down the canal a gondola is approaching the Customs-House from the open lagoon. The small black cabin is closed and there is no one visible but the two gondoliers. The sentries have turned to watch the approaching gondola and are paying no attention to the small sandolo on the other bank. The gondola comes to a stop against the mole, and a hand emerges with a white envelope which is passed up to the sentries.

Bepi: "Basso, Siorina."

Winifred lies back down in the bottom of the sandolo. Bepi goes on rowing for some time, his hands crossing in the slow ballet-like motion at the end of each stroke. She hears reeds sliding along the bottom, and once the sandolo slows and falters as it touches on the mud. Then they are in open water again and Bepi increases his pace, bending forward against the two oars with a push of his whole body at the end of each stroke. There is a plash of water slipping rapidly by the planks under her ear.

Winifred raises her head tentatively, looks back past Bepi's legs, and sits up again on the thwart. The Customs-House is only an outline in the haze behind, and the two figures on the mole are barely visible. The gondola has disappeared.

Bepi: "Franzesi, Siorina."

He says nothing more during the two hours that follow as they cross the placid, yellow, somewhat rotten-smelling lagoon. Gradually the sun burns away the mist and objects are visible in the distance: a low green island with a white monastery on it, then a church tower that seems to stand by itself in the water, then the houses and cupolas of the city itself. Only when they have passed the Giudecca, and the steeple of San Giorgio and the tall Campanile come into view, and the gilded domes of the Basilica, does he speak.

Bepi: "Ecco, Siorina. Venecia."

It is wholly fantastic and insubstantial, a city that might have crystallized like salt out of a solution, and might dissolve again almost as easily. It is not clear how the colors—everything is colored—can be all pastels, and yet so vivid. The buildings seem all to be of marble, although marble in Venice looks no more solid than clouds in London. Since Bepi has the air of presenting it to her, as though it were his personal possession, she responds with a polite murmur in English, forgetting even her Italian in the tremor of the moment.

Winifred: "How beautiful."

Bepi: "Xe bela, sì."

They are going down the broad channel with the Giudecca on one side and the houses of Dorsoduro on the other. He inquires for the first time where she wants to be taken.

Winifred: "To the Molo. No, to . . ."

She tries to remember the address of the English Residence. Oh, that M. Carnot! He was enough to drive anything out of your mind with his arrogance.

Winifred: "To Campo Santi Apostoli. Do you know where that is?"

Bepi: "Siorina, sì."

The sandolo penetrates into the city, down a narrow slit of water that Winifred hasn't even noticed between two houses. For a half an hour or more it winds its way through a series of small, rather evil-smelling canals with decrepit houses on both sides and drying laundry hanging from one side of a canal to the other. She notices with interest what seems to be a dead dog floating in the canal. Bepi brings her finally to a stone landing with a small square and a church facing it. At the end she tries once more to give him one of the gold coins, but he will not take it.

CLOCKS ARE A NUISANCE FOR

Clocks are a nuisance for a story-teller. Their hands go about always in the same direction, and if you interfere with them you are in danger of damaging the mechanism. Furthermore they describe any given circle on the face only once. This is not in accord with ordinary human experience, as everyone knows. It is possible to have the same experience many times, in one's mind, in anticipation and then in recollection; in fact it is possible even if the experience never really happens. Just as God exists out of time and is not obliged to take account of it, neither is the novelist. He can cut the story up with scissors and rearrange the parts, as he pleases. Of course this is playing fast and loose with human beings. But it is no more than what God did with Jonah—first sending him out to sea in a leaky boat, then not very plausibly having him eaten by a great fish, and then shriveling the tree over his head.

Of course that was only a God in a story. But let us face frankly what everyone senses but no one recognizes openly, that the story-teller is always a character in his own story, whether he conceals himself cleverly like Defoe, or comes out swaggering all over the page like Rabelais. If nothing else can be seen, at least his hand is visible, tracing out the weary thread of the narrative, and losing his patience now and then at the pen. This particular story-teller, we can see, is a harmless fellow, fond of Venice, mildly interested in history but more in people, knowing a great deal more about ships and sailing than he can ever get into any story, a bit of an erotomaniac although he successfully manages to conceal this in real life, that is, the life in which he is not telling stories and has to take account of policemen. Likes a good yarn and likes to tell one, but is baffled by the intricacies of fiction technique as these are delineated by the specialists in ivied halls, the detectives of metafiction and detectors of Derridian structures. Not very tidy, to judge by the coffee-spots on the manuscript. There he is, lost under all those badly arranged heaps of paper: Tentori's *Raccolta*, the *Memoirs* of Marmont, a proclamation or two of the Army of Italy, De Brosses's *Letters from Italy* and Mrs. Thrale's *Glimpses of Italian Society in the 18th Century*, the photographs of the model of the *Pandora* from the Museo Storico Navale. And, as if all this weren't enough, there are the characters to deal with. These puppets, molded from a little clay found in a corner of the workshop, are set into motion and begin to totter and jiggle about the stage. But all robot stories, all Coppelias and Frankensteins, have the same ending. The puppets somehow acquire a soul, they begin inventing their own gestures, departing from their roles, and soon they are out of control.

As an instance of this annoying behavior, let us regard Malcolm. He is a simple enough bloke, all of one piece, and you would think his actions would be fairly predictable. But, on the morning after his trip up the Brenta—the same morning of the twenty-first in which the French complete their occupation of the Terra-ferma—Malcolm oversleeps. This is unusual for him and entirely out of keeping with his character. It was after three in the morning when the gondola brought him back to his house in San Trovaso, but ordinarily he is up at daylight no matter what the circumstances. Yet there he is, lazing in bed, while the sun shines brightly and the old woman fusses around down below in her kitchen.

At a certain point, his body taking form out of a mass of somnolent sensations that are perhaps only the bed-clothes, he finds himself opening his eyes and looking straight upward. The light reflected from the rio plays on the ceiling of the room, and there is the sound of water lapping. He can hear Siora Bettina setting down a spoon on the marble table, chopping something with a knife, knocking about with a broom. Everything is exactly as it should be. It is an ordinary day, except that for some reason he doesn't get up. Instead he lies in bed with his eyes open, looking at the ceiling and thinking, or not thinking exactly but musing. About what? Nothing in particular. This is definitely not his ordinary behavior. Perhaps he is catching something, a fever or an ague. But this is not an ordinary sickness. He feels that, when this fever finally comes upon him, his mind will travel in strange lands and his eyes feast on luxuries. A strange longing for this sickness comes over him. He wants to be sicker. He feels a premonition of—what? As though a kind of imp has penetrated into his chest and lies there pulsing softly, harmlessly. As though a strange new liquor has filtered into his blood—honey—no, wine—no, perhaps ichor.

What Horsefeathers! Here he is, a forty-year-old sea-captain with grime between his toes, lying in bed comparing himself with a god, an Apollo. He has probably only caught something from diving into the lagoon after that goose of an English girl. It would be a miracle if he didn't, since the lagoon serves as a sewer for ninety thousand Venetians, as well as a repository for fish-entrails, offal, sweepings from the campi, and anything else anyone feels like throwing into it. He gets out of bed, still feeling strange, and dresses in breeches, shirt, and waistcoat. He washes his face in a basin and combs his hair with the fingers of his right hand, and ties the hair at the back with a piece of string. He puts on his coat and stands there for a moment, dreaming again. Then he remembers the packet. He feels for the shape in the right-hand pocket—it is still there. Taking his hat in one hand and dangling his saber by its sling in the other, he goes down to breakfast.

This consists of a cup of black coffee and a rusk, which Siora Bettina brings him in the tiny salon which also serves as dining-room. With the breakfast is a letter. A man came with it about an hour ago. He was still sleeping, the Poverino, so she didn't want to wake him. He came in so late. She lingers about, emitting a large odor of dishwater and onions, her oversized breasts floating over the table, while she explains all this in the dulcet murmur in which one speaks to children.

Malcolm looks at a large official envelope, with a wafer of wax on it stamped with the seal of the Signoria. Across the front is his name in an elaborate rococo hand: *Ill.mo Signor Capitano Langrish de la Marina Militare.* He gazes at this stonily for a moment, then slits the envelope open with the table-knife. Inside is a quarter of fine parchment folded in four.

The balloon-like breasts are still becalmed by his elbow. She is pretending to pour his coffee, but she is really waiting for him to open the letter.

He turns and fixes her with a look. She sighs, and goes off to the kitchen. If there is anything she has to reproach the captain with, it is that he is secretive about his private affairs. If she takes in a boarder it is really only for company, and surely he might confide in her a little more. He is a foreigner and a naval officer—he has traveled in many places in the world—and undoubtedly he has many interesting things to tell. But it is his nature—he is an Anglosassone—and northerners take no pleasure in talk. They don't confide. They are cold. There is no intimacy in them.

Malcolm knows all these thoughts of Siora Bettina, but he has other things to concern himself about than the unhappiness of old Venetian women, and he prefers to read his letters alone, especially those that arrive by special messenger with the seal of the Signoria. He unfolds the parchment. It is covered with the same elaborate hand as the address on the envelope, all scrolls and curlicues.

1797. 21 Aprile in Pregadi. (That is, in the Senate.) After a number of preliminary fanfares and flourishes the letter embarks into its argument, the gist of which is that the Signoria and the Council of Ten wish to congratulate the Most Illustrious Signor Captain Langrish and the crew of the S.M. Galeotta *Pandora,* as well as the Most Illustrious Signor Commander Pizzamano of the Castel Sant'Andrea, for their heroic defense of the lagoon on the Twentieth Instant against the attempted unlawful and piratical incursion of the French frigate *Liberatore d'Italia,* which by the Grace of Heaven and the courage of the Navy and the Militia of the Serenissima has been captured and its crew and officers remanded into custody; by reason of which the Signoria is pleased to confer on the Most Illustrious Signor Commander Pizzamano the Order of San Nicolò of the second degree, and on the Most Illustrious Signor Captain Langrish the Order of San Nicolò of the third degree; and to grant from the funds of the appropriate Naval and Militia accounts an extra month's pay to all the Fanteria (that is enlisted men) concerned.

Malcolm folds the parchment and puts it back in the envelope. At least they have spelled his name right—no mean feat for a secretary of the Senate who knows no English. As for the Order of San Nicolò of the third degree, he would just as soon have an extra month's pay along with the crew. It is difficult to see what the heroism of Pizzamano has consisted of; he was safe inside his fort and did nothing but fire his batteries at the wrong time, completely missing the French vessel (which he notices the Senate has promoted to a frigate) and almost hitting the *Pandora* herself. The commendation says nothing of the fact that there were several French casualties. As for poor Fioravanti, he gets neither a month's pay nor a medal, only a grave in the naval cemetery on the Lido. In fact, as he thinks about it, the commendation gives the curious effect of skirting carefully around carnage and bloodshed and preferring to discuss heroism in purely abstract form, as though it were something like a chess-game. It also occurs to him, as he slips the letter into his pocket, that the engagement at the Lido took place only late yesterday afternoon, yet the letter was delivered to him, Siora Bettina said, before noon. This means that the Senate has already held a session on the matter, a most unusual procedure, since patricians as a rule do not like to get up early in the morning. He reflects on this for a while without reaching any conclusions.

He stands up, buckles on his saber, and finds his hat. Summoned by the almost inaudible click of the saber, the damp apron appears in the doorway.

Siora Bettina: "Ah, you're going out."

Malcolm: "You guessed it."

Siora Bettina: "Poverino, you haven't touched your rusk."

Once he is outside in the sunshine he feels better and forgets his queer symptoms upon waking up. It is a fine spring day; the air is crisp and a few clouds float lazily over the roof-tops to the west. There are Militia stationed all over the city with the yellow-and-blue cockades of the Republic in their hats. On the Molo a twelve-pounder has been installed pointing out into the lagoon. The militiamen are armed with obsolete muskets, their uniforms are not very clean, and they seem bored. Probably their presence in the city is meant more to reassure the population than anything else. The cannon on the Molo could hardly hit anything except the

Isola San Giorgio, a few hundred yards across the water. Everything else in the city is exactly as usual. The market-stalls in the Piazzetta are thronged—black gondolas creep along the Canal—there are ships at anchor with limply hanging sails.

Malcolm crosses the Piazzetta and goes on around the corner of the Ducal Palace, where he disappears for the moment. And now let us linger a little behind him and have a look at this famous Piazzetta. From this vantage—just by the three great masts where the standard of St. Mark is flown on holidays—the library of Sansovino is on the right, and on the left the Basilica and the Ducal Palace. The four bronze horses on the balcony of the Basilica were stolen from Constantinople at the time of the Fourth Crusade. (Constantinople was a Christian city, and the Pope came near to excommunicating the whole lot of them in this business, but it is still called a Crusade.) The porfiry kings at the entrance to the Palace were also stolen, from Acre in the Levant, and likewise the carved stone pillars before the doors of the Baptistery. A list of things the Venetians stole would be very long. The two antique columns at the end of the Piazzetta were also stolen from Constantinople, where they were said to decorate the Hippodrome. On one of them is an effigy of San Todaro standing on a crocodile. The other has on top of it something that looks like a stone dog with an ape's head, sprouting wings, which is popularly taken for a representation of the winged lion of St. Mark. It is here at these columns that executed criminals are displayed, and sometimes in the morning a wretch of a corpse will be bound hanging upside down from a line strung between them. Thus the expression, fra Marco e Todaro, to be between the Devil and the deep blue sea. Not far from the columns, down the Molo toward the Ponte de la Paglia, is an apparatus for another sort of misfortune: a kind of trestle or open table on which the bodies of the drowned are laid out until they can be identified by relatives or others. In short, the Piazzetta is a place of public entertainment and spectacle, the center of the civic life of Venice.

The two sides of the Piazzetta are devoted to different purposes. The side over by the library of Sansovino, where the market-stalls are set up, is frequented by plebeians and commoners. The other side, under the portico of the Ducal Palace, is reserved for patricians, who walk up and down it in the afternoons discussing Politicks and conducting their various intrigues. It is called the Broglio; thus an imbroglio, a complicated involvement or conspiracy, one of the ten words bequeathed by Venetian to the other European tongues. (The others are gondola, regatta, ghetto, sequin, lazaret, arsenal, lagoon, casino, and gazette.) The fish and poultry markets in the Piazzetta are never cleaned. Mrs. Thrale, an English visitor of the time, reports that "St. Mark's Place is all covered over in the morning with chicken-coops, which stink one to death, as nobody, I believe, thinks of changing their baskets; and all about the Ducal Palace is made so very offensive by the resort of human creatures for every purpose most unworthy of so charming a place, that all enjoyment of its beauties is rendered difficult to a person of any delicacy, and poisoned so provokingly, that I do never cease to wonder that so little police and proper regulation are established in a city so particularly lovely to render her sweet and wholesome." And she is comparing it to a London which is none too sweet-smelling itself. Flies swarm, and gnats hang in the air like tiny wavering spots.

But, instead of lingering in the Piazzetta along with Mrs. Thrale and her sensitive nose, let us follow Malcolm on down the Riva degli Schiavoni, the chief and fashionable waterfront promenade of the city; named, not for the Corybantic nudists, but for the merchants from Istria and Dalmatia who traditionally moor their vessels there. The way goes along the side of the Ducal Palace for a while, then we stop and look to the left down a rio. High in the air, connecting the Palace with the next building, is a kind of enclosed corridor of marble, the celebrated Bridge of Sighs. Over it (or through it; it is sealed like a casket) the unfortunate accused of Politickal crimes have for centuries been conducted from the Palace to the Ducal Prisons. In the Prigioni, an elegant building designed by the same Antonio da Ponte who also made the Rialto bridge, there are accommodations for every sort of criminal. Some chambers, the so-called Quattro, are light and comfortable. If the incarcerated has money, he may have meals brought in or even entertain his friends. At the top and bottom, however, the building touches the two absolute extremes of discomfort. In a kind of attic at the top are the Piombi, so-called from the lead roof which efficiently conducts the heat of the sun to the inside. It was from the Piombi that Casanova escaped, in the incident described in his *Memoirs.* Anyone who complains of the temperature in these apartments may prefer the Pozzi, or Wells. These, as their name implies, are windowless dungeons at the bottom of the building, half full of water. Certainly there is never any discomfort here from the sun. The torture chambers, by the way, are not here in the Prisons; they are in the Palace, thus saving the Inquisitors, who are usually old gentlemen who may be in frail health, the trouble of walking back and forth incessantly over the Bridge of Sighs. However the garrot is. The jailer was kind enough to exhibit this machine to Casanova when he was a guest in the place. "You see, sir," he explained, "when their Excellencies order someone to be strangled, he is seated at the stool, his back against the wall, and that collar around his neck; a silken cord goes through the holes at the two ends and passes over a wheel; the executioner turns a crank, and the condemned man yields up his soul to God." It was perhaps not on account of this that Casanova escaped, since he was not under a capital sentence, but still it can hardly be cheerful to live in a place with such devices around. Of course the garrot is used only for criminals of the baser sort; when the Doge Marin Falier was found guilty of treason he had his head chopped off on the steps of the Ducal Palace.

But we are losing sight of Malcolm; there he goes, just over the Ponte de la Paglia and on down the Riva teeming with its morning traffic.

After crossing several more bridges he turns left along a canal just beyond the Ca' de Dio or municipal workhouse. After a short distance there is a drawbridge for pedestrians across this canal, an odd-looking rickety affair which splits in the middle and can be drawn up to either side by cables. A little farther down the canal are the two square medieval towers of the Arsenal. The canal continues between them, but the way is closed by a pair of massive wooden gates, broad enough that the largest man-of-war or galley can pass out through them. To the left of the canal-towers is a smaller portal for those entering on foot. It is an elaborate affair decorated with statues, sculptured lions, and worn Corinthian columns. Over the portal is a winged lion of St. Mark with the inscription *Victoriae navalis monimentum MDLXXI.* The naval battle referred to is the victory over the Turks at Lepanto in 1571; the mistake in Latin can be attributed to Venetian indolence, or to the imperfect scholarship of the sixteenth century.

A few yards from this portal is another statue of a lion, a

queer-looking animal, long and gangling, but imposing. This beast was brought as a trophy from Athens by the Doge Francesco Morosini, who is famous in the history of art for having blown up the Parthenon; but it was the Turks' fault, for storing powder in it. This lion is a story all by himself. At one time he guarded the entrance to the Piraeus, which for that reason was called the Port of the Lion; but when the Venetians got him to the Arsenal they discovered that his chest and flanks were covered by some peculiar inscriptions, not Greek, and not even Arabic or Chaldean. No one knew what they were, until there arrived an erudite Dane, who pronounced them to be Norse runes. "Haakon, combined with Ulf, with Asmud and with Orn, conquered this port," he translated. In addition to this Norwegian lion there are a number of other statues; but none quite so curious. Malcolm passes in through the portal. The two militiamen on sentry duty come to attention, rather ineptly, and present arms.

The *Pandora* is not in her usual berth in the Bacino Vechio. It takes Malcolm some time to find his own vessel. The Arsenal is immense; it is the largest shipyard in Europe. The walls around it are forty feet high and two miles in circumference. A large man-of-war, the *Vittoria,* is moored in the Bacino Novo. There are several more deep-water ships, but they are not in a state to go to sea; their yards have been sent down and their armament is in the gun-shop. There is a stagnant and lackadaisical air about the place. Not much work is going on. The Arsenal was in its prime back in the days of Lepanto, when a new and fully armed galley came out through the great gates every day for a hundred days. Now it has begun to run down, like a watch. It needs a good twist on its winder. Malcolm finally finds the *Pandora* in the far end of the Arsenal, tied to a dirty stretch of quay around behind the rope-walk where bottles and scraps of wood are floating in the stagnant water.

The Schiavoni catch sight of him when he is still on the quay, and raise mock cheers. Evidently they have heard about the extra month's pay. A flask of wine goes hand-to-hand and disappears under the bulwarks as Malcolm comes aboard.

Malcolm: "What's happening here, you Jailbirds? Why is no work going on?"

Mark Anthony: "Carpenter shop, Copn, dey coming to fix de

bump on dis ship. Dey come when dey get round to it. Hoppen tomorrow, hoppen by Saint John Day."

Malcolm goes off on the quay to look. On the larboard side the cap-rail is splintered where it struck against the French brig, and there are some gouges in the planking. This makes the muscle quiver at the side of his jaw. He goes back on board again, in a rotten temper, and his eye is caught by an irregular dark stain by the mainmast.

Malcolm: "Turn to and man buckets and swabs. Wash off all that muck."

His experience has taught him that if there is nothing better for a crew to do it always benefits from washing down decks. A general camaraderie results from the taking off of shoes and rolling up of trousers, and a clean ship is good for morale. When the water starts flying from the buckets he goes ashore and sets off down the quay. A ragged chorus of shouts follows him.

Schiavoni: "Viva el Capitàn! Viva the Order of San Nicolò of the third degree!"

Mark Anthony: "You fellows better cut out de capers, and wash off corpse-spot of dat Greek. Dat trouble de copn in his mind. He very sensitive bout such matters. He delicate as a young girl."

It is even more difficult to find the brig. They have hidden her away in a remote corner of the Arsenal where there is not even a proper quay to tie her to, only a rickety wooden dock. He finally catches sight of her spars over the top of a shed, with the broken yard dangling from the foremast. The Schiavoni haven't sent the yard down as they were told. Glancing about him and finding nobody in sight, he goes on board.

There is a good deal of carnage along the main-deck from the *Pandora*'s nine-pounders, but he isn't interested in this. He climbs up to the quarter-deck and, with another furtive look around behind him, goes down the companionway-hatch to the after cabins. In the passageway at the bottom of the ladder it is warm and rather close. There is a diffuse milkiness from the half-open skylight over his head. He looks around.

There are two small cabins, one on either side of the passageway. Farther aft, at the end of the passageway, is a great-cabin extending the width of the brig. He goes into the great-cabin and inspects it briefly. Everything seems intact; clothing hangs on hooks and the berth is made up. There is a sea-chest he doesn't bother to examine. On the table are a chart of the northern Adriatic and another of the Venice lagoon, a fine Swiss watch in a case, and navigation instruments.

Malcolm touches nothing. He leaves the great-cabin and goes down the passageway to the smaller cabins. In each one there are accommodations for two officers. In the cabin on the starboard side, however, only one berth has been made up. He steps over the raised sill and enters. He is aware of a faint odor or essence, elusive and not readily identifiable, but enough to hint in some way of the female sex.

The cabin is almost bare. All the possessions of its occupant have been packed ready to go ashore. On the floor by the berth is a worn green portmanteau, one of the old-fashioned kind that folds in the middle so it can be used as a pair of saddlebags, and next to it a hat-box. He looks around to see if there is anything else in the cabin. Propped in the bookcase is a wine-bottle with a crude flower made of colored paper and wire stuck into it, probably the gift of some sailor or steward. He holds the flower and looks at it for a moment, then he opens the porthole and drops the flower and bottle overboard into the fetid water of the dock.

He feels unmistakably odd, and yet he doesn't leave this place that makes him feel this way. Being in the cabin causes him a little twinge that is something like pain and yet gives him an odd kind of pleasure that makes him want to go on feeling it and thinking about it, the way a person might touch a loose tooth now and then to see if it still hurts.

Mark Anthony is right; he is as sensitive as a young girl. It is all very well for him to yell at the Schiavoni and call them Buggers and Turkeys, but when he is by himself the most extravagant fancies find their way into his head. For instance: he has only to close his eyes, and he sees a sugar-plantation in Jamaica. A dark green island, almost black, surrounded by some white sand, and then a pale green sea with surf beating. Some ragged palms that look like feather-dusters, and sough in the trade-winds. He beholds himself with a double-edged axe, felling trees for a house; then the house rising, with palm-leaves for a roof; then another figure somehow besides his own, tall and cool in a linen dress, causing perhaps a thread of smoke to emerge out of the chimney which he has built out of chunks of coral; then some sharp treble cries, and a number of small tow-headed animals bolting out of the doorway into the tropic sunshine. These progeny, growing to size, eventually take axes of their own and build more houses. And so on. There is no end to this sort of private Magic Lantern show, once you surrender your mind to it.

It is probably only this ague or fever he is catching. He claps his hand to his forehead: it is cool. Still it is all nonsense, this standing around with your eyes shut beholding non-existent scenes in Cloud-Cuckoo Land. An even stronger term occurs to him, a vocable used by Massachusetts farmers for the excrement of farm animals. Taking the hat-box and the green portmanteau with him, he leaves the cabin and goes ashore.

The sun arches down over the Giudecca, sending the shadows of Santa Maria de la Salute and the Customs-House out over the Canal. The Marangona booms out the end of the day, and the workers trickle homeward out of the Arsenal in twos and threes. Under the portico of Florian's patricians sip tiny cups of chocolate. In the house in San Trovaso, Malcolm lies on the bed with his boots on, reading. There is a shimmer of light on the ceiling. From the kitchen below come the usual sounds of the old woman fixing dinner: a stove being lit, the slow plop and bubble of polenta. Yet he is hardly aware of all this. The trivial and mundane buzz of the senses—all that Aristotle calls the accidental—falls away like a film, and he is lost in the world of the invisible, the world of ψῡχή. The book he supports on his chest.

> "I am Odysseus, son of Laertes, who for my wiles
> Am of note among all men, and my fame reaches heaven.
> I dwell in sunny Ithaca. A mountain is on it,
> Neritos, with trembling leaves, conspicuous.
> Many islands lie about it quite close to one another,
> Dulichion and Samê and wooded Zakynthos;
> She herself sits low-lying, farthest out to sea
> Toward dusk, and they are apart toward dawn and the sun."

The whole incident of the Phaeacians is calming. Odysseus tells the King and Queen about his various wanderings over land and sea, and he also helps Nausicaa collect her laundry. There is a good deal of eating and drinking. Alcinoos and Arete, the King and Queen, don't spare on the victuals: smoking ox-thighs, honeyed wine, pears, pomegranates, and figs. White-armed Nausicaa is a charming companion, although she and Odysseus hardly get farther than that. In spite of her complexion she is not really pretty; this is evident. But she is a Princess, and it is not necessary for a Princess to be pretty. Malcolm imagines her as somewhat tall, with a long face and large and calm, rather bovine eyes. (Hera is called ox-eyed even though Nausicaa isn't, so perhaps Nausicaa would be ox-eyed too.) Alcinoos and Arete are very respectful, even though they are Monarchs and he is only a castaway sailor. As for Nausicaa, she takes quite a fancy to him, although anything serious between them is out of the question, owing to her birth and the necessity of his getting on with other things. She even tells her companions, "Beforehand he appeared to me unseemly" (this is when he is just washed ashore, all over mud and sand and hiding his shame with a bush), "but now he seems like one of the gods who possess broad heaven. Would that a man of this sort might be my husband." And this even though he is old enough to be her father. In fact he has a son her age who is out looking for him somewhere in another part of the ocean. But it is not for nothing that he is called Odysseus of Many Wiles. He is not ready for Telemachus to find him just yet.

Another bell—the vespers toll from the church of San Zuane across the city. The slow brazen thud and the lengthening shadows put him in a reflective mood, metaphysical although not religious. The thoughts that come to him are not of spiritual duty but of night, inevitable Night. He is too much a child of his century—and a pupil of old Father Dottle—to trust in Pascal's gamble, and in any case he is unable to derive much solace from the notion of being borne away by wings to join a transcendental harp-choir. Better endless Night than boredom, some part of him tells the other part. Nor is he much impressed with the modern notion of prayer, a formula in which a person, after declaring his unworthiness, asks to have the laws of the universe suspended for his benefit. One must not expect too much from omnipotence. And one can't expect miracles anyhow from the tortured Man-God, with his following of wailing women, who exhorts us to be chaste and turn the other cheek. No, old Zeus is better, not too high overhead, perched on a cloud, fond of chasing a skirt now and then or a beaker of wine, like Odysseus himself, very much like

Odysseus in fact, with all his wile, the great-bearded old Scoundrel. Malcolm doesn't trust him either. Still he isn't a bad sort to have as a Commanding Officer. One could find worse in the world. So Malcolm considers, still lying on the bed and contemplating the slightly muddy toes of his boots, while the last notes of the vespers die out over the roof-tops.

The old woman calls up the stairway: Come and eat four grains of rice.

This is only a Venetian saying, although the supper that appears on the table is almost as parsimonious. This evening it is Polenta e Osei; that is to say, roasted larks with corn meal mush. It does not occur to Malcolm that there is anything Homeric about this menu. The larks are gathered out on the marshes, by people who stretch out nets and then come by every so often to collect their victims. Malcolm rather admires this. The Venetians have found a way of extracting meat, so to speak, from the empty air, at no cost to themselves and at negligible cost to the universe, which always seems to be able to provide larks in sufficient quantity for their modest needs. It is a thing that might be done in his own New England, if people had the patience to make nets so fine they couldn't be seen by a flying bird. It is true there is not much meat on a lark—not as much as on a smoking ox-thigh. On the plate before him is something that resembles a handful of used toothpicks with, clinging to them, the meat the user has picked out of his teeth. But Siora Bettina isn't rich. She is not Queen Arete.

Malcolm pushes back his plate. There really is something wrong with him, he decides. Reading Homer has not calmed him as it usually does. He begins to feel odd again as he did in the cabin of the brig—that slightly feverish pleasure-in-pain like touching a loose tooth, imagining Nausicaa with her white arms, with her large eyes, smoothing his bed, offering him honeyed wine.

SUPPER IS OVER AND MALCOLM

Supper is over and Malcolm is in his room looking out the window, with his forearms resting on the sill. The window is on the side of the house, facing Rio San Trovaso. It is quite dark. The starlight filtering through the clouds gives the impression that everything has been washed in a thin watery milk. The houses across the rio are visible through a kind of luminescent quality, as though they themselves were giving off a faint light. Just under Malcolm's foot, against the wall, is the green portmanteau swallowed up in the shadows; but he has not touched it, and he has half forgotten it. Far out over the roof-tops, beyond the Giudecca, something white jaggers for an instant: lightning over the sea.

At this time of the night the working-class quarter is almost deserted. By looking around to the right out the window Malcolm can see a small piece of Rio Ognissanti with its quay. At the place where the two rii meet there is a small shrine of the Madonna with a lamp set into the wall. Occasionally somebody going by along the quay appears in the light of this lamp. An old man with a cat goes by, and a boy in a leather apron. After that there is a long pause.

The next person to appear in the lamplight is a young man in a gilded tail-coat, pink breeches, and a fawn-colored tricorne with a gilded brim. He carries his gloves in one hand and a stick with a silver head in the other. He seems uncertain of his surroundings.

He stops and hesitates, and Malcolm gets a good look at him in the light from the lamp. He is thin, with a pale oval face and dark lashes like bird-wings. There is something almost feminine in the delicacy of the features. After a moment he turns and goes back the way he came, disappearing from the lamplight.

Then a little girl appears and crosses over the bridge to the other side of the rio. She is wearing a white frock with a dark cloak over it and she has a tin milk-can in her hand. Malcolm knows her. She lives in the house exactly opposite his window across the rio, and she comes home every evening about this time carrying the milk-can. But this time for some reason she doesn't go into the house. Instead she stops and stands in the doorway, quite motionless, looking at something around the corner in Rio Ognissanti. Her expression is watchful, concentrated, and very interested. There is an adult gravity to her manner, even though she can hardly be more than ten. She never raises her eyes to Malcolm, yet he senses that she is aware of his presence.

He makes a slight noise, by shifting a flower-pot on the sill. She only raises her glance slightly, not enough to reach his window. But he is able to read in her face, as though in a mirror held at just the right angle, what she is watching around the corner of the house. The gilt on the young man's coat and hat are conspicuous, a flag, signaling the presence of something exotic to the neighborhood and therefore, perhaps, inimical to its inhabitants.

Malcolm turns away from the window and pulls out his watch, an old-fashioned onion which he carries on a leather lanyard. A quarter to nine; time to go. He blows out the lamp. In the inky darkness he takes down the saber hanging by its sling on the wall, fits it over his shoulder, and puts his coat on over it. Then he goes out, carrying his hat in his hand.

Down below at the door of the house he pauses to put his hat on and jam it down over his eyes. As he expects, the young man in the gilded coat is dimly visible in the doorway on the other side of the rio. Malcolm stares at him for a moment, but he is elaborately engaged in looking the other way. Malcolm sets off to the right down the quay.

After a short distance he comes to Campo San Trovaso. Describing a wide arc, he crosses the campo diagonally, goes on down the lane behind the boatyard and past the church, and comes out

again on the rio. Occasionally he catches a glimpse of the brown
coat with its gleams of gold behind him. He loses it, however, in
the dark streets between the rio and the Carità. He comes out into
the campo and crosses it to the tragheto landing.

Under the pergola it is dark and he turns to look behind him
into the campo. A few drops of rain patter on the leaves. The wall
of the Scuola de la Carità, across the campo, is a vertical sheet of
darkness. In the shadow at the bottom of it is something like a tiny
glowing ember. Malcolm can hear his watch ticking. The tragheto
has just left to cross the Canal and it will be five minutes before it
comes back. The rain rustles softly on the leaves overhead.

The spark of gold remains motionless. Malcolm fingers the
saber under his coat. After a while he hears a noise behind him;
the tragheto has returned and comes to a stop with a bump. Three
passengers step from the narrow black craft onto the pier. Malcolm stands aside for them to pass, then he gets in. At the last
moment there is a shout and another passenger, a short blocky
man in a frock-coat, comes hurrying across the campo. The ferryman waits for him. He drops into the boat, breathing heavily, and
the ferryman pushes away with his oar.

Across the campo the figure in the gilded coat is still standing
under the shadow of the wall. But Malcolm is more interested now
in this man who came rushing down the pier to drop into the
tragheto at the last moment. He can't see much of him in the
darkness. He is simply a squarish silhouette, with now and then a
gleam of an eye under the hat. The two of them stand at opposite
ends of the boat. Malcolm still has his hand on the saber-grip. He
senses that the fellow is watching him, while pretending to be
wrapped up in his shadow and half asleep.

Across the water in San Vidal the tragheto lands in the open
space by the stonecutter's workshop. Malcolm steps out before
the gondola has quite reached the plank. He sets off quickly across
the untidy field littered with blocks of marble, which gleam like
crazy gravestones in the darkness. The blocky man is a little slower
getting out. Malcolm can hear the footsteps a hundred yards or so
behind him. In absolute blackness he goes down a street which
turns to the right and then to the left again, and comes out in the
large open rectangle of Campo Santo Stefano. The sound of
footsteps behind him has ended. It is not clear where the man has

gone. From the marble workshop, which is enclosed on all sides, there is no place to come except out into the campo.

The rain falls steadily now, with a sound like a great whisper over the roof-tops. A woman scurries by holding a piece of canvas over her head. Rather warily, glancing around now and then behind him, Malcolm sets off through a series of narrow streets in the direction of San Fantìn. There is nobody in sight. The streets are deserted and the shutters of the houses are closed. He goes on down a dank alley with the wall close on one side, then he stops suddenly and waits in a doorway, watching a patch of wet street behind him illuminated by a votive lamp. A minute goes by, perhaps a little more. The lighted circle of pavement remains empty. A puddle in it is dimpled intermittently with rain. Malcolm slips out of the doorway and continues on over a small bridge, with Campo San Fantìn visible just beyond.

At this moment a lumpy sort of shape whirs out of the darkness on his left, as though it has come out of the blank wall. It strikes his shoulder with a shock and Malcolm is almost knocked over. He manages to get out his saber, but there is a bump from the other side, catching him off balance this time, and he goes down on the pavement. He is on the point of rolling off into the rio; he can feel the edge of the stone with his boot. Something gleams like quicksilver, just out of the frame of his vision on the left. The gleaming thing hisses and he feels a sharp sting at the base of his throat. This makes him angry. He wrenches himself to his feet, kicks the indistinct shape away with a push of his boot, and follows with a violent saber-slash.

It is suddenly quiet, except for the sound of Malcolm himself panting. On the pavement in front of him is a cat the size of a small mastiff, almost cut in two and exuding a pool of black blood, its lantern-eyes gradually dimming. It stretches out its white nails toward him; they grate on the stone and gleam like teeth. Then it dies.

Malcolm looks around. It is silent; the raindrops plunk down steadily into the rio. He has the impression that the blocky man in the frock-coat has somehow turned himself into a cat at the last moment, or that at least it was he who sent the cat at him and that he is still lurking there somewhere in the shadows. He even thinks he sees something, and takes a cut at it with his saber. But there is nothing; he is slashing at darkness. In a paroxysm of irritation he goes back to the cat lying on the pavement and chops it in two. But this is foolish; he has probably only turned the edge of his saber on the stones. He washes the blade off in the rio, dries it on his breeches, and fits it back into the scabbard.

He turns and stalks away angrily into the darkness. He is late for his appointment and also there is a small wound on his neck, which pricks like a bee-sting. He can feel a stickiness there with his fingers. The quay stretches out ahead of him, almost invisible in the darkness, and on the right is the rio with raindrops catching the grayish gleam from the sky. After a while he turns into a courtyard. He finds a laundry-tub by the wall of the house, and next to it a bucket of water. The courtyard is dimly illuminated by the light from a shuttered window. The rain sifting down from above is caught in the yellow gleam.

He takes off the bloody neck-cloth and throws it away. Then he dabbles at the cut with cold water from his hands. The bleeding has almost stopped. At the far end of the courtyard he sees a line of laundry, hanging under the shelter of a balcony. He pulls off a shirt and dries his hands on it. With luck there may be a clean neck-cloth. Unfortunately all the other garments on the line are feminine, and of a generous size. But at the end is a string of diapers. The soft linen rags are two feet or more long and half as wide. He pulls one off, winds it around his neck, and buttons his coat over it. The linen is only slightly damp. It coolness feels good against his slightly feverish throat.

THIS IS CALLE DE LA

This is Calle de la Màndola, or Almond Street. The name is obscure; perhaps almonds were once sold here. Or perhaps it is a mistake for mandòla, a mandolin. For why shouldn't a street be named after a mandolin? As well as to name it after a nut. But the word mandolin itself is enigmatic. It is evidently connected to mandora, mandura, pandura, pandora; all from the Greek pandoûra, a musical instrument with three strings. If this is so, then what the indiscreet lady released from her box was perhaps music. In Almond Street is an inn, the Locanda de la Cortesia. No one knows why it is called that either. The servants are not more courteous here than elsewhere. The best explanation is that the inn takes its name from a nearby bridge, and the bridge (in medieval times) was named after a family called Cortese. Nothing else is known about this family, however, and perhaps it didn't exist.

From the street the inn is a dubious affair. The door is a kind of hole, and there are no windows. There is a sign with a barred lion, and a branch over the door to indicate that wine is sold. Malcolm, keeping a wary watch around him, comes down under the shadow of a wall and ducks into the hole. It is almost as dark inside as it is out on the street; there is a guttering lamp at a table in the rear. The place is deserted.

Finally a servant appears out of the Stygian gloom. He is wearing a leather apron and has no forehead. He glowers all the time; the fact that he glowers at Malcolm is not significant. After the two of them stand silently confronting each other for a time, a hand emerges from the apron and points up the stairs.

At the top of the stairs are a number of rooms. Everything is pitch dark. There is a bar of light under one of the doors. Malcolm tries it, finds it unlocked, and enters.

Contìn is sitting in a room furnished with nothing but a table, a hanging lamp, and a pair of chairs. He rises and offers his hand in the English manner, then sits down at the table again.

Contìn: "You received my note, evidently."

Malcolm: "Yes."

Contìn: "No one saw you come here?"

Malcolm: "No."

Contìn: "You met no one?"

Malcolm: "There was a cat in Campo San Fantìn."

Contìn: "A cat?"

He smiles. He doesn't see the joke, if there is one, but he understands what is expected of a *sense of humor,* a term which he thinks of in English. He seems not to notice Malcolm's unorthodox neck-cloth. Malcolm also has small amounts of mud and filth on his clothing from lying on the wet stone pavement, but Contìn makes no comment on this either. Probably he doesn't expect sartorial elegance from a foreigner. He is friendly, well-bred, courteous, and even democratic in his manner, showing no sign that he considers himself superior to Malcolm or to anyone else, even though he comes from a thousand-year-old family and inhabits a celebrated palazzo on the Grand Canal.

Contìn (suddenly solicitous): "But you will take something? A glass of wine, or—"

Malcolm: "Don't trouble yourself."

Contìn: "A brandy perhaps."

The beetling waiter is summoned, and Malcolm orders a grappa, Contìn an Armagnac. Contìn is silent until the waiter has gone. He studies Malcolm, who is sitting somewhat stiffly in the chair and has not even taken his hat off.

Contìn: "You'll notice that I prefer the brandy of our enemies. One of the small ironies of our times."

He takes a small sip from the glass, sets it on the table, and ignores it for the rest of the conversation. He launches into the business at hand, in a fluent and grammatical Italian, with a minimum of fine language and circumlocution. He speaks Venetian only to his friends.

Contìn: "First, my congratulations on the engagement at the Lido."

Malcolm: "I've already had them from the Senate."

Contìn: "I know. It was I who wrote them. You carried out your orders precisely and there is nothing whatsoever to be reproached in your action."

Malcolm: "Why should there be anything to reproach?"

Contìn: "I didn't say there was. In fact I said specifically that there wasn't. Still," he adds in his most plausible and diplomatic tone, "there are some complexities, or shall we say niceties, of the situation that I might explain to you."

Malcolm, still stiffly upright in the chair, stares across the table with his Basilisk expression.

Contìn: "When I gave you your orders last week to take the *Pandora* to Chioggia, I didn't explain that there was a difference of opinion in the Signoria as to whether the *Libérateur* should be intercepted."

Malcolm: "You mean there are people that wanted her to enter the lagoon?"

Contìn: "I mean there is a body of opinion in the Senate and even in the Council of Ten that, shall we say, wishes to avoid a provocation."

Malcolm: "Defending the lagoon is a provocation?"

Contìn smiles in a blasé way, and lifts his shoulders. He goes on.

"In any case, Lallement, the French Minister, has protested the seizing of the *Libérateur*. His note was delivered to the Signoria this morning. He contends that the *Libérateur* entered the lagoon peacefully, to take shelter from an Austrian squadron, and was fired upon and then attacked without provocation."

Malcolm: "That's a ball of Chicken Feathers."

Contìn: "Yes. We needn't go into all that. I only wanted to keep you informed of what has been going on. Still, Lallement's protest has had a certain effect in the Palace. As I am sure you understand, there are two parties in the government in respect to the French Question."

Malcolm: "I don't know what the French Question is."

Contìn: "The French Question, Captain, is simply whether the Revolution is a great popular movement that will bring freedom to Europe, or a stampede of mad dogs bent on exterminating us. Some people think we should make an alliance with the French. The two Republics can divide up Europe, or what's left of it. Perhaps they would let us keep at least some of our mainland territories. In any case we shouldn't do anything to annoy them, like fortifying the lagoon, or deploying the ships we've got in the Arsenal. This is the so-called Party of Unarmed Neutrality." He smiles faintly. "The neutrality of the hare toward the fox." He unsmiles. "There are quite a lot of these people. And they are"—he lowers his voice only slightly—"encouraged at the highest level."

Malcolm: "You mean the Doge?"

Contìn: "Manin is astute. A man of ability in many ways. But he is indecisive. He has bad advice. And he is a coward."

Malcolm restrains an impulse to look around. The room is empty except for Contìn and himself. However the beetling waiter is very likely behind the door.

Malcolm: "And the other party?"

Contìn: "It's called the Party of Armed Neutrality. It is led by Francesco Pesaro, a Senator and a member of the Council of Ten, and a man of great influence. He believes it's nonsense to talk about an alliance with the French. The Directoire in Paris may be in favor of it, but General Bonaparte has other ideas. He *wants* Venice—perhaps to protect his right flank against Austria, perhaps for its art treasures, perhaps merely out of vanity. And he is supported in Paris by Carnot, who is in charge of military affairs in the Directoire. So Pesaro is convinced that the attack will come, and that Venice should start arming itself as quickly as possible. This party too has a lot of adherents. Although not many are as outspoken as Pesaro."

Malcolm shifts uneasily in his seat. He transfers his weight to the other cheek, and crosses his legs. He stares warily across the table.

Malcolm: "Why are you telling me all this? A foreigner—the captain of an unimportant vessel."

Contìn: "And I, Captain? A minor councillor of the naval ministry. We're two unimportant persons, having a private chat."

Malcolm: "Let's skip the jokes."

Contìn: "You're right, of course, Captain. Even though you're a foreigner there is a particular reason why I must talk to you about these matters. First a question I hope you won't find too personal."

Malcolm: "Too personal?"

Contìn: "Who is Miss Hervey?"

Malcolm: "She's an Englishwoman. She was on board the *Libérateur*."

Contìn: "We believe now that she may have been an agent who was carrying dispatches, either to the French Legation or to French sympathizers in the city."

Malcolm: "She's English."

Contìn: "Yes. But precisely for this reason she might be more useful as an agent. If the *Libérateur* were captured, Carnot might have expected that she wouldn't be treated as an ordinary prisoner of war. In this way she might be able to carry certain documents into the city with less chance of detection."

Malcolm's arm is resting on the right-hand pocket of his coat. He shifts in the chair again and moves the arm slightly.

Contìn: "Yesterday afternoon she seems to have landed on the Molo. After that there's no trace of her. Do you have any idea . . ."

Malcolm: "She went off in a gondola."

Contìn: "And no attempt was made to stop her?"

Malcolm: "No."

Contìn: "That's very unfortunate, Captain."

Here he waits. Malcolm seems to have nothing to say. He remains impassive under his hat. Contìn goes on.

Contìn: "The French are preparing something. One evidence of this is that Lallement sent off his protest over the Lido incident at nine o'clock this morning, when the details were hardly known. The protest was prepared in advance. We also know that the French are active in stirring up opinion in favor of themselves in the city. We suspect that they will make some kind of move in the next few days—a military action from the Terraferma, an uprising from within the city, or both. We must know what these plans are. This is why the documents Miss Hervey was carrying may be of the greatest importance."

Another pause. He looks hopefully across the table. But Malcolm only uncrosses his legs and crosses them back the other way.

Contìn: "Her present whereabouts are not known. If she's in

the city she'll have to make contact with the Legation or with French sympathizers. It's known who these people are and they'll be watched. If she should attempt to communicate with you, inform me immediately. Have nothing to do with the Inquisitors or the Council of Ten. Send a message to me, or directly to the Provveditore da Mar. You're a naval officer and you need have nothing to do with matters of state."

Malcolm: "You mean even the Council of Ten doesn't know what's going on?"

Contìn: "I don't quite follow you, Captain."

Malcolm: "On Wednesday you gave me orders to take the *Pandora* to Chioggia, follow the brig down the Lido, and prevent it from entering the lagoon. Who originated those orders?"

Contìn: "The orders came from Pesaro, who is a Procurator and a member of the Council. They were concurred in by the Provveditore da Mar and those in the naval office who were responsible for carrying them out."

Malcolm: "But the Doge didn't know about them. Eh?"

Contìn: "There was no need for that. They were part of the normal defense of the lagoon. The decree of the closure of the lagoon, voted by the Senate itself, dated from the seventeenth."

Malcolm: "And the citation I received this morning. Which you wrote yourself, as you told me. The Doge didn't know about that either, did he?"

Contìn: "Dozens of such documents are issued every day."

Malcolm: "Sounds to me like I'd better lay low for a few days."

Contìn: "You put everything so bluntly, Captain. You might leave the city and take a little vacation if you like. I plan to do so myself. The countryside is charming at this time of the year."

IT IS STILL AN HOUR OR TWO

It is still an hour or two before daylight when Contìn, provided
with a laisser-passer issued by the French Legation and signed by
the Minister himself, leaves the city on a highly important and
confidential mission, the first step of which is to take him to his
uncle's summer villa at Oriago on the Brenta. Once past the
Giudecca it is very dark out on the lagoon. The pale ghost-city
behind gradually dwindles and vanishes; the crooked stakes marking the channel steal up one by one, slip past the gondola, and
disappear astern like the city. Finally the sky to the east begins to
turn milky. On the horizon ahead, to the west, a vaporish line
gradually clots and turns into a lumpy marsh spotted with trees:
the Terraferma, exactly as always and yet with an odd look to it
now that it is occupied by the French.

At Fusina the gondola is challenged by pickets on the mole by
the Customs-House. The laisser-passer is read and Contìn is allowed to pass immediately. Except for the soldiers the countryside
is deserted. The gondola encounters nothing during the passage
up the canal; only near Fusina a sandolo with a boy in it, probably
searching for crayfish, slips past along the other bank of the canal
and disappears in the haze of the lagoon.

At eleven o'clock he is at Oriago. His uncle has been up since
dawn, but nothing much has been accomplished. The four-

wheeler is standing in the dusty courtyard, but the coachman is nowhere in sight and the two grays have not been brought out of the stable. His uncle is in his chamber, fussing with a valise that he is unable to close, and quarreling with the servants. He suffers from rheumatism and hobbles painfully about the room. He can only stand up with the aid of a cane. His head is so spotted and shriveled that with the wig off it resembles a nut-meat. His eyes are set in deep sockets which might have made him look cadaverous except for the irascible and badger-like look which no corpse could ever have. A childhood accident (he fell out of a tree where he was waiting with a blunderbuss for ducks) has left him with a slightly bent nose and a permanent fear of heights. He is standing in the middle of the vast chamber with its decorated ceiling wearing nothing but his shirt, waistcoat, and drawers, these last not very clean.

Contìn: "Uncle, we've got to leave by noon at the latest. We ought to be in Udine tonight."

Paternian: "I know, boy. I have too many things to see to and nobody will do anything but me. I have to dress and they can't find my velvet breeches. The plum-colored ones. My greatcoat must be found too. It will be cold in the mountains."

In actual fact the old Senator has done nothing all morning except complain to the servants and interfere with their efforts to get him ready for the journey. The greatcoat has been left behind in the palazzo in Venice. It won't be needed anyhow, since it is not as cold as all that in April and they will be traveling mostly in the daytime. The scarlet toga and cap, which will be needed for the formal meeting in Graz, are carefully folded in paper and packed in a separate trunk. Contìn finds the plum-colored breeches, claps the old gentleman's short wig on him a little crooked, tells the servants to stay out of his way as much as possible and finish packing when he isn't looking, and goes out to see to the carriage. It is a four-wheeled clarence on the English model, with a high seat forward for the driver and footman. It has glass windows and steel springs, and inside are panels painted with nymphs in the manner of Rubens. It is almost new and in good condition, but it hasn't been used since the summer before and is dusty both outside and inside. The Senator dislikes land conveyances of all kinds, greatly preferring a gondola, and the carriage is seldom used except for visits to the villas of other families during the season of the villegiatura. On the door is the family crest of the Paternians, a pelican and the constellation of Orion, in yellow and blue enamel picked out in gilt.

Contìn has the carriage dusted. The grays are brought out and hitched. The lazy coachman Lazzaro appears from behind the shed, hatless and with his coat unbuttoned. The usual footman is down with the tertian, so the boy Zulio will go in his place. Zulio is dressed up in a travesty of a footman's costume: breeches too large for him, a shabby coat in the yellow family livery, and an old hat of his father's. By some miracle everything is ready by noon. The housekeeper comes out of the door of the villa guiding the Senator. The valise and trunk are put in, along with Contìn's small traveling-bag, and Lazzaro and Zulio mount to the seat. Lazzaro cracks the whip. The grays wheel to the left and start off at a trot, leaving a cloud of dust in the courtyard behind them. In it the housekeeper waving her handkerchief is invisible.

It is eight leagues to Mestre, where they will change the grays for post-horses. Paternian is still in a querulous mood. He dislikes traveling and this journey particularly he finds to his distaste. He is determined to find somebody else at fault for his discomfort and his general dissatisfaction with the state of things, and now that the servants are gone he tries half-heartedly from time to time to pick a quarrel with his nephew.

Paternian: "D'you have the letter from the Council of Ten?"

Contìn: "Yes."

Paternian: "You'd better give it to me. I'm the one who's supposed to deliver it, you know."

Contìn: "I'll take care of it, Uncle."

Paternian: "D'you have the laisser-passer?"

Contìn: "Yes."

Five minutes or so go by. He looks irascibly through the small glass window at the front of the carriage from under his tipped wig.

Paternian: "Eh! eh! that's not our usual footman. Who's that boy?"

Contìn: "It's Zulio, Uncle."

Paternian: "Ah, Zulio."

The monotonous landscape goes by: marshes, canals, dikes, occasional fields of Indian-corn. At Mestre, at the post-station, it is necessary to show the laisser-passer again, to a rather hostile sergeant of gendarmes with a bruise on his cheek. He says nothing and doesn't bother to salute; he simply hands the letter back. The post-horses are hitched and the grays sent back to the villa.

Twelve leagues to Portogruaro. They make good time now along the good road over the delta of the Piave, but it is sunset before the new horses are put in and they are on their way again. In the gathering darkness they cross the Tagliamento and enter the Friuli—a feudal territory of Venice, although not part of the Veneto.

Paternian: "Manin, you know, is a Friulian. Heaven curse the day when we made that foreigner a Doge."

The Manins are inscribed in the Golden Book and the family has been Venetian since the Middle Ages, but Contìn decides not to quarrel. At least the Senator has found the right thing to complain about for a change.

Contìn: "One man or another doesn't matter. It's history, Uncle."

Paternian: "Ah! ah! Pesaro. If only we had elected Pesaro."

This is what Contìn thinks too, but he says nothing. He had no part in it. In 1789, when Manin was elected, he himself was only eighteen and too young to vote in the Consiglio. The trouble with Venice is the same as the trouble with the Papacy. It is governed by octogenarians—one of whom he dearly loves. The Senator is still muttering to himself in dialect about Manin.

Contìn: "Your wig's on crooked, Uncle." This is malicious, since it was he himself who set it on. Contìn is not in a very good mood himself.

Paternian: "I ga fato Doxe un furlan! La Republica xe andada."

Then in his old man's way he seems to grasp something that Contìn has said two or three sentences back. "History? What d'you mean history?"

Contìn: "It's like ancient Rome. There's a man named Vico who's written a book, Uncle. *La nuova scienza.* History turns like a wheel. First there's the Age of Heroes, then the Golden Age, and then the Decadence. Venice rose up with the wheel, but the wheel turns, and now we must come down. That's what I mean by history."

Paternian: "You talk like a Jacobin yourself. Who's this Vico? A Milanese, I'll wager."

Contìn: "A Neapolitan. We can't hope to hold the Terraferma, Uncle. We should fall back and defend the Dominante. We're still strong on the sea."

He is aware as he says it that this contradicts the theory of Vico. No matter; the old man seems not to notice. He is off on another track. Certain words are like triggers, setting off a match-lock inside his head and making him angry again.

Paternian: "The Terraferma? What about the villa then?"

Contìn: "Let them have it."

The Senator makes no answer to this. He shifts about in his seat, and sets the skewed wig to rights—or tries to—by pushing it over onto the other side. He moves his mouth around into the shape of several words, but changes his mind and is silent for a while. He looks out through the glass at the Friulian hedges and rice-fields going by. Then he remembers what he was thinking about, and gets his mouth in order again.

Paternian: "Tell me something, Alvise. What do the young people think?"

Contìn: "Young people? Some think one thing and some think another."

Paternian: "You know what I mean. What do they think. About Venice."

Contìn: "That it's very old."

Paternian: "And when you're very old. You die. Eh? Is that it?"

Contìn: "I didn't say that, Uncle."

They stop for the night in a rather vile inn in Udine—the best that is to be had. It is a whitewashed two-story building with mud-stains around it at the bottom. It is in fact only a kind of large farmhouse conceived according to the local notions, with people above and animals below. They sleep in a rather chilly room in the upper story. There are French soldiers quartered below in the stable. Paternian is irritated at the Friulian dialect of the servants and pretends not to understand it. He is even crosser the next day, as the carriage leaves the valley of the Tagliamento and begins climbing up into the mountains. He is Venetian to the core, and he believes that the land of God's earth was meant to lie flat and not heap itself up into all these crags and precipices that look as though they might cut your throat if you fell on them. There is water, but it is a different substance from the friendly yellow water of the lagoon with its smell of mud and vegetation. This water is cold and violent—blue or black except when it shatters into icy white shards on the rocks. The river booms in the valley below. The road is bad and the going is slow. Zulio puts a monogrammed rug over the old man's knees. But this, like any other stimulus, only sets off another one of his half-chewed jeremiads.

Paternian: "The Council might have found somebody else for this business. At my age. Fit to catch a flux in the limbs. If nothing worse. All I asked was to be left in peace."

Contìn refrains from quoting Scriptures to the effect that it is no good crying for peace if there is no peace. There is a wealth of things that Contìn thinks of replying to his uncle, on this journey, and doesn't say. Instead he looks out of the window and thinks of the French infantry who fought their way up these steep mountain defiles only a few weeks before, hungry and tired, undersupplied, driving back the crack troops of the mightiest monarchy in Europe. Paternian, snug in the carriage with its glass windows, the rug over his knees, complains of discomfort. And he, Contìn, is uncomfortable too. He has to admit it. Perhaps there will be a fire in the inn tonight. This journey is a mistake; he knows that now for a certainty. The Venetians should meet their enemies at sea, as they did at Lepanto and Chioggia. Venice is fire and water, the water of the lagoon, the flame in the glass-furnaces of Murano, the fire flashing from the guns of Sant'Andrea and the *Pandora,* driving the French brig on the mud. Here in the mountains it is earth and air—the rocks jut upward into the air, and there is too much empty space. He, Contìn, begins to grasp something now about the century that is to come. The man they are going to meet is a man of the new century. It will be a century in which people are haunted by a dream of emptiness—the eternal silence of infinite space—nothingness. Some will be able to live in it and breathe this new atmosphere, but they will be a new kind of men. This is what the Revolution means. It has nothing to do with Politicks.

It is after midnight when they arrive at Tarvisio, at the summit of the pass. The inn is impossible. Not only is there no fire but there are no beds, and they are invited to sleep on a heap of straw in a horse-stall. Contìn orders the post-horses changed and they continue on, through the towns that have names now that ring strangely in the ear—Arnoldstein, Villach, Velden, Pörtschach.

They pass the night or what is left of it at Klagenfurt. They are awakened at dawn by the bugle of the French infantry battalion quartered in the Rathaus, and set out again in the carriage. Lovely sunshine—a smell of manure and prosperity. There is *too much* sun—in the clear air everything is outlined piercingly, so that it hurts the eyes. There is none of the comfortable softening of the Venetian air, the glassy refracting light of the lagoon. Austria is intact. The war hardly seems to have passed over it. The country is a series of fertile valleys, with mountains in the distance. All this land too the French have taken in only a few days, almost as fast as they could march. By noon the carriage has passed into Styria. At sunset—this is the third day—they see ahead of them the tiled roofs and onion-shaped steeples of Graz, the capital of the province and the second-largest city of Austria. The French occupied Carinthia and Styria ten days before and halted here, only three days' march from Vienna, while the Armistice of Leoben was signed. An artillery encampment straddles the road on the edge of town. Hundreds of guns with their caissons—wagons, tents, piles of provisions—cover the fields up to the edge of the forest on either side. Contìn shows the laisser-passer again. The sergeant of artillery refuses to allow them to pass. It is not permitted to anyone, civilians of whatever nationality, to enter the city unescorted. The Senator mutters of barbarians and diplomatic privilege.

Contìn: "Never mind, Uncle."

They are obliged to wait. Some soldiers stare at them—not without irony as it seems to the Senator—perhaps on account of Zulio's hat. Finally an officer, young and tanned, very friendly, appears and mounts to serve as their escort. He has a fine bay, glossy from Austrian oats.

Officer: "To which part of the city do you wish to go, gentlemen?"

Contìn: "The Schwarzer Adler."

With the officer trotting by the side of the carriage, they enter the city by the Kärtnerstrasse and Brückenkopfgasse and cross the river to the Hauptplatz. Once he has seen them safely to the inn the officer salutes and leaves. The inn is comfortable, not to say luxurious, after the hazards of the journey. But the old Senator is querulous and uneasy and complains of everything, of trivialities, of the German-speaking servants who snap "Zu Befehl!" so sharply that they seem to be barking at you, of the Black Eagle over the door that is the hereditary sign of the Habsburgs. It is the Austrians who are the traditional enemies of Venice and not the French. Paternian has served as Ambassador to the court of Louis XV, he speaks French fluently, and his combination of pro-French sympathies and anti-Revolutionary principles is well known. It is probably for this that he has been chosen for the mission to Graz. His own opinion, which he expresses to Contìn before going to bed, is that it is to punish him for his equally well-known contempt of the present Doge.

In the morning they are served excellent coffee and Viennese rolls in a window overlooking the Hauptplatz. There are no French in the city; they are quartered in the villages on the outskirts or bivouacked in the surrounding countryside. The Oberkellner who serves them breakfast is a little surly and bangs the crockery on the tray as he clears away the table. It is unlikely he knows they are Venetians; probably he takes them for French.

Paternian: "They hate us, these Sausage-Eaters."

Contìn: "Probably he just has a stomach-ache."

Paternian: "I know Austrians."

After breakfast the Senator goes up to his room and changes to his ceremonial cap and toga. Contìn sees to the horses, and inspects Lazzaro and Zulio to be sure they are clean and respectable. Then they set out for Schloss Eggenberg on the western outskirts of the city, where the General is waiting for them.

THE GENERAL IN CHIEF OF THE

The General in Chief of the Army of Italy has been installed in Schloss Eggenberg for a little less than a week. On the eighteenth he signed with the Austrians the Armistice of Leoben, certain secret articles of which were not published at the time. His relations with the Directoire in Paris are difficult, and he is always in danger of being removed and replaced with a more conservative and less impetuous commander. His successes in northern Italy and Austria have made this less likely. Still he has many things to consider: correspondence with the Directoire, disposal of his forces stretched along a precarious line from Trieste to the Alps, and preparations for a final treaty to end the Austrian campaign. The interview with the Venetian envoys is only one of several pieces of business on his calendar for the day. This is why it has been scheduled at this hour which, to anyone familiar with protocol, is totally lacking in prestige: ten o'clock in the morning. He receives them in the state chamber of the Palace, a hall exaggeratedly long and narrow in its proportions, decorated in red with a frescoed ceiling and heavy crystal chandeliers.

Contìn and Paternian find themselves at one end of this room, gazing as it were down a long square tunnel lined with red damask and crystal. At the other end is a group of officers who turn toward them as they enter. Paternian is almost lost in the bulky scarlet toga. On his head is a loose cap of red taffeta. The officers stare. Nothing like these garments has been worn since the Middle Ages, in any place except Venice. The Senator hobbles down the red carpet, supporting himself on his silver-headed stick. Contìn follows. The group at the other end of the room includes a dozen or more generals and aides-de-camp: Junot, Marmont, Duroc, Louis Bonaparte, Sulkowsky. The generals are identifiable by black neck-cloths, the staff officers by the red-and-white brassards at their shoulders.

In the heavy and ornate décor of the hall there is something almost flower-like about the arrangement. The generals are in black but surrounding them are officers of gendarmerie in red coats. In the center, a little shorter and slighter than the others but dominating them—coming to view like the pistil of the flower as the others draw aside to make way for the visitors—is the General in Chief. Bonaparte is twenty-seven. He is dressed simply, in a tight-fitting jacket and the black neck-cloth of a general, with no other insignia of rank. In spite of the slightness of the figure the head is large, with alert gray eyes and dark hair which he wears loose and hanging almost to his shoulders. His nose is Grecian, so long that it almost overhangs the mouth. The firm chin is rather prominent. Paternian identifies him instantly; he is one of those lank-haired youths with lean faces and smoldering eyes who sit all day in the Caffè de la Spaderia discussing Heaven knows what, and fall silent if their elders approach. Twenty-seven! He is no older than Alvise. There is a page at the Senator's arm, some kind of subaltern, tugging at the sleeve of the toga, wanting to know how he wishes to be announced. He mumbles the formula.

Subaltern: "The Provveditore Straordinario of the Republic of Venice."

Another voice (cool, and slightly ironic): "Good-day, Senator."

Paternian: "I am the bearer of a letter from the Council of Ten of the Republic to the General in Chief himself."

He draws himself up slightly inside the toga, which touches the floor a little unless he holds himself perfectly erect, and steps forward tentatively in an effort to present the letter, which is on parchment in an elegant portfolio of tooled leather.

Bonaparte: "Never mind the letter. I haven't got time for letters. What does it say, your precious letter?"

Paternian finds himself glaring fixedly into the eye of the General in Chief and holding his breath. How is he to conduct himself with such a person—he, a Senator and a descendant of Doges, a member of a thousand-year-old family, with a palazzo of forty rooms on the Grand Canal? He calms himself and begins speaking with dignity, in fluent French with only a slight accent.

Paternian: "The Council requests"—with diplomatic exactitude he chooses the verb *demander,* which is slightly stronger than *solliciter* but not as peremptory as *exiger*—"that the French forces bring to an end the atrocities and looting which have taken place against the Venetian population of the Terraferma. . . ."

Bonaparte: "There have been no such incidents."

Paternian: "Second, it requests the French forces to vacate the Venetian territories on the Terraferma, so that order may be restored."

Bonaparte: "The occupation is necessary to ensure the security of my army engaged at the present against Austria. The French troops will see to maintaining order."

Paternian: "Third, it presumes to recommend"—(here his diction is a little more cautious; *ose recommander*)—"that the French provide Venice with military assistance in defense against their common enemy, the Austrian Empire. An alliance at this point is to the advantage of both parties. The Council ventures to point out to the General in Chief that, while on land the achievements of the French forces are impressive, at sea the Venetians—"

The face under the lank hair whitens; the edges of the mouth go tight. He does not allow Paternian to finish this sentence.

Bonaparte: "You demand, you recommend, you request. I will tell you what I demand. I've done your work for you and driven your enemies the Austrians out of the Terraferma. I demand a subsidy from the Senate of a million francs a month for six months, for the maintenance of my armies in Venetian territory."

Paternian: "The Venetian treasury is depleted."

Bonaparte: "Then use the funds deposited by French émigrés in Venetian banks. Do you think I don't know about that? Every petty tyrant in France—every count and duke who escaped the guillotine—has fled with his gold to Venice. What about the Comte de Lille, eh?" Here he really becomes incensed. His paleness has disappeared and a flush begins to appear on his face.

There is a film of perspiration on his forehead and upper lip. "Do you know who the Comte de Lille is, you Venetians? Do they teach you in your schools who the Comte de Lille is? Eh?"

Paternian continues to hold himself erect, feeling a hotness mounting into his own face. Bonaparte goes on, speaking more rapidly and loudly.

"I'll tell you who he is, the son of a bitch. He's the brother of Louis XVI, who was given asylum in Verona, in Venetian territory, and used it as a headquarters to intrigue against the Revolution. His house in Verona is a refuge for every syphilitic reactionary in Europe. After the death of the Dauphin he even had himself crowned in a silly charade as Louis XVIII. The stupid prick!"

Contìn: "The French government demanded of the Senate over a year ago that the Pretender be expelled. On March 31 of last year he was asked to leave, and did so."

The General glances at him only briefly. It is not clear whether he knows who Contìn is. He continues with his diatribe, growing a little warm.

"On April 17 there was an uprising in Verona, instigated by Venetian agents. French troops were slaughtered in the streets. The whole God damn Terraferma is up in arms. In the countryside they're all sharpening their scythes and running around shouting 'Death to the French.' Many hundreds of the heroes of the Army of Italy have already been killed. These are my comrades, you bastards! How the hell can you shirk the responsibility for these atrocities? Do you think that because I'm off here in the middle of Germany I can't cause the French nation—the first people of the universe—to be respected? Do you think we're going to sit around and do nothing about these murders you've encouraged? You come to me with demands and your hands are dripping with blood. You're a bunch of bandits, all of you. You stole Greece and the whole fucking eastern Mediterranean, until the Turks came and took it away from you. Well, now the shoe's on the other foot. You can take your pick—peace or war."

Paternian is about to reply that it is precisely to offer an alliance between Venice and France that he has journeyed over all these mountains. While he is casting about how to form this into the proper diplomatic language the General goes on.

Bonaparte: "Get this straight, you bunch of crooks. Before I'll accept any letters from the Council of Ten, or demands, or offers of alliance or whatever, all the French and pro-French in Venetian prisons have got to be set free. And anybody else who's in jail for political opinions. This is the age of Liberty, Equality, and Fraternity, haven't you heard that? Turn those poor bastards loose! And you've got to cut your garrison down to what it was a year ago, before you began arming against France. Get rid of all those Dalmatian cut-throats. And the British Minister! You come offering me an alliance, and the British Minister is still in Venice."

Paternian: "Only a Resident."

Bonaparte: "Only a Resident! And what the hell difference does it make, as long as he's still there doing his business against me? Get rid of the fucker, or I'll come in and take him myself."

Contìn: "You've got to get across the lagoon first. Our navy will blow you out of the water."

Paternian (alarmed): "Alvise!"

Bonaparte: "Who is this pup?"

Contìn: "I'm a member of a delegation that's come to work out a treaty with you, if you haven't noticed. My name is Contìn. I'm a councillor of the Provveditore da Mar."

Bonaparte: "The what?"

Contìn: "I'm telling you that all you've beaten so far is a bunch of land-powers. Venice is a sea-power. We've got an Arsenal full of ships. You'll never get your artillery across the lagoon, so let's talk about a treaty. You take the Continent, and we'll take everything east of the Adriatic. The enemy is Austria—together we can put them out of business. Pesaro already made this point, when he talked to you a month ago in Gorizia."

The General can not believe what he is hearing. He stares at Contìn with flashing eye, and a piece of the lank hair falls down over his forehead. He tosses his head to fling the hair aside. The generals and aides-de-camp draw away a little, as though to give him more room to rant.

Bonaparte: "I never heard such God damned insolence in my life. Who are you, some pen-pusher in the navy office? It's an insult to me, do you hear, an insult, to send such crummy characters to me as a delegation. Why can't the Doge come himself, eh? The Doge! If he wants a treaty so badly."

Contìn: "You are a General in Chief. My uncle is an Ambassador Extraordinary. Your ranks are exactly equal."

Bonaparte ignores this. "And Pesaro! I know this character. He's the leader of the anti-French party in the Senate. Don't think we don't have our intelligence. Who picked him to come to Gorizia anyhow? It was a deliberate affront. While the Venetians pretend to offer me treaties, this son of a bitch plots to betray me. He's got to be removed from office and put under arrest. As long as he's walking around free your envoy is a sham—a fraud."

Standing with his feet apart, he puts his hands on his hips and makes as though to move forward toward Contìn. But then he seems to realize that, if he is going to assault anybody physically, it ought to be the head of the delegation. He turns back toward Paternian.

Bonaparte: "And then there's the affair of the Lido."

Paternian sighs. This is the part of the interview he has been dreading. There is no doubt that the Venetians behaved correctly in the matter, once you concede that they have the right to close their own lagoon. Still . . .

Bonaparte: "What d'you have to say about that, eh? Just last week a French vessel, the *Libérateur d'Italie,* tried to take shelter in the lagoon to escape from the Austrians, the poor devils. They were fired upon by the fortress, and then attacked by a galley manned by a bunch of Dalmatian convicts, and led by a renegade of an American. The French commander, Laugier, tried to surrender but he was cut to pieces along with five of his crew, and the others thrown in the dungeon. This final atrocity, Senator, I can not tolerate. I demand and insist that those responsible be brought to account."

Contìn reflects that if the French know all these details they could only have learned them from some Venetian source. The survivors of the French crew are imprisoned on the Isola San Giorgio; the crew of the *Pandora* have been ordered to say nothing. It is possible that someone high in the government—even in the Council of Ten—is in communication with the French. This doesn't surprise him. Nothing that takes place in this ornate and operatically voluptuous room of red damask surprises him; in fact he finds he is hardly paying attention. Probably it is the fatigue of the journey. He remembers this sensation of slight vertigo, of dizzying clarity, from times when he was sick as a child. Everything draws away from him and becomes tiny and distant. There is a buzz. Or rather a silence like a buzz, through which the voices penetrate only thin and strained. Along with this is a sense that the Palace is unreal, the whole countryside around a panorama erected to please children—the generals toy soldiers who, as in an only moderately frightening nightmare, are suddenly seen to have the faces of well-known personages. With an effort he clears his vision and focuses on the French uniforms before him.

Bonaparte: "I demand"—his verb is *exiger*—"that the criminals of the Lido be punished. The thing was done by the direct orders of the Inquisitors. I demand the arrest of the three Inquisitors of State. They are"—he turns to his aide-de-camp Junot, who passes him a sheet of paper—"Agostino Barbarico, seventy-two years, Anzolo Maria Gabriel, sixty-five, and Cattarin Corner, eighty-eight." It is unclear why he insists on the ages of the Inquisitors; perhaps merely to suggest the general senility of the Venetian aristocracy. "I demand the arrest of the commander of the Castel Sant'Andrea, Pizzamano. And I demand the arrest of the American captain of the *Pandora,* Langrish."

He glances again at Junot, who confirms the accuracy of all these names with a nod.

Bonaparte: "I demand the release of the *Libérateur d'Italie,* which is illegally held according to the rules of international law— the liberation of its crew—and their safe conduct to Ancona. From now on the Venetian navy is to stay in the Arsenal, including the galley that carried out this shitty attack."

Paternian: "It was hardly a galley, General. Only a small vessel, a galeotta."

This really enrages the General, as does any suggestion that the French navy is inferior to the Venetian. His face goes from white to red again, and his lip curls like a snapping flag.

Bonaparte: "What do you think I care about that? What does it matter, since it was large enough to murder my comrades? These atrocities and massacres have got to stop. I've got eighty thousand men, and I've got boats to cross your mud-pond in an hour. Tell that to the old farts back in the Senate. The Revolution has come, you bastards. No more Inquisitors, no more Doge. I will be an Attila to the State of Venice!"

IN SPITE OF THE ACRIMONY OF

In spite of the acrimony of this interview, protocol requires that the Venetian envoys be offered a refreshment, a small collation of state, before their departure. First Paternian is politely led to a small convenience off the corridor (old men's bladders are weak), then the footmen swing open the doors and they enter an enormous dining-hall large enough for a hundred. In the center of this space, dwarfed by the baroque ceiling, is a table set with only a dozen covers. Again the motif is red: the floor is parquet with strips of red carpet, the velvet of the chairs is red, and the long rear wall is hung with red damask. On the other wall are French windows looking out onto a park.

They take their places; Junot adeptly guides the Venetians to the proper chairs. In many respects the collation is an even more uncomfortable experience for Paternian and Contìn than the interview that preceded it. Partly this is on account of the table arrangements. Although the collation is occasioned solely by the presence of the two Venetians, they do not seem to be the guests of honor. Bonaparte himself occupies the head of the table. At his right is his chief aide-de-camp Junot; at his left his brother Louis, who is nineteen but looks hardly more than a child. Then come the two Venetians, Paternian on one side and Contìn on the other. There follow Marmont, Duroc, Sulkowsky, a pair of staff officers, a secretary, and—occupying the other end of the table facing Bonaparte—a major of gendarmerie in a red coat. The reason for the presence of this military policeman is not clear. Perhaps Bonaparte is afraid the Venetians will steal the spoons, or attempt to assault him physically. The gendarme officer keeps his sword on during the meal, as do the staff officers and Contìn—the latter because there has never been any convenient moment for him to remove it.

Contìn gazes with some curiosity at Junot: not only a brilliant strategist and an intimate personal friend of Bonaparte, but a notorious erotomane who accompanied Mme. Bonaparte on her journey from France to Italy and, beyond any doubt, enjoyed the favors which—if rumor is correct—she is by no means parsimonious in distributing among the generals and staff of the Army of Italy. Bonaparte, who commands the most powerful army of the world, is unable to command his own bed-chamber. Perhaps (Contìn thinks) this may account for his nervous jerky manners, and his tendency to ventilate his temper on innocent targets. Junot is bland, composed, and articulate; not jerky at all.

In rapid succession they are served a carp in white sauce, a cutlet breaded in the Viennese manner with egg and lemon, and a pastel-flavored ice. There are only two wines. Paternian hardly notices what he is eating. Every time he raises a bite to his mouth Junot asks him a question and he is obliged to set down the fork and reply. The young aide-de-camp is the soul of French politesse—a quality Paternian has always admired while at the same time sensing in it a certain artificiality, a cutting-edge hidden under the flow of elegant language with its Parisian accent. Politics are carefully avoided. Junot inquires about Paternian's years as an ambassador in Paris, asks him to explain the difference between a Senator and a Procurator, commiserates with him on the rigors of the journey to Graz. (He himself, in spite of his elegance, has done it on horseback and in the face of enemy fire, but he doesn't refer to his accomplishment.) He raises his hand to the footman whenever there is room in Paternian's glass for even a few drops of wine.

As for Bonaparte, he has the manners of the young savage he is, or seems to be to Paternian. He ignores his food for long periods of time and then, when he notices it on his plate, consumes it rapidly in a few animal-like gulps. (His behavior in bed with women, so the whispers have it, is similar.) Occasionally he says something in a low tone to his boy-like brother. In the intervals he interrupts Junot to browbeat Paternian in his manner of earlier in the morning; that is, to address to him heavy questions of a peremptory nature to which there is no possible answer. To do this he has to raise his voice over the clatter of the luncheon and the conversation of the other speakers, almost to shout.

Bonaparte: "Those Prisons of yours in Venice. The Pozzi and the Piombi. Eh? What are they exactly? Tell me about them."

Paternian: "The Prisons . . ."

Contìn (under his breath): "We keep Corsican bandits in them."

Bonaparte: "These famous Inquisitors of yours. What do they do exactly? Eh? What do you have them for?"

Paternian: "The function of . . ."

Bonaparte: "The Bridge of Sighs. A remarkable architecture, I've heard. Why is it called that? What does it connect, exactly?"

This passes for table conversation with the General in Chief. It is a kind of parody of Junot's polite inquiries about Venetian customs and the journey to Graz. Junot's aplomb never leaves him. He pauses silently during Bonaparte's interruptions, sips his wine, then goes on with his faultless causerie as though nothing has happened. Contìn, across the table, understands that all this has taken place many times before—that the table arrangements, Bonaparte's rude questions, and Junot's politesse are a concerted technique that has been applied to many delegates who have come to this imperious and self-assured young man bearing letters from the governments and left with empty hands. Bonaparte's anger has left him; he is only pale and contemptuous now. Except for the raising of his voice when he speaks to Paternian, which is necessary because of the arrangement of the table, he shows no emotion. The eyes in the large head, as they turn from one object to another at the table, are detached and almost indifferent. Contìn observes that they are rimmed with red, perhaps from lack of sleep.

Bonaparte: "And your estates. All you patricians in Venice have estates on the Terraferma, I understand. Isn't that right? Manin himself has a couple, they tell me."

Paternian: "The present Doge has a villa in Maser and another in Passeriano, both in the Friuli."

Bonaparte: "And you?"

Paternian: "I possess a villa on the Brenta, at Oriago, and several farms near Vicenza. You may call them estates if you like."

Bonaparte: "And you'd be sorry to lose them. Eh?"

This is too much for Paternian. He pushes back the chair and gets up, standing erect before the table in his heavy toga. The major of gendarmes rises too, and the two staff officers. Bonaparte himself remains slumped in his chair with one knee over the arm.

Paternian: "I enjoy my villa during the summer. It is one of the rewards of a long service to the Republic. But let me tell you, General, I am ready to surrender all I possess on the Terraferma, and to sacrifice my own personal liberty and life, if only the security and independence of the Dominante are preserved."

Bonaparte: "The Dominante. What is that?"

Paternian: "The city of Venice itself, apart from its possessions on the mainland."

The General in Chief exchanges a glance with Junot, who if he is amused shows no sign of it.

Bonaparte: "A very old term, no doubt. Senator, you are a courageous man, and your respect for French civilization is well known. I myself will personally guarantee your estates on the Terraferma, if my message is conveyed to the Senate and my other demands are met."

The Provveditore Straordinario stands with his lips pursed and his eyes slightly narrowed, his most badger-like expression, staring down at the figure in the chair.

Paternian: "General, I am present here not as an individual but as a representative of my government. I ask for nothing for myself, and could accept nothing from the French government under the present diplomatic conditions."

A kind of large smile spreads inside Contìn. On the outside he shows nothing. Not only has the Senator had the last word, but he has said exactly the right thing and snubbed the most powerful general on earth without departing a single syllable from the language of protocol. It is particularly adept that, while Bonaparte spoke of personally guaranteeing his possessions, he has replied that he could accept nothing from the French government, thus tactfully reminding the General that he too, Bonaparte, is in the end responsible to the Directoire and can offer nothing in his own name. The fifty years he has spent in diplomacy have not been lost. Even the imperturbable Junot gazes at him thoughtfully, perhaps in admiration, at the end of this speech.

The collation is over. The guests are escorted down the corridor, with another visit to the convenience for Paternian on the way, and out to the gothic portico where their carriage is waiting. The assemblage has dwindled away, in the trip down the corridor, until now there are only two: Junot and the major of gendarmes. Bonaparte himself has never left his chair in the dining-hall.

On the porch the major of gendarmes draws away tactfully. The two Venetians and Junot are left in a ceremonial arrangement, a few feet apart. Junot's uniform, that of a colonel of artillery with a staff brassard, is impeccable. His tight-fitting white breeches clearly show the bulge of his male organ, which like most men of the century he prefers to wear in the right leg. He stands blandly, with his heels together, waiting evidently for the Venetians to make some conventional remark so that he may conclude the visit by bidding them farewell.

Paternian finds he is still holding the leather portfolio. Awkwardly, white with annoyance, he comes forward like a figure in a Swiss clock, thrusts the portfolio at Junot, and backs away again. Junot takes it with the smoothness of a majordomo accepting a gratuity. Paternian does not pronounce a word.

The two Venetians get into the carriage, and the door is shut with exactly the right pressure, firmly but without slamming.

Junot: "Bonjour, Messieurs, et bon voyage."

Contìn raises his hand; Paternian makes no reply. Lazzaro's whip snaps and the carriage runs down the gravel drive through the oaks with a slight crushing sound.

Paternian's diplomatic presence has left him now. He is only an angry and exasperated old man slumped in the corner of the carriage, seeming very small in the toga that envelops him to the chin. The carriage reaches the end of the drive and turns out onto the highroad for Klagenfurt. It is a mile or two before the old man has anything to say.

Paternian: "Langrish! I never heard the name before, and now it seems that the whole Republic is in peril because of this foreigner—this—this—Inglese." He stares at the painted nymphs on the panel in front of him, working his lips around to form the next sentence. "Somebody in the Navy lost his head. They say the

French captain was cut to bits. Is that true, Alvise? Maladeto! Would to Heaven that Pandora's box of a galeotta had never been sent to the Lido!"

Since it is characteristic of the Venetian government that, out of fear of excessive power, it never allows its left hand to know what its right hand is doing, the Senator is not aware that it was his own nephew who prepared the orders to send the *Pandora* to Chioggia. But Contin is not thinking of this. Instead, as the carriage rattles down the long white road between the trees, a kind of minutely detailed panorama unrolls in his mind, a sort of reverie in which he himself remains thoroughly in control of the story. Night—the dark lagoon—the distant gleams of light from the city. The twenty thousand French board the barges at Fusina and Mestre. Weighted down with their haversacks and muskets, they flounder in the dark along the improvised planks laid out in the mud, and go aboard one by one. The barges move out into the lagoon, the heavy shapes dotting the water like a swarm of insects. The oars rise and fall; the splashes are visible in the darkness. But in the city the massive gates of the Arsenal are opening and the galleys are slipping out. Past the gloomy splendor of San Marco, past the Giudecca, they steal across the lagoon toward the Terraferma. The French do not know the channels through the shoals. It is a hopeless labyrinth. The barges go aground, others bump into them and go aground in their turn, there is confusion and the chain of command is broken. Then the galleys come slipping up out of the night, their lateens like hawk-wings against the sky. The thud of gunfire rolls over the water. The flashes, staggering out in all directions, illuminate the white plumes that spring up around the barges. It is Lepanto again: San Marco, stiff and archaic with his gilded medieval wings, hovers over the galleys. Darkness, fire, and water; the fire of Murano, the holy fire of the Saint in the mosaics of the Basilica, the ancient yellow water that washes the feet of the city. The galleys slip along the channels and skirt the edges of the shoals. Even in the dark the Venetians know the lagoon as they know the palms of their hands, as they know the bodies of their own wives. The French rally and cry out orders; there is an answering rattle of musket-fire. The light galleys tack, with a clatter of rigging, and come ghosting back through the confused fleet of landing-craft to fire again. The barges tilt and settle, slowly spilling their contents into the water. Yells, splashes, the acrid smell of gunpowder. The gun-flashes illuminate a broken litter of wood and débris. Men flounder under the weight of their heavy packs and muskets. The ones who do not drown struggle waist-deep in the muddy water to clamber out in dozens, in hundreds, soggy and discouraged, their weapons abandoned, to retreat back on Mestre again.

Then, like those peep-shows in which a strip of painted canvas goes round and round until its end is connected once more to its beginning, the whole thing is repeated again in Contìn's mind. The great doors of the Arsenal swing open, and the galleys come out and steal down on the light wind toward the Terraferma. The flashes, the crump of gunfire, the shattered wood, the cries in the darkness. The canvas turns; day breaks over a lagoon littered with broken wood and débris. The sun of noon beats on a body floating in a blue coat and white bandoleers, swollen like a balloon, half-caught in weeds by a muddy bank. The wheels clatter on stone. They are in a town, probably Köflach. A French sentry, haggard and tattered, gazes curiously through the dusty glass as they go by without stopping.

IT IS THE MORNING

It is the morning market-hour in Campo Santi Apostoli. A green-grocer is doing a lively business from a table set up in the open air by the church. Women with straw market-bags go by, and merchants in twos and threes stand around chattering in the sunshine. Winifred feels conspicuous. She is wearing low slippers, the Contessa's linen gown, and the military cloak which comes only to her knees and reveals the skirt of the gown below. Her clothes are muddy and the cloak is soaked from lying on her side in the wet boat. She still has a cold too. Her nose is stuffed and her eyes are scratchy in their sockets. This puts her in a bad humor. She decides it is unwise to stand this way in the open campo any longer than necessary. She goes up to one of the women with the market-bags, selecting a younger one about her age.

Winifred (briskly): "Per favore, dov'è il Residente Inglese?"

The woman understands almost immediately and points to a house across the way, opposite the church. The house is small, but it is cleaner than the other houses in the campo, and there are graceful ogival arches over the windows. Set into a kind of niche by the door is a small majolica plaque with the Royal arms: a lion and a unicorn rampant supporting the crown. Over the plaque is a wooden bell-pull attached to a wire. She seizes the handle firmly and pulls it.

The window opens over her head.

Voice: "Chi xe?"

Winifred: "I wish to see the English Resident."

It is not the hour, she grasps from the woman's Venetian. A ora pontada—it is necessary to have an appointment.

Winifred: "I wish to see Mr. Birdsell, and immediately. Please let me in."

This violation of the ordinary etiquette in such matters, evidently, so startles the servant that she comes downstairs immediately and opens the door.

The woman understands no English but there is no difficulty in comprehending what Winifred wants. She is also impressed, evidently, with her costume, which gives her the effect of a shipwrecked voyager or a person who has undergone some other bizarre disaster. She leads her up a flight of stairs, shows her into a small waiting-room, and vanishes.

After only a short time—ten minutes perhaps—Mr. Birdsell himself appears. Like the city itself, he too gives rather an impression of sugar-candy—a phantom of an Englishman, a gentleman from a children's book with illustrations by a somewhat odd or eccentric artist, rather than a solid human being. He is immaculately clad in a smoking-jacket, a cravat, and a dressing-gown, and his black shoes have been polished to a glassy surface. He has evidently been interrupted at breakfast, because he is carrying a napkin which he touches one last time to the corner of his mouth before he tucks it into the pocket of the dressing-gown. He is narrow-shouldered, a little less than average height, with soft gray hair which he trims close to his head, evidently because he is frequently required to wear a wig in his official capacities. His face is a pale pink, reticulated with fine lines the color of claret. There is no question now that he has been eating his breakfast—he smells of toast.

The two of them examine each other in silence, rather diffidently on both sides. She waits for him to ask her business, but he seems to be waiting for her to speak. Finally she introduces herself. It takes him some time to understand that her name is not Harvey, or Hervé; the latter of which suggests that he is perhaps not quite convinced yet that she is really English.

Birdsell: "Related to the Hervey-Boyntons in Sussex?"

Winifred: "I don't know. I've never heard of them."

Birdsell: "I wonder how Sir Charles is. I was with him at Harrow. Haven't heard from him in years."

There is another pause. His eyes, she notices, are exactly the color of robin's eggs, a very pale blue. He manages to direct these eyes away from the vision of Sir Charles Hervey-Boynton, probably as he was as a schoolboy at Harrow, and back to Winifred again. She is not angry yet but a certain *firm* feeling she has now and then is coming over her; her lower lip stiffens and presses against her teeth. She begins explaining her situation, or perhaps predicament is a more accurate description of it. She says nothing about the Villa Baraoni, the Contessa, or the two days that have passed since her arrival in the French brig. She doesn't believe in telling lies, but there is no point in bothering Mr. Birdsell with matters that don't concern him.

Birdsell: "Your fiancé is English?"

Winifred: "No, French. His name is Jean-Marie Fontenay."

At this he stiffens perceptibly. She has not imagined there was anything stiff in him, but this is because she has no experience of diplomats.

Birdsell: "Then my dear young lady, I don't understand what I have to do with the matter. The French and English governments at this time, you understand, are not very—are not quite on amiable terms."

Winifred: "I'm not concerned with the terms the French and British governments may happen to be on. I'm a British subject."

Birdsell: "I understand that. But—"

Winifred: "This matter has nothing to do with the French government. M. Fontenay is a composer and musician. He has come to Venice to study music. I was to follow him here in the spring for our marriage, but since he was unsure of where he would be lodging, it was agreed that he would leave his address with you."

Birdsell: "But why with me? Why not with the French Legation?"

Winifred: "Because if I went to the French Legation some fool of a Resident would be sure to ask me, 'But why me, my dear young lady, since you are a British subject?'"

He examines her a little more carefully, in what might be described as a kind of calm alarm, and adjusts his cravat. Decidedly she is more formidable than he expected. Although her odd costume, and her impropriety in forcing her way into the house at unsuitable hours, ought to have warned him. Young women are certainly different these days. It is the reading of novels, and the influence of French ideas. This one frankly admits to being involved with some Frenchman. A musician! Venice is full of French agents pretending to be musicians, Royalist émigrés, admirers of Palladian architecture, and Heaven knows what. A thing like this could have what are called international repercussions, even though slight ones detectable only by the fine instruments of the Foreign Office. Mr. Birdsell sighs inwardly, in a way that reveals no outward sign. Outwardly he is a British gentleman, adjusting his cravat and examining her with his pale blue eyes. She is undoubtedly an attractive creature in a wild sort of way. Another minor thought that occurs to him, tucked into an obscure spot in the left-hand corner of his mind toward the rear, is a sense of satisfaction that he has never married. He begins speaking in a cautious way, pausing when necessary to be sure he is saying exactly what he intends.

Birdsell: "My dear Miss . . . Hervey. You are quite right that as a British subject you ought to have come here. These are not our ordinary reception hours, but it makes . . . little difference." (He still smells of toast.) "It would be better to have nothing to do with the French Legation. Please forget that I ever mentioned such a thing. I don't know why I said it. As for Monsieur . . . as for your fiancé, it is a question what to do. One should be very careful in having any sort of relations with French citizens in these days. My best advice, I think, would be to reconsider carefully whether this . . . relationship is in your own best interests. I will think what it is best to do. I imagine your immediate need is for some sort of lodging. You have funds?"

Winifred: "Yes."

Birdsell: "And you hold a British passport?"

Winifred: "It's still aboard the ship that brought me here, in my baggage."

Birdsell: "I would advise you to retrieve it as soon as possible. If you will bring it here this afternoon in our proper visiting hours, between four and six—"

Winifred: "Mr. Birdsell, has M. Fontenay, my fiancé, been here to leave his address?"

Birdsell: "Not that I'm aware of."

Winifred: "And who would be aware of it if you weren't?"

Birdsell: "I don't know, I'm sure."

Winifred: "Then I have nothing more to ask of you. I'm sorry to have bothered you. Please go back and finish your toast."

She is gone before he can say anything else. She does not flounce, slam the door, or in any way dramatize her exit. She simply goes out through the door and shuts it, but the set of her mouth and the wisp of hair straying from her forehead suggest that there is a force working inside her that might be dangerous if one weren't careful. How did she know that she had interrupted his breakfast? And that he was having toast? It occurs to him for the first time that she may not have had any breakfast herself—that the gentlemanly thing would be to invite her to take something—at the very least a cup of tea. The expression *fraught with complications* occurs to him. He is not sure whether he means diplomatic or personal. Mr. Birdsell has never had any lady to a meal in his private chambers; least of all for breakfast.

IT IS A LITTLE MORE DIFFICULT

It is a little more difficult to find the French Legation. It gives her a pleasure to do so, however, since it is a direct violation of Mr. Birdsell's instructions. She is now beginning to be aware of some of her difficulties. She has been aware before that there were difficulties, but now she has become *fully* aware—the difficulties present themselves to her as large concrete menacing creatures, with jaws and watchful eyes, whereas before they were only abstractions. There are two of these creatures in the main— although there is perhaps another and smaller one represented by Captain Langrish. The first is that she has entered Venice illegally, on a French vessel, dressed in a military uniform, and she is quite probably—in fact almost certainly—liable to arrest by the Venetian authorities. She is dimly aware of Inquisitors, dungeons, and other matters not really suitable for explaining to young ladies. On the other hand there is the French foreign service with its Cabinet Noir, as it is called—its intricate system of informers, assassins, and undercover agents spreading over Europe from Vienna to Cádiz like a spiderweb—which she seems to have fallen foul of in ways that seem to her no fault of her own. It is true that she has lost the packet confided to her by M. Carnot. Or rather it was taken from her by violence—no one suggested to her that her arrival in Venice was likely to be so sanguinary for others and so full of indignity and discomfort for herself. M. Carnot gave the impression that, France and Venice being technically at peace, the *Libérateur* would simply dock at the Molo and she would step ashore as a passenger. Still—the packet was weighted and she knew clearly what she ought to have done. When she was in the water—it would have been a simple thing to slip it inconspicuously from her clothing and let it sink. But first she was preoccupied merely trying to keep herself afloat—she had expected swimming would be easier even though she had never tried it—and later she was too busy trying to push Captain Langrish under water or otherwise free herself from him to think about the packet. Now she has lost it—under the worst possible circumstances—and as soon as the Legation tracks her down in Venice she will have to account for it. It will not take them long to trace the whole business, from the people in the osteria to Bepi and his sandolo.

Winifred is unwilling to be threatened simultaneously by these two beasts—the Inquisitors on one hand and the Legation on the other. It fills her with a sense of indignation, of injustice. Surely one persecutor at a time is enough. What would a woman do who was True? This is the way she prefers to put it to herself. She has undertaken a task for M. Carnot and made a botch of it. How much trouble she has caused she doesn't know. But from M. Carnot's tone, in her interview with him at the Luxembourg, she imagines it is a great deal. And someone at the Legation, no doubt M. Villetard, seems very worked up about it too. Sending that unsavory-looking pudgy man all the way to the Brenta after her—he looked quite capable of inflicting some harm on her, if necessary, to recover the packet. But it is not really herself she is concerned about. If the packet fell into Venetian hands, M. Carnot had said—what had he said?—it would be *dire* for Jean-Marie. At this point a small panic rises in her again. But she quickly subdues it. Bother them all! The time has come to beard the lion in his den—to go straight to the Legation and explain to them frankly what has happened. Only in this way can she be True, even though she has made something of a botch of the matter so far. She would prefer for Jean-Marie to assist her in this, but Jean-Marie is unfindable. Either that, or that robin-eyed idiot Birdsell knows where he is and is concealing it, for the reason, no doubt, that well-brought-up young ladies should have nothing to do with Frenchmen. Well, she will have to do without Jean-Marie.

How to find the French Legation? She has no notion of its address, and besides the streets in Venice do not seem to have names as they do in other cities. To find Mr. Birdsell was easy, slight in value though the finding was. But Bepi brought her to Campo Santi Apostoli, only a step from the house, and besides Britain is a country more or less friendly with Venice at the moment, whereas France, as Mr. Birdsell pointed out, is not. To go about asking in bad Italian, in English, or in French for the whereabouts of the French Legation might only end in her falling into the jaws of the wrong beast, that is the Inquisitors. If only there were another Bepi!

A gondola, the thought occurs to her. By this time, through following what seems to be more or less a main thoroughfare (it is the width of the meanest back alley in London), she has reached the Rialto. She goes directly to the quay by the bridge, where there are a number of gondolas bumping docilely against the stakes. There is only one gondolier in sight, and he seems an honest enough looking fellow.

Winifred: "Légation Française."

Gondolier: "Franzese. Sì."

Here at least she has done the right thing. Not only does the gondolier know the location of every embassy and palazzo in the city, but gondoliers are the most discreet of Venetians, as discreet as Swiss bankers or English diplomats. As the Président de Brosses tells us in his celebrated *Letters,* a gondolier who betrayed a lady to her husband, or a political secret to the Signoria, would be thrown into the canal by his colleagues. This one conducts her smoothly down the Grand Canal, turns out of it into the Canareggio, passes under a bridge, and continues on down a quarter of a mile or so to another bridge. This second bridge is a curious structure. There are three semicircular arches, and the bridge itself is rather broad, so that the passageways underneath are like long elegant sewers. It is a quiet and, as it seems to her, slightly ominous part of the city. The gondolier offers her his hand to help her onto the water-stair.

She realizes for the first time that she has nothing to give him but a gold sovereign.

Winifred: "Wait here. Aspetta."

Gondolier: "Bene, Siorina."

He doesn't seem concerned about the fare. He will wait. He

even points out to her where the Legation is, using the typical Venetian gesture: he holds out a hand with fingers together and moves it up and down in a sawing motion. "Tuto dreto, Siorina." There is no straight ahead because, once over the bridge, the quay turns either to the left or the right. After a moment of hesitation she chooses the way to the right.

The Legation has for almost a century been installed in the Palazzo Surian Bellotto, a fine baroque palace with columns and carved putti on the façade. It was here that Rousseau was a secretary, fifty years or more ago, and he describes the place in his *Confessions.* Winifred in fact has no difficulty finding it; there is a plaque with a bell-pull, and also someone has written *Death to the French* on the wall. She pulls the wooden handle and there is a discreet jingle from within.

The door opens and Winifred begins speaking fluent French, with a sense of relief at having found—at last—someone she can communicate to with precision. The servant is a man in a striped apron. He is perhaps Provençal, or perhaps only speaks French with an Italian accent. Before she has half explained who she is he has conducted her rapidly into an inner waiting-room, motioned her to an armchair, and vanished.

After a while another person appears. This is a young man with excellent manners, a kind of clerk or undersecretary—very elegant, in beige breeches and a morning-coat.

Undersecretary: "Mlle. Hervey?"

Winifred: "Oui."

Undersecretary: "Auriez-vous l'obligeance de me suivre."

After pronouncing this elaborate phrase, with its ceremonious flavor of the Ancien Régime, he leads her through a series of connecting chambers to a rather large anteroom, with stucco decorations and a frescoed ceiling. There is a Persian carpet and a Murano chandelier. The clerk or undersecretary is adept and self-assured, and conducts himself with a minimum of words. He shows no sign that he notices her odd boat-cloak or the muddy skirt. At the end of the anteroom is the door of the bureau, a heavy oaken affair with gorgons. In the middle of the door is a bronze knocker in the shape of a human hand. He raises this slightly macabre object and allows it to fall.

Villetard: "Eh bien?"

Undersecretary: "Mlle. Hervey."
Villetard: "Faites-la entrer."

M. Villetard's study is not so large as the anteroom, but it is even more elegantly furnished. Another Murano chandelier and a carpet. Two armchairs in Louis Quinze style; an upholstered tabouret for seating persons of lesser importance. By the door, a credenza and a chair for the undersecretary. Before the window opening on the water is a rather long table of dark wood, inlaid with ivory and ebony. At the table is M. Villetard—a lean and bony, rather pale man with a narrow face. He rises as she enters, but doesn't come around the table to offer his hand. Because of his withered arm? No, that is the left; and besides why should he offer his hand? This is an English custom, and the French manner would be to embrace her on the cheek—a gesture she would resist vigorously if he made any sign of attempting it. Instead he inclines the upper part of his body slightly.

His next action, even before he has greeted her, is to motion for the undersecretary to leave. The door closes discreetly and noiselessly.

He sits down again and she, without being invited, takes one of the armchairs.

Villetard: "I am happy to see you have returned safely to Venice. There were no incidents on the way?"

Winifred: "There were French sentries at Fusina."

Villetard: "And they let you pass?"

Winifred: "They were busy with something else."

He seems to make a mental note of this, as though it is a matter he plans to attend to later.

Villetard: "And you arrived when?"

Winifred: "This morning."

Villetard: "And how have you passed the time until now?"

Winifred: "Going about the city and trying to find the Legation."

Villetard: "And how did you find it?"

Winifred: "In the end I took a gondola."

Villetard: "Where is the gondola now?"

Winifred: "Waiting."

Villetard: "Where?"

Winifred: "In the canal, by the bridge."

He seizes the velvet cord hanging behind him at the window and pulls. The undersecretary appears almost immediately.

Villetard: "There's a gondola waiting by the Tre Archi. Send the man away with a scudo and tell him to say nothing."

The door closes silently as before. With his right hand M. Villetard lifts his withered left arm and sets it on the table. Then he arranges the right arm on the table beside it, and regards Winifred carefully.

Villetard: "You didn't go to the English Resident then?"

Winifred feels the color flowing into her face. She has omitted mentioning Mr. Birdsell because she knows that the French and English missions are not on good terms. But she has forgotten that her instructions were to go to the Resident for Jean-Marie's address, and to deal with the French Legation only through Jean-Marie.

Winifred: "Yes. But I—"

Villetard: "I see. Never mind. Did Birdsell provide you with the information you requested?"

Winifred: "No."

Villetard: "I thought not. M. Fontenay has been diverting himself in other ways instead of paying attention to business. What did you tell Birdsell about yourself?"

Winifred: "Simply that I had come to Venice to rejoin my fiancé, and wished his address."

Villetard: "Excellent. And then you came directly here?"

Winifred: "As you see."

Villetard: "It was perhaps the only thing to do, Mlle. Hervey, considering the information you had available. The trouble is that the Legation is constantly watched by agents of the Inquisitors. It would have been better, for example, simply to write a note and have it delivered by a gondolier."

Winifred: "I didn't know."

She is careful not to say that she is sorry, since she doesn't see that any of this is her own fault.

Villetard: "Of course. These things are not important, Mlle. Hervey. They are details. Other things are important. The dispatches, for example."

Winifred: "I don't have them."

She sits looking at him across the table, her lips compressed a little.

M. Villetard's manner has changed—or rather, since she doesn't know him well enough yet to say that his manner has changed, his manner is not what she expected. She has expected him to be ominous, and to use a language laden with veiled and obscure threats. Perhaps there is something ominous in his narrow chin and pale lofty brow, the ferret-like quality of his eyes, but the general impression he gives is that of an overworked bureaucrat who has so many things to think about simultaneously that it would exasperate an ordinary man. He looks also as if he does not get enough exercise. There is a great patience about him. Not a philosophical patience, but the patience of a man who knows the imperfections of the world and has lived in it too long to be surprised and annoyed by them, yet still finds them rather wearying. It is the patience of a small clever animal waiting by the hole for its prey, and knowing that it will be a long time, perhaps, before it comes out. She observes now for the first time that the serenity of his brow is marred by some very faint wrinkles, beginning in a V between the eyes and spreading out into little lines of vexation that show only when the light from the window strikes them.

Villetard: "Where are they?"

Winifred: "I don't know."

Villetard: "You don't know? Don't speak in that idiotic way. Where are they?"

He doesn't seem to be angry; at least he shows no sign of it. He is merely describing her behavior factually.

Winifred: "They were taken from me by Captain Langrish."

Villetard: "Ah. Then the Signoria has them by this time, no doubt. The whole thing has been blundered—botched. I'm the one who will have to answer for this, you understand."

He sighs and settles back into his chair, placing the left arm in his lap. Then he evidently cogitates, in his beady way, without taking his eyes from her. Winifred has been vexed with him for the past few moments—all through the discussion of the dispatches—and now she realizes why. No one, either M. Carnot or M. Villetard, has ever deigned to explain to her what is contained in the packet. For M. Carnot it was a petit rien, a little gift. She was to deliver it to Jean-Marie and ask no questions. M. Villetard has suggested the importance of the dispatches only through his exasperation—an exasperation he is almost successful in concealing. And this is because she is a woman. A male agent would have been informed—at least in a minimum degree—of the contents of the packet and the possible consequences of it falling into the wrong hands. But if they are willing to tell her only that it is a little gift, then she has given the gift to Captain Langrish, that is all. A feminine whim. She is firmly resolved in her mind to say no more about it and not to defend herself in any way.

M. Villetard is still thinking. He is a more thoughtful person than she would have imagined him to be. One doesn't think of Legation secretaries, somehow, as persons of a philosophical cast. He rearranges his various arms on the table again: the one that works, the other that doesn't.

Villetard: "It would have helped if we had known about this earlier. Why did you run away from Mme. D'Artigny on your own, in that foolish way?"

Winifred: "I didn't care for the appearance of the man who was sent for me. Or his manner either."

Villetard: "Your sensibilities are very delicate."

He still shows no annoyance. It is a comment on a trait of her character. He thinks again for a moment.

Villetard: "But we don't know, of course, that the packet has left Captain Langrish's hands."

Winifred: "No, we don't."

Villetard: "What was his reason for taking it from you?"

Winifred: "I don't know."

Villetard: "What did he *say* his reason was for taking it from you?"

Winifred: "He's not a very talkative person. He simply detected it on my person, and told me that if I didn't give it to him he would take it for himself."

Villetard: "How did he detect it on your person?"

Winifred: "Because I was soaking wet."

He doesn't ask her why she was soaking wet.

Villetard: "Why do you imagine he took it?"

To this she is silent. Although in truth she has some idea about the matter. If she hadn't been so foolish as to jump overboard, Captain Langrish's attention would not perhaps have been drawn to her and it wouldn't have occurred to him that she was carrying something important on her person. Also, if she hadn't been wearing the uniform it wouldn't have been necessary to jump overboard. No one would have thought of searching the clothing of a well-bred young Englishwoman who was only traveling on board the *Libérateur* as a passenger. But there would be no useful purpose in explaining all these subtleties to M. Villetard; in fact they would only give him a lower opinion of the feminine sex than he already seems to have.

He considers—his lower jaw moving slowly from side to side. The button-like eyes are still fixed on her. There is a good deal about him, she reflects, of the boa-constrictor; although, when one comes face-to-face with such animals and examines them objectively, one sees that they are not ominous in themselves but simply the way that they are. They can't help weaving back and forth; this is the way they plan out how to fix their coils around you.

Villetard: "Thursday evening. Two days ago. If the Venetians had the dispatches there would be repercussions by this time. We have our sources of information in the Signoria. So far there is nothing. This means—this suggests—that perhaps Captain Langrish hasn't yet given the dispatches to his superiors. But if not—why?"

Winifred: "I haven't the least idea."

He hasn't expected her to have the least idea. He is conducting the dialogue with himself.

Villetard: "He's a foreigner. It's not clear exactly what his allegiance is. It's possible he's serving as a double agent—for the English perhaps."

Winifred: "He's American."

He doesn't seem to regard this as an important distinction. He ignores it and goes on.

Villetard: "Perhaps he merely hopes to sell them. To someone else, or to us. If so, he may simply be waiting while he thinks how to get the best price. Most of these mercenaries in Venetian service, you know, are little better than pirates."

She considers remarking that his behavior to her in the gondola wasn't that of a pirate, but thinks better of it.

Villetard: "It's clear what must be done. What are your own relations with Captain Langrish?"

Winifred (coloring): "Relations? No relations at all."

Villetard: "Excuse me. I mean—on what terms are you with him?"

Winifred: "Courteous terms."

Villetard: "He took you to Mme. D'Artigny, at my instigation, and behaved to you correctly?"

Winifred: "Perfectly correctly."

Villetard: "And yet he took the packet from you, by force."

Winifred: "He only *said* he would take it by force if I didn't give it to him."

This isn't the line that M. Villetard wants to pursue. He wants to find out whether the relationship—his term, not hers—between Winifred and Captain Langrish can be pursued to some advantage.

Villetard: "Mlle. Hervey, you have put us to considerable embarrassment in the matter of the dispatches. It was only on account of the dispatches that you were enabled to come to Venice to rejoin your fiancé. You can, if you like"—(there's no question of whether she likes or not; this is what he is instructing her to do)—"compensate for all this difficulty you've caused by helping us in the matter of Captain Langrish. First you must leave here, as inconspicuously as possible, and rejoin M. Fontenay. Then, with his help, you must seek out Captain Langrish, since you already have an—acquaintance—with him, and make an effort to find out what he has done with the dispatches. If they are still in his possession, do nothing, but inform me immediately. Not by presenting yourself here, of course. M. Fontenay is cognizant of the proper means for communicating with the Legation. Remember that you have nothing to do with the Legation and are in Venice only as a private British subject, M. Fontenay's fiancée. You have already compromised yourself by coming here in broad daylight and ringing the bell. But it could be explained that you simply came to ask for M. Fontenay's address."

Winifred (crisply): "And where may I find Captain Langrish?"

He gazes at her for a moment before he answers. Clearly he has not fathomed this odd foreign creature—this odd feminine foreign creature—completely as yet, and is moving warily. These blunt questions about delicate matters—perhaps it is only the English manner of doing things.

Villetard: "We are aware of where Captain Langrish lives. M. Fontenay will inform you at the proper time. As for M. Fontenay, his lodgings are in Ca' Pogi, in the San Pantalon parish. A Legation gondola will conduct you there. All this, of course, is to be carried out in the utmost confidence. Have nothing to do with Venetians of any sort."

The interview seems to be over. He rises from the armchair and Winifred rises too. He moves toward the bell-cord behind him, then turns again. The left arm, with a baby-hand at the end of it, bumps against his hip.

Villetard: "One more thing. In your impression, what were Captain Laugier's orders in regard to entering the Venetian lagoon?"

Winifred: "I don't know. The ship was to come to Venice and I was to disembark there."

Villetard: "Did Captain Laugier know the port had been closed on the seventeenth by order of the Senate?"

Winifred: "I have no idea."

Villetard: "Did he have orders to attack the Castel Sant'Andrea?"

Winifred: "He never spoke to me about his orders."

Villetard: "Who fired first?"

Winifred: "Is all this important?"

Villetard: "Very important."

Winifred: "There was a great deal of confusion. I believe the fort fired first. But someone said they were only warning shots. They came nowhere near the ship."

Villetard: "In the engagement between the *Libérateur* and the *Pandora,* which was the aggressor?"

Winifred: "What is the *Pandora*?"

Villetard: "The *Pandora* is Captain Langrish's vessel."

Winifred: "I'm not an expert on naval matters. There was a battle and a great deal of shooting. Then Captain Langrish's crew jumped on board our ship and captured it."

Villetard: "And did Captain Laugier defend himself?"

Winifred: "I don't know what you mean by defend himself. The Venetian sailors dashed up with their cutlasses. Captain Laugier was on the quarter-deck. He fired his pistols, and then he surrendered."

Villetard: "Ah! You're certain?"

Winifred: "He cried out 'Je me rends.' Then one of the sailors with the cutlasses—struck him."

Villetard: "After he cried out 'Je me rends'?"

Winifred: "Yes."

Villetard: "Splendid."

Winifred can't see anything splendid about what the cutlass did to Captain Laugier, but she is ready to believe that the sequence of events is important, at least for a diplomat. M. Villetard doesn't seem exactly pleased with this piece of information, but he seems interested. He says "Ha!" to himself several times. After he has seized the bell-cord he almost, but not quite, comes around the table to escort her to the door.

The undersecretary in the morning-coat appears again. Winifred passes into the corridor and turns to go out the way she came in, but a hand, elegantly draped in lace, rises to point the other way.

Undersecretary: "Par ici, Mademoiselle, si vous vouliez bien."

With his perfect courtesy—like an automaton demonstrating the manners of the court of Versailles—he escorts her to the rear of the palazzo and a small doorway with water-steps. A pergola with vines almost hides the doorway from the houses opposite. There is a gondola waiting at the water-steps. She slips into it, and it moves away without a sound.

VILLETARD IS LEFT ALONE

Villetard is left alone; which is the state he prefers. He is not a gregarious person. His masters have hired him not to be gracious and go to levees and receptions, but to think. To be gracious is for Lallement, who was raised to be a marquis, and would have been except for the unfortunate accident of the Revolution. Lallement is the Minister. Excellent for Lallement. But he, Villetard, is responsible for the real working of the Legation. And the Legation exists for one purpose only, to bring about the fall of an obsolescent and reactionary Venetian Republic. All this rests on one man. And on the delicate and carefully balanced machinery he has assembled to carry it out. And so, once the undersecretary has shut the heavy oaken door with its gorgon-carvings, he thinks.

He walks back and forth on the marble floor, looks out the window, and returns to stand pondering before the table. He says "Ha" to himself several times. His left arm annoys him and he puts it in his pocket. That goose of a girl! Couldn't she have put the packet—somewhere—where it wouldn't have been found? It is more valuable to his enemies than it is to him, Villetard. He knows more or less what is in it. Far better for it to be destroyed than for the Venetians to have it. The point is—why did Carnot entrust it to a woman, and an amateur? And why did he send it in this roundabout way, a way full of risks, instead of having someone simply slip into the city secretly with it from the Terraferma?

He divides the question in his mind. First of all, the choice of a courier. Carnot, he reflects, is a ladies' man. (He knows a great deal about Carnot, from his own intelligence sources, even though he has never met him.) Not only that, but something even more foolish, he is a sincere believer in the principles of the Revolution and the Rights of Man, and envisions a perhaps Utopian society in which women occupy positions of responsibility equal to those of men. For Villetard, firmly held principles are simply a weakness in character, like cowardice, or forgetfulness. He himself is loyal to nothing in particular except the techniques of his own métier. He has served under the Bourbons, under the Revolutionary Assembly, and now under the Directoire, all with equal efficiency. He is an old professional of the Cabinet Noir, and he is cynical about women and thoroughly convinced of their fundamental weakness and triviality; and he has plenty of evidence from his own experience to support this view. So it doesn't surprise him that Mlle. Hervey has lost the packet.

But one can hardly believe that Carnot gave the packet to her simply because he was thinking with his testicles instead of his head. He is not a complete imbecile. In fact, he is perhaps not an imbecile at all; there is evidence for this. Let us take now (he asks himself) the matter of why Carnot has sent the packet all the way around from Marseille to Rome to Ancona, instead of through the usual and proven clandestine lines. Carnot has behaved almost as though he wished the packet to be delayed, or not to arrive at all. And—it is necessary to examine all alternatives—would Carnot in fact be disconcerted if the packet were delayed? Or if it fell into Venetian hands?

First of all, what is in the packet? Villetard knows a good deal about this, or can guess. One thing he hopes for and has long expected is the full text of the Armistice of Leoben, including the secret clauses, which involve the plans for the eventual disposition of Venice at the end of the hostilities between France and Austria. Bonaparte has never deigned to reveal to the Directoire what he intends to do with Venice if he gets his hands on it. He confides only in Carnot, his protector in Paris. There are many possibilities. He could establish a democratic government and then set it free. He could incorporate it into the Cisalpine Republic. Or he could give it to his wife for her birthday. (June twenty-third; Villetard's information is excellent.) She would probably be pleased; she is fond of jewels. Villetard could manipulate things much better if he knew what was in this infernal Armistice.

More important, Villetard has requested, and has been promised, a list of patricians and members of the Maggior Consiglio who might be sympathetic to the French cause, or might be willing to betray their vote for a price—a list supplied by the Venetian Delegate-Extraordinary in Paris, who has sold himself to the French. With this list, Villetard can manipulate the vote in the Maggior Consiglio to cause Venice to pass, quite harmlessly and without the least violence, into French hands. His own hands itch for this list—at least the right—there is no feeling in the left.

But suppose—ahah! This is where the keen cerebration begins. Suppose that Carnot intended the packet to fall into Venetian hands. This would explain a good many things; for example, the choice of the roundabout route and the inept courier. This would be an ingenious and even fiendish device, and one that Carnot is quite capable of. It is a simple but devastating way of undercutting all the carefully laid plans of the Legation. For Carnot, and Bonaparte his protégé, have other plans. If Venice should fall without resistance, through diplomatic means, no credit would accrue to Bonaparte. And Bonaparte wishes another coup—a brilliant and unorthodox military victory—to add to those of Lodi, Castiglione, and Rivoli. The publication of the list of traitors would throw panic into the Venetians. No one would be trusted. There would be summary trials and executions. Opinion would turn violently anti-French, and there would be a wave of military hysteria. The remaining patricians would be obliged to behave in a rabidly chauvinistic way to show that they were not pro-French; in short a declaration of war. The French and Venetian armies would clash somewhere on the Terraferma, in a battle of purely symbolic nature, as sanguinary as it was unnecessary. The French would win, naturally, and Bonaparte would emerge from the carnage with another laurel. It might be enough to make him a Director, or even—who knows what the madman has in his head?—Consul, or Emperor, some delirium or other resurrected from ancient Rome. In that case he, Villetard, would be cooked. For he is not in sympathy with these Corsican flamboyancies. And the Bonapartists know it.

The packet must be found. If it is in Venetian hands, then that must be determined. But the most probable case is that Langrish still has it. This Langrish, he is beginning to realize, is an infernal pest. He sent that silly fop Fontenay after him, and Fontenay lost his nerve. Then he sent his own man after Fontenay and he bungled it too—complaining about his gout, and that the American walked too fast. Now he will see if the female English can do it. If not . . .

Working slowly and doing one thing at a time, with his right hand alone, he opens the drawer of the table and takes out a goose-quill pen, a sheet of foolscap, and finally an inkwell. He arranges the sheet in front of him and sets his tiny left hand on it, to serve as a kind of paperweight. Then he begins writing. The pen scratches its way down the sheet, without haste but also without pausing, in a column neatly aligned on the left. When he is finished he looks over the list to see if he has forgotten anything. No, he has them all. He gets up and pulls the bell-cord.

Undersecretary: "Monsieur?"

Villetard: "These are certain friends of ours in the city, whose names may be compromised. These persons must be confidentially advised to leave the city for a while. For a few days—until the situation is stabilized. You know how to do all this. When you are finished, of course, destroy everything written."

Undersecretary: "And the others?"

Villetard: "The others?"

Undersecretary: "The agents who are not on the list."

Villetard: "They are not important people. They're screwed, that's all. Foutus."

THE GONDOLA DEPOSITS WINIFRED

The gondola deposits Winifred in Campo San Pantalon. The gondolier evidently has instructions not to take her directly to Jean-Marie's house, since neither she nor Jean-Marie is supposed to have any connection with the Legation. As he helps her out onto the water-stair he gives her explicit directions. Ecco Siorina: across the campo, down the calle past the church, a turn to the right, and so on. Tuto dreto. She recognizes him now as the same gondolier who took her with Captain Langrish to the Villa Baraoni, the night of her arrival in Venice. He is a slender youth in a purple jacket and loose trousers in the Turkish manner—quiet, with a dark childish kind of beauty—a figure out of an Oriental tale, so it seems to Winifred. He replaces his round straw hat and nods to her, respectfully and with dignity. Then he fixes his oar in the water and the gondola moves off silently down the rio. The campo is almost empty and no one has noticed her landing.

It is a little after three. The directions are precise but Winifred still manages to lose her way once. This doesn't bother her. She feels blithe. Perhaps along with the cold she has a slight fever. How could it bother you to lose your way in a city so phantasmagorial and unreal that it might dissolve at any instant and turn out to have been only a dream? There is something corrupt and innocent about the city—innocent and corrupt—the decaying palaces, the grave dark-eyed glances of the children—and she feels corrupt and innocent too. She feels a sense of guilt that gives her no discomfort at all—instead she is vaguely pleased with herself and at the same time afraid, like a child who has stolen sweets. She is uncertain why this is. Probably it is because she has disobeyed Mr. Birdsell, and because M. Villetard treated her like a child instead of speaking to her intelligently like one human being to another. In all ways she feels she is a child again and having a child's dream. The city is made out of sugar-candy. But there are dog-droppings in the street and the wall is smeared with something unspeakable. The sugar-candy is dirty, and so is she. Exactly as in a dream. Her skirt is splashed with mud and her slippers are sodden. She takes a grave and malicious pleasure in this state of things. If the adults don't like it—let them pour the hot water in the tub and set her in it. She will splash them and make them cross. She will be a bad girl. It lifts her up to remember the joy of being a bad girl when she was six. She *is* feverish. What on earth is she thinking about? But she feels good, not bad, in spite of the bad-dream quality. If you *know* it is a bad dream you are having, it doesn't bother. You know that it isn't real and that you can wake up whenever you want. Presently she identifies at least a part of this secret and complicated euphoria—it is because she is going to meet Jean-Marie again. She has almost forgotten why she is plying her way back and forth in this maze of streets. Perhaps Jean-Marie would have a bath. Although Venice does not look like the kind of a city where baths are known.

Speaking of cleanliness, she seems in some way to have set her foot in a yellow and sticky sort of cheese, with an odor like all the effluvia of Dante's Inferno. Oh, now that is really horrid! She sits down on the quay and dips her slipper in the water. Then she finds a stick and scrapes the stuff off. She is very business-like about this. Rinse again. The water is not very much cleaner than the—stuff itself—but it can't be helped. Venetians evidently love animals. No doubt they are a kind people. She is feverish! She stands up and looks about her. It was this narrow and dank lane off to the left that she meant to follow.

Finally—after ending once more in a cul-de-sac and retracing her steps—she finds the right street. The calle, after it turns, comes to a door with a pair of worn lions on either side, and an antique marble frieze set into the lintel. For a bell-pull there is a scrap of wood attached to a rather rusty wire that disappears into a hole overhead. She gives this a pull. There is a sound from inside as though someone has dropped a pan.

There is a long wait. She pulls again and there is the same clunk of the broken bell. She glances around, not nervously exactly but watchfully—the calle is deserted. Finally the bolt is slipped from the inside, a chain loosened, and the door opens. There appears a pretty curly-haired youth, in a striped waistcoat and breeches. He regards her out of his velvety eyes, saying nothing.

Winifred: "M. Fontenay, if you please."

Boy: "No ghe ne xe."

Winifred: "Is M. Fontenay in? I am Mlle. Hervey."

Boy: "Nya pah."

Winifred: "When *will* he be in?"

Massimo is intimidated. He has never seen anyone so tall. That is, not a woman. In addition he is impressed by her costume—no, baffled. No, bemused is the right word. She is wearing a long cloak with a damp linen skirt showing under it—her shoes are muddy and her hair has come loose and strayed down her cheek. Also she smells like dog-shit. Perhaps she is a Gypsy. He is familiar with Gypsies. But this one has gray eyes and a long pale face, and is half again as large as an ordinary Gypsy. Besides she doesn't have the air of someone who would pick your pocket, or read your palm. She is an Inglesina, he decides from his imperfect knowledge of racial type. Englishes are all a bit mad. The cold in those parts addles their brains. What does this one want? His master has an active sentimental life and it is not for him, Massimo, to keep track of all his ladies. Massimo has his own gallantries to think about— the baker girl in Campo Santa Margherita, a certain ballerina at the Fenice, and so on. Besides the Paròn (the Moussou) is asleep now and doesn't want to be disturbed. It is hard to believe that this odd creature is a person of interest to the Moussou. If he were to disturb him in the middle of the Siesta—there is an ebony stick with a silver head upstairs—Massimo has felt it before. On the other hand, suppose this muddy castaway *were* a person of importance? In that case the Moussou would be angry that he has not admitted her, and he would feel the stick anyhow. Still this second contingency is unlikely. The best thing is to get rid of her before she begins making a fuss and the Moussou wakes up. His French forgotten anyhow, he repeats the Venetian gargle which he is sure she finds incomprehensible: "No ghe ne xe." Then he shuts the door.

MARK ANTHONY ENTERS THE

Mark Anthony enters the Arsenal through the portal under the monument to Lepanto, past the sentries who know him well and pay no attention to him, even though he is carrying a white rooster upside down by the feet. He is wearing a short wig, and on top of it a large felt hat with the brim turned up on one side and fastened with a pin. In recognition of the rain of the night before, he has donned a long cloak that comes below his knees—perhaps it is some kind of a toga—and a pair of military boots with the toes cut out, since no shoes on this part of the world are large enough to fit him. The rooster seems to find no objection to being carried upside down; he hardly stirs a feather. In his mechanism for perception, perhaps, it makes no great difference whether the world is inverted or not. He only blinks once in a while, and cranes his head around to see where he is going.

Once inside, Mark Anthony continues on down the quay past the great roofed sheds, where a dozen galleys can be built simultaneously under cover even in the winter. Now there is only the graying skeleton of a galley commenced a year or so ago and then abandoned. He crosses a bridge, goes around the magazine where pyramids of cannon-balls are gleaming in the dark interior, past the rope-walk and the victualing-shed, and comes out into the Bacino Novo. Alongside the quay a light galley called the *Astrologo* has been careened, that is, turned up in the water with her mast hauled down to a barge so that one side of her bottom can be caulked. The caulkers are prying shipworms out of her and throwing them to the small rust-colored crabs that scuttle on the wall of the quay.

Not far from her is the *Bragadin,* named for a commander who was flayed alive by the Turks after surrendering honorably at Cyprus. His skin, stolen from the mosque at Constantinople by an enterprising Venetian, is still preserved in the church of San Zanipolo—a kind of odd naval trophy. The *Bragadin* is hauled up on the ways and there are several planks out of her bottom. The Arsenaloti found some rot in her, when they set out to recaulk her several weeks ago, and are waiting for new planks to come from the carpenter's shop. Mark Anthony stops and gazes through the opening into the damp bowels of the vessel. All he sees is an oversized cat with hunched shoulders—the only creature on board. The cat seems to regard the *Bragadin* as his private territory. He raises his claws threateningly at Mark Anthony and makes a little hiss; the saucer-eyes widen in the gloom. The rooster bumps his wings and thrashes. He emits sounds of alarm, which come out upside down and resemble yelps more than the cries of an ordinary fowl.

Mark Anthony: "You hush now. Dat cat not hurt you. He de tutelary spirit of dis ship. Maybe he duppy of old Admiral Bragadin."

The rooster quiets, but still cranes his head around to stare into the hull with one eye. Mark Anthony waits until the rooster and the cat are done looking at each other, then he continues on down the basin. Just beyond the *Bragadin* is the *Pandora.* There is no one on board her either. The Schiavoni have been sent on shore to sleep for a few days in the great stone barracks beyond Castello, and the carpenters have finished repairing the cap-rail and gone away with their tools. Everything is covered with dust and there are scraps of wood and other shipyard junk lying around on deck. There is no gang-plank. Mark Anthony finds a length of timber on the quay and lays it over to the rail. Seen in perspective, from a few yards down the quay, he is a giant boarding a toy ship. His weight on the rail causes her to sink down in the water a tiny fraction of an inch, and then tilt slowly back and forth like some great pendulum.

Mark Anthony: *"Pandora* ship too, she alive, just like you and me."

With the rooster craning his head around to see where they are going next, he bends his head to pass in under the tweendecks. Here it is shadowy and quiet. There is a faint creak of timbers, and a watery reflection playing on the beams overhead. In the mixture of smells certain individual odors can be made out, like the voices of instruments in a medley: oakum, tarred cordage, turpentine, charcoal, cooked mutton, saffron, and the slightly acid scent of gunpowder.

Mark Anthony: "Dis where we live on de ship."

There is no proper cabin. Covering the after third of the vessel is the raised quarter-deck, and under it is the tweendecks, a kind of shadowy den with the great shoulders of the ship's skeleton cutting into it on the sides. The comforts are primitive. The *Pandora* was originally a chebeck of the Barbary corsairs, cunningly designed for speed under sail, especially to windward and in light air. In succession she passed into the hands of the Maltese, the Spanish, and then the Turks, who cut the rowing-ports in the bulwarks and added the benches for oarsmen. They used her to raid the islands along the Illyrian coast, until, some ten years or so ago, they had the misfortune to run afoul of a Venetian galley off Corfu. Spots of Turkish blood can still be seen here and there on the decks, in corners where the holystone doesn't reach. She is a kind of palimpsest of Mediterranean naval history: carved into the thwarts and deck-beams, scrawled in faded ink on the bulwarks, scratched with knives and nails in every part of the vessel, are names and inscriptions in all the languages of the men who have sailed in her—Arabic, Spanish, Turkish, the indecipherable Maltese tongue akin to Phoenician, demotic Greek, and for some reason one crudely scratched legend in English: *Iohn Braithe farr from Plymouthe 1765.* There are still some rusty eyebolts in the timbers—the Turks chained the oarsmen to the benches.

Loaded muskets are stored in racks under the deck-beams. Near them the rows of cutlasses and boarding-pikes gleam dully in the half-light. The two sides of the tweendecks are divided into doorless cabins, leaving a broad passageway down the center. In one of these half-open cubicles is a square of bricks full of cold ashes, with something like a large wrought-iron funnel suspended over it to carry away the smoke. This is the galley, such as it is.

Mark Anthony, pulling up the cloak, reaches into his breeches pocket for a length of string. This he fixes onto the leg of the rooster, and ties the other end to a stool. Set aright, this animal begins making sounds more common to his species, but in a subdued way, as though he still feels disaffected.

Mark Anthony: "Maybe you duppy of Turk who skin old Bragadin. Hoppen a mon do wrong, sooner or later he suffer. Whole universe a big balancing machine. You born as a chicken to punish you."

He finds some kindling, arranges it on the cold charcoal, and strikes a light. When the flames begin to crackle he goes off to look for a hammer and nails. In the earthen pot in which the cutlery is kept—such was the custom of the Greek—he digs around for a small knife with a worn-away blade, of the kind used for paring vegetables. The fire is burning briskly, and the rooster is examining it.

Mark Anthony: "We wait for him to burn down to coals. Dat de proper way to do it. My Granddaddy old mon in Kingston Town, he teach me Africa way when I a little boy."

While he is waiting he unties the rooster and inspects him once again. He is perfect and unblemished, with a fine red comb that erects whenever something catches his attention.

Mark Anthony: "You not Jamaica chicken, but Jamaica chicken not obtainable in dese parts."

He examines the coals, and finds they have died down enough. Holding the rooster still in his left hand, he reaches into his pocket with the right, and comes out with a tobacco-bag full of twigs, leaves, and crumbs of vegetable substance. He dumps it out onto the coals. There is a sharp flare of greenish flame, a billow of smoke, and a heavy odor like musk or civet. Holding the rooster upside down, he thrusts his head into this gas. The beast flops his head around, soundlessly. After a while his convulsions cease, and he hangs motionless with his beak open. His eye is dull.

Mark Anthony: "I like to try dat for myself some time. But I fraid I not come back from de place where you go."

He sets the rooster down on the stool, where he lies limply. Yet he is still aware; the glazed eye follows Mark Anthony as he turns away to pick up the hammer and nails. Mark Anthony seizes him, by the neck this time, and arranges him against the curved planking of the ship. He nails one wing to the planks, and then the next.

The same with the feet. The rooster makes a sound not very often heard from domestic fowl, a kind of wail like an unattended baby. Mark Anthony takes the nails from his mouth one by one as he works. When the nailing is done he sets the hammer down, arranges a basin on the deck under the rooster, and takes up the knife.

Mark Anthony: "Harenji harenji. Obai na' gobodo."

The knife-blade flicks in his hand. There is a gush of scarlet, which he stands back to avoid. To be touched by the blood is bad luck, or at least it spoils the business. When the arterial spurting has stopped he approaches again and makes an incision from breastbone to anus, in a single stroke.

Mark Anthony: "Orobu na' oku. Banjee, banjee. Renkedu mankedu, moto harenji."

Sticking away the knife for the moment into the planks, he inserts his fingers into the warm entrails. He pulls out various purple tubes, organs, and whitish masses and examines them, taking the knife again to separate them. The liver and gizzard he studies with particular care; he gives the heart only a glance.

Mark Anthony: "One die by water. Anudder by fire. One or two more dey get off scot free. Hoppen dat be Mark Antony."

He goes out on deck to empty the basin over the side, then comes back in, pulls out the nails, and throws the rooster on the fire. There is only a little blood on his fingers, and he wipes it off with a piece of tow. The string he puts back in his pocket, and he also restores the hammer to the tool-box.

Mark Anthony: "Place for every ting in de universe. Place for hammer. Place for each mon. It all one big machine. Some born chicken, some born mon. Why dat be? No mon know. But Machine, he know."

When everything is cleaned up he leaves the galley and makes his way aft, bending to avoid striking his head on the deck-beams. In the very end of the vessel he is able to stand up again. He is in a kind of lazaret, extending the full width of the hull, although here at the stern this is only ten feet or so. There is no door, and only a crude stool to sit on. There is a table with a chart, an inkwell, and a rusty knife for cutting pens. The berth is a shelf of planks provided with a donkey's breakfast, that is, a canvas bag loosely filled with straw. Over the berth is a brass lamp hung on gymbals.

Mark Anthony: "Dis de copn's quarters. He lie in here and read books when he sposed to be tending to business. What good is reading books, I ask you dat?"

The lamp has left a smudge of soot on the beams overhead, and oil has leaked from it onto the berth. It is a trick to get close enough under the lamp to read by it, and still to dodge the drops of oil. In the daytime the light comes in through a pair of fine brass portholes—far too fine for an Algerine pirate—and in fact this hardware was removed from a Dutch merchantman confiscated by the Venetians for smuggling, and broken up for its fittings. Mark Anthony gazes out through the dirty glass. He sees framed in it a broad gelatinous face, surmounted with a cocked hat, staring into the *Pandora* from the dock. Mark Anthony is acquainted with the Missier Grande from several other encounters. Behind Cristoforo himself are other persons: a bulky sbirro with a small head and a sword down to his ankles, and another who looks as though he might be a clerk, with a cheesy complexion and an ink-smudge on his cheek—in fact he is carrying a leather wallet under his arm, the badge of his trade.

Clerk (shouting): "Hey you there, Black Fellow. Come out."

Mark Anthony sniffs, looks around for something to put in his hand, and thinks better of it. Taking his time, he slouches out on deck where he can get a better look at the three. The Constable himself—the Missier Grande—is clad in his ceremonial cap and toga. Although he is imposing in all parts, the most striking feature about him is the nose, which is like a great gnarled oak. Since he is slightly strabismic, the eyes give the impression of two fey creatures peeping around this trunk, each trying to see the other without being seen. One or the other of these eyes fixes with a glare on Mark Anthony as he comes ashore down the improvised plank.

Cristoforo: "Speak to him in English."

Clerk: "His Excellency say, you are to say where is your captain."

Mark Anthony: "He not aboard right now. Last time I see him more dan two days ago."

Clerk: "But you know his wheres. Eh?"

Mark Anthony: "No, he not bliged to keep track of where I am at all times, and I not bliged to keep track of him."

Cristoforo: "And the Inglesina!"

Clerk: "Where is the English female person?"

Mark Anthony: "Not sure who you are speaking bout."

Clerk: "L'Inglesina! How to say? Girl of England. She is on the board of *Liberatore.*"

Mark Anthony: "Dey a young midshipmon on de French brig. I not notice he a girl."

Clerk: "But that is the her! The Inglesina in travesty!"

Cristoforo: "He's making a fool of you. Ask him about the packet."

Clerk: "The Girl of England has got the pacheto, eh. How to say. The involto. The bolgia."

Mark Anthony: "He not bulge very much, hoppen you mean de midshipmon. He built bout de same as you. No chest before, not much behind."

Cristoforo: "What is chest?"

Clerk: "Cesto. A basket."

Mark Anthony: "No, not dat kind of chest."

Clerk: "El petto."

Cristoforo: "What is this idiocy? Petto! Petto! Take this fellow in charge."

Feeling the warm sunlight, Mark Anthony stretches upright. In this posture he is a head taller than the others.

Clerk: "There's a lot of him. I'd recommend that you send for another man or two."

Cristoforo: "I'll not be mocked! To the Pozzi! Ask him again about the packet."

Clerk: "Girl of England is carrying a small bundle in front. Inside her panza—how do you say, the belly."

Mark Anthony: "Sound to me like she going to be mudder."

Cristoforo: "Never mind this cretin. Let's go on board."

Clerk: "Stand backward, Black Fellow. Authority of Inquisitors will search this ship."

Mark Anthony: "Watch out for dat plank."

Cristoforo turns away with great dignity. The toga floats like a purple Montgolfier across the three feet of water to the *Pandora*'s deck. The sbirro lingers behind for a moment, staring at Mark Anthony as though he wishes to memorize his face. His eyes are set close together in the small head, with ears that stand out from the skull: the head of a bat. Even the hair that shows under the hat, short and furry, is bat-hair. A blink, and he turns and follows his master. The clerk comes after, carrying the wallet and teetering on the narrow plank.

Something is going on at the entrance to the Arsenal, and a small crowd has collected to watch. At the end of the campo, behind the skinny lion, the massive canal-gates are being cranked open. Inside the gates, looming over the towers on either side of the canal, some tall spars are creeping up with the slowness of a clock-hand. The rickety drawbridge across the canal has been drawn up on its cables.

Mark Anthony: "Ship coming out. Hoppen dey going to fight de French."

The gates open only very slowly. It is five minutes or more before they are turned at right angles and fitted into the mortises set into the walls. Then a large man-of-war comes out, towed by a pair of cutters each manned by a dozen or more oarsmen. It is necessary for the yards to be trimmed so they won't strike against the towers of brick and white stone. Orders are shouted, and there is a creak of braces running through the blocks. The yards braced, she moves out into the canal at the pace of a walking man.

Looming over the houses and the small figures in the campo, the *Vittoria* seems immense. She is a palace, but a palace that moves slowly and with dignity down the canal. The gun-ports are closed, the anchors catted, everything ready for sea. The upper works are ornately carved and gilded. The aftercastle, a rococo structure eighteen feet or more above the water, ends at the stern in a massive gilded lantern. Above it the red-and-gold banner of St. Mark floats on a long staff.

And in truth she is a splendid thing. Never mind if Venice has lost all her Levantine colonies, or if there is nothing in particular for a ship-of-the-line to defend in the Adriatic, or no particular enemy worthy of all this gilt and circumstance—simply as a spectacle, a product of human craft and love, she has a magnificence. It is a commonplace that, even after artifacts have lost their functional value, they retain a beauty which, in a certain measure, is enhanced by their very obsolescence—a suit of armor is an example, or a Roman wick-lamp. And so the *Vittoria*—unconscious of any irony in her name, or in her lady-like dignity choosing to ignore it—passes on down the Rio de l'Arsenale toward the lagoon.

The great shadow falls over the houses. There is a touch of breeze from the north, lifting the red-and-gold banner. The crowd in the campo looks on, but nothing breaks the silence. They are all kinds of people—shopkeepers, an Arsenaloto or two, a baker's-boy with his hair sticking out from under his cap, a patrician in a red toga. Then someone lifts his voice. The baker's-boy impulsively cries out.

"Viva San Marco!"

Another voice takes it up, with a catch on the r, and a characteristic lingering and slight rise of pitch.

"Viva San *Mar-rr*-co!"

Then there are several voices, never in chorus, a kind of jagged and erratic staccato of shouts that only gradually dies away.

"Viva San *Mar-rr*-co!"

". . . San Marco!"

" . . . arco!"

If each one cries out for himself it is because the cry is a thousand years old and comes from inside him, from an inchoate stir in the veins, and not from the others. The catch on the r with its rising note is an affirmation, a defiance: it is the cry of the victories of Chioggia and Lepanto, of the long war with the League of Cambrai, of the centuries when Venice ruled the Levant and the red-and-gold banner flew over Cyprus, Candia, and the Morea.

There is silence again. The ghost of history, having passed through the crowd, departs, leaving them bewitched and a little suspicious of each other. The *Vittoria* reaches the end of the canal and the cutters cast off their tow-lines. The topsails drop to the light breeze, then the courses are loosed. She passes out into the lagoon and turns in a wide sweep to the left, toward the Lido and the open sea. In three days, perhaps four, she will be at Corfu.

Mark Anthony: "Dat a very fine ship. Copn of her, he no doubt a nobleman of some old family. Foreign copn, he not hope to have a ship like dat."

The *Vittoria* heels to the breeze and slips away down the channel. After a while she disappears behind the houses at Sant'Elena; only her topsails are visible now. The crowd disperses, rather sheepishly. Mark Anthony turns and goes off up the Riva in his cloak and wavy hat.

MALCOLM LIES ON THE BED WITH

Malcolm lies on the bed with his boots on, wearing a pair of Franklin glasses with half-lenses perched on his nose. Even though they are tiny, these two beans of crystal transform him completely. The Sea-Captain disappears behind them, and the Scholar emerges. From every appearance—except, perhaps, for the boots on the bed—one would take him for a cranky recluse who has spent his whole life among books. At the moment he is in Book Eleven. This is the part in which Odysseus finally escapes from Circe's island, although not without leaving behind some casualties. In some ways he is a completely incompetent commander. Always losing his companions through some stupid blunder a child could have foreseen, and then grieving and pouring down swelling tears. He does know how to speak about handling a ship, however.

"And when we came down to the ship and the sea,
First of all we dragged the ship to the godly water
And set up the mast and the sails upon the black ship.
We took sheep and brought them on board, and we ourselves
Went on, grieving and pouring down swelling tears.
Then a driving wind full in the sails, a good companion,
Did the fair-braided Circe, dread god with a singing voice,
Send on for us from behind the dark blue-prowed ship.
And when we had tended to the gear through the ship, piece by piece,

We took our seats. The wind and a pilot steered her.
The sails were stretched all day long as she fared on the ocean.
The sun went down and all the ways were shadowed."

Those fellows always had the wind abaft the beam, he thinks skeptically. It is easy enough when you have the wind behind you, even with a squaresail. They had the gods on their side, that was the thing. If you could call the fair-braided Circe a god, the slippery bitch. Still, why they didn't use a lateen for beating up through those islands he can't imagine. The winds in the Aegean are variables, mainly out of the north, and plenty of currents. They use lateens nowadays. Reflecting over this, he arrives at no particular conclusion except that you need a better rig when the gods aren't on your side.

He closes the book, gets up from the bed, and moves over to the table. He finds a sail-needle and sets it by the lighted candle. Then he spreads his coat out on the table and begins inspecting the seams carefully through his glasses, pressing the cloth apart with his fingers. He heats the needle in the flame and stabs. There is a hiss, a tiny thread of smoke, and an odor of burning insect. He proceeds patiently down the seam until he finds another, aiming at it through the glasses on his nose. He heats the needle again and pricks.

This keeps him busy enough for twenty minutes or so. He is aware of various familiar sounds. The water under the window slaps lazily at the wall. There is a cry of *Ah-o-é* from a gondolier in some distant rio. Then, after a long and faintly buzzing silence, the old woman calls up the stairway.

"Capitàn. Xe El Moro."

Mark Anthony comes in, stooping to pass through the doorway.

"Good day, Copn."

The bass voice fills the small room to its corners. There is a rich odor, not unpleasant, something like a medley of roasted nuts and olive oil. Malcolm glances up and goes back to slaying lice again.

Malcolm: "Why aren't you in the Arsenal?"

Mark Anthony: "Bad smell today in de Arsenal. What dey call in Venice miasma."

Malcolm: "What are you talking about?"

Mark Anthony: "Dat Mister Grand, he looking all over town for you. He perspicating round de *Pandora* asking questions."

Malcolm: "Did he ask you any questions?"

Mark Anthony: "Dat he did, Copn."

Malcolm: "What did he want to know?"

Mark Anthony: "He very curious bout de English Leddy. He already find out a good many tings bout her."

Malcolm: "Such as what?"

Mark Anthony: "He know she carrying a certain packet when she come to Venice. Mister Grand, he very interested in dat packet. I spect he have a notion in his head dat you might have it now."

Malcolm: "Why doesn't he come and ask me for it then?"

Mark Anthony: "Dat I can not say. Hoppen he not like to climb stairs. He a somewhat old person."

Malcolm: "Does he know where the English lady is now?"

Mark Anthony: "I spect he do not, from de questions he ask. But I do."

Malcolm: "You do? Where is she?"

Mark Anthony: "She sitting in Caffè Bertazzi, drinking tea."

Malcolm: "Damn! Why didn't you say so at first?"

He approaches the place rather warily. It is in a street just off the Boca de Piazza. The street is busy at this hour, and the café itself is full. There doesn't seem to be anybody watching from the street. He goes in and finds her sitting at a table in the rear, clearly visible to anybody who puts his head in the door. There is a silver tea-service on the table in front of her, and the remains of a dish of cakes.

He goes to the table and sits down without a word, leaving his hat on. The waiter comes up immediately to ask if he will take something.

"Nope."

He waits until the waiter has gone.

"Get up and follow me. Don't say anything to anybody."

She: "Why?"

Malcolm: "Cristoforo is looking for you."

She: "Who?"

Malcolm: "The same fellow as before—the Missier Grande."

She: "Oh. That horrible constable who—puts people in the Pozzi?"

He nods stiffly.

"I see. But I haven't . . . done anything wrong," she lies, brightly, and not very convincingly.

Malcolm: "Neither have I. He's looking for me too."

"But *you're* not in the Pozzi," she points out smoothly, even with a little smile.

Malcolm: "I haven't been sitting around in cafés."

She: "Isn't there a danger in your being seen with me?"

He only makes a gesture as though he were brushing away a fly. He has an angry expression for some reason.

She: "I don't think they put women in the Pozzi anyhow."

Malcolm: "We'd better leave immediately."

She: "Very well."

She gets up quite simply, leaving a few coins on the table. She is still wearing the boat-cloak he gave her, with a kind of muddy nightgown under it. A conspicuous costume. She is bareheaded, and a lock of her dark hair has strayed down her forehead over her eye. She follows behind him out of the café, seriously and even a little primly, as though she is not conscious of any danger but wishes to do exactly the right thing. Luckily he finds a gondola quickly in the rio nearby and gets her into it.

She: "Where are you taking me?"

She still shows no alarm or even diffidence. There is only a kind of curiosity, as though she is interested in the proceedings and wants to have each step explained to her.

Malcolm: "To my lodgings."

She: "Oh." And then: "Why?"

Malcolm: "Your portmanteau is there. You can change into something that doesn't make you look quite so freakish. Then we can decide what to do with you."

She: "I don't quite understand why it's *you* that has to decide what to do with me."

He doesn't reply to this because he doesn't know the answer himself.

Siora Bettina shows no surprise. The captain often has strange visitors—Moors, other Englishes like himself, characters in odd garb who might be Turks or Greeks. He has never had a woman before, but this is not exactly a woman, it is an Inglesina, wearing what appears to be a naval cloak, a nightgown, and some dancing-slippers. Contrary to her expectations, the captain does not take the Inglesina up to his room. She asks if she might bring something, coffee or chocolate. There is no chocolate but she could go out to the campo and get some.

Malcolm: "No. Leave us alone."

He waits until the old woman is gone, then he sits down on one side of the table and she on the other. He examines her uncertainly, drumming his fingers on the table. He has the air of a man who has unexpectedly found a pearl in the street, and is afraid it might roll away in the gutter, or dissolve if he tries to pick it up.

Malcolm: "What are you doing wandering around the city? Why aren't you at Villa Baraoni?"

Winifred: "It was dull there. I was bored and the Contessa was quarrelsome. Besides a man came to ask for the packet. You know, the one you took from me and were so rude as not to give back."

Malcolm: "What kind of a man?"

Winifred: "From the French Legation. I was threatened with some vague fate if I didn't give it to him."

Malcolm: "Give what to him?"

Winifred: "The packet. Are you listening to what I'm saying?"

He clears his throat. He would like to get off this subject of the packet, which is an awkward one for him.

"Then what did you do?"

Winifred: "I left by the rear exit, and came back to Venice. A wonderful boy brought me in a boat. Then I wandered about the city for a bit. I had various adventures. I called on the English Resident."

Malcolm: "Why?"

Winifred: "Because he was supposed to have the address of my—intended. But he didn't have it. So I went to the French Legation."

Malcolm: "I don't think Villetard wanted you to come to the French Legation."

Winifred: "He didn't. He was very unhappy about it. He also wasn't very happy about the dispatches"—only slightly flustered, she corrects herself—"you know, the little packet. He ordered me to become acquainted with you and—persuade you to give it back."

Malcolm: "Did he order you to tell me this?"

He doesn't know what to make of her. She gives the impression she is making fun of him, or perhaps of Villetard. She seems slightly delirious. There is even a hectic flush in her cheek. She goes on, blithely.

"He gave me my intended's address. Then he put me out the rear door, once again. I went to Ca' Pogi, where M. Fontenay lives. But there was nobody there but a boy. He spoke only Venetian and what he imagined was a few words of French. He wouldn't let me in. He was an insolent boy, really."

Malcolm: "Then what?"

Winifred: "I didn't know what to do then. I went to a café and ordered tea."

Malcolm: "You picked a poor one. The Barnaboti go there, and officials from the Palace."

Winifred: "Well, the people were very nice. I had nothing to pay for the tea but a gold sovereign. They didn't have change of course. But they were very honest and said they would send off to a Mosaic person to change it. A boy went off to the Mosaic person and came back with the change. I had more tea and sat there for quite a long time. Then that enormous black man put his head in the door. I recognized him as one of the crew from your ship."

In short she has wandered around the city all day in her freakish costume, giving her name to people, displaying English gold to strangers, making a fuss at Residencies and Legations, leaving a trail so broad a blind child could follow it.

Malcolm: "What do you intend to do now?"

Winifred: "Wait until tomorrow, I suppose. Then go to Jean-Marie."

Malcolm: "Until tomorrow? Where?"

Winifred: "I have no idea."

Malcolm: "Better go back to the Villa Baraoni."

Winifred: "Oh, the Contessa is a nuisance. She lectures me, and besides there's nothing to eat there. It's terribly boring. I'll stay—somewhere. Why not here?"

Malcolm: "Here?"

Does she understand that there is only one bed-chamber in the house? What *does* she understand? Perhaps she expects him to sleep in the kitchen. Or perhaps—he remembers that M. Villetard has told her to—how did she put it? become acquainted with him, and get the packet back. He treads cautiously, like a man skirting a lighted bomb.

Malcolm: "The best thing would be for you to go back to M. Fontenay this evening."

Winifred: "But the boy said he wasn't in."

Malcolm: "Blast the boy! The boy is an idiot. If you will go up the stairs, just there"—he points—"and turn to the right, you'll find a bed-chamber. In the chamber is your portmanteau. Change into something more suitable and—refresh yourself." He feels the red mounting into his cheeks. Blast and Perdition. He has no experience in talking about such matters to women. "Then we'll take a gondola to Ca' Pogi, and I'll have a word with this whelp who won't let you in."

To his surprise she does exactly as she is told. Except, perhaps, for the recommendation about suitable costume. When she comes down in half an hour she is clad in a blouse, a short coat cut somewhat in the military fashion with brocade facings, long narrow pantaloons that come down to her ankles, and short English walking-boots. The coat is chestnut and the pantaloons beige. She has tied her hair in the back with a broad yellow ribbon. She holds the hat-box in one hand and carries the cloak over her arm.

Winifred: "Captain Langrish, will you be kind enough to go up for the portmanteau? I can't manage it on the stairs."

Malcolm: "That your idea of inconspicuous dress?"

Winifred: "These things? I bought them all in Paris. Except for the boots. So they must be correct. Everyone in Paris goes about en style sans-culottes."

Malcolm: "Not in Venice."

Winifred: "Well I can't pass for a Venetian so why try? Besides I enjoy wearing trousers. They're comfortable and they're practical."

He can do nothing with her. She is in an impulsive, blithe, headstrong, and slightly feverish mood, probably because she is going to rejoin her fiancé after a long separation. It is possible that she doesn't understand the risks in going about the city so conspicuously. He knows little enough about well-brought-up young ladies, except that he has a certain sense of the respect due them even in one's thoughts. Still most of them don't go around wearing trousers. He does as he is told, goes upstairs and gets the portmanteau.

Malcolm: "Stay here, and don't come out until I have the gondola alongside the quay. Then come out quickly and get into the gondola with as little fuss as possible. It'll be enough of a circus as it is."

Winifred: "I don't understand why *you* should be cross with me too."

She removes a hat from the box and puts it on, verifying its exact tilt in the glass. It is a kind of beige hunting-cap with a short brim turned up on one side, and a feather.

LIKE ALL GONDOLAS THIS ONE

Like all gondolas this one is provided with a broad double armchair or sofa at the rear of the felze. Before when Malcolm occupied a gondola with Miss Hervey he left the sofa to her and took the chair facing her at the other end of the felze. But the arrangement of a gondola is contrived essentially for two persons. This is one of the charms that have made it famous, but it also occasionally raises awkward questions of etiquette. The small wooden chair is provisional; it is without upholstery, hard, narrow, and not very comfortable. It requires its occupant to sit bolt upright, almost leaning forward—a posture that is not only tiring but gives the impression somehow that he is preparing to lunge at the occupant of the sofa. When Malcolm sat in this chair before on the trip to the Brenta, it seemed a deliberate unfriendliness and also left the feeling in the air that she was in some sense or other a prisoner and he was sitting there to keep his eye on her. If there is some slight grain of truth in this last, it is all the more important to avoid the suggestion. After a moment of indecision he takes his seat on the sofa beside her. Since she is on the left, his saber lies between them. She gives no sign that she has noticed the change in the arrangements.

The door of the felze is closed, and the shutters narrowed to slits. No one on the outside can see anything of the interior; from the inside they can see only small fragments of a rio or a palazzo going by the shutters. With some embarrassment he sits stiffly on the sofa, his elbow almost touching hers. The portmanteau and hat-box occupy the chair at the other end of the small cabin. Her composure seems total; the slightly hectic, feverish manner of before has disappeared. She hardly glances to the side to look out through the shutters. A small Renaissance smile plays now and then on her face, a smile of Leonardo or Guido Reni. The ambiguity of this expression corresponds to the ambiguity of her emotions. She is in the custody of one strong and virile man, older than she is but still at the peak of his vigor, and she is on her way to meet a younger and even more elegant male person who is shortly to become her husband. It is a late April afternoon—the air is tepid—the water splashes along the gondola only a half-inch from her hand. She has also got those filthy clothes off, finally, and is dressed in something which she believes to be attractive. This does no harm at all to her sense of composure.

Malcolm is able to guess, at least, at these bifurcated reasons for the smile, and it only contributes to his sense of malcontentment combined with vague physical stimulus that he has felt from the beginnings of his relations with this elusive and exasperating phantom. As he has told himself—and as is borne in upon him even more forcefully now—he has had very little experience in the world with creatures such as this. On the whole he has endeavored to avoid entanglement with such. And he has even worked out a device to this end. Supposing you encounter a young person whose attractions, whatever they are, tend to cloud the senses and interfere with the clear exercise of reason—the thing to do is to attempt to divest her, in your mind, of the purely feminine and see her in male guise; or, to put it another way, to imagine that you are looking at her brother. Through this technique of demystification, it is often possible to see that the female in question is quite an ordinary person. But this does not work very well with Miss Hervey. Since she already looks like somebody's brother, this is discounted from the start, and there is no gainsaying that she is unmistakably a woman, even though a rather odd one. So Malcolm has no other recourse than to avoid looking at her as far as possible, and to go on sitting somewhat stiffly with his back not quite touching the sofa, which is inclined to the rear at what seems to him an excessively indolent angle. (He knows, as she doesn't, that if a pair of hooks at the rear are released the back will fall almost to the horizontal.) Ordinarily, when he is seated, he rests his left hand on the saber-scabbard in order to prevent it from clanking or interfering with the person seated next to him. But this might result in a part of the hand, a knuckle perhaps, coming into contact with the chestnut coat at his left—an unthinkable catastrophe. He keeps the hand on his knee, where both of them can see it. He says nothing during the short journey to Ca' Pogi, and neither does she. The gondola goes on down the Grand Canal, past the great houses with their imposing façades of gilt and marble, and curves to the left into Rio Ca' Foscari. In the neighborhood of Campo San Pantalon it bumps to a stop by a great wrought-iron grille. It is not the door that Winifred called at before, of course, but the other entry on the rio.

They get out and stand on the mossy stone. There is no bell-pull. The gondolier calls out.

Ao.

Presently the insolent boy of Winifred's account appears. To persons arriving by water, according to Venetian custom, he is more civil and more ceremonious than to those who ring at the street-door. He unlocks the wrought-iron grille and allows them to enter the atrium. The portmanteau and hat-box are passed in and set onto the mosaic floor of a Pompeiian magnificence. The gondolier waits.

The boy explains that the Sior is at home but not receiving. At least his story is consistent. The sounds of baroque chamber music can be heard floating down the marble staircase: a pair of silvery violins, the deeper gold or bronze of violas, in a fretwork of intricately contrived harmony exactly suited (Malcolm feels) to the elegant and slightly corrupt décor of the palazzo. His senses detect a faint aroma of coffee.

She, the goose, does nothing. She only stands there at the bottom of the stairs with her hands entwined, wearing her Gioconda smile. Malcolm begins dealing with the boy in Venetian, and without hair on his tongue, as the local saying has it. "This is Siorina Hervey. She is the fidanzata of Sior Fontenay. She has just come a long distance, all the way from London"—(there are inaccuracies or oversimplifications here, but it will do for the boy)— "and she wishes to refresh herself and also to speak to Sior

Fontenay. Please tell Sior Fontenay all these things, and that we wish him to come down, or I will box your ears for you."

Massimo is perplexed and somewhat thunderstruck. First of all to see the Inglesina return, when he thought he had got rid of her permanently and in such a satisfactory way earlier in the day, and in a different and more elegant costume. Second, to learn that the Moussou has a fidanzata; he has never confided this detail to Massimo. Third, to find her accompanied by this Inglese who seems to be a formidable person, and fourth that the Inglese speaks Venetian and roundly too; he makes Massimo's head ache. He makes a little bow and retreats up the stairway, wrapping himself as best he can in the vestiges of his dignity.

The music upstairs stops. The heavy note of the viola da gamba goes on a little longer than the others, then it trails off into silence too.

Winifred: "He *does* have guests."

Malcolm: "Blast his guests."

Winifred: "Still, it is rather rude of us, when I was told . . ."

Malcolm: "Please be so good as to leave everything to me."

She turns away from him and says nothing more. In any case it is just at this moment that Jean-Marie appears at the head of the stairs. He and Malcolm recognize each other instantly. Jean-Marie's clothes are different, and the glimpse Malcolm caught of him the night before in the glow of the votive lamp was imperfect, but there is no mistaking the person. He glowers up the staircase without a word.

As for Jean-Marie, he feels a double shock. Massimo did not explain that there was a gentleman accompanying the Inglesina. He mentioned earlier in the day that an English lady had called, and Jean-Marie of course understood that it was Winifred. But he has not expected her to be accompanied. A second little twinge passes down his spine when he recognizes her escort as Captain Langrish. He feels so many emotions simultaneously that it is difficult to sort them out: a pleasure at seeing Winifred, an annoyance that his musical has been interrupted, a perplexity what to do with Winifred now that he has the exquisite pleasure of being reunited with her, a resentment at this person who seems to have captured her when she first set foot in Venice and now carries her around the city as though she were his personal possession, a diffidence of Langrish's tall frame, broad shoulders, and saber, a mild panic over how to get rid of Angelìn and the others upstairs without offending them, a wild alternative plan that the thing to do is to get rid of Winifred instead while he thinks out what to do about the rest, and a small satisfaction, the smallest of all the emotions and the least perceptible to Jean-Marie's own consciousness, that he is presenting himself to Winifred in a costume that is informal and has the air, almost of improvisation and yet is elegant and shows him to the best advantage: the English smoking-jacket, a black waistcoat with discreet silver brocade, the loose Turkish breeches, and black-and-silver slippers to match the waistcoat.

He decends the stairs with a smile that increases as he comes, his hand trailing along the marble balustrade. Three steps from the bottom he stops, extends his arms, and breaks into a kind of silent laugh, with his head inclined to one side.

Jean-Marie: "Ma chère Clélia."

He trips down the last three steps, she moves forward, and they are in each other's arms. Winifred murmurs something, her head half-hidden in his shoulders. Malcolm is baffled at the name he has used to greet her. Has he two fiancées and is confusing them? The embrace to tell the truth is more conventional and less passionate than it seemed at first. Perhaps this is because of the presence of a third and a fourth party; Massimo is at the head of the staircase learning more and more from his master. A French grip of shoulders, a touch of each cheek, and they separate, both a little embarrassed now.

Jean-Marie: "Mais comme tu es chic."

He steps back a little to examine the short coat, the pantaloons of latest Paris fashion, and the hunting-hat. Perhaps he expects her to reciprocate by saying the same of him, but if he does he is disappointed. Winifred is endeavoring to control her joy and compose her face into a mask of seriousness, and this involves compressing her lower lip and assuming a look—almost—of severity. These English! they are so complicated. They laugh at adversity and frown when reunited with their fiancés. Instead of expressing joy (which to Winifred goes without saying, it is part and parcel of the situation) she launches into a long explanation of why her arrival at Ca' Pogi has been delayed for two days.

Winifred: "You see, Jean-Marie, first it was necessary to take me to—another place." (It seems that no one is to be entrusted with names and addresses in this sly city full of secrets, perhaps not even Jean-Marie himself.) "Then, when I finally came back to Venice"—(she flushes, having given away the secret that the Other Place was not in Venice—"Mr. Birdsell didn't have your address." (The fault is Mr. Birdsell's; it does not occur to Winifred that Jean-Marie himself might have neglected to call at the Residency and leave his address, since this would not have been True on his part, and it is part of her way of being True that she is obliged to believe implicitly that he is as True as she.) "In the end I went to the Legation, which I wasn't supposed to do and which made M. Villetard very cross" (she is still speaking French and this is *fort agacé*). "But he gave me your address and"—this is the difficult part of it to explain—"Captain Langrish was kind enough to help me find the palazzo, since I . . . don't know Venice very well," she concludes lamely.

It is not a very satisfactory account of her behavior during the day—in fact regarded with severity and rigor it isn't True at all. Winifred is aware of this, and Jean-Marie too, although in his case it takes the form not of jealousy exactly but of annoyance (he is *légèrement agacé*) combined with mild alarm at this formidable figure with his saber, his square shoulders, and his unappetizing scar who seems to be able to go about the city as he pleases, immune to interference both by the French Legation, whose dispatches he has appropriated, and by the Inquisitors and the Council of Ten. Not to mention having appropriated Jean-Marie's fiancée. Jean-Marie doesn't know whether to be grateful or not that Captain Langrish has been so kind as to help Winifred find the Ca' Pogi. He can hardly approve of her going about the city with another man in a gondola. He knows very well the reasons for the felze, the drape that covers the opening at the rear, and the adjustable shutters at the sides. And another idea. With his polyphonous mind he is capable of dealing with many ideas simultaneously. Very fleetingly, and only for an instant, it crosses his thoughts that circumstances have arranged a very curious and unexpected fortune for him in juxtaposing, in a single point in time and space, the two present poles of his existence—the sentimental and the Politickal. Both have fallen into his hands, so to speak, in a single bundle: Winifred is in his arms, or was only a moment ago and is still standing before him, and Captain Langrish, whom he is supposed to be pursuing and separating in some way from the confounded dispatches he has appropriated, has had the temerity to penetrate his house and is standing only an arm's-length away. If he were really competent at his métier he would offer the captain a cup of tea with a suitable drug slipped into it, and then, when he had fallen into a harmless sleep, go through his pockets carefully and extract, if not the dispatches themselves, at least the key to his lodgings where they were sure to be found. The captain, according to this imagined little drama, would awaken a few hours later in the back room of some locanda at the other end of the city, whose proprietors knew only that he had been left there by an anonymous gondolier who has been paid to keep his mouth shut. Unfortunately Jean-Marie has no tea in the house, let alone the proper drug, the name of which, or how to procure it, he hasn't the least idea. All this occupies his thoughts, perhaps, for no more than a second. The impulse that succeeds it is a more practical one, and a good deal stronger: to get rid of Captain Langrish as quickly as possible.

The critical quality of the whole moment—the equilibrium of the situation that is, so to speak, swaying precariously in the balance—is driven home to him even more forcibly when he turns his head to see Angelìn peeking curiously around a column at the head of the staircase, and that fool of a Massimo standing up there too with an asinine grin on his face.

Jean-Marie: "Winifred—Clélia ma chère—I am sure you must be tired. What shall we do with you?" He assumes his most charming apologetic smile. "Unfortunately I live upstairs in a tiny room or two and have no proper accommodations for guests. But there are apartments here off the atrium"—he makes it clear with a gesture of his hand to all, to Winifred herself, the captain, Massimo, Angelìn, even the gondolier himself, that the apartments in question are nowhere near his own quarters—"where you can at least refresh yourself and take a little supper until we find some more suitable arrangement. There is a serving-woman, I believe, who can attend to your needs. Massimo, go fetch the serving-woman, Elena or Elisa or whatever her name is. In the meantime we can only thank Captain Langrish for having so kindly . . ."

Malcolm: "Quite. Good-bye, Miss Hervey."

He turns on his heel and plunges into the gondola.

* * *

The dark little cabin smells of leather, of old perfume, and of salt-water and decaying wood. There is a rhythmic swish as the water goes by outside. Malcolm slumps on the sofa, surveying his boots which are propped on the chair opposite. He is not angry exactly. What is wrong with him? It is as though someone has attached a string to some vulnerable place inside him and is pulling at it. It is that loose tooth! but the tooth is inside his chest. He tugs at the string himself, now and then, to see if it still hurts, but the hurting gives him an odd kind of pleasure. He *is* angry too—he is annoyed at himself in some way for his behavior—although it isn't clear to him precisely how his behavior has been at fault, or how he might have acted otherwise than he did. He feels he is trying to do five or six things at once and doing all of them badly. One of the five or six is what he ought to do, and another—perhaps—is what he wants strongly to do. But—strangely enough—he is unable to identify which of the five or six these two are. He is like a dog chasing a half-dozen different rabbits. They run off in different directions, and in the end he only stops and barks. He bites the side of his finger in the darkness, and finds that he enjoys this too. At last he identifies the disease he is suffering from. It is not a fever at all. It is called Melancholy—an Englishman named Burton has written a book about it. It is caused, it seems, by an excess of black bile in the bloodstream.

He dismisses the gondola in San Luca, not far from the Piazza. The sun has just set but there is a little light left in the sky. He knows the streets in this part of the city perfectly, so well that he could follow them with his eyes shut. He tries it—in fact he is able to go along with his eyes shut, making all the turnings without a mistake, only occasionally brushing his hand against a wall. Pedestrians, not comprehending the game, skirt with Venetian politeness around him. Calle dei Fuseri, the Frezzeria, the Boca de Piazza. He goes through an arched passageway and comes out abruptly into the open. There is a feeling of vastness overhead—he opens his eyes.

He is standing in the middle of the Piazza. A pair of swallows sweep down toward him, bend away sharply, and fleet off upward into the sky like two bullets on a string. And the soaring of these tiny spots, into the boundless infinity of the vault overhead, sets off something inside him. The Piazza twangs and vibrates. He says "Hah!" to himself several times, and inside his chest he begins to feel heart-barks. (A fine Homeric expression—κραδίη δέ οί ἔν-δον ὑλάκτει—his heart is barking within him.) He feels odd, disembodied, light, as though he too might suddenly lose weight and become a thing of the sky like the swallows. His melancholy of a few moments become a joy; or rather he understands now that there can be a kind of melancholy that is a joy, or like a joy. He is content with his unhappiness; he considers it a great privilege and pities the ordinary mortals passing in the Piazza who do not possess it. Clutching it to him, he makes his way across the great open space and in under the arches of the Procuratie on the other side.

Inside the portico it is dark. He floats along, hardly aware of what he is doing, even though his senses are keenly alert. Gray chunks of Piazza go by on his left, alternating with columns. A shadow follows along in these uprights, like some enormous bird perching first on one and then on the other. He watches it out of the corner of his eye. Then he stops and whirls against the wall with his saber drawn.

Malcolm: "Come out of there! Whoever the Blast you are."

Mark Anthony: "Only me, Copn."

Malcolm: "What the Devil are you following me around for?"

Mark Anthony: "Cause you not capable of taking care of your-self. You walking round de city wit your eyes shut, playing blind mon buff wit spooks."

Malcolm: "Well you can clear out now. Your help isn't needed."

Mark Anthony: "Copn, are you quainted wit a person dey call Pipistrelo?"

Malcolm: "Who?"

Mark Anthony: "He de sbirro who go round wit Mister Grand. Big mon but wit small ears on head, resembling to a bat."

Malcolm: "What about him?"

Mark Anthony: "He come to San Trovaso house to inquire after you, just after you leave wit English Leddy. Den he cotch sight of you when you get out of gondola by San Luca, but he lose you again in Frezzeria."

Malcolm: "How could he lose me in the Frezzeria?"

Mark Anthony: "Hoppen because he trip and fall in canal."

Malcolm: "What the Hell have you done? Before these charac-ters were just chasing me. Now we're both in the same pickle."

Mark Anthony: "Dat what I trying to tell you."

Malcolm: "Well, come on then."

They go off together down the portico, keeping close in the gloom under the columns. From the porch of Sansovino's library they launch out into a Piazzetta like an etching, everything in black and washed over with a thin gray. At the Molo a half-dozen gondolas are knocking sleepily against the stakes. There is no one in sight. After a moment a single gondolier takes shape in the gloom.

Malcolm (barking from under his hat): "San Francesco del Deserto."

Gondolier: "Paròn, xe lontàn. That's a long way. Two hours or more on the water."

Malcolm: "Can you take us there or not?"

Gondolier: "Paròn, sì."

ZULIETTA ARISES LATE FROM HER

Zulietta arises late from her couch, which is a kind of Moorish pallet, low to the floor, with rococo scrolls and decorations. Languidly, trailing a scarf, she moves about through the vast marble apartments opening the shutters, which let in not only an orange-colored sunlight but also the ends of a number of snaky vines that are always endeavoring to come in through the windows. She breakfasts on a rusk and tiny cup of coffee, still in her nightgown. The old palazzo where she lives is in a quiet corner of the city near Campo San Cassan, not far from the Rialto. She values her solitude and knows how to enjoy it. It is her private reward to herself for the intimacies she dispenses, to anyone who is able to afford them and who catches her fancy a little, later in the evening.

After breakfast she turns her attention to her toilette. First she removes the nightgown and regards herself critically in the rather tarnished Murano mirror, as the greengrocer might look over his lettuce to be sure it is still fresh, or as the jeweler examines a diamond through his loupe. The glass has patches of gray and gold in it, like continents in a faded chart, but she is accustomed to these and discounts them in appraising the effects of time on form and complexion. She can not reasonably be dissatisfied with what she sees. Anyone's body is a calendar, and on hers the years are clearly marked off, but there are not too many of them (thirty-one to be precise; her most carefully concealed secret is that she was born on the nearby island of Burano in 1766), and their signs are not excessively evident. Partly this is because she is in excellent health and has a naturally perfect complexion. But what strikes the eye in the glass (the outward and glancing, Zulietta in her phenomenal aspect) is a combination of nature and art; and, as time goes on, art tends more and more to take the place of nature. She is realistic about this, and also expert. In short she is competent at her trade—but this is far too crude and ungallant a way to put it. It is not a trade with Zulietta, or even a profession. It is a social state and at the same time a role in the scheme of existence—even the existential scheme if the modern reader prefers—a complex of behavioral tendencies which add up to a coherent and self-consistent although by no means simple character that is immediately recognizable to anyone with a slight knowledge of the world—in short what will come to be known in later epochs as a personality. If it were a trade she would be competent at it. Since it is not a trade it can only be said that she perfectly fulfills her personality. She is all of one piece—but a very special and expensive piece—only for the most discerning collectors.

Zulietta does not take a bath, either in the morning (her morning—that is a half-hour after noon) or at any other time of the day. Baths as everyone knows are unhealthy and a practice confined to Turks, Russians, ancient Romans, and other degenerate races, along with eccentrics like the English. Instead, still standing naked before the mirror, she begins rubbing a certain cream into her face, beginning with a daub on each cheek and then working it outward, downward, and upward with supple motions of her fingers. This if properly done takes ten minutes or more, but ensures the perfect paleness and softness of her hands and face. Then she exchanges the cream for a bottle of cologne-water, pours her left hand full of it, and plashes it liberally over her throat and downward to her breasts and the rest of her body, with especial attention to the places where bad odors might tend to accumulate. As the cologne-water dries she carefully applies kohl to the rims of her eyes with a tiny brush, in such a small quantity that it would require a bigoted spinster of exaggerated prudery—and of excellent eyesight—to accuse her of this cosmetic at all. When all this is done she turns away from the mirror and dresses. This is simple: a sleeveless linen gown cut low around the neck and falling to the ankles absolutely without ornament. For there is still more toilette to do.

For this it is necessary to go up on the roof of the palazzo. And here something has to be explained that is rather complicated. Venetian women of the patrician class have been famed for centuries for the color of their hair, a light auburn touched here and there with glints of gold; a color which in time comes to be known as Titian blond, although it can be seen in the canvases of Tintoretto, Guardi, Canaletto, Veronese, and other painters of the Venetian school as well as those of Vecellio Tiziano. The reason for this phenomenon is in dispute. It may be, as the patricians contend, that they are descended from the ancient Romans, whose frescoes of Pompeii and Herculaneum show women with hair of the same color. Historians are suspicious of this because the patricians emerged from the merchant class and mingled freely with it before the closing of the Golden Book in 1506, and geneticists because there is no scientific evidence for hair-color as a hereditary trait appearing only in the female, as hemophilia does in the male. What is more likely is that the patricians of Venice acquired knowledge of a certain cosmetic, and the means to obtain it, before the other classes did. At any rate, whatever the reason, by the eighteenth century golden-auburn hair has become a mark of superior birth and therefore of beauty (there are other examples in history—the Habsburg nose, the Spanish lisp), and is widely counterfeited by those of other social classes who can discover the secret, or afford to purchase it.

In actual fact there is more than one biondella, as the water that effects this transformation is called. It depends on the original or natural color of one's hair, the method of application, and the technique of insolation that follows, and on the expense one wishes to go to. Some use henna, usually to bad effect, and others India tea mixed with a little potash. The biondella preferred by Zulietta is an infusion of the herb called by Venetians centurea minore—to distinguish it from the common blue-flowered gentian which is used as a tonic—and known to botanists as Gentiana centaurium. Some go to hairdressers to have the thing done, but she, preferring her privacy, performs the ceremony herself. When she is ready, therefore, she calls Marta, the old serving-woman she shares with several other tenants of the palazzo, and together they go up to the roof of the building, Marta carrying the flask of gentian-water and a basin and Zulietta some other things. Marta sets the gentian-water and basin down and leaves. Zulietta is left alone on the altana, a kind of wooden loggia or terrace on the roof of the palazzo, open to the sunshine except for an arbor of vines at one end where one can sit with a book or otherwise take his leisure if the sun is too hot.

For what Zulietta wishes to do the sunshine is necessary. She wraps a kind of light linen towel around her shoulders (it is made especially for the purpose and is called a schiavenetta) and tucks it in place in front. Then, leaning over the basin, she takes a handle with a little sponge at the end of it, dips it into the gentian-water, and begins soaking it into her hair, allowing the excess to fall into the basin and wringing out a dripping lock now and then. This has to be done carefully to ensure an even tinting of the hair. Each part has to be just as wet as every other part. There is no rinsing. When the hair is uniformly wet with gentian-water, and wrung out enough not to drip, Zulietta passes a comb through it briefly. Then she puts onto her head a kind of crownless hat, or more precisely a circle of straw in the form of a hat-brim, called a solana, on which she spreads out the hair to be dried in the sun's rays.

It is a warm and windless day, the air absolutely clear: she can see the large red-and-white mass of the Campanile in San Marco, a half an hour's walk away, as though it were near enough to reach out and touch. Beyond it is the narrower steeple of San Giorgio Maggiore, and a little farther to the left is the squarish bulk of San Zanipolo. The sun, almost exactly overhead, bathes the city in that kind of luminous clarity that suffuses in and around the objects, rendering each one distinct and lucid against its background, and turning everything to bright enamel. All this is not lost on Zulietta, who is an expert in matters of beauty, but the sun also serves to dry her hair. An incidental neatness of Zulietta's day is that, getting up late because of her personality, she arises just at the time when the sun is in a position to turn her hair to Titian blond. If she were an early riser her hair would be a dull brown. And if her hair were a dull brown she would not stay up late at night, and not be able to afford gentian-water. In this way, reflecting the universal symmetry of the Newtonian universe in which she lives—a universe as yet undisturbed by Einsteinian doubts and shadows—her life is a perfectly architectured structure of cause and effect.

Zulietta sits in a wicker armchair in the sunshine, her hair spread out on the solana and the towel around her shoulders. While she waits for the hair to dry she reads a French novel, but since she is not a linguist she reads it in an Italian translation. Although it is perhaps not really a French novel but only pretending to be so because French novels and everything else French are fashionable just now, and perhaps this Rousseau who claims to have written it is really a Russo who wishes to make his name look like French by misspelling it. On the other hand who ever heard of an Italian novelist? So perhaps it really is a French novel. At any rate the action takes place in Switzerland in a château by a lake, and the characters have names like Julie, Saint-Preux, and Wolmar. It is all fairly well done, although privately she considers that this Julie, or Giulia or Zulia, is a little goose for letting herself be drowned simply because she can not choose between her lover and her husband. What is there to choose? If one likes chestnuts can't one like cherries too? One is for the winter, the other for the summer. At any rate, between Julie's whimpering and the young tutor's elaborate and rather affected love-speeches, it passes the time while waiting for one's hair to dry. Zulietta shuts the book up at the point where Julie allows herself to be kissed by Saint-Preux, or in some way is regaled by "a sudden fire darting from his frame," and instantly regrets it. "One unguarded moment has betrayed me to endless misery. I am fallen into the abyss of infamy, from which there is no return." And this trifle, *Julie oppure la nuova Eloïsa*, has cost eight lire at Bonciani's, the bookseller in the Merceria, because it is a forbidden book and its importation or possession punishable by the Inquisitors. Zulietta is familiar with the hypocrisy of Inquisitors because she has had at least one of them in her bed, and he a man of seventy-two.

Zulietta removes the solana from her head, combs out the hair again a little more carefully this time, takes the solana, the sponge, the towel, and what is left of the gentian-water, and goes downstairs to her apartments. There she spends an hour dressing carefully but in an unostentatious and even demure mode, so that when she is finished she might easily be taken for a zentildonna who, while not a patrician, is still of a prosperous and respectable class. Then, taking her purse and a short grayish-blue cloak, she goes out to the Rialto market and spends the rest of the afternoon shopping. This she does in a passive and lazy mood and yet with competence, intuitively rejecting shoddy or overpriced merchandise and resisting the temptation of fine things she has no use for or already possesses. On the Rialto bridge she considers and rejects a necklace of finely spun woven gold, the manufacture of which is a Venetian secret, and the goldsmiths who possess it forbidden under penalty of death from leaving the territory of the Republic. Such a thing would be an investment, but it is one that requires a month's income and is not convenient just now. Instead, in the nearby Ruga Vechia, she buys a pair of low shoes in gilded Florentine leather, with tongues that rise gracefully in the back and cling to the Achilles tendon—a fashion called Grecian and only lately imported from France.

As the sun begins to sink into the lagoon Zulietta goes home. She is mildly hungry, but she is so used to the sensation that she is hardly aware of it. She eats frugally, for professional reasons: a man with large hands might encircle her waist with them. She takes only a rusk for breakfast and nothing at all at midday (that is, for her, at five o'clock). In the evening she gracefully accepts whatever supper comes her way, and if nothing does, orders a little white meat of chicken and a glass of wine at Crespi's. She is not a self-indulgent person but a dedicated one, as much as an athlete or a concert violinist, more (far more in fact) than the average monk of her time. If objection is made to her conduct on moral grounds, reflect that at the time of the visit of the Président de Brosses to Venice in 1739—and things have not changed much a half a century later—three convents were quarreling furiously over which was to have the privilege of supplying a mistress to the newly appointed Papal Nuncio. De Brosses does not record which carried the day. Zulietta is obliged to be skillful because her profession—her personality—is under heavy competition from amateurs. Not all of them are nuns, unfortunately. If they were the situation would be simpler, since they at least are obliged to keep to their convents.

UNDER A NIGHT SO CLEAR THAT

Under a night so clear that the stars seem to shake, Jean-Marie and Balbi glide down the Rio de la Frescada. The two friends sit side by side on the broad leather armchair. Neither feels like talking. Jean-Marie examines his fingers and chews at a hangnail. Balbi, thoughtfully, smokes a long ivory pipe. There is a rhythmic groan as Iseppo turns the oar in the forcola.

A little beyond the Frari the gondola turns into a smaller rio and bumps against the quay. They get out and enter a rather gloomy-looking building with a shrine-lamp burning fitfully in the wall. There is an enormous ogival portal, then a long and dank corridor in lieu of an atrium, then a turn to the right and a chapel with a vaulted gothic ceiling.

The chapel itself is not lighted, and the only illumination comes from the choir-platform at the far end, where a number of lanterns with purplish lenses are set about on tripods. On the wall behind the choir is a crucifix, a rather sanguine one which looks more like a medical illustration than an object of worship. Jean-Marie finds this rather forbidding. He wonders whether he is going to enjoy himself or not. It is not the right atmosphere somehow for music. Still, Balbi has recommended it.

But the audience reassures him. The chapel is only half full, but those who have come seem to represent the very flower of Vene-

tian fashion. Their dress is impeccable—Jean-Marie has thought
that his own umber coat with gold facings would impress, but he is
far from being the most elegant in the chapel. He recognizes a
number of Senators, the wife of a Councillor with a young escort,
and the octogenarian admiral Zusto with some younger officers.
Some people are in masks. There is a pair of priests in lilac
cassocks—they go everywhere together—Jean-Marie knows them
to be on intimate terms.

He and Balbi take their seats, on side-chairs in the Louis Quinze
manner with red-velvet upholstery. For the audience, it seems,
everything is of the very best, but except for these furnishings the
chapel is austere. The Tortured Christ gazes at Jean-Marie re-
proachfully, the clotted blood seeping from the wound in His side
and down into His loin-cloth. There are rattles and coughs, the
usual preliminaries to a concert.

Then, from some gloomy opening in the wall to the left, the
orphans appear, shepherded by a pair of severe Sisters in gray and
white. They trickle up in twos and threes into the choir carrying
their instruments. Finally there are twenty or more of them,
turning and groping about in the confined space, attempting to
find their chairs, grappling with the larger and more unwieldy
instruments like the viola da gamba. They are all female children,
but beyond that there is a great variety. Those that strike the eye
most immediately, perhaps, are the albinos, and those born without arms or legs. But also there are hydrocephalics, giants,
hopelessly obese, and chlorotics. Some have white eyeballs, like
half-curdled eggs. Some are six-fingered. There are mutes: one of
astonishing beauty. There are blue children with defective hearts,
and a completely hairless one. Another is perfectly formed except
that her legs are only a hand's-breadth long, so that her feet begin
just below her torso. She comes in on a platform with wheels, is
helped up to the choir, and rolls along to her chair with her
mandolin. They are all clad identically, in blue smocks, all with
their hair cut to exactly the same length; except the one who has
no hair, or eyebrows either, and is provided with a kind of mob-
cap to hide her shame.

When Jean-Marie tires of looking at the orphans, he raises his
eyes and finds himself exchanging glances with the Christ hanging
on the wall. He sighs. He is too well bred to slump in his chair, but
he begins examining his fingernails again. Balbi, puffing at his

ivory tube, comments on the audience. Everybody comes to the concerts at the Incurabili. It is a custom as Venetian as gaming at Crespi's, or taking the Fresco at sunset in a gondola. He points out Cecilia Tron, a well-known courtesan. Not the kind that frequents ridotti; she has a magnificent palazzo of her own. And there is Marina Querini Benzon, a famous beauty, the one they wrote the song about, *La biondina in gondoleta*. Jean-Marie cranes his head to look. He is not impressed. Ah, says Balbi, but you should have seen her twenty years ago. He himself was only a lad then, but . . . He puffs his pipe in a violent fit of recollection. Still, it is the music they have come to hear. The program tonight is Vivaldi. They are in for a treat. Vivaldi, he explains, was once music-master in this same orphanage.

Jean-Marie: "It was the Pietà, I believe."

Balbi: "What's the difference? It was some orphanage or other."

Jean-Marie: "It's not their fault, perhaps, if they are orphans. But music is not for children."

Balbi: "The Pope has a boy's choir, as I've heard, that makes heavenly sounds."

Jean-Marie: "They are boys who will never be men."

Balbi: "What's a testicle or two among friends? The angels too are sexless."

Jean-Marie: "Be serious, will you?"

Balbi: "I, my friend? I'm always serious. Art comes only out of suffering. There's a Latin proverb for that, but I've forgotten it."

Jean-Marie allows himself to comment only that the material is not promising. It is hard enough to play an instrument if you have all your arms and legs in place.

Ah, but the discipline, explains Balbi. The little girls get up at dawn, eat their polenta, scrub their dormitory and all the other rooms, go to the bathroom to the sound of a bell, and then practice their instruments the rest of the morning under the severe direction of the Sisters. In the afternoon the Dottore comes for rehearsals. To be invited to a rehearsal is an especial privilege; only the most competent lovers of music are accorded this honor. Notice, Balbi suggests, the instruments. The orphanage depends on generous benefactors to provide the best of everything. The post-horn which the albino girl is holding is an authentic Jacob Schmid from Nuremberg. He also points out a Zugtrompete, a curious machine with a sliding mouthpiece that goes in and out, the only example in Venice.

Jean-Marie makes no reply to this. Evidently he is not impressed by the German machine. Balbi puts his pipe back in his mouth. And besides, he adds, just because one has no pigment in the epidermis, that doesn't mean one can't play the post-horn.

There is a stir in the choir. The Incurables arrange the music. Everything is ready.

Then Rossi, who is called the Dottore because he has studied the science of harmony at the Academy of St. Cecilia in Rome, appears and strides briskly to his place on a kind of pulpit with a carved rail, a little higher than the choir. He turns and glances sidelong at the audience—his version of a bow—which produces a flutter of applause. He is a nervous person in an old-fashioned black coat a little too large for him, with a pink and splotchy complexion like underdone veal. His expression is simultaneously harassed and furtive. He resembles, perhaps, one of those anonymous Flemish sinners in the landscapes of Hieronymus Bosch who are afraid to look over their shoulders because they fear, correctly, that some unspeakable demon is following in their tracks. He raps on the stand in front of him, with a kind of rattan crop which might be used for training small animals.

In the hushed silence the Incurables embark on the Fourth Bassoon Concerto in C Major. The bassoon, which is called a fagotto in Italian, is managed by a blind girl who plays with a certain desperation, as though she is barely keeping ahead of Rossi and the orchestra, and yet somehow manages never to miss a note. The first movement of the concerto, an Allegro, consists of four Tutti and three Solo sections. The opening ritornello which sets the pace is full of vivid impetus. It is not easy to maintain this pace on such an unwieldy instrument, but the blind girl, with little creases pulsing around her mouth, follows helter-skelter along with the orchestra. There are descending broken triads, then the same notes turn and go back up the other way. Everything is symmetrical; the whole thing would balance on the point of a pin. The movement ends in a vigorous tutti chord. The blind girl removes the instrument and wipes her mouth with the back of her hand.

The second movement is very fine. It is a Largo divided into three sections: a short prelude by the orchestra including sackbut trills, then a long Solo passage, then a restatement of the prelude by the whole orchestra again. The iambic motif of the opening measure is reiterated in the other two sections. This Largo is as stately as a minuet. The bassoon is not ordinarily considered a lyrical instrument, but in the hands of the blind girl it assumes a sepulchral and primitive dignity, something like a poem of Ossian. The blind girl only chews her lip at the end of this movement. Rossi raps for attention.

The third movement is another Allegro. Again the four Tutti sections embrace and present the three Solos. The tone is gay and insouciant. Rossi saws the air with his rattan crop. The Incurables, at least those that have vision, keep an uneasy watch on this object. It is clear that their knuckles have felt it, when they made mistakes in rehearsal. The creases work around the blind girl's mouth, and the bassoon plunges up and down a series of trills. Rossi too sings the part: "Bibibibi bobobobo bum-bum-bum-bum." Jean-Marie notices for the first time that the two viole da gamba have been consigned to a pair of girls with uncontrollable tremors in their limbs. The vibrato they produce is impressive. By applying every ounce of their determination, they manage to bring the shaking down to exactly that amount of vibration demanded by Vivaldi. Still there is a kind of wild desperation to it, barely in control. It is hardly pleasant to watch, and Jean-Marie turns instead to the giant girl playing the tromba marina, an enormous bowed instrument over seven feet tall, called for some reason, perhaps in irony, the nun's fiddle. She seems totally in charge, and her task is easier since she has only one note to play for every four of the bassoon. She pulls at the bow with gravity, not looking at the audience.

The movement ends to a ragged clatter of applause. Rossi is morose. He has the impression that the concerto was not very well received, perhaps because the winds are not quite up to the triplets yet. Never mind! he will see to it in rehearsal.

There is a brief intermission. The second half of the program consists of the Concerto in C Major for Diverse Instruments, with Mandolins. Vivaldi here has a certain problem of instrumentation, which he has attacked with mastery and converted into a problem for the Incurables. The mandolin is incapable of producing sustained notes, or widely spanning melodies of a lyrical character in slow tempo. The very nature of the instrument demands that it be plucked rapidly. Thus the soloists (there are two, the beautiful mute and the girl with no legs) play mainly semiquavers in the quick movements, and demisemiquavers in the Largo during which the bass is silent. The beautiful mute and the girl with no legs bend over their instruments, their fingers flying so fast they are invisible. The last movement is a kind of ritornello, in which the rapidly plucked mandolins and the rest of the orchestra politely exchange the motif, as though with bows. It ends in a single drawn-out note, the C of which Vivaldi is so fond.

There is a little more applause this time, and Rossi jerks his head to acknowledge it. The Incurables gather up their instruments. The girl with no legs rolls herself to the edge of the choir, carrying the mandolin in her lap. The Holy Victim on the wall holds His arms wide apart, as if to say "What can I do?" Jean-Marie and Balbi stand up while the applause is still trickling through the chapel, and make their way out before most of the others. They go down the corridor and out through the gothic portal, and emerge into a night of heady coolness. Tiny stars like diamonds spring out over the roof-tops—each one a universe like our own, billions of miles away. The two friends are silent. They go slowly down the lane to the bridge where Iseppo is waiting. Balbi has let his pipe go out and is trying to puff it into life again. Finally he gives up.

"Well, my friend?"

Jean-Marie: "The bassoon is not my favorite instrument."

Balbi: "I suppose it's not the favorite of anybody, except bassoonists."

Jean-Marie: "Still there were passages of a certain brio—a stiff unwitting elegance, one might say."

Balbi: "The world is not a perfect place. Vivaldi must work through Rossi, who isn't perfect, and then Rossi must work through the blind girl. Finally the blind girl must work through an instrument which, as we say in Italian, is only a faggot. And out of this there come—'passages of a certain brio'—ah, you are not a philanthropist, my friend."

Jean-Marie: "No, I am a musician."

Balbi: "And the mandolins?"

Jean-Marie: "Mandolins are for country fairs."

Balbi: "I bow to your expertise. But they seemed to me charming."

They have arrived at the bridge. Iseppo inquires where the Paroni wish to be taken.

Jean-Marie: "To the Frezzeria."

Balbi: "O, la, la."

Jean-Marie: "What's the matter with you?"

Balbi: "I beg your pardon?"

Jean-Marie: "Why are you making that odd noise?"

Balbi: "I don't know. It was involuntary. Are you sure you don't want to go back to Ca' Pogi?"

Jean-Marie: "What for?"

Balbi: "I hear rumors of a happy arrival, my friend."

Jean-Marie: "Don't joke. Who told you?"

Balbi: "Villetard."

Jean-Marie: "You are acquainted with Villetard?"

Balbi: "In a diplomatic way. It's perfectly discreet."

Jean-Marie: "Then stick to diplomacy, and leave private affairs alone."

Balbi: "Ma foi. You are a little bit heated."

Jean-Marie: "Why not? My private life is sacred to me."

Balbi: "Oh my Heavens. The cock has his feathers ruffled. A thousand pardons. I never heard of the blessed business."

Jean-Marie: "Are we going to Crespi's or not?"

Balbi: "Very well. But if I were in your shoes, my young friend . . ."

IT IS A SLOW EVENING AT

It is a slow evening at Crespi's. There are only a dozen or so guests, and by eleven o'clock most of these are gone. The times are uncertain and people are preoccupied with other things, Crespi himself complains. What these other things are he doesn't specify. It is not customary in such places to speak of Politicks or other serious matters, and besides everyone knows that a Venetian delegation has been sent to Bonaparte in Austria and that, until it returns, the course that events are to take will not be known. You might expect that if people had troubles they would want to divert themselves. But—the gilded rooms with their green baize tables are half empty. Crespi sips a glass of excellent Malvasia and sighs. He confides to Zulietta that Venice was different when he was a young man. "How?" "Ah—people were more carefree then, my dear girl. One thought of nothing but—pleasure, beauty, music. Now . . ."

Zulietta accepts a glass of wine from him and drifts away across the room carrying it in her hand. All men Crespi's age, she has noticed, complain that Venice was different when they were young men. In her experience there is no lack of interest in beauty, pleasure, and music in present times. Venice is always the same. What people like Crespi mean when they say that Venice is no longer what it used to be is that *they* are no longer what they

243

used to be. Zulietta is in a position to know this even if they themselves don't. That Inquisitor of seventy-two—but never mind anecdotes.

Things become a little more lively, at least, when Zanetto and his friend Balbi arrive a little later in the evening. They take a table with two guests who were about to leave but now change their minds: a bony and morose individual who is patently a priest in secular dress, and a plump young man in calico breeches. Zulietta slips into a chair at the table, but declines with a polite smile when she is offered a hand. The game is panfilo. It is more complicated than faro, and to tell the truth she doesn't understand it very well. There is no banker and each player takes only four cards. The ace of spades is dominant, and if a player manages to acquire the king and ace of the same suit (especially in spades) the others have to pay him a forfeit. This sketchy knowledge, however, is not enough to keep Zulietta interested in the proceedings. She notices only two things: that Zanetto is winning again so that there is a considerable pile of sequins by his elbow, and that he is—not in bad sorts, exactly, or melancholy, but listless. He discards a card, takes another, selects two cards from his four and lays them on the table: the king and ace of clubs.

Balbi: "You're a necromancer, my friend. A sorcerer."

Jean-Marie: "H'mm."

Priest: "Another hand."

The three coins slide across the table and are added to the stack. Zanetto, neat in all things, sees that the pile of coins is about to topple and makes two piles out of it.

Matters go on in this way for several hours. Zulietta plays a hand or two, but quickly loses her own sequin and another lent her by Balbi. (Who is perfectly selfless in this gift, never having had anything to do with Zulietta except speak to her casually in the gaming-rooms.) Zanetto seems to have forgotten to eat. Finally he orders his English bread with meat, but ignores it and the glass beside it as he goes on playing. Zulietta cuts off the end of the sandwich with the knife, eats it carefully to the last morsel, and removes the crumbs from her fingers by licking them one after the other. Zanetto looks up, sees what she has done, and finishes the rest of the sandwich and drinks the wine, rather distractedly.

There *is* something on his mind. It isn't the game either. He is playing to forget whatever it is that is on his mind. And he keeps on playing, beyond his usual hour, so he won't remember what it is that he is playing to forget. Calico Breeches quits, but Zanetto, Balbi, and the disguised priest play on. Zulietta stifles a yawn. Not a yawn of sleep—she is never sleepy at night—but of boredom.

Finally—Zulietta is getting out of sorts herself and has almost decided to abandon the field and see what is happening in some other room—they slap down the cards and rise from the table. All except Zanetto and Zulietta herself. He remains by his pile of coins as though plunged in thought, and she regards him critically from across the table.

Zulietta: "You are hungry?"

He shakes his head.

Zulietta: "You would like to look at the view from a window?"

Jean-Marie: "Perhaps."

The starlight shimmers on the ceiling. The shutters are closed, but the light from the sky reflects on the rio below, then filters through the cracks to make a kind of wavery aqueous effect on the stucco, which is slightly concave with a cornice like a rococo picture-frame running around it. The paint is peeling here and there from the ceiling. There is no sound but the lapping of water, and a kind of faint crackling or whisper that seems to come from the walls.

After a long while they slither apart. Zulietta lies propped on her elbow with one leg crossed over the other. Jean-Marie remains supine for some time with his eyes fixed on the ceiling. She regards him for a while, and then speaks in a deliberately blithe tone.

"Never mind, Zanetto. Perhaps you just don't feel—amiable tonight."

For an answer to this he only sits up and pulls on his drawers.

Zulietta: "And it happens to everyone."

Jean-Marie: "It's the first time."

Zulietta: "Well, it's probably the last."

For a while at least, she thinks—remembering the Inquisitor. She lights the candle. It reveals Zanetto in his shirt, looking about in a lackadaisical way for his breeches, which are on the chair behind him.

Zulietta: "On the chair behind you. You have something to-night, eh, Zanetto?"

Jean-Marie: "Have something?"

Zulietta: "You are thinking about something."

Jean-Marie: "Why shouldn't I think about something? That's my affair."

Zulietta: "Yes, but tonight you are thinking about something that distracts you. You are here but your mind is somewhere else."

Jean-Marie: "Mind your own business, will you?"

Zulietta: "But you see, Zanetto, this sort of thing is my business."

Zanetto, who is adjusting the fastenings of his breeches, glances at her and then turns his back. She knows that he doesn't like to be watched when he is putting on his clothes. What men don't realize is that they look even more ridiculous from the rear, under these conditions, than they do from the front.

Jean-Marie: "Why don't you get dressed? Since, as you point out, I'm thinking about something else."

She rises from the bed stark naked and floats about the room towing a scarf. She can do this free from care because—that part of her—is also Titian blond. She is attentive to every detail.

Zulietta: "Don't forget the—you know."

Jean-Marie: "Even tonight?"

Zulietta: "Of course. The sad fact about failures in this world, my friend, is that we have to pay for them just as if they were successes."

He gets out the four sequins and sets them on the table by the bed. Turning, he finds her regarding him with a long stare, and he takes out another one and adds it to the pile.

Jean-Marie: "Stop prancing around the room with that scarf. You're making me nervous."

Zulietta: "Where are you going now, Zanetto?"

Jean-Marie: "Home to sleep."

Zulietta: "Have you ever been to the Rialto at dawn?"

Jean-Marie: "No."

Zulietta: "Ah, pecato. Then you are not really a Venetian. Come."

She puts her own clothes on, with an insouciant kind of languor, as though she were taking them off to entice him, only in reverse. Her many charms disappear one by one.

* * *

The sky is graying a little now in the east. He has no idea why she is hurrying along so fast—Calle dei Fabbri, San Salvador, the Merceria, Campo San Bartolomeo. He has to exert himself to keep up with her, at her elbow and a little behind. Up and over the Rialto bridge, the shop-fronts gray and deserted, the whole thing insubstantial as though it were made out of mist. On the other side of the bridge it is quite different from the San Marco quarter. It is not elegant at all. There are bad smells, and the pavement is littered with rotten fruit. But Zulietta seems perfectly at home here, in spite of her elegant gown and cape and her gilded slippers. It is a new Zulietta. In place of the nocturnal Zulietta there is—not a diurnal Zulietta exactly—but an auroral Zulietta, born out of this grayish light like a figure of Botticelli.

Lightly, holding her chin high and looking around to see if he is following, she leads the way into Campo San Giacometto with its vegetable market, and its queer little church which is supposed to be the oldest in Venice. A roughly clad crowd is pushing and shouting its way through the campo. Porters are bumping along with enormous crates of vegetables, crying "Ai piedi!" and forcing people to squeeze over to one side. The chests of the porters gleam with perspiration through their unbuttoned shirts. Jean-Marie feels queer. He has never been up so early in the morning; or rather he has never done anything so early in the morning except go straight home to bed. He is suddenly conscious of his clothes. He is dressed with perfect correctness for the evening, but it is no longer evening. But no one so much as glances at him, or at Zulietta either.

The way is too narrow and he has to fall behind her. They cross the campo, pushing their way through the stands heaped with baskets of tomatoes, eggplant, melons, peaches, and grapes. All about are strings of onions, heaps of fennel and lettuce, the jagged green of dandelions. Zulietta seems to know exactly where she is going. On the other side of the campo, emerging finally from the hurly-burly of the market, they go down a short street and come out onto a quay with a broad expanse of water before them: the Grand Canal just before it makes its great curve toward the Rialto bridge.

It is suddenly quiet. Across the water is an unexpected apparition: the Ca' d'Oro, an improbable faery-palace, with its delicate and lace-like columns of stone gradually catching the pink from the sky. Along the quay are the barges that have brought the produce during the night from the islands of the lagoon. The boatmen are still heaving crates out onto the quay, but the work is almost done. And now Jean-Marie sees that other well-dressed couples, most of them young, have come to the market for the same reason: to take a breath of fresh air after the long debauch of the night, to watch the barges being unloaded, and to look at the Ca' d'Oro in the dawn.

Zulietta is hungry. She has taken nothing since breakfast except a glass of wine and the end of Jean-Marie's sandwich. She calls out to a porter, a grimy rascal with a bent back and long dirty fingernails. The fellow evidently knows her. He grins, puts down the crate, and tosses her an orange.

"Sì. Prendi, bela. Ciao."

She catches it deftly and digs into the thick rind. There is a pungent, slightly acrid odor from the oil that springs under her fingers. When it is peeled she breaks it into segments, puts one in her mouth, and offers another to Jean-Marie.

He shakes his head.

Zulietta: "You're afraid you'll spoil your fine clothing."

Jean-Marie: "It's not that."

Zulietta: "Explain your trouble to me, Zanetto, and maybe I can tell you what to do."

Jean-Marie: "I don't think so."

Zulietta: "Explain to me anyhow, because I'm very curious about people's secrets."

Jean-Marie: "You see, I have a . . . fidanzata. A betrothed."

Zulietta: "Is that all? What a terrible tragedy. Everybody has that at one time or another."

Jean-Marie: "Yes but you see, this one is difficult. It's an English."

Zulietta: "Well. What's so difficult about an English?"

Jean-Marie: "This one is difficult. She came all the way from Paris to . . . join me. And now she's here. She is a *lady,* you understand." He uses the English word. "She's very intelligent. Perhaps too intelligent. She is easily bored. She demands to be entertained at all times. It is impossible to have her—where I live."

Zulietta: "Where *do* you live, Zanetto?"

This playfully. He will never tell her where he lives. He imagines it is a secret. But everyone in Venice knows where Zanetto lives. He goes on without answering.

Jean-Marie: "I need privacy. I have friends who come there. I've put her into some rooms on the pianterreno. She has a servant—everything she needs. But she complains she is a prisoner. She bothers me night and day. I don't know what to do with her."

Zulietta: "Perhaps I am stupid, Zanetto, but why don't you marry her?"

Jean-Marie: "It isn't—convenient just now."

Zulietta: "She has lots of money?"

Jean-Marie: "No."

Zulietta: "Then again, pardon my stupidity, but why do you want to marry her?"

Jean-Marie: "I'm not sure I do."

Zulietta: "Then why have you got engaged to her?"

Jean-Marie: "That was in Paris, you see. Things were different there. We used to talk a lot. We talked about fine ideas. She is interested in fine ideas and she speaks well. Somehow there isn't so much to talk about in Venice. And when the talk ends"—he shrugs helplessly—"one doesn't know what do do with her."

Zulietta: "And you haven't—yet—have you, Zanetto?"

Jean-Marie: "How did you know that?"

Zulietta: "I know. But you love her, eh, Zanetto?"

Jean-Marie: Così. She is a very—precious person. Very fine. She makes me better when I am with her. When I am with her I have to think hard, to think of interesting things to say. But that's hard work, you see, Zulietta. She makes me feel—affectionate. One wants to be kind to her. But I'm not sure I could—how can I explain this? It's very embarrassing. You see, she is—" He makes a shape in the air like a long narrow box, about the width of Winifred. "If I married her what would happen? It might be a terrible—what is the word?"

Zulietta: "Fiasco."

Jean-Marie: "Exactly. And in any case, you see, I'm not sure the English are interested in—*that*."

Zulietta: "They seem to have gone on making Englishes all the time."

Jean-Marie: "Yes, but out of a sense of duty. So there she is in the rooms on the pianterreno, and she threatens—" He stops. This thing he is explaining is a very difficult one in all respects. "You see, she entered Venice in a way that was—not quite conventional. The Inquisitors are curious about her. They think she is an agent of the French, which is ridiculous. But what will you? You know how it is. The Inquisitors are suspicious of everybody. Too many people know she's in the house. A gondolier—the servants."

Zulietta: "Gondoliers are not very talkative."

Jean-Marie: "No, but there's also a pesky American captain who follows her about for some reason."

Zulietta: "American?"

Jean-Marie: "American, but a captain for the Venetians. He's already made a nuisance of himself. He knows where she is now. It would be best to get her out of Venice. But one can't leave Venice just now because of the—situation."

He stops, feeling himself on the brink of the risky bourn of Politicks. They go slowly on down the quay toward the fish-market. The sky over the Canal is pink now, shading upward into a pale blue. Then, exactly over the Ca' d'Oro, a blob of flame leaks upward, crawls, wrinkles, and collects into a distorted silver of a circle. Jean-Marie feels the faint warmth on his cheek.

Zulietta puts the last segment of orange into her mouth, even though she has not quite finished the one before it and her mouth is a little too full. A spurt of juice appears. Her effort to restrain it is impeded by her smile at her own bad manners, and the juice descends in a slow trickle onto her chin.

She stops the juice with her fingers, and licks her fingertips. When she is able to speak again she regards him thoughtfully, as though she is pondering. "Well, Zanetto."

He waits for her to go on, but she has nothing more to say. They turn and go off slowly toward the Pescaria. She dips her fingers into a fountain in the fish-market, splashes a little water on her face, and borrows his handkerchief to dry herself. Then she leads him over a tiny bridge and through a series of small connecting streets. After a time they come out in a place where Jean-Marie has never been before: it is Campo San Cassan. Instead of crossing the campo she turns left into another calle, so narrow that he has to fall behind her. She tows him with her hand, which is still cool and slightly damp from the fountain. On the right is the high wall of a palazzo that is difficult to see because the street is so narrow. Presently they come to a heavy iron-bound door. The arch over the doorway is stained with grime. Zulietta produces a pair of keys from the pocket of her cape. She takes the larger one—it is the size of a small spoon—and thrusts it into the door. They enter.

Jean-Marie: "What is this?"

Zulietta: "This is where I live, Zanetto. You won't tell me where you live, but this is where I live."

Jean-Marie: "Ah, then you don't live at Crespi's?"

Zulietta: "Don't be foolish. How can one live at Crespi's? Even Crespi doesn't live there."

What they have entered into is a kind of dank abyss partly open at the top: the atrium of the house. On the left is a broad marble stairway going up to the other floors. At one side of the stairway is a small door, and some pails of slops are standing against the wall. At the far end of the atrium is a kind of wavering grayness in the shape of an ogive—the other door that opens onto the rio. The stones are damp and smell faintly rotten.

Zulietta: "Wait here."

She disappears into the small door at the side. He can hear her quarreling with someone, evidently a servant. The other voice is sleepy and petulant, Zulietta's is adamant. After only a short while she emerges with a triumphant little smile. She holds up a forefinger. Around the finger is an iron ring, and attached to the ring are two keys like her own.

"Come."

She leads the way up the broad and elaborately carved stairway to the piano nobile. Beyond this the stairs are narrower and less elegant. Once they have left the light from the atrium it is almost dark. He follows her quite blindly. After several flights she stops on a landing with three or four doors on it. Zulietta goes to the last door and opens it with the smaller of the two keys on the ring.

Inside a thin light penetrates through the shutters and Jean-Marie is able to see something for the first time. There is a salon, a dining-room, a small bed-chamber, a kitchen and a pantry, and a cubicle with a mattress on the floor and some carpenter-tools. The furnishings are worn and somewhat shabby but of good quality, in the style of the century before. Everything is in place: books in the shelves, a prie-dieu in the chamber, candles in the bronze candlesticks, even pens and ink on the writing-table. There are paintings that are evidently family portraits. The floors are marble and cold.

Jean-Marie: "Who lives here?"

Zulietta: "Nobody, now. Before, Austriacanti." Which is what the Venetians call Austrian sympathizers. "When the French came too near, they were afraid and went to Vienna. Don't worry. They won't come back for a while."

Jean-Marie: "But—whose house is this?"

Zulietta: "A crazy old woman. My good friend. You can trust her. She's too crazy to tell anybody anything. No one would believe her. Your Inglesina will be safe here. A servant can bring her meals. You can visit her, and . . ."

Jean-Marie: "What?"

Zulietta: "Talk about things. Your fine ideas."

She seems to be in an excellent mood. She is smooth, slightly amused at something, almost pert. She holds out the keys with her finger through the ring, as though it were a game. He takes them and puts them in his pocket.

Out on the landing she takes her own key and goes to another door. When the door is opened she turns back to him for an instant. Her face is a pale blur in the darkness.

Zulietta: "So good evening, my friend. Or rather good morning."

He finds himself excited by the darkness and the silver liquidity of her voice. He moves forward and slips an arm about her waist. He is aware of the faint scent of orange—not the juice but the bitter fragrance of the rind.

Zulietta: "You forget, Zanetto. I've already told you I live here."

At the expression on his face she makes a little laugh—not regretful exactly, on the contrary playful, perhaps even with a faint nuance of irony. He manages a smile himself. She is about to close the door but he holds his hand against it.

Jean-Marie: "Listen. That nuisance of an American captain. He may find her even here. You understand, the Americans speak English too, so he can"—he finishes the sentence rather lamely—"speak to her in her own language."

Zulietta: "But what would he do if he found her?"

He says nothing.

Zulietta: "But you say the English don't do—*that*. And besides you don't want to. So what do you care, Zanetto?"

WINIFRED IS TRANSLATED TO

Winifred is translated to San Cassan this same morning, in a gondola accompanied by Jean-Marie himself and by Massimo who comes along to carry the portmanteau and the hat-box. There is no sign of Zulietta. She is out, or remains tactfully asleep behind her locked door. Jean-Marie opens the apartments with the key provided, stays for a few minutes to be sure everything is satisfactory and the portmanteau is set in a convenient place for Winifred to unpack, and then most tenderly takes his leave, embracing her in the continental manner and almost, but not quite, deciding to kiss her on the lips. (Massimo is standing there looking on, the nuisance.) The serving-woman appears, inquires as to Winifred's wishes as to meals, and also provides bed-linen and other necessities. Then she goes away. The apartments are vast and empty.

The whole business—the palazzo with its leprous gothic decorations, the ivy that grows on it as thick as a man's arm, the rio under the wall—seems to Winifred most romantic. She greatly prefers her new lodgings to Ca' Pogi, even though it means being separated for a time from Jean-Marie. (Besides for Winifred, in spite of her advanced ideas, there is something slightly questionable about inhabiting the same house as one's fiancé; even in Venice, and even when one occupies different floors. There is—no one to *supervise* at Ca' Pogi. No duenna like the aunt in Paris. It is awkward. Even though Jean-Marie behaved like a perfect gentleman and hardly showed himself during the two days she spent there.) San Cassan is quiet, in a remote part of the city. In the silence you can hear the water lapping at the decayed and slightly foul-smelling stone under the windows. Now and then a little sunlight manages to touch the rio, and the reflection plays delicately on the ceiling with its heavy wooden beams. Winifred feels at home, for the first time since she left the house of her uncles in London. Even more than in London—since for some reason she feels from the beginning that these rooms in this gloomy and dilapidated old palace are hers. It is a common sensation of sojourners who stay in Venice for more than a few days that in some way they have *always lived there.* It sometimes happens that there are places and landscapes familiar to us not because they exist but because we inhabit them every night in recurring dreams. Venice has many characteristics of these dream-cities: it is insubstantial, the vistas resemble each other and are interchangeable, you lose your way and find yourself in a street you never knew existed even though it is only a few steps from your door, and so on. And also there is the quiet, the absence of carriage wheels, or of vehicles of any sort. "I have dreamed of this house," thinks Winifred.

According to Marta (who resembles a decrepit sibyl, and must know a good many things), the house is called Ca' Muti Baglioni, and it is owned by an old lady who in some way is entitled to bear a salamander on her coat-of-arms. She is simply the Parona; she has no other name. The quality that Marta attributes to her is chiefly a very old age: "Xe vechia, sa." Since Marta herself seems to have at least seventy years, this information is impressive. The Parona must be very old indeed. Marta says that she has, perhaps, a century. Or possibly she is only mumbling something about supper. The two words are similar: cena, cento. There are many mysteries, as there always are about things romantic.

Ca' Muti Baglioni is, in truth, a rather curious and interesting palace, if such a grandiose term can be applied to it. As early as 1604 it is cited in Stringa's description of the city as one of the most remarkable houses of Venice: "Stupendous and singular, but even more marvelous would it appear to all if it had been built along the Grand Canal." In fact it is a curious place to erect so pretentious a house. It has a magnificent façade facing the water, but the tiny rio is barely wide enough for a gondola to pass, so that the façade is invisible from any point except the roof-top opposite. A small fragment of it can be glimpsed if you stand at just the right place in Campo San Cassan. On the other side, Calle Muti is so narrow that you can touch both sides of it with your hands. The palazzo is only a wall rising up in a dank alley and disappearing into the shadows overhead. Yet this façade, and the other on the water, are both patently intended to be seen. One explanation is that the builders planned to pull down the houses around and create a broad campo in front of it, but reckoned without the profound inertia of the Venetians, who never pull anything down until it falls of itself. At any rate, by the middle of the seventeenth century it was well enough known that it had given birth to a popular saying: anyone who sat silent in a corner would be taunted, Vien de Ca' Muti, he comes from the House of the Dumb. The name of the place itself is obscure. It may have been built by the Muti, and then bought by someone else named Baglioni. Or perhaps the name merely means, "The Baglioni who never say anything."

The next reference after Stringa's is over a century later. A Venetian diary in the Biblioteca Marciana (Codex 58, Class XI) records that when Francesco d'Este, Duke of Modena, was chased out of his territories by the King of Sardinia, he stayed for a time in the house, for which he paid a rent of a thousand ducats a year. The owners must have come down in the world by this time, since they were ready to rent out their palace and move to more modest quarters. At any rate, by the end of the century any pretense that it was a seat of aristocracy had been abandoned. Neither the Muti nor the Baglioni ever appear in the Golden Book. The house, like many other fine palazzi in the period of the decline of the Serenissima, was subdivided into apartments. The only other reference to it in history is the fact, recorded in the municipal archives in the Ca' Grande, that it caught fire in 1736. This is perhaps why there is a salamander over the doorway.

Winifred, as near as she can tell, is free to come and go as she pleases. She spends the rest of the morning exploring her new lodgings—a lengthy undertaking in itself, since there are many rooms. Far more than she has need of, and countless wardrobes, cabinets, closets, cupboards, and chests, any one of which might contain something fascinating and valuable, although as it happens none of them do. At midday the old woman appears with cold veal, polenta, and bread, along with a flask of wine.

Winifred: "Tea. I don't drink wine."

The old woman doesn't understand.

Winifred: "Tè inglese."

The old woman takes the strange monosyllable for a second-person pronoun, an ungrammatical one. No, she isn't English, she replies crossly. "So' de San Polo, io."

Winifred dismisses her, flings off her clothing, opens the portmanteau, and puts on the long narrow trousers, military coat, and English walking-boots. In this large city, a city as large as Bristol or Manchester even though it is full of foreigners, surely there is some tea to be found, and she will find it. Standing before the mirror, she adds the beige hunting-hat. All the mirrors in Venice are tarnished but this is the worst. It resembles, perhaps, a magic sea into which many treasures are sunk, its surface rippled by a faint breeze. She is pleased. Her reflection stirs like a wraith under the silver surface, and smiles. The hat is at exactly the right angle. She goes out.

The fact is that she has seen little of the city during the three days she has spent in it. (Four if you count the night she landed on the Molo with Captain Langrish.) Most of the time she has spent moping, reading, or pacing impatiently in Ca' Pogi. The exception is the day she spent searching over the city for Jean-Marie. But then the new scenes were so confusing, and the search so distracting, that she noticed little except that the streets were narrow and there were no carriages. Now for the first time she has the leisure and the peace of mind to absorb some sense of the place, like the observant young woman that she is.

The first thing that happens is that, at the Ponte de le Do Spade only a few steps from the palazzo, she is stopped by an old man who insists that she buy a lemon. He is a mythological figure, a kind of Charon or transcendental janitor. A lemon is good, he tells her. Fa bene a la salute—it is good for health. One can put it on fish. Or you can put it in your tea. And so on. Finally, in order to be able to pass, she buys it and eats it like an apple as she goes along.

For two hours or more she ranges more or less at random, from Campo San Polo to the Rialto, looking for tea. Or pretending to—this search has now been submerged in the intoxicating new-ness of the sense of place. She is in the humor of the newly arrived tourist to whom everything is a delight, even things that are exactly as they are in his own country, such as the street-lamps and the dogs who wander about sniffing in gutters. The novelty of it, and the charm and difference from London, is that in the milder climate everything is done out of doors. The whole city is like a great domicile in which people carry on their lives without leaving the house. The narrow streets and canals are the hallways, the campi the rooms. From one street to another they bargain, dis-pute, quarrel, or make love as they would inside a house inhabited only by a few families. Carpenters, cobblers, and blacksmiths work in the open air, sometimes stretching a canvas overhead to protect them from the sun. The streets are festooned with laundry; Winifred has to step nimbly, sometimes, to avoid the drops from a bed-sheet far overhead. Tiny children barely able to walk stand half-naked in doorways with their fingers in their noses, watching her gravely as she passes. The older ones play quoits with rough loops of rope, or hopscotch on lines crudely chalked on the stones. Everywhere there are smells. Jutting from the walls of some houses, over the canals, are little closets that serve as privies, with their openings just above the water-line. The smells are bad, but so are the smells of London, and these smells are different from London smells, because they are *foreign*. Some cheeses smell bad too, but they are expensive and come from abroad, therefore good. So Winifred reasons—her mind working against her slightly outraged olfactory sense. She makes her way back up the street, away from the stench of the canal. The street is even worse.

In Campo San Polo a fritter-vendor has set up shop, with a brazier of charcoal and a tub of boiling grease. A boy helps her by scooping out the fritters with a sieve and setting them on a bench. Nearby is a vendor of boiled tripes and offal. Everybody, it seems, is either buying or selling something. All Venetians wish to be shopkeepers, but since some are too poor to keep shop, they become instead itinerant artisans and peddlers of all kinds. Buzzola-vendors go about carrying their ring-shaped buns stuck onto long sticks. There are knife-sharpeners, vinegar-vendors, costermongers, and peddlers of all kinds of second-hand junk and ironwork. The chimney-sweeps are like those in London except that they wear close-fitting breeches like juggler's tights, and flowing caps instead of top hats. The vendor of rat-poison carries a staff with three dead rats hanging from it like flags, to indicate the efficacy of his product. Dogs follow him barking; little children are afraid and have to be reassured by their mothers. The flint-vendor cries: Azzalini mi gho per batter fuogo! He wears a tricorne like a French gentleman, but all battered and greasy. Another man, if Winifred understands his cry, will repair your broken pottery or castrate your cat, according to your need. All this activity seems to be in no whit discouraged by Politickal events or the fact that Venice is to all intents a besieged city. Food continues to come in from the islands of the lagoon, and the Venetians go about their mild and honest commercial ways, making money and spending it, eating polenta and little birds, crossing themselves in front of churches—just in case, even though they aren't believers.

By the church of San Polo a man urinates against a wall while his dog, taking advantage of the opportunity, defecates in the middle of the campo. Winifred doesn't care for *that*. She wanders back again toward the Rialto, asking for tea along the way. No one has ever heard of it. It must be found somewhere in the city, since it is served in Caffè Bertazzi. And the old man, the Lemon-God, said there would be tea. At least she thinks he did. It isn't quite clear what sort of shop it would be sold in anyhow; there don't seem to be any grocers. In Campo Sant'Aponal a mountebank has set up his outfit and is offering miraculous nostrums, guaranteed to cure fever, toothache, and impotence for only a few coins. A little farther on an astrologer is doing a brisk business in horoscopes, which he writes out inside a black box with curtains in the front, like a tiny theatre. She decides not to have her horoscope written. To know one's fate! One doesn't want that. Instead she crosses the street to watch a poultry-vendor plying his trade. He looks like a chicken himself; he has a bright and piercing look, and there are hairs on his bony Adam's-apple. Without taking his eyes off Winifred, he removes a chicken from the wicker box. Still staring straight at her, he wrings its neck—without changing his expression. She flees.

By way of the Ruga Vechia she comes out presently in the Rialto, where the market, at this hour, is broken up into a squalor of abandoned crates, vegetable-ends, and rotten scraps of fruit. A lone vendor who has not yet sold his five Mazzorbo melons is doggedly staying on until someone takes them at the price which he refuses to reduce.

Winifred: "Tè?"

Melon-vendor: "Cossa?"

Winifred: "Tè inglese?"

The man, shaking his head and even scratching the stubble on his cheek in thought, tells her politely he has never heard of it: "Xe cossa che no gho mai sentìo."

She crosses the campo to the other side, which is a little more promising. Here under the portico are shops with ham, dried codfish, barrels of sardines, cheese, olives, rice, and sweet Malvasia wine.

Do you know where one may buy tea?

She stares at the Venetians, they stare at her. They observe her with the same detached curiosity that might be aroused by a hen laying eggs of some novel shape, pyramids for instance. H'mm, look at that. Her costume, they feel, is a thing worth examining for at least a few moments before one goes on one's way. Xe inglese, sai. She hears them calling her the Inglesina. Her hunting-cap with its feather provokes some admiration. Evidently the Venetians are connoisseurs of hats. Their own hats are of all kinds: soiled and bent tricornes, turbans, long flowing stocking-caps, others that are simply cylinders of canvas like oversized fezzes.

An inspiration comes to her.

Tè cinese?

Since she can not possibly be saying to a person, You are Chinese? even in bad grammar, this is quickly grasped. Ah bene, Chinese tea. For that you have to go to the speziarìa. And where or what is that exactly? All of them raising their arms together, they point off across the campo and into the street on the other side. Tuto dreto, they assure her. She knows that tuto dreto! Nothing is straight in this city that seems to consist entirely of corners, dog-legs, and streets that come to an end in dank court-yards. A half-dozen or more offer to show her the way—children follow along, and a stray dog or two. The speziarìa proves to be in Campo Sant'Aponal, where she stopped earlier to watch the astrologer. It is a kind of shop where drugs and spices of various sorts are sold, a place with a medicinal smell, a mortar and pestle on the counter, white-enameled jars labeled with the names of specifics, in short a kind of apothecary. Here she is quickly sold a handful of tea wrapped in a twist of paper.

The collection of guides explain this to each other. You see, it's tea that she wanted. Chinese tea. No, it's English tea. The English drink tea as we do coffee. Bah! it's medicine. Paese che vai usa che trovi, they conclude—no telling what foreigners will do.

This small entourage trails her for a little while as she leaves the shop, but evidently the fun is over. By the time she has crossed the Ponte de le Do Spade and entered the narrow and crooked street beyond it, only a small boy is still following. She turns around and stares him down. He stops, his finger in his mouth. She goes on alone. She is a little uncertain about the way, but she believes that by following this street she will come out after a while in Calle dei Botteri. There, she does. Now one enters the small lane to the right, hardly more than a passage, and in a few yards—

Her way is blocked by a muscular person of the lower classes. She has never actually seen a bravo, yet instinctively she knows that this is a bravo. Behind him is another figure with a pale broad face. Winifred recognizes him instantly as the pudgy man in the frock-coat who came to Villa Baraoni for her. He does not look any more savory now than he did then. An odor of male perspiration and unclean linen assails her nose. She turns, but one is on one side and one on the other.

Frock-Coat: "Siorina, you will follow me, please."

Winifred: "I'll do nothing of the kind."

Frock-Coat: "Please to follow me."

She attempts to slip into a doorway—it is a flower-shop and she observes with clarity a wisp of straw on the pavement, a carnation crushed and soiled underfoot—but Frock-Coat seizes her by the arm. Bravo does nothing, he only stands there with his ape-like arms hanging down, but patently he is capable of doing the same or more if she resists. The pressure on her arm makes a shock run through her, as though she were touched by something repugnant and toad-like. She stifles an impulse to scream. This would be futile and it might even be contrary to her interests. It would only result in more violence like a hand over her mouth—a thought she can not abide. She turns and goes back down the lane with them. Frock-Coat still holds his hand on her arm. There is not room for three to go abreast and Bravo follows behind. She thinks she can feel his breath on her neck, but this is probably only imagination.

They only have to go a little distance. After two or three turns to right and left (in the emotion of the moment Winifred neglects to notice exactly where they are going) Frock-Coat stops before a doorway, taps on it once with his fingertips, and the door opens silently. Winifred is made to go inside. Frock-Coat still holds her left arm, and Bravo is on the right almost touching her. He *is* touching her if she makes the slightest move in that direction. With a kind of snail-like convulsion she pulls an inch or two away.

There are no windows in the room, or the shutters are closed. It is a place where the poor live. The furniture is rudimentary. Straw is strewn on the floor, and there is a sour smell of cooking. On a rude deal table across the room a candle-end gutters in a saucer. In its light she sees before her a strong-armed brassy woman who looks as though she might have been a streetwalker, before she grew too old and fat for it. Her hair is drawn back tightly with a comb, making her eyes seem to protrude. Her breasts are enormous. Two great udders strain at the blouse and pull it apart at the top where it is laced with a cord.

Frock-Coat at last releases her arm.

Woman: "Come, Siorina."

She leads Winifred into the bed-chamber. It is very small, only large enough for a brass bed, a chair, and a chamber-pot, this last in plain view. There are no windows and it is dark. A faint yellow light comes through the half-open door. It is better to have the door open, even though Frock-Coat and Bravo are only a few steps away in the other room.

In three minutes or so the woman satisfies herself that Winifred is carrying nothing on her person except her money, a handkerchief, the keys to her rooms, and the small package of tea in its twist of paper.

Woman: "Where is it, Siorina?"

Winifred makes as if she doesn't understand.

The woman motions toward the doorway. In the other room she exchanges a look with the waiting men. No one says anything. Frock-Coat, after a hesitation during which Winifred wonders what will happen next, goes to the street-door and opens it. Winifred, as in a dream, passes through the door and out into the sunlit street: an ordinary world, the usual laundry hung out to dry, a child playing in the gutter, an inquisitive dog who looks up at her as she passes. She still feels odd, as though she has been suddenly chilled by some ice-apparatus and then warmed up again. She is feverish and cold at the same time. The place on her arm where the pressure of fingers has enclosed it still burns.

She is totally lost and has to ask a woman sweeping out a doorway for Campo San Cassan. Tuto dreto, Siorina. She follows over a strange bridge, under a passageway, around a jog to right and left and, instead of coming out in the campo as she expects, finds herself in the narrow street before her own doorway.

She makes certain that the heavy door is latched behind her. Then she goes up the broad staircase to her rooms. As soon as she enters she senses that something is different. The rooms have been ransacked and everything turned upside down. The doors of the wardrobe are open, the clothes flung out. The covers are stripped from the bed. The portmanteau is tipped over and its contents strewn out on the floor, but the purse with her money is intact.

She sits down on the wreck of a bed. She will have to call the old woman, she thinks, to put everything straight again. No, it would be better to do it herself. No, better call the old woman. And tell her: the Inquisitors, you see, have turned my rooms upside down, and you must help me set them to rights. She must know about it anyhow, since things could not have been turned so hugger-mugger without a great deal of noise. In fact she must have lent them a key, since the door is unbroken. But perhaps it was not the Inquisitors, she now sees. More probably it was M. Villetard himself who arranged to have her rooms ransacked while Frock-Coat was holding her safe in that dingy den. Yet she feels no particular rancor toward M. Villetard, or the Inquisitors. Her rancor is purely physical. It is directed toward Frock-Coat and the grasp on her arm. Noli me tangere! She begins to form a reverie in which she and Frock-Coat meet again in the same circumstances, except that Winifred is able to produce a loaded pistol from her coat and level it. She sits on the bed for some time rehearsing this little drama. Pistols are quite simple—she has never worked one but she would know how. You pull the trigger, the flint snaps, and there is a flash and a loud noise which you have to brace against so it doesn't throw off your hand. She wouldn't really fire though.

She dislikes loud noises. What would she do? She would require Frock-Coat to mount onto a bridge and step into the canal. She imagines him bubbling, his hat floating over his head, until he manages to claw his way back to the air in a pool of sewage. It is a satisfying thought. It makes the itchy circle on her arm feel better.

After a while she gets up, rings for the old woman who comes to clean up the mess without a word, and makes herself some tea. The tea is vile. It *is* Chinese tea, probably of the kind drunk by coolies. She enjoys it very much, and makes something almost like an English high tea out of it, with some veal and scraps of bread left over from the meal at noon. With the tea inside her the last of the coldness is gone. She feels English and confident again, but not in the same way; she is changed. What has happened has affected her profoundly: not only the nasty episode in the bed-chamber but that other oneiric and insubstantial charm of the city—the mountebanks, the wandering vendors, the poison-man with his rats, the insistent and curious but not unfriendly procession that followed her when she bought the tea. Even the scene in the bed-chamber is gradually transformed in her mind and loses its sharp edges. The woman did not really touch her in any immodest way. She was very skillful and even performed her office with a kind of respect, a deference. The whole thing—on reflection now with the tea inside her—seems very Venetian to Winifred, as she understands Venetian. Sinister and polite at once, with the complicated flavor of the decadent—smelling bad only because the stones of the city are very old. It is true that the bread is bad. It crumbles into a kind of plaster when broken and has no taste at all. But Winifred eats it dutifully and will hear nothing against it, even in her own mind. It is *her* Venice now, she has lived in her palazzo for a whole day and the city already belongs to her in the secret landscape of her dream-mind: even if the dream is faintly tinged with nightmare.

TOWARD EVENING THERE IS

Toward evening there is another event or development, also slightly dream-like: as her scale of existence improves, things slide off more and more into the realm of the improbable. There is a knock on the door—it is the old woman. Still cross (she isn't really cross perhaps, or at least not cross at Winifred, it is simply the way her face is made), she mutters something about a gondolier. What about the gondolier? The gondolier is here. How, here? What gondolier? The old woman has no English, Winifred only a few words of dialect. The two of them grope in a thick cloud of misunderstanding. The gondolier is below. The old woman points to the floor. Well, have the nuisance come up! Faites-le monter! cries out Winifred in French, exasperated. The old woman grasps the verb, a cognate in all the Latin tongues, and goes away to make the gondolier mount.

After a few moments he enters timidly: a young man in baggy trousers and a worn and faded purple jacket, carrying a round straw hat in his hand. He stands by the door, hardly daring to enter the room, saying nothing.

Winifred is perplexed. "But you're the gondolier from the Legation." "Siorina, sì. But not anymore. Now I am the Siorina's gondolier." "Mine? And . . . but what about M. Villetard?" "Sior

264

Villetardo has several gondoliers. For a time I am to serve the Siorina." "I don't understand. Who says?" "Sior Villetardo." "I see. And how do you call yourself?" "Nando."

And so Nando is her gondolier. Like a fine lady, like any patrician, she can come and go as she pleases, not only by the land-network of the streets but by the water-network that interlaces it, the way of the rich and privileged. But where is she to go? She has no errands, and no one to visit.

At this hour, Nando explains (it is five o'clock), the thing to do is to take the Fresco.

What is that exactly?

Ecco, Siorina.

Holding a hand out behind him like a dancer, and looking around to see if she is following, he leads her down the staircase—across the gloomy atrium—the gondola is waiting at the water-stair. The small cabin has been removed and it is open to the sky like a barouche. He lifts his hand to help her into it: his touch is cool and he arranges her delicately on the black upholstery, as though she were an expensive vase that might break. He sculls away with a stroke of his oar from the two large ornamental pali, set into the mud not quite straight, with traces of gilt-and-blue paint still clinging to them. They go down the rio and come out onto the Grand Canal. A wide curve to the right; Nando turns his oar and allows it to trail in the water.

Nando is right that the thing to do is to take the Fresco. The air is tepid and motionless, faintly chill when the gondola slides under the shadow of a wall. The water of the Canal, slightly oily, has a gleam like shot silk. There are other gondolas on the Canal, most of them open like hers so that the occupants can inspect each other from a respectful distance as they pass: a bewigged gentleman and a young lady who is perhaps his niece, two gallants with a mandolin, families with children sitting primly upright on the chairs, a solitary old countess with a fan. Winifred is an object of especial attention, with her military jacket and hunting-cap. Who is this long-faced calm creature—the yellow feather in her hat exactly matching the ribbon that ties her hair in the back? Not a German, she is too chic. Not a French, she is too odd. Not a Chinese or a Persian or an Esquimau. An English, they decide with their unerring instinct about foreigners. Ecco! xe un'Inglesina. You see all sorts of things on a Fresco. It is worth doing, not only

for the air but for the things you see. There is always something to
see.

Beyond the Rialto bridge there are more gondolas—dozens,
scores. If there is a war on the Terraferma these Venetians have
not heard of it, or think it better manners to ignore it. The more
elegant gondolas, or those with families, have two gondoliers. Is
she infra dig. in having only one? She isn't sure. Nando is perhaps
not dignified but he is certainly decorative, even though he is
hardly more than a child. His manner is deferential, but offhand and
a little shy. He wears his straw hat tilted a little to the front, at a
rakish angle somehow at odds with his quiet, easy-moving, modest
character—*fragile* is the word that occurs to her even though he is
lean and strong—his quiet and fragile character. And somehow
too—there are all kinds of somehows in this business of Nando—
they understand each other, since Nando—perhaps out of shy-
ness, or because she is a foreigner, or simply because it is his
way—speaks slowly and distinctly, forming each sentence, explaining things over again when he sees she doesn't understand. Since
both hands are occupied with rowing, he points things out with his
hat. Ecco, Siorina, Ca' Foscari. Ecco the church of San Samuele.
Ecco the house of Desdemona. Bah, says Winifred. Desdemona is
only a story. Yes, but this is where the story was. This is Desdemona's house. Ecco, Siorina, the church of the Salute.

They reach the cornucopia-shaped mouth of the Canal, where it
emerges finally into the open lagoon. On the right is the
Customs-House with its odd weathervane, a gilded ball with a
female bronze figure on it, one leg cocked like a dog, catching the
wind with a bit of bronze drapery she has removed from her
person—Xe la Fortuna, Siorina. His serious face offers no comment either on her nudity or on the metaphysical implications of
this uneasily balanced Fortune: which way do the winds blow?
From the Terraferma, from the west.

On the other side, to the left, it is not necessary to call attention
to the vista. The Piazzetta calls attention to itself, with a kind of
visual fanfare—a clash of cymbals deafening to the sensibility and
even a little excessive in its gorgeousness. The great Basilica is
more like a mosque than a church—a pile of polychrome pastry,
all gilt and circumstance, with a collection of cupolas arranged
more or less at random on top. The cupolas are like a heap of

convex objects for some mysterious purpose, gilded and expensive, for sale on a merchant's counter. The Basilica is preeminently a feminine thing, almost embarrassingly so. Nando makes no comment on the gilded breasts. He does, however, remark on the Campanile, which rears straight upward on the other side of the Piazzetta, connected to no church, immensely high, red and vigorous, ending at last in the slender pyramid of stone at the top: We call him El Paròn de Casa, Siorina, the master of the house. The blood mounts lightly to Winifred's face.

The Piazzetta is behind. Now it is the Ducal Palace. Winifred feels a frisson at the thought of the dungeons. But, as she herself told Captain Langrish, they probably do not put women in the Pozzi. They go on down along the Riva with the broad expanse of the lagoon on the right. Here and there a patch of trees, or a slightly leaning steeple, appears improbably out of the water in the distance.

Winifred: "And those islands?"

Nando: "Ecco, that one is San Lazzaro. And San Servolo. And the Carmini."

Winifred: "Ah! there are Carmelites?"

Nando: "Sì, Siorina. They are nuns. Mùneghe."

Winifred: "And what do they do?"

Nando: "They pray, and take care of the unfortunate."

Winifred feels a little twinge of—what? of nostalgia, remembering the Sisters in Passy who were so kind, who knew everything, who assuaged one's little sorrows. She would like to ask Nando more about the Carmini, but the simplicity of his phrase seems to end the discussion. They are both silent for a while. The gondola has left the lagoon and turns back into the complicated clutter of the city. They go down a rio with houses on both sides, linen draped from the windows, a camel-backed bridge which they slip under in absolute silence, broken only by the murmur of the trailing oar. Without seeming to pay very much attention to what he is doing, he guides this long-necked black bird exactly where he wants it to go. The monuments of interest in these parts, which he points out with his hat, are chiefly churches. Ecco, Santa Marina. And that one, Santa Maria dei Miracoli. (A real miracle—a tiny shrine of pink-and-gray marble, as if carved from rock-salt and then tinted.) These spectacles are mingled in her mind with the mysterious bird-like cries which Nando emits at crossings, or at places where the view ahead is hidden: Ah-o-é! Or sometimes: Valo de là? is anyone coming? If someone comes, the two gondolas slide past each other in silence, although the occupants stare at each other while pretending not to—a Venetian art.

Unexpectedly they come out on the Grand Canal again at a point not far from the Rialto. The Fresco is almost over. There are only a few gondolas left now on the Canal. The sun has set; the palaces still glow faintly in the gray light. Winifred turns to look behind. Nando's left hand is on the oar-handle, his right farther down on the shaft, pushing in the odd steady rhythm with the twist at the end that leaves an oily swirl in the water. The wake astern, spreading and dissipating slowly, is as straight as a pencil-line across a not very clean piece of paper.

Winifred: "But how can you make it go straight when you are rowing always on one side?"

Nando: "Very difficult, Siorina."

Winifred: "But how?"

An English is a funny thing. Not to be understood. She *would* find out. And the next day she does. For a Venetian of quality to take an oar in his hand is unthinkable. For a lady—you don't even think of thinking of it. But although the Siorina is clearly a milady, she is a foreigner and she does not quite count either as a woman or a patrician. She is *more*—she can do things they can't. And less. Anyhow she doesn't count. She can do anything she wishes. She wears trousers! Two Venetian young women, in 1790, were sent to a convent for no more, and nothing further was ever heard of them. Ogni forestier mato in modo suo—each foreigner mad in his own way. The next day on the Grand Canal, in full view of everyone, and to the slight embarrassment of Nando which he manages to conceal by tilting his hat a little more to the front, the Siorina takes the oar.

First of all she puts it into the wrong notch in the forcola. Winifred sees now that the curiously shaped gnarls in this wooden post are purposeful. Each of the notches has its use—one to turn right, another left, another to go straight, to hold water, or to turn the gondola around in its own length. She fixes the oar into the notch near the top. Her English boots are set firmly onto the scrap of carpet. The oar, which now seems enormous, extends out over the water to the right. She attempts a tentative stroke. The gondola, as might be expected, swings to the left.

Nando: "Premi, Siorina!"

Winifred: "I don't know what that means."

Nando: "Premi is to push on the oar with a twist at the end, so that the gondola goes straight. Ecco, Siorina."

He takes the oar and shows her. You push forward, with your left knee bent, and the oar-blade digs into the water. But at a certain point you push *down* on the oar, and at the same time rotate it by turning down your knuckles, ecco, like this, so that the oar-blade makes a little twist and pushes the water sideways, to keep the gondola going straight. And to make ready for the next stroke, you pull the oar back feathered, so that it slips through the water like a knife.

She takes the oar once more. It is too big and heavy for all these subtleties. It is like knitting with a tree-trunk. And the bending of the knees and the pushing of the handle low, below the waist— although it seems graceful when Nando does it—is not a very feminine pose. Never mind—she bends her weight against it, crouches, pushes outward, and somehow the gondola goes straight for a little distance. But the Canal, meanwhile, is turning to the right! Nando: "Stali, Siorina."

Winifred: "I don't know what that is either."

Nando: "Stali means that if you wish to turn to the right, you put the oar in front of the forcola, ecco, and let it drag in the water a little."

She tries Stali too. She can make it go to right or left! It is absurdly simple—like most of the secrets that men guard to themselves so childishly. In an access of power, of dream-like power, she glides on down the Canal. Of course it is tiring; her arms ache and she stops for a moment. And now she notices something else that has not struck her before. Between strokes, allowed to drift ahead by its momentum, the gondola curves off all by itself to the right—ready for the next stroke that will send it back to the left. It is not *only* the twist of the oar. It is something about the gondola.

Winifred: "But it doesn't go straight. It turns to the right."

Nando becomes confidential and lowers his voice. "I will tell you something about the gondola, Siorina. Something that only the gondolier knows. The bottom of the gondola is not straight. It is curved like a bird's-wing, ecco." He makes a long graceful line in the air with his hand. "It has more curve on one side than on the other, and so it turns to the right. But with the oar we make it go straight."

It isn't as simple as she thought. It is more like some odd musical instrument than like a boat. It's like a violin—a big black violin—graceful—balanced—delicate. A violin is very hard to play. It takes much practice, and only one trained can do it. But anyone can pick it up and draw the bow across the strings. Even produce a thin little sound, oddly beautiful.

Winifred: "It's like a violin."

Nando never contradicts. "A violin or a bird's-wing, whichever you like, Siorina. But if it were not for the curve of the bottom, ecco Siorina, it would not be possible. Sometimes the curve of a gondola isn't perfect and it won't go straight. The boatbuilder throws it away. This one is perfect."

He is perfectly serious, she is perfectly serious. A gondola is a serious thing. Otherwise he would not have told her these things. Some of them secrets.

"Bene, Siorina. Now that you can turn, you can go back into the rio, ecco." Nando is perhaps a little anxious to get out of the Grand Canal, the theatre of Venetian amusement and a rather conspicuous place for a lesson. People have indeed come to street-ends and out onto their balconies to watch the Inglesina in her odd hat struggling manfully—that is the only word—with the oar. A little shakily she guides the long bird into Rio San Cassan. Premi! Keep close along the wall, otherwise, should you meet another gondola, there will not be room for your oar. In fact there is a hollow cry from the rio ahead.

Nando calls back: Ah-o-é. Surely there is not room to pass! And it is at a corner too. The other gondola appears. The occupants and gondolier stare only briefly at Winifred as they pass. Somehow the two unwieldy oars slip over and under each other instead of tangling, as Winifred has imagined, like insects' limbs. There is the palazzo! The great blue-and-gold pali stick up like tree-trunks. Winifred bumps the wall, pushes against it with her oar, and manages to swing the gondola, which has suddenly become very large and unwieldy, against the pali and the water-stairs.

Nando explains, almost apologetically, that it is not very good to push against the wall with an oar. Sometimes it has to be done, if one makes a mistake. But the place for the oar is in the water. One can go anywhere, with the oar in the water. The impersonal form is a kind of tactful reproach, and yet reassuring. *One* can, perhaps, but not Winifred. And yet if *one* can, then Winifred may too, in time. Winifred is sensible of the nuance, and appreciates it.

Gentle and taciturn Nando, a child, and yet with all a man's assurance and a man's deftness of hand, a man's strength (he is wiry under the leanness), a man's mild and respectful contempt— contemptuous respect—for the vagaries of females. What does Nando think of her? Why should she care what Nando thinks of her? Nando is a servant. One is civil to servants, even solicitous, making certain they are provided for and no injustice is done them through oversight.

Winifred: "M. Villetard pays you, doesn't he?"

Nando: "Don't preoccupy yourself, Siorina."

Winifred: "Where do you sleep, Nando?"

Anywhere. It doesn't matter. He gestures vaguely toward the darker end of the atrium. Does he sleep on the stones? She will not ask if he has enough to eat. They part in a curious state of wary friendship or truce, each profoundly altered by the encounter although they maintain their outward aplomb, Nando imagining now a world he has never dreamed of full of Inglesinas who wear trousers and do things that in Venice are done only by men, Winifred thinking that a gondola is no more hard to handle than an English jumping-horse and a good deal more docile. Still—she reflects as the old woman fusses about serving her meal—a hunter is a live creature, a male (any horse, even if it is a mare, is a kind of male), and a gondola is only a *thing*. But Nando is not a thing. It has never occurred to her before that a man is like a horse. She knows at once with a little cold creep of insight, like a chill except that it is not unpleasant, that her *body* enjoys being on a horse, just as her body enjoys being with Nando in the confined space of the gondola, doing something muscular, pushing at the heavy oar, while Nando, the soul or mind of the gondola, tells her what to do, just as the horse itself tells her how to ride it. What foolishness! She is tired and eating her supper in her sleep.

But she is not really sleepy. After supper, in total darkness, she steals down the great staircase to the atrium. The gondola is still there, outlined in the starlight, bumping gently and fitfully against the pali as though it were asleep. The great iron halberd at the prow is erect like a horse's head. It is divided into six blades, Nando explained, one for each of the sestieri of Venice—San Marco, Castello, San Polo, and so on. At the top is the large broad blade that stands (perhaps) for the whole city; Nando was not clear on this. One thing she has discovered by herself: this ferro at the prow is exactly the right height so that, slipping under a bridge, it indicates that the gondola with the felze mounted will slip under it too, even if the gondolier has to stoop a little. Like a cat's whiskers, it is a feeler for small openings. She touches it gently. It feels more like a horse's muzzle than a cat's whiskers, but it is harder, hard like a man. Winifred wishes that she were hard. It isn't enough merely to wear trousers and speak in short sentences, omitting foolishness, like a man. What is a man? She has lived among them all her life, and yet suddenly she does not know them any longer. They are as strange as giraffes, as fabulous as griffons. Julie lived in the château with two men, in love with both, while she . . . it is all very strange. Winifred ponders: What is it to *be in love?*

There is a Very Special Person in the world. The body of this person is magic; the mind of this person is a delight, an unexplored empire. And this, the body and the mind, belong to *one's self*—but one's self belongs to the other too. And this last part is a mystery to Winifred. For how can that be, and how can that be a delight?

The night is cool and still—absolutely quiet—as though the city were enchanted. She goes back up the broad staircase to her rooms, takes off her clothes in the darkness, and puts on a white gown with lace at the throat, so long that it comes to her feet and trails on the floor. Barefoot on the cold marble, she wanders through doorways, trailing her hand along the walls, feeling her way with her soul's whiskers through the darkness. In the bedchamber she swings open the casement. There is no moon. The starlight floods in, surprisingly bright, in color a kind of mauve rather than gray. Only a few yards away the wall of a house takes faint fire in this illumination—a pink wall—it is perhaps this that has turned the starlight violet. From below, between the palazzo and the house opposite, there is the lapping of water. She feels an urge to surrender herself to this, to all of it, to the starlight, the chill air of evening, the pink wall opposite that is only a shadow that one could pass through by magic, the fluid insistent murmur of water. But if one passed into those shadows one would be only a shadow too. A tremor passes through her, a danger. She is suddenly afraid. She goes to bed.

THE ISLAND OF SAN FRANCESCO DEL

The island of San Francesco del Deserto lies about five miles east of Venice, in a remote and inaccessible part of the lagoon surrounded by marshes. It can be reached only through two narrow channels navigable by small boats, one leading from Venice and the other from the island-town of Burano about a mile away. For the rest, there is nothing for miles around but a plain of brackish water.

The convent is nearly as old as Venice. In 1228 the patrician Iacopo Michiel donated the island to the Franciscans, in respect of the tradition that St. Francis of Assisi once took shelter here from a storm and planted his staff in the soil, whereupon (tradition quickly sliding off into legend) it sprouted into a pine, the relics of which are still revered by the Brothers. As a matter of fact there are many pines on the island, which, along with the cypresses in the graveyard, make it visible for several miles across the lagoon.

The Frati Minori, as the Franciscans came to be known in Italy for their modest ways, built a church and a cloister on the island, and have lived there ever since according to the rule of their order. They observe vows of poverty, chastity, and obedience, they wear habits of coarse brown cloth with a cord about the middle, and they are not allowed to ride horseback. From its earliest history the island has been virtually self-sufficient. The

Brothers dug wells, laid out orchards, and planted vegetable-gardens. If they have need of other things, such as salt, wine, or trifles like needles or eyeglasses, they obtain them from Burano by trading vegetables for them. The order is renowned for its charity. Also, even though the Dominicans and Jesuits are considered the true scholars among the holy orders, the Frati Minori are not without learning. They possess a considerable library and are sometimes consulted by the Patriarch of Venice on theological questions. They have the reputation of being somewhat more virtuous than other orders. For one thing, they are too far away from Venice for temptation.

Here Malcolm and Mark Anthony are able to take refuge for a few days, at no danger to themselves, and in no discomfort except for a certain degree of boredom. It is very quiet. The wind whispers and sighs in the rushes, and at intervals the Brothers can be heard singing their offices in the chapel. Mark Anthony, confined on this tiny scrap of land (it is only about a half-mile long), suffers from lack of exercise and stands on the beach whooping, throwing rocks at the sea-birds. Then again, he sits with the Brothers in chapel, listening intently as they intone their offices. Moved in some way by these Gregorian intervals, he throws back his head and howls—as a dog will sometimes at the sound of a violin—in a controlled but eerie kind of ululation. Perhaps there is something atavistic in this unexpected welling-up of sensibility, some racial memory of the melodies of a dark and lost kinghood. The Brothers pay no attention to him. There are many ways of witnessing the Glory of God. Malcolm has a small cell with whitewashed walls and a single window, or rather an unglazed hole; God's fresh air comes through it at all hours and purifies the lungs. In the cell it is even quieter than outside. There is only the sighing of the wind around the old walls and the faint sound, every four or five seconds, of a kind of whistle on a fixed note. For the most part Malcolm passes his time reading. He is still in Book Eleven, the later part where Odysseus tells of encountering the ghosts of the dead in the Underworld.

"First came the soul of our companion Elpenor,
For he had not yet been buried beneath the wide-traveled earth;
We ourselves had left his body in the hall of Circe,
Unwept and unburied, since another labor drove us on.
I wept when I saw him and pitied him in my heart."

This keeps him occupied for a day or two. When he tires of reading, he is quite at liberty to walk about where he pleases. He stands under the pines, with the wind soughing over his head, and looks across the lagoon at the distant city. He wanders around the cloister, glances into the kitchens, and peruses the library, which has an impressive collection of antiquity, including the thirty-eight volumes of the *Thesaurus Antiquitatum Sacrarum* as well as an incunabulum Homer. And there is Fra Mauro to talk to—a monk who has acquired a considerable renown as a mathematician and cartographer, and for this achievement is provided with his own study instead of having to live in the dormitory with the others. Fra Mauro takes an interest in Malcolm because they share in common the art of navigation; Fra Mauro is one of the half-dozen scholars in the world who have mastered Maskelyne's method of determining longitude by observing the distance between the moon and sun, using Hadley's quadrant. This instrument he keeps in a shelf along the wall together with various astrolabes, some with Arabic inscriptions, telescopes, azimuth circles, a drafting-machine capable of making any curve either on flat or spherical surfaces, a spirit-level, a barometer according to Torricelli's design, and compasses of various sorts. For, as he gently explains to Malcolm, Etiam vir sanctus scientiam non abhorret, even a holy man does not scorn knowledge. Another wall is lined with books, and under the bookshelf is a long cupboard with artifacts of various sorts arranged along the top: quartz spear-blades and arrows from the marshes of Aquileia, a Pompeiian box, an almost intact Greek krater with decorations, antique statuettes from Sardinia, an Attic lamp, and a number of small Roman bronzes, at least one of which is obscene.

It is not this, however, that catches Malcolm's eye. Directly over the table, just by Fra Mauro's elbow, hangs an armillary sphere made in the previous century, probably, by some Flemish craftsman. It consists of a set of bronze rings and circles, bars, swivels, pivots, balls, and graduated scales which in their conglomerate form a kind of mechanical model of the heavens. One major ring represents the horizon, another the meridian, another the ecliptic. The parts are pivoted in such a way that all the motions of the celestial bodies can be represented and predicted, provided the rings and scales are set properly.

Malcolm is not invited to seat himself. In any case there are no chairs except for the one at the table. The old monk makes a kind of a twitch. "I see you are looking at my armillary."

Malcolm: "An interesting machine."

Fra Mauro: "A machine made out of circles. The circle is a figure with extraordinary qualities, including that of perfection. God has been defined as a circle whose center is nowhere and whose circumference is everywhere."

Malcolm: "Defined by whom?"

Fra Mauro: "By myself, among others. I have the scales set for the present date. You will notice that Mars is in ascension."

Malcolm (getting out his glasses and examining the machine more carefully): "However, I see what seems to be a sun at the center."

Fra Mauro: "And why not?"

Malcolm: "I seem to remember that, according to Christian doctrine, the earth is supposed to be the center of things."

The old monk sighs, rather feebly. He suffers occasionally from tertian fever and is still wan from his attack of the night before.

"You are right that my armillary is somewhat heretical. However, I doubt that any theologian is capable of noticing it. In any case, the real question is not whether the earth or the sun is at the center of things, but whether the earth moves. Even the great Galileo had to recant on that point."

Malcolm: "But later he said, 'Nevertheless it moves.' "

Fra Mauro: "Yes, but under his breath. The judges didn't hear him. Poor Bruno was not so fortunate. They burned him, even though he was a monk. It is better not to have business with wheels unless you are sure what you are doing. Fio Mio, have you seen our Hospital?"

Malcolm: "Hospital?"

Fra Mauro: "Come."

He arises slowly from the table, beckons to Malcolm with a bony finger, and leads the way out of the study. The door opens onto the cloister, which consists of a square of columns enclosing a garden with some scraggly cacti in it. Fra Mauro seems even more wavery out in the sunshine. On the other side of the cloister he pushes open a rough timber door which Malcolm for some reason has not noticed before. Behind it is a long whitewashed corridor, at the end of the corridor is another door, and beyond this door they enter a large gloomy hall with a beamed ceiling and unglazed clerestory windows. Around the walls are cubicles, some open and others closed with doors. There are also cages, of the kind used in menageries for confining animals. In the center of the room are work-tables, benches, and chairs, some of the chairs upside down or broken. There are perhaps fifty Unfortunates in the room. (Fra Mauro calls them Fortunati, but perhaps he only misspoke himself.) Some are seated quietly in their cubicles or lying on cots, some are working at various things at the tables, and some are confined in the cages. There is an odd sound, not loud but insistent and penetrating, consisting of a medley of hums, disconnected speech, groans and moans devoid of any particular emotional content, and a single whistle at exactly even intervals, about four seconds apart. It is this whistle that Malcolm has heard, coming through the clerestory windows and over the cloister to his cell.

Fra Mauro: "Ecco, Fio, our Hospital."

Malcolm: "I thought that madmen were kept at San Servolo."

There they are violent, Fra Mauro explains. These are of a harmless sort, those that are capable of humming to themselves and making things with tools. A young Brother with dark expressive eyes moves gently and systematically among the Fortunati, as though he were tending flowers, giving one a cup of water, cleaning up another who has soiled himself, taking away from a third an awl he has acquired somehow, which might be dangerous to himself or others. The man with the awl shows no signs of aggressiveness, in fact; he is only curious about the tool, and watches it go off longingly but in a distracted way. The Venetians, in conformity with their gentle nature, go mad quietly and with understatement. The man who whistles, Fra Mauro explains (he points him out, a small inoffensive octogenarian with a shock of white hair, his lips distorted into a permanent pucker), does so because he believes that if he does not make this small sound every few seconds the world will stop and all the people will fly off. He is a saint—a savior of mankind—without him the race would perish. The Brothers agree with him solemnly on this. And when he sleeps? He does not sleep, or believes he does not. Probably, Fra Mauro concedes, he dozes off for a few minutes every now and then. "It is a curiosity to see him eat. He is dexterous at doing both things at once. You could come back at dinner-time if you like, to see how this is done."

There are other eccentricities worthy of attention. Fra Mauro points them out. A man who keeps a store of quite invisible objects, which he sells to invisible clients in return for invisible money. When asked what kind of store it is he says it is a Pharmaco-Polyopticon. Another who believes he is a Doge and has been endeavoring for several years to poke a protuberance into his hat to make it into a Corno. Another who suffers from the delusion that he is sexually violated by angels. He lies quite happy on his cot, in a permanent state of erotic excitement. The inmates—they are all men—seem quite content with their lot and do not rave or engage in violence in the way lunatics are popularly supposed to do. Even those who growl or roar—those confined in the cages—merely seem to be trying out their voices in various ways as they might a musical instrument, a bass viol or a horn.

It is not any of these, however, that Fra Mauro has brought Malcolm to see. Instead it is the Omo de le Rode, or Wheel Man. He has a shock of hair that sticks out on one side, and he occupies a large table at the far end of the workshop. There he busies himself with his collection of wheels and wheeled objects: a child's toy carriage, various tops and gyroscopes, a spinning-wheel, a knife-sharpener's stone driven by pedals and a leather belt, and a small adding-machine on Pascal's model in which sums are calculated through the rotation of brass disks. Many of these things he has collected, but others he has made himself, with no other tools than a pen-knife and a little hammer. At the moment he is attempting to construct a perpetual-motion machine on the overbalancing principle as proposed by Worcester and Orffyraeus, in which a flat wheel enclosed with linen on both sides contains a system of curved spokes and balls, so that the balls on one side will always roll to the rim of the wheel, while those on the other side will return to the axle:

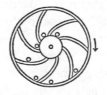

This, however, has proved to be too difficult a challenge for his pen-knife. He works on it diligently, with a puzzled but contented air, taking off the linen on one side to see whether the balls have really fallen into the proper positions. He replaces the linen with tacks and a small hammer and fits the wheel again into its axle. It still doesn't turn.

Malcolm: "But why is it necessary to confine such a man?"

Fra Mauro: "Because he is mad."

Malcolm: "But some of the greatest thinkers of our time have concerned themselves with such matters."

Fra Mauro: "You can conclude what you want from that."

Malcolm: "If he is mad, then you ought to confine every wheelwright in Europe."

Fra Mauro: "There are no wheelwrights in Venice. If this man were not a Venetian, he would not be mad."

He delivers these explanations in a detached and scientific tone and in full hearing of the Wheel Man, who does not bother to turn his head. He goes on tacking: tap tap. There is nothing more to be seen in the Hospital. Fra Mauro turns and leads the way out the door and down the whitewashed corridor to the cloister. The groans, cackles, and whistles behind them gradually die away. They go around the square of cacti on the gravel path. Back in his study Fra Mauro seats himself heavily at the table, pulling the cowl from his head. He is bald except for a reddish tonsure. He is perspiring a little from his walk in the sunny cloister. The fine vellum of his head shows every bone of the skull under it.

Fra Mauro: "Fio, you are a Lutheran, I believe? Or something of the sort."

Malcolm: "I'm not a believer."

Fra Mauro: "Have you heard, you Lutherans, of the Sin Against the Holy Ghost, for which there is no forgiveness?"

Malcolm has heard about it from Father Dottle. But this was years ago.

Fra Mauro: "There is much disputation about this. I have my own opinion. Which, I ought to make clear, is not shared necessarily by the Holy See. My opinion is that the Sin Against the Holy Ghost is the making of the wheel. Only God is allowed to be perfect. The circle is forbidden to man."

He scratches his head, as though he has lost the thread of his discourse. Then he continues.

"In England, as I understand, there are factories run by wheels in which thread is spun and cloth is woven. You, Fio, who have been in England, can tell me if this is true. A Frenchman named Cugnot has already contrived a carriage which is worked by steam. No horses are needed; it goes along by itself. There is also a round gun which fires many balls as its drum revolves. It is very clever. They say it can kill twenty men. These toys, Fio, are all made of circles. It is because we have made them that God is displeased with us, and we are unhappy. Perhaps," he interrupts himself timidly, "these ideas seem strange to you, or like a madness. If a Spanish Inquisitor heard about them, he might consider them heretical."

Malcolm: "He might break you on a wheel."

Fra Mauro: "Exactly."

It is their little joke. However neither smiles.

Fra Mauro: "A great deal is said these days about General Bonaparte. We here are somewhat isolated from events on the Mainland. But about this general I have heard two things. First, that he is successful and has swept all other armies before him. Second, that where previous armies fought with the musket, he is an artillerist and defeats his enemies with cannon which he is able to bring into action more swiftly than any other general."

Malcolm: "Both of these things are true."

Fra Mauro: "Now tell me, Fio. How is a cannon different from a musket?"

Malcolm: "First, it is larger. Second, it has wheels."

Fra Mauro reaches up to feel his skull again. He scratches. Perhaps he suffers from eczema.

"It's a new way of things, Fio. Cugnot's carriages will cover the face of the earth. Men will shoot each other with revolving guns. We are coming to a time in which gentle folk like the Venetians will either die or go mad."

Malcolm: "If they all go mad together, perhaps they won't notice."

Fra Mauro: "In my opinion this has already happened to the rest of Europe."

There is a silence. Malcolm finds himself looking at a point in the air just over Fra Mauro's shoulder. The collection of bronze circles, catching some faint breath of air, twirls slowly in the gloom.

Fra Mauro: "Ah yes. I'm a great sinner."

A monomaniac, thinks Malcolm.

MALCOLM IS CLUTCHED IN A VAST

Malcolm is clutched in a vast boredom, a condition which, as the theologians tell us, is a fertile ground for sin. He walks around the island, which takes only a few minutes, and sits sometimes for an hour or more on a piece of wall with a muddy beach at his feet, looking out across the marshes. There is not very much to be seen. To the north, seeming to float a little above the water through some trick of refraction, is the town of Burano, with a campanile sticking out of it at a slight angle to the vertical. Beyond it is the more massive square tower of Torcello, a city once more powerful than Venice until finally it succumbed to the fever and the silting-up of the lagoon around it. The sky is clear, with only a few clouds over the Terraferma. On the horizon to the west there is a kind of wavering excrescence on the water—a few dots, squashed or elevated by the lens-effect of the air. A tiny stick identifiable as the Campanile of San Marco can be made out, the oblong bug of San Zanipolo, and another grayish insect that is perhaps the Gesuiti. From five miles away the rest of Venice is submerged.

In fact, Malcolm calculates, from five miles away a point on the earth's surface is three and a half feet below the horizon. What is he doing anyhow, sitting on this sharp piece of stone doing arithmetic in his head? There is still the possibility that he contracted some sort of fever, a week or more ago when he jumped into the lagoon after that Ninny of a girl. This would account for a good many things. But he has the impression that it is the world about him that is feverish, while he himself regards it quite clearly, noting the tendency of things like distant churches to heave up and down. Perhaps, he decides, Fra Mauro is right, and men have got the world completely out of adjustment by rolling over it on wheels. But it is not only the world that is out of joint. He himself has difficulty focusing his thoughts. A Plague! It is probably only some kind of miasma or other peculiar to this island. After a while he gets up and wanders back over the warm sand toward the buildings of the convent, which also appear slightly gelatinous in the quivering sunshine.

In his cell it is cool and gloomy. Whatever light there is seems to come, not from the hole of a window, but from the whitewashed walls themselves. From the chapel comes the thin and reedy sound of the Brothers intoning some office or other, perhaps Sext, or Tierce. His watch has stopped—he has forgotten to wind it since he arrived on the island. Has he taken his noonday meal or not? He has forgotten. The Brothers have voices like spiders, and they insist on the same vocables over and over, as though they were building a sort of complicated web out of them. "Gaudeamus omnes in Domino. . . . Deus in adiutorium meum intende, Domine. . . . Domine. . . . Domine ad adiuvandum. . . ." Over this sound, at intervals, comes the distant basso of Mark Anthony yelling at the sea-birds. The Whistling Man is still at it; the world will not end for a little while yet. Malcolm takes off his hat and hangs it on a nail, scratches at his damp hair with his fingers, looks vacantly around the cell, and goes through the pockets of his coat looking for his Homer, which in fact he has left under the cot. Instead his fingers encounter the packet wrapped in green cloth.

Fra Mauro is in his study, but he is not writing. He is at the bookshelf examining a large volume bound in red morocco, which he shuts as Malcolm comes in.

"Excuse me. I was verifying a passage in—Eratosthenes," he explains in a thin and timid voice, as though apologizing for the erudition of the reference.

Malcolm clears his throat. He is not interested in Eratosthenes. "I have a thing here which you can perhaps give your opinion on. A matter of conscience."

Fra Mauro: "Of conscience?"

Malcolm: "It involves a promise made to a member of the—female sex."

Fra Mauro floats like a butterfly to his chair, sits down, and regards him nervously.

Malcolm: "I have come into the possession of some papers which belong to a young lady. It is very likely that the papers deal with matters of state. I believe your order has nothing to do with matters of state?"

Fra Mauro: "Less than nothing."

Malcolm: "But I can't examine the papers, because at the time I came into possession of them I promised the young lady that I wouldn't—violate any of her modesties." Seeing that Fra Mauro doesn't quite follow this, he plunges on. "I don't know what I said. That I wouldn't delve into her intimate secrets. Something of the sort."

Fra Mauro: "But what do the papers contain? Matters of state, or intimacies of a young lady?"

Malcolm: "That's what I don't know, you see."

Fra Mauro: "Why don't you return the papers to her?"

Malcolm: "That would be contrary to my duty."

Fra Mauro: "Then perhaps you should give them to your superiors."

Malcolm: "I can't do that either, because of my promise."

Fra Mauro: "Oh, Fio Mio. I know even less about young ladies than you do."

Malcolm: "H'mm. The thing is. It's all right for you to look at the papers, don't you see. Because you've taken certain—vows."

Fra Mauro: "You mean that this is a matter that can be proposed only to a eunuch."

Malcolm: "I express myself poorly."

Fra Mauro: "You express yourself splendidly, Fio. In fact a monk is only half a man. Still I'm perfectly familiar with the matters of which you speak. I was raised on a pig-farm near Treviso. We are all born between urine and faeces, as the Saint reminds us. It is a madness that we should come into the world in this way, but such is God's will. Show me your papers. I will tell you whether there are any young lady's intimacies in them."

Malcolm hands over the packet.

Seated at the writing-table, Fra Mauro looks around for his spectacles, which are made of brass to resist the damp air of the marshes and have left a green line across his nose. When he finds them he puts them on with exasperating slowness. Then he turns to examining the packet. He attempts to untie the green ribbons, finds they are stuck down with sealing-wax, and slits them with the small knife he uses for sharpening his pens. With the same knife he breaks the wax sealing the folds of cloth.

Malcolm turns his back and begins studiously examining the spines of the books on the shelf. Behind him he hears a trickling on the table and then a series of tiny bumps on the floor, a rustling like raindrops. Fra Mauro has just discovered the lead shot in the end of the packet. There is another sound, evidently that of Fra Mauro endeavoring to catch as much of the shot as he can in his hands and put it somewhere or other, perhaps into his inkwell. The table is slightly inclined and anything round will roll off of it.

Following this there is a long silence, lasting perhaps three-quarters of an hour. How in the name of Thoth can so much writing be contained in a small packet the size of a man's hand? Malcolm turns his head once and finds Fra Mauro examining the finer script with a magnifying-lens. A dozen or more papers are spread about on the table. Malcolm goes back to examining the books, the titles of which by this time he knows by heart. He remains with his back turned for another ten minutes or so. At last the silence is broken.

"Well, Fio Mio."

He turns abruptly.

Fra Mauro: "There is much writing here and I am afraid my eyes are not as good as they used to be. Some of it is not clear to me even when I can make it out. There is nothing that has to do with the intimacies of a young lady."

He attempts to fold the packet up into its former state, but this is impossible because the ribbons have been cut and the wax broken. He makes the neatest bundle of it that he can and passes it to Malcolm in his two hands.

Fra Mauro: "I am sorry. These little bullets . . ." Some of them are in a saucer, the rest on the floor underfoot.

Malcolm: "Don't worry about it."

Back in his own cell he shuts the door carefully, stares out the window to be sure nobody is watching, then sits down and spreads out the papers on the table. There are perhaps two dozen sheets, all of the same material, a fine tissue so thin it is almost transparent and yet as strong as parchment. He finds his own spectacles and puts them on.

Most of the sheets are written on both sides, and some are cross-written. The script is so tiny that even with the spectacles he can barely make it out. The first sheet that comes to hand is in a kind of cipher. "Scamandros must be accomplished by 1 Floréal. The peace with Bithynia will be concluded by that date. Our friends in the city, who are privy to the plans, indicate that Aiaie will oppose the Scamandros Game with force. Troilus is not aware of this. The Scamandros Game" (Jeu de Scamandre in French) "is essential to the subsequent neutralization of Aiaie by Achilles. Greek heroes will fall at Scamandros, and their fate will be useful."

As it happens, Malcolm is better equipped to deal with this code than the average sea-captain. Scamandros is a river by Troy, the scene of a mythic battle. 1 Floréal, he calculates with a few scratches on the table-top, is April 20, the date of the engagement at the Lido. Troilus is therefore the unfortunate Captain Laugier, whose government did not warn him that his attempt to penetrate the lagoon would be met by force. Aiaie—this is not very difficult either. It is the island of Circe, where men are turned into swine. Aiaie is Venice, Bithynia is no doubt Austria, and Achilles can only be General Bonaparte, who is to "neutralize" Venice in some way or another through the Jeu de Scamandre, a game in which French deaths will be useful. Laugier cries out "Je me rends!" and a moment later he is lying on the deck with his body going one way and his head another. The sun shines brightly outside the cell, making a few motes dance in the hole of a window.

He goes on to the other sheets. Several of them are concerned with the activities of French agents in Venice. For them the Homeric code is abandoned and they are identified by names borrowed (a typical Revolutionary touch—a strain of sentimental romanticism) from the pastoral romance: Mélibée, Corydon, Alexis, Anacréon, Clélia, Galatée. One sentence catches his eye: "Clélia has instructions to deliver this present only to Corydon, who will transmit it to Alexis unopened." A single word of this, to his annoyance, makes the back of his neck prickle. He tries it again—Clélia—it does the same thing.

Corydon is that idiot Jean-Marie, and Alexis is clearly Villetard himself. This cipher too is not a very difficult one. A child could see through it. The French give the impression that they are playing at a pageant of Watteau. Mélibée, it seems, is an intimate advisor of the Doge, and Galatée is the wife of a Senator who enjoys the confidence of the Council of Ten. She is evidently willing to pass on information to the Legation because her lover, identified only as Anacréon, is French. Venice seems to be infested with these shepherds and shepherdesses who are privy to the innermost secrets of the Signoria. "Attempt to have Galatée elicit from the Council of Ten the Venetian expectations regarding the disposal of the Ionian Islands. It is important to determine whether the Council would regard the seizure of Corfu as casus belli, provided it were feasible by naval means."

Malcolm does not think it is feasible by naval means, but nobody has asked his opinion. In any case the Venetians seem to have anticipated this move on the chessboard by sending the *Vittoria* to Corfu. He takes another sheet and begins piecing it out. It is a copy of a letter written by General Bonaparte to Carnot on 4 Ventôse An V, that is, February 22, 1797.

"Since the discovery of the Cape route to the Indies and the rise of Trieste and Ancona, Venice has been on the decline. It will hardly survive the blow. This wretched and cowardly population, unfitted for freedom, without land or water, must, of course, be handed over to those to whom the hinterland is allotted. First of all, we shall take the ships, empty the Arsenal, carry off the ordnance, and close the banks; we shall also keep Corfu and Ancona."

The reference to hinterland evidently means that Venice, after its "neutralization" by General Bonaparte, is to pass into the hands of the Habsburgs, who are supposed to be the enemies of the French. Malcolm has believed that he is cynical about Politicks, but the degree of this perfidy astonishes even him. He mutters "Dangled Frogs" between his teeth.

Following this comes the full text of the Armistice of Leoben. This is cast in tedious diplomatic terms and he doesn't bother to read it. He goes on to the next sheet, a letter from Carnot to Villetard on the subject of the arts.

"The Museum presently being organized by Citizen Denon in the Louvre ought to contain the most celebrated examples of all the arts, and France will not neglect to enrich it with all that it may expect from the conquests that the Army of Italy has already effected and from those of the future. . . . Much of the great art of the Nation has been destroyed in the violence of recent years, before the reestablishment of order under the present government. This loss must be restored, and at the cost of the enemies who sought to destroy the Nation in the hour of her greatest need. The Directoire therefore requests you to search out, survey, and inventory the most valuable objects of art, both in the city of Venice and in the dependent territories on the mainland, to the end that, after the agreement concluding the establishment of a democratic government in Venice and a new relationship between this government and the Republic of France, the necessary steps may be taken to remove the said works of art to France."

The sons of bitches seem to have everything neatly planned. The next sheet that comes to hand is a letter from Bonaparte, forwarded by Paris to the Legation in Venice. "The General in Chief, Army of Italy, requests a special surveillance of the patrician Francesco Pesaro, Procurator of San Marco and a member of the Council of Ten. Since An I" (that is, 1793) "he has been the chief instigator and leader of the war faction directed against the French. As a delegate to Gorizia he was pleased to be insolent to the General in Chief. His activities in Venice, according to intelligence, are still inimical to French interests and reactionary in nature. He is to be arrested immediately upon the installation of a democratic government in Venice. An attempt on his part to leave Venice should be prevented by any means. The General in Chief, Army of Italy, regards the regulation of this insult by Pesaro as a matter of personal honor." Pesaro had better lie low for a while too. Perhaps the monks at San Francesco could find a cell for him.

Finally, there is a sheet headed, "Nobles of the Venetian Republic known to be sympathetic to the cause of the Revolution, or who have in the past rendered confidential services to France. List provided by His Excellence Antonio Zeno, Venetian Delegate-

Extraordinary to the Directoire." There are eighteen names on the list, all Senators, Procurators, or patricians inscribed in the Golden Book. One of them is Paternian, the uncle of Contìn. Malcolm imagines the scrap of paper flying across the water to Venice, fluttering down the Riva and over the Ponte de la Paglia, twinkling in the sunshine like a pigeon. In the wall of the Ducal Palace, under the shady portico, is a marble bas-relief of a lion with his mouth open, and under it the inscription *Denontie Secrete contro chi Tradita lo Stato*. This is the celebrated Boca de Lion, for anonymous denunciations to be brought to the attention of the Inquisitors. The small scrap of paper, entering into this hole, would be the death sentence of the eighteen. They are the cream of the Venetian aristocracy. Liberals, perhaps. But men anyhow.

Paternian, he knows, is no traitor. But the publication of that list will throw panic into the Senate. In the wave of anti-French madness the guilty will perish with the innocent. After the beheadings on the great staircase, more hysterical denunciations. No one would be safe. Malcolm finds himself torn in several directions by five or six motives, all of them strong. His thoughts are confused, but vehement. God-dangled Frogs. They're sneaky devils. As for that upstart Bonaparte, someone should kick his rear. Contìn is a decent sort. His uncle is innocent. Liberty and Fraternity! Translation: les aristos à la lampe. Malcolm thinks a number of black thoughts about Revolutions. Along the line of omelets and eggs. On the other hand, to give the list to the Venetians would break the eggs into an even messier omelet.

He takes the sheet by the corner, gingerly, and examines it again. Only now does he notice that someone who writes in a much larger hand, perhaps Carnot himself, has scrawled across the bottom of it: "N.B. Alexis. Clélia, who carries this, seems a little goose. If she is compromised, she should be removed from the scene."

The language is that of the theatre. *Si Clélia se fait compromettre, qu'on l'ôte de la scène.* When actors play their parts badly how are they removed from the scene? Ophelia and Desdemona, not understanding their parts, end pale as wax, the lovers who have slain them haunted by guilt. There appears to Malcolm a white patch of face in the darkness, surrounded by some damp hair, and lower down the indistinct form of the boat-cloak, the garment of a man slain the same day. There is a rustle of water along the thin boards, and the flat, slightly angry voice held steady against any tendency to quaver. "Perhaps the gondolier has a light." Before his eyes the image sinks slowly, strangled in the water. Floats just under the surface, eyes staring open, like Ophelia among the lilies. Captain Langrish, say the eyes, you gave me your promise.

He gets up from the table, crams the papers into his pocket, and leaves the cell, taking with him the unlighted candle from the table. In the refectory two Brothers are at work cleaning the pots from the midday meal. Brushing past them without a word, he goes to the stove and lights the candle from the still smoldering embers. The two Brothers stare at him curiously.

Shielding the candle with his hand, he walks across the sand to the edge of the water. There is only a faint breeze from the south. In the shelter of the broken wall he arranges the contents of his pocket in a little pile. The papers themselves flare up almost immediately, but the waxed cloth does not burn quite so well. He stirs it with a stick. A bell tolls from the chapel: ". . . consummatum est . . . per omnia saecula saeculorum. Amen." The Brothers are at one of their mysterious offices, probably Vespers this time. Fra Mauro, however, is evidently not required to attend. His pallid face, with the cowl of his habit fallen down, is visible over a hedge, the gleam of his spectacles fixed in Malcolm's direction.

ON THE EVENING OF APRIL

On the evening of April twenty-ninth the Venetian envoys return from Graz. The next day orders are issued for the arrest of Pizzamano, the three Inquisitors of State, and the captain of the *Pandora*. The Council of Ten debates the arrest of Pesaro as well, but decides not to concede this much to the petulance of the General, at least not for the present. Pesaro is one of them, after all, and their wives and daughters all know each other. It would be embarrassing. They take courage, by fits and starts. Death rather than dishonor! The arrests of Pizzamano and the three Inquisitors are carried out, and they are confined to the barracks on the Isola San Giorgio. The American captain is unfindable.

A new set of Inquisitors is appointed, of necessity, and they go on with their task of sniffing out subversion. But subversion has undergone an odd transformation overnight; it has now become any sentiment which might be suspected of being anti-French, or which might annoy the General sulking in his Styrian fastness. Rumors spread through the city—not like wildfire, the usual simile, but like embers creeping slowly through a vein of coal, with little spurts here and there. The French army still occupies the Terraferma, only a league from the city across the lagoon, and there is the sound of sporadic gunfire, evidently from the campaign against peasant guerrillas.

On the evening of the thirtieth the Council of Ten meets again, in the Doge's private apartments in the Ducal Palace, to discuss the possibility of constitutional reforms. There are many opinions and the meeting takes the form, for the most part, of hand-wringing. But if we concede this, and concede that, will it save us? Let the Terraferma go, say some. And our villas? A plague take the villas! Let him have them. Ah no, my villa at Stra? A constitution then. Your villas or your togas; you must give up one or the other. But even if we give up both, will that save us? This General is an Attila, a mad dog! He'll take both!

The mutter of cannon is clearly audible from the Terraferma. The old Doge, his face sagging like a bloodhound, frets that he is no longer safe in his bed—"Sta note no semi sicuri gnanca nel nostro leto." Although Italian is customary on such occasions, in the excitement of the moment everybody breaks down and speaks Venetian. Pesaro himself—who discreetly absented himself from the Council earlier in the day when his own fate was debated—is present at this meeting, and in a state of high emotion. "I see that for my country all is finished. I can give her no more help. But any country can be a home for a brave man. Among the Swiss, even, one might find something useful to do." The councillors and secretaries try to comfort him, and dissuade him from the flight he has almost decided upon. He composes himself, at least in appearance, and consents to take some snuff. The Senators and other Illustrissimi depart, not speaking to each other, each thinking his own thoughts.

On the walls of the city the first graffiti appear, crudely scrawled in charcoal: 𝗔 i franzesi. The two v's, upside down and over-lapping, are shorthand for an inverted viva. Down with the French! But this is the work of dubious elements—riffraff who do not even own villas on the Brenta.

On the evening of the thirtieth—the same night that the Doge pulls the covers over his head in order not to hear the sound of cannon—Jean-Marie and Villetard meet furtively by the columns in the Piazzetta and make their way together down the Riva. At a certain point, where the street-lamps end, they encounter a boy waiting with a lantern. After filing along for some time after the lantern, turning left and right, they stop. The lantern is put out. Jean-Marie has not been in this part of the city before. They are somewhere in Castello, a dubious quarter inhabited by sailors and Arsenaloti. Finally, after a certain amount of whispering in the dark, they ascend a stairway in the flickering light of an oil-lamp fixed into the greasy wall. No one greets them and they open the doors themselves. The house seems deserted. They penetrate into it, along the dingy corridors, like phantoms entering to haunt the sleep of some dreamer.

They arrive at a kind of anteroom. It is unlighted and some figures can be made out, waiting. Someone speaks in a low tone. After a short wait they are conducted into the room beyond, a kind of empty storeroom devoid of furniture. It is lighted with lanterns set on the floor. Perhaps thirty people are present. Jean-Marie recognizes a number of well-known French sympathizers, including the surgeon Lamberti, a celebrated eccentric whose practice includes the highest circles of the nobility but who is also—as it is termed these days—a philosopher. At his elbow is the grocer Tomaso Zorzi, who has served as informer for the Legation and has also sheltered in his house various persons sought by the Inquisitors until they could be spirited out of the city. These activities do not seem to have enriched him very much. He is a small dumpy man, rather shabbily dressed, with what appears to be a smudge of flour on the shoulder of his frock-coat. However he has a great air of self-importance. He holds himself erect and stares at everything fiercely out of his splotchy pink face. Everyone waits. There are no greetings, except that Dr. Lamberti inclines his head slightly to Villetard.

After ten minutes or so the person they are waiting for is announced in a whisper. Paternian enters, rather fearfully, gazing around at everything out of a beady and slightly clouded eye. Are these phantoms that he perceives? Perhaps he is the dreamer himself, entering into the place of his dream. He is almost lost in a large red toga. Behind him is Contìn.

They are introduced to the others, or at least to Lamberti, Zorzi, and Villetard, the last of whom they are acquainted with. There is an awkward moment. No one speaks. This lasts for some time. In the back of the room someone clears his throat.

Dr. Lamberti: "Senator, we thank you for coming. We are sensible that the place is out of your way." (A note of sarcasm creeps into his voice at this point, and stays there to the end.) "You are aware, I am sure, of the deplorable state of the Serenissima Republic. The provinces of the Terraferma are in revolt and have raised the standard of true liberty. You know the ineptitude of the government and the suffering of the people."

Paternian (muttering): "I know everything."

Dr. Lamberti: "The Navy and Militia have been allowed to decline. Venice is defended only by foreigners and ruffians, who are not reliable. Commerce is in ruins. The state of public morals—"

Contìn: "There's no need to give the Senator lectures on the state of Venice. Proceed."

Lamberti concedes the point, and even makes a little formal smile in Contìn's direction. He is most polite. "Senator, I am only a simple citizen, but I seek the good of Venice and all its citizens. It is in the name of the citizens of Venice that I speak."

He harps on this word, Contìn notes. It is a French importation, a catchword of the Revolution. There are no citizens in Venice; there are only Venetians.

Lamberti: "There is much unrest, as you know. So far the Dominante has been spared these uprisings, but there has been much bloodshed on the Terraferma. There is no question that the unrest will spread to the city itself."

Paternian: "So now you're threatening, eh?"

Lamberti (imperturbable): "You will avoid these internal disturbances, and you will do a great favor to the city and to humanity, if you recommend to the Signoria that it conclude the agreement with the General in Chief of the Army of Italy, who is anxious to guarantee the freedom and security of all Venetians under a more liberal form of government. Monsieur Villetard" (he points, Villetard bows, and Paternian returns his irascible ferret-look) "has been kind enough to compile a protocol of conditions indicated by the General for the restoration of order in the Republic."

Zorzi passes him a sheet of paper.

Dr. Lamberti produces a pair of spectacles from his breast-pocket and puts them on, without hurry. He begins reading.

"First, there will be necessary an alteration in the form of government. The antiquated oligarchy" (he offers a cheerful smile to the Senator in his toga) "must be terminated. In its place the General recommends a Provisional Municipality, with representatives from all ranks of the people. All political prisoners to be released. The prisons to be thrown open for inspection by the people. The Tree of Liberty to be set up in Piazza San Marco. The Militia to be disarmed. The Schiavoni to be dismissed. The Fleet to be recalled from Corfu. The Bourbon refugees in the city to be arrested, and the funds deposited by them in Venetian banks to be returned to their rightful owners, the people of France. And a garrison of four thousand French troops to be invited into the city, to keep order and to protect the establishment of real liberty in Venice. Is that all, Monsieur Villetard?"

Villetard murmurs something.

Lamberti: "Ah yes, and Pesaro has not yet been arrested. Neither has Langrish."

Paternian: "Who?"

Contìn: "The American captain."

El Meregano! grits Paternian to himself.

Contìn: "These are the conditions of bandits. No Venetian could accept them."

Lamberti: "The people have been made aware of the conditions, and find them acceptable."

Paternian: "The people?"

Lamberti, with his long graceful surgeon's fingers, indicates himself and the others behind him in the room.

Paternian stares at these persons. One or two of them shift uneasily. Zorzi clears his throat.

Contìn: "And the alternative?"

Villetard: "If the conditions are not accepted, then we can not be responsible for the actions of those patriots who rise up against the tyranny of the present Venetian government."

Contìn: "Patriots? The scum of the streets. A handful of paid agitators. A grocer or two."

Villetard: "I beg your pardon, whom are you speaking of?"

Contìn (hotly): "Those who are betraying our country to its enemies!"

Paternian: "Alvise!"

Contìn (between his teeth): "Uncle, this is shameful. It's blackmail."

Lamberti (drily): "We have come to hear from—His Excellency."

Paternian looks around. They are all waiting for him to speak. He seems to draw himself up a little and falls into his old diplomatic manner, choosing his words carefully. "Gentlemen, these are delicate matters. I am grateful for the deference you—you illustrious gentlemen have shown me" (the liberals exchange glances, and Zorzi makes a face) "in inviting me here tonight so that you can—express to me your opinions. I have no authority, as you know, to speak for the Senate or for the Maggior Consiglio. I am here simply as a friend of our—two nations—hoping to mediate in their common interest. The conditions you enumerate seem to me—h'mm—harsh ones, but reasonable in the light of the conditions of the time. The Fleet . . . you want us to recall the Fleet . . . the Militia . . . the garrison . . ."

He has started well, but here he seems to lose the thread of his thought and forget what he is talking about. "The garrison. . . . Let us hope that the armed forces of our two nations can join hands in friendship and serve together as brothers. I doubt it, but . . . as brothers. Let's hope. As for the Schiavoni, I . . . I concur in the matter of their dismissal, and why, gentlemen? Because their . . . loyalty in these days is doubtful anyhow, and it's a wonder . . . they haven't already gone over to our enemies. . . ." Here he stops and begins coughing. "That is to say, I mean . . . our friends . . ." He coughs again. ". . . who are determined to save us at all costs."

Lamberti and Villetard exchange a glance.

Paternian masters his fit of coughing and goes on, a little flushed, perhaps from coughing or perhaps out of shame. "In short, gentlemen, I find this protocol of conditions acceptable—to me personally, I mean, I reiterate that I have no authority to speak for the Consiglio and . . ." Here he stops and seems to reflect on something for the first time. "You speak of a provisional government, gentlemen. Chosen from the people. But the Doge?"

He looks about inquisitively, and even gropes with his hands in the toga, as though he has lost some small object, a key, and is hoping for someone to find it for him. There is no response. They wait for him to go on.

"H'mm. So I will conclude, gentlemen, but . . . accepting this protocol from your hands and . . . I most heartfeltly trust that it will meet with the approval of the Consiglio, the Senate, and the . . ." He abandons the sentence finally without mentioning the Doge. "And that its—promulgation will bring . . . full liberty to the people of Venice and that our two nations will join in friendship so that we will once again be . . . a single family of . . . equal and happy citizens."

He pronounces this last word almost with a sob, but it is greeted with applause and a few bravos.

Dr. Lamberti makes a few polite claps of his own, holding his hands at an angle and touching the palms together lightly.

"Senator, I bow to your eloquence. We are grateful for your generous and most fitting words. Let us take heart that a world redeemed by justice is preparing for us a worthy place, honored and independent, at the great banquet of peoples, and that the liberator of Italy, the enemy of all tyranny of Europe, himself offers us his hand to lift us from the abjection into which we have fallen. Senator, will you sign the protocol?"

Paternian: "Sign the protocol?"

Lamberti produces a pen and inkwell from somewhere. The room is entirely bare of furniture. Is he expected to get down on his knees and sign it on the floor?

Paternian: "I don't understand."

Lamberti: "Simply as a receipt, Senator."

Paternian: "But if I am to carry the protocol to the Senate, for their consideration, then I don't see the use of a receipt."

Lamberti: "It is only to indicate that you have taken note of the terms."

Paternian: "Taken note of the terms . . . that I have, of course. But—it seems to me . . ."

Lamberti: "Here is the pen, Senator."

From somewhere a hand produces a tray and sets the paper on it. It is presented to the Senator.

Paternian: "It seems to me, Alvise—that since it is simply a receipt—although I don't see the point of a receipt, since I am to carry the thing to the Signoria. . . ."

Contìn: "Sign whatever you want, Uncle."

He signs. The tray with the pen and inkwell are whisked away and he is left with the protocol, which he is obliged to hold awkwardly in his hands, since there are no pockets in a toga.

Lamberti: "And now, citizens, it seems to me fitting that we should not allow the Senator to return alone to carry out his important task of delivering this document to the Signoria, especially since this neighborhood is not a very savory one—it isn't the fault of the inhabitants, they are very poor—instead we should constitute an escort of honor to be sure that the Senator arrives safely at the Ducal Palace and delivers the protocol as—he has agreed."

Paternian: "How? I don't require any escort."

Lamberti: "No, but we wish to honor you."

What an honor! Paternian suspects that they only want to compromise him publicly, either in order to put him further in their power, or simply as another humiliation. And from that horse-butcher Lamberti! A curse on the day he ever allowed him to treat his wife for fibroids. Paternian allows himself to be pushed out into the anteroom, and down the stairs.

The escort is quickly made up. It consists of Lamberti himself, the grocer Zorzi, the boy with the lantern, and a somewhat wild-eyed young poet named Foscolo, who has said nothing coherent during the meeting but has taken a vigorous part in the murmurs and bravos. Leaving the others behind, this procession sets off down the unlit street. The Senator's gondola is nearby in Rio de l'Arsenale, but it is decided to go on foot, since there is not room for all in the gondola. This is a slow business, because of the Senator's bad legs and his limp. The poet emits Delphic yips as they go along. Perhaps he is composing an ode for the occasion. He has already written one to Bonaparte, as well as a tragedy in the Ossianic manner, *Tieste,* which has achieved a certain celebrity. No one pays any attention to him. The barrel-shaped Zorzi is excited. His head bobs in the collar of his frock-coat, and he makes gestures. Near him is the tall figure of Lamberti in the darkness, with his hands thrust into his pockets.

Zorzi: "We've done great things tonight. Great things."

Lamberti: "I fear we have made a great hole in the water."

Zorzi: "Eh? What? A hole? How?"

Lamberti: "I'm a doctor, Signor Zorzi. My profession is to diagnose illness. I'm afraid our good intentions may not have sufficient root in the people."

Foscolo (at the top of his voice): "Citizen, don't despair of virtue, like Brutus!"

Lamberti: "You have the protocol, Senator?"

Paternian: "I have everything. Don't concern yourself."

Contìn: A bridge, Uncle. Can you manage it?"

Paternian: "What will you? I have no choice. The Schiavoni too! They want us to cut off our fingernails, so we won't scratch those who are strangling us."

ON THE ISOLA SAN GIORGIO, JUST

On the Isola San Giorgio, just across from the Piazzetta, some militiamen are ramming a bag of powder into a nine-pounder with an old-fashioned flaring barrel, like a trombone, and large spindly wheels. They push some rags down on top of it, then touch a smoking rope to the match-hole. There is a kind of bump. A flower of white smoke blooms out and is pushed away by the breeze—the last shot to be fired by the Republic. A few pigeons fly up in alarm, on the pavement in front of the Basilica, and then settle down again.

The gun is the signal for the convocation of the Maggior Consiglio, consisting of all the nobles of the Republic whose names are inscribed in the Golden Book. There are about sixteen hundred of these, and six hundred are required for a quorum. The meeting takes place in the Sala del Maggior Consiglio of the Ducal Palace, a room that rivals the Salle des Glaces at Versailles in every way, and is superior to it in its decorations. As the Doge sits in state, on a dais at one end, he has behind him the great *Paradise* of Tintoretto, the largest oil painting in the world. Directly over his head in the ceiling is another large painting, one of particular irony for the occasion: the *Venice Crowned by Victory* of Veronese. There are a number of other large paintings which are described in every guidebook. The cornice, under the gilded ceiling, is decorated with the portraits of all the Doges of Venice from the founding of the city in the seventh century, with a blank place for Marin Falier, who was decapitated for the treason of conducting secret negotiations with commoners. The last portrait is that of Ludovico Manin, the present Doge. After that there is no room for more; an oversight on the part of the architects, or perhaps an omen.

Since it is a warm day the windows are open onto the Riva, allowing the sea-breeze to enter. Nothing can be seen through the windows, because the hall is on the second floor, but the sounds of voices and occasional shouts float in from below. Every so often a Senator sticks his head out of the window to see what is happening. There is an air of nervousness in the hall, and sentries have been posted at the doors of the Palace, an unprecedented precaution. Must the flower of the Serenissima now be protected from its own people—its children—its faithful servants? Matters have come to a fine pass. In the Caffè Bertazzi the destitute Barnaboti grumble over their tiny cups of chocolate. A meeting of the Cabinet, and we lose a city. A meeting of the Council of Ten, and we lose a province. Now the Maggior Consiglio is meeting. What will we lose next? Cowards! Testicle-heads! Traditionally the Barnaboti live by selling their votes, but today, in the confusion, no one has remembered to pay them. So they refuse even to come to the Palace; they sit in the cafés and grumble. Perhaps there won't even be a quorum, and nothing will happen.

Those who can't even afford a cup of chocolate—boatmen, artisans, and shirt-sleeved workers from the Arsenal—are gathered in little groups in the Piazza to wait for the news from the Consiglio. There are several hundred of them, perhaps a thousand or so, but even so they hardly fill the immense open space. Large patches of empty pavement are showing. Now and then a kind of dog-like howl arises, echoing from the façade of the Procuratie.

Abbasso i franzesi-i-i!

Or sometimes:

Viva San Marco-o-o!

It is impossible to tell where these yells are coming from. The sound seems to emerge from the paving-stones. A waiter comes out of Florian's, with a towel over his shoulder, and looks speculatively at Quadri's across the way. From one of the side streets comes another cry, not very loud, but with a derisive lilt.

Viva la libertà!

Heads turn in the Piazza. There is a murmur of disapprobation. Who was that? Nobody knows.

In the great hall of the Palace these cries are barely audible. Contìn is aware of them, but Paternian is not. The old gentleman's hearing is not what it once was, and in any case nothing much can be heard in the rustle of whispers and conversation. Someone is making a speech, but nobody is paying very much attention. Paternian fixes his irascible glance on the dais at the end of the hall. "That's a Doge? He's not even a Venetian!" He is speaking louder than he realizes. Contìn attempts to quiet him with a gesture. Manin, dressed in his rich ducal robes, is seated on his high chair of office under the canvas of Tintoretto. The Corno on his head resembles a Cardinal's berretta, except that it has a protuberance in the top which a phrenologist might identify as a bump of sagacity or authority, but which in plain Venetian is simply a mark of impotence. Under this headpiece is a long and rather lugubrious face, dark Venetian eyes with bags under them, and a mouth that works about in a nervous way. The secretary, who has been reading the articles convening the Consiglio, now finishes, and the Doge rises to his feet all pale and trembling to propose the business of the day.

This is the protocol prepared by M. Villetard in accordance with the desires of the French Directorate and the General in Chief of the Army of Italy, he explains in an almost inaudible voice, and transferred into the hands of a member of the Council for delivery to the Signoria. (Everyone knows this is Paternian, but he has insisted that his name not be mentioned.) He goes on to read the conditions. He can hardly be heard, but it doesn't matter. They are already well known, and printed versions are circulating in the city, clandestinely distributed by the French.

Following this there are other speeches. One of these—the only surprise of the day—is made by Pesaro. No one has expected him to have the courage to show himself. He is a small jug-shaped man with a round chest and a determined look, in spite of his rather weak chin. He steps onto the dais in order to make himself more visible. This in itself is without historical precedent. The dais is traditionally reserved to the Doge. Manin's mouth works.

It is possible to catch only a part of what Pesaro is saying. The floors are marble, the old hall is full of echoes, and the whispers and murmurs continue while he speaks. "Fellow Venetians, why are we gathered here like cowards to cringe before the demands of the invader? If the land so beloved to us" (*my villa,* says someone through his teeth) "has been usurped by the Corsican, the sea is still ours. The Arsenal is strong. Venice is impregnable while stout hearts man the galleys . . . it is not yet too late. If we are to die, let us die like men and not like dogs." Out of the walls a single voice, in a conversational tone, comments, "Bravo." Heads look around to see who has spoken. It was a ghost, an echo; perhaps some old Doge from the paintings around the wall.

Much of the rest is lost in the murmurs. ". . . A thousand years of history . . . our nation which is wedded to the sea . . . heritage of Lepanto and of the League of Cambrai . . . sacrifices . . . with the Grace of God eventual victory." And so on. The echoes resound from the marble for a moment after he ceased speaking. "Ventual victory. Victory. Ictory."

Paternian's mouth works. He is not very tall and can barely see over the others. "Cossa dise, Alvise?"

Contìn: "It's Pesaro, Uncle."

Paternian: "He's the fellow we should have elected."

Contìn: "Yes. Be quiet now, Uncle. The Doge has something more to say."

Paternian: "That Friulian!"

Manin rises again, tottering a little, to reply to this oration. He reviews the deplorable state of the Militia and the lagoon defenses, the depletion of the Treasury, and the sufferings that would be attendant upon a prolonged and pointless siege. He refers to the heritage of ten centuries of art contained in the city, the destruction of which would be a heavy charge upon their heads. Then, stifling a sob, he declares himself resigned to the Divine Disposition, and ready if such is the will of Heaven to accept the system of provisional government as proposed by the French, concluding by advising the Consiglio to recommend themselves and their city to the mercy of the Lord God and His Most Holy Mother. At this he breaks frankly into tears and has to be led to his chair by a secretary.

This spectacle is so astonishing that the whisperings and murmurs stop. Everyone is silent. There is no more discussion. At this moment there is a rattle of musketry from outside, shaking the windows a little.

"The vote! The vote!"

It is only the dismissed Schiavoni, departing from the Riva in barges, offering their final salute to the Republic. But this is not understood, and the result is panic. The Doge rises in consternation and makes as if to descend from the dais. A group of patricians forms around him crying, "The vote! the vote!" The urn is brought forward. It is an immense affair of bronze, all in gilt, with allegorical figures on top of it. The patricians rush for the black or white balls and deposit them in the urn. Only after half the votes have been cast is it made clear what they are voting for. The secretary announces that the question is "the acceptance of the Provisional Representative Government, always provided that this meets with the approval of the General."

Paternian: "I don't see that we need to put that in, Alvise."

Contìn: "Cast your vote, Uncle."

Paternian: "But I don't know which."

Contìn: "The black."

The murmurings and whispering in the hall rise to a kind of rumble as the votes are counted. A quorum of six hundred is required and only five hundred and thirty-seven members are present, so any vote taken is null and void. In the confusion of the moment this detail is ignored. It is announced that there are five hundred and twelve votes in favor of the protocol and twenty opposed.

At this announcement there is a kind of vast exhalation, like an enormous beast lying down to die. This is followed by a certain amount of uncoordinated streaming back and forth over the vast floor of the hall by persons in velvet togas. Some patricians hasten to leave the Palace, while others are not sure this is advisable at the moment. Those who are believed to be wiser, or to have special information, are consulted. Where is Manin? He hurries away down the marble corridors, followed by his attendants who have to struggle to keep up with him. He passes through the door into his private apartments, the guards presenting their halberds. Once in his chamber he takes off the ducal regalia, the Corno, the ermine stole, and the toga, and flings them to an attendant—"Tolè, questa no la doperò più"—Take this away, I won't be needing it anymore.

Down below in the courtyard the patricians are streaming out of the Palace, some of them leaving their togas and wigs on the floor of the antechamber. No one dares to lay a hand on Pesaro. They have done enough shameful things for one day. His toga is a rich scarlet, as conspicuous as a flag. He launches out into the Piazzetta, his small chin set firmly in the collar of the robe, and disappears in the direction of the Molo.

Paternian can not make up his mind what to do. Finally he hands his toga to an attendant, but leaves on his short wig. Contìn doesn't remove his toga, since it is black and only resembles a long robe such as might be worn by any well-to-do person. They go down the great stairway and out through the portal. To Paternian's consternation the Piazzetta is filled with a large crowd of folk in shirt-sleeves, who are unmistakably agitated. They can not move very fast because of the old gentleman's hip. The way is blocked, and they find themselves surrounded by a crowd of small wiry men the color of honey.

Contìn: "Aren't you Arsenaloti?"

They are. It is their privilege, in times of crisis, to escort the Doge and carry his large violet umbrella. They wish now to escort him to the Arsenal and show him the galleys they've made, with cannon to toast the mustaches of the French.

One: "Is that the Doge there, eh?"

Contìn: "No, he's not the Doge."

Another: "He looks feeble enough to be the Doge."

Another: "Viva el Doxe!"

They hold a coat over Paternian's head, in lieu of the umbrella, and insist on escorting him to the Arsenal. One of them plucks him by the elbow, and he frees himself irritably. The crowd does not actually do any harm. But the old gentleman is buffeted from all sides. Some militiamen with cockades in their hats look on passively, leaning on their muskets.

It is impossible to get out through the Piazza, or to the Molo where gondolas are waiting, and if they are to go home to Ca' Paternian they will have to go the long way round. Contìn leads his uncle around the Basilica and into the narrow alleys of the San Lio quarter. A straggling procession follows them, shouting vivas for the Doge and for San Marco and explaining to passers-by that these are two gentlemen they are escorting home to their palace so they will take no harm from the evening damp. They make sporadic efforts, in fact, to hold coats over the heads of Contìn and Paternian. If the two slow down at all they are bumped from the rear. Some people drop out, others join on, but the raggle-taggle behind remains about the same size. A piece of melon sails over Paternian's head and smashes on the stones. Evidently they are not far from the Rialto market.

A head in a window: "And the Consiglio?"

Arsenaloto: "They've sold us to the French."

Contìn is wearing his sword, but he resists the temptation to hit somebody with the flat of it. They go over a bridge and down the other side, past the Miracoli, across a campo, and into the street beyond. They can't really steer themselves, and are swept along like chips in a flood. The crowd, becoming a little less amiable as it grows in size, falls onto people who are going about business as usual and showers them with fisticuffs. They are particularly incensed by an elegant young man in a gondola who, for the delectation of a middle-aged patrician sitting beside him, is singing in a sweet falsetto and accompanying himself on a guitar.

> "Vien co mi, montémo in gondola
> Andarémo fora in mar."

They pitch him into the canal, also his middle-aged friend, and then the gondolier. The guitar sails in after them.

"Viva San Marco! Abbasso i franzesi!"

Where are they exactly anyhow? Somewhere near San Canciano. They pass the house of Bernardin Renier, a patrician known to be in sympathy with the French. The shutters are torn off and the house is burning. There is no sign of anyone; only a servant out in the street flapping her apron in the hope, evidently, of extinguishing the flames. The crowd cheers.

Paternian: "Alvise, these people are ungrateful. At Graz, you know, I risked my neck. The General—"

Contìn: "Keep moving, Uncle."

They cross the Canareggio. From the bridge, looking down to the right, they can see a mob throwing fruit and pieces of offal from the street at the French Legation. Across the canal they continue down the Lista de Spagna, the procession still sweeping them along. After a few steps Contìn and his uncle manage to take shelter in the Spanish Embassy, slipping sideways out of the crowd in the way one might beach a boat from a flooding river. A servant clangs the grille shut behind them. Safe! There are shouts, birdcalls, and ironic farewells from the street behind.

* * *

In Campo San Bartolomeo, near the Rialto, a crowd has gathered to listen to a speaker. He is a thin and perfervid young man in a white blouse, standing on a crate somebody has brought over the bridge from the market. A wine-shop in the campo has been doing a brisk business and the crowd is bumptious. For the most part they are clerks from the shops nearby and porters from the Rialto. Nobody recognizes the young man. Still, he speaks excellent Venetian. "Citizens," he demands of them with a dark intensity, "what does a man want?"

Nobody knows, and after a while somebody suggests, "Bread."

"Citizens, the Bread of Liberty is the most healthful of all. Every man has a right to it, because what is a man if you deprive him of bread and liberty?"

The crowd: "Bread! Polenta!"

Speaker: "A man without liberty and bread is like a mad dog. Like a dog without a master."

Crowd: "Viva! He's right! Polenta, polenta! We're like mad dogs! He speaks well, this one."

It is not clear how a man without liberty, that is to say with some kind of master or other, is like a dog without a master which therefore has all the liberty it wants. But this is no time to get lost in sophistries. The speaker goes on.

"And citizens, who has taken your bread? Who has taken the bread out of the mouths of your children?"

Since polenta is made from maize, and the maize-fields are all on the Terraferma, the answer is, "The French."

Voice: "Non tuti i franzesi son ladri ma Bona Parte"—not all the French are thieves but a good part. There is laughter at this.

Speaker: "No, citizens, it is not the French. It is the patricians, the ones with their names in the Golden Book. The patricians have fine palazzi on the Grand Canal, and where does a poor man lay his head?"

Voice: "In the Frezzeria." More laughter.

Speaker: "Citizens, you have been told that Venice is a lion. But the lion is high up in the air, on a column in the Piazzetta. Go and look at him. Instead of attending to the needs of the people, he is reading a book. In the book it is written, Pax tibi Marce. But there is no peace. The lion has turned the page, and now it is written, Liberty, Equality, and Fraternity."

There is some kind of commotion at the edge of the campo. It is the Arsenaloti, who are on their way back from escorting Contìn and Paternian to the Spanish Embassy. The leader is a wiry caulker who walks with his arms a little apart from his body and his fingers spread out, as though he is about to grab something.

Caulker: "What's he saying?"

Porter: "He's talking about liberty."

Caulker: "Oh, fine."

Speaker: "You should be thankful to God that you have the Provisional Government. Now there are no more masters. It's the Revolution."

Caulker: "Revolution, what is that exactly?"

Speaker: "The reign of justice, fraternity, and liberty. Government by all men."

Caulker: "It's by Zorzi the grocer, from what I hear."

Speaker: "He's been elected or appointed by somebody. It's all in the protocol. There are no more masters now. Everybody's free."

Caulker: "That's a lot of balls. What do we need of a freedom imposed by foreigners who don't have our interests at heart, but their own? Why should these French want to make us free? Would we want to make them free, if we had the power?"

This perfect cynicism strikes home to the crowd. As shopkeepers they are ready to believe that everyone is motivated by interest. "Yes, why?" They turn on the speaker with angry shouts.

Crowd: "He isn't one of ours! Who ever saw him before? It's French money he's taken! Assassin of St. Mark! Kill him! Beat the shit out of him!"

They pull him down from the crate and treat him roughly. Like a ball he bounces from one to the other. A large blue patch appears on his cheek. He falls, gets up and runs, but the crowd pursues and drives him against a wall, where several more take turns at him as though he were some game of strength at a fair. Finally he manages to limp away up the lane.

In the campo his departure is hardly noticed. The discussion turns onto what exactly a Provisional Government might be.

"They're going to give us provisions, man."

"Testicle-head you are and always were. It's provisional for a while, and then comes something else."

"What?"

"Well, they've not told us that yet, you see. We have to wait and see."

"He said they were going to give us polenta."

"He said the Bread of Freedom. Try to eat that. It's nothing but a nun's fart."

"Ay," says a porter in a ragged canvas jacket, "in '93 they freed a precious lot of people. They freed 'em from their heads. They have a very fine machine for that. They set it up in the piazza, and thwack! a fellow is freed from his head once and for all. It's called the Encyclopedia," declares this expert firmly. "Ay, it's in the Gazette that you can read about it," he goes on, sure of himself since he has never read the Gazette, first because he can't afford to go to cafés and second because he can barely read the proclamations put up on the walls in large print. "Not only the patricians, you know, but the new ones when they came in charge, they cut off the heads of the ones who had taken charge at first, and so on. Oh, they were up to their ankles in freedom there, around that machine in Paris."

After night falls the crowds go on roaming through the city. There are numerous fires. The house of Zorzi in the San Lio quarter is burned and ransacked, and the French pamphlets thrown out into the street. The authorities attempt to restore order. The government, like all governments, announces that looting will be severely regarded. There are rumors of some mayhem or other from the Rialto, and constables are dispatched. Under the command of Renier, who has been appointed police-chief, the militiamen set up a cannon on the Rialto bridge and fire a burst of grapeshot into Campo San Bartolomeo, hitting a dog and an old lady who has gone out to collect droppings for her flower-pot.

The cries echo in the streets.

"Viva San Marco! Abbasso i franzesi!"

From somewhere off the campo there is an answering yell.

"Viva la libertà!"

Feet pound after it. There is the thud of fists. Most of these Jacobins, that is to say lovers of liberty, are dumped unceremoniously into the canals; but one at least is torn apart and beaten over the head with his own arm. Still it seems there are a lot of the sons of bitches.

"Viva la libertà!"

Another one! They run off after him in the darkness. Fistfights in obscure courtyards, in the corners of campi. An old woman, holding a cat with dangling legs under her arm, looks on. "What is it?" "They've voted in the Consiglio, Granny. We're all going to speak French." "And the Doge?" "Gone off to Paris, to kiss Bonaparte's arse." Well, a good voyage to him, she concludes, going back in the house with her cat.

The disorder increases toward midnight. The mob, with perfect impartiality, seeks with homicidal intent not only the exponents of the new democracy but the corrupt aristocrats as well. The great houses of Grimani and Battaja are burned. Renier, the new police-chief, is caught by a crowd in Calle Larga and barely escapes with his life. Now and then there is a rattle of musketry. A body lies in the Piazza, inspected by two saucer-eyed cats with electric whiskers.

To the early hours of morning the yells go on echoing in the streets; some in favor of liberty, others for the Saint. Now and then there is a thud of running feet, or a crash and a shatter of glass as some piece of furniture or other is dumped from a window. Toward dawn the Militia and the constables succeed in restoring some kind of order. But the spectral cries go on echoing through the streets, at longer intervals now. It is impossible to tell where the yells are coming from. They seem to arise from the stones, and hang in the air on a note of operatic anguish or defiance, like the howls of demons who have made themselves invisible but retain their vocal cords.

"Viva San Marco-co-o-o-o!"

"Viva la li-ber-TÀ!"

"San MAR-co-o-o-o!"

AT SUNSET THE NEXT DAY, WHILE

At sunset the next day, while a giant orange firework blooms in the sky to the west, Malcolm, Mark Anthony, and a half-grown novice from the convent go down the path to the creek. The boy, tucking up his skirt, wades out in water up to his knees to untie the sandolo. He wears the coarse brown robe of the order but without a hood. His head is tonsured like the others, which gives him an odd look, the look of an old man who has stayed young, a giant dwarf.

Mark Anthony, since he is the larger, gets into the stern of the sandolo and Malcolm into the bow. When the boy gets in too the tiny craft sinks almost to its gunwales. He pushes away and rows off down the creek, which is so shallow that the oars grate on the bottom. He rows standing up and facing forward, with his wrists crossed. Questioning him, Malcolm finds he is from Chioggia and the son of a fisherman; this accounts for his skill with the oars.

Malcolm: "So now, instead of being a fisherman you want to, h'mm. Give yourself to God?"

Boy: "At home there isn't much to eat, Paròn. Too many children. Six besides me."

After a while he adds, "Besides it's not so bad, serving God. They might be right, Paròn."

Malcolm: "Who?"

Boy: "The priests."
Malcolm: "That's true, they might be right."
Boy: "Where do you want to go, Paròn?"
Malcolm: "To the Fondamente Nove."
Boy: "Bene."

After that he says nothing, only goes on rowing the sandolo with swift and bird-like motions of his wrists. There is a half-inch of dirty water in the bottom of the craft. It slips along like an eel, responding to the rhythm of the oars with little forward jerks. The light in the sky is fading. A gray bank of clouds hangs over the horizon to the west, catching the sunset along its lower edge. Overhead a gray skein of clouds is slipping away in the other direction, as though the sky itself were sliding off toward Istria and the Dalmatian coast. Down below, on the lagoon, it is calm. The air is almost oppressively warm. The water smells of mud and rotten weed. A grassy island goes by with a piece of wall still standing on it: an abandoned convent. Then, after another half-hour or so, it is dark and nothing more can be seen. The city ahead is a line of lumps on the horizon.

Murano goes by: some ghostly white houses, and a flare of orange here and there from the glass-furnaces. The strung-out lumps on the horizon gradually coalesce and assume shape. On the left hand is the Zanipolo like a sleeping elephant, and the other way is the great bulk of the Gesuiti. Malcolm decides it might be better not to land at the Fondamente Nove after all. It is a conspicuous place, the landing for the tragheti that ply constantly back and forth to Murano. Instead he points out a rio for the boy to enter, farther to the left toward the Mendicanti. Once in between the houses it is black as Styx. There is no light except for the yellow gleam of a shrine here at the corner of a rio. A small church goes by, and a palazzo. Everything looks different in the darkness. The plashing of the oars is reflected with an odd loudness from the walls.

The sandolo bumps against the stone. They are somewhere near Campo San Canciano, at one of those landings where the quay comes down to the water in steps, like an Indian ghat. Malcolm and Mark Anthony get out and slip into the dark street opposite. Behind them the boy pushes off without a word. The sandolo dissolves.

They go along in single file up the street, which is like a ravine filled with ink. Malcolm looks around to see if Mark Anthony is following and can make out only a pair of white spots, astoundingly high, as though they were seven feet in the air. The street turns to the right, then to the left again, and comes out in Campo San Canciano.

At one side of the square is a wine-shop. The door is open, and there are lights, the clatter of crockery, and voices. A man is sitting at a table inside, with a plate before him and a bottle of wine at his elbow. As they pass the doorway he is staring straight at them. His fuzzy skull with its small ears is silhouetted in the light from behind.

With Mark Anthony following, Malcolm crosses the campo and goes on over the bridge toward Santi Apostoli. When he glances around he can see an outline with a misshapen tricorne on top of it, passing under a street-lamp a few hundred yards behind. Malcolm and Mark Anthony increase their pace. At Campo Santi Apostoli they go off to the left, around the inky mass of the church, and into the street beyond. Their footsteps ring with an extraordinary loudness on the pavement. Malcolm puts his hand under his coat to steady his clanking saber. This street, after a short distance, brings them to Campo Santa Sofia, a broad lane leading down to the water on the left. At the end of it is the tragheto landing.

Under the arbor there is a bench and a table where the gondoliers sit in the daytime to drink wine. With the vines overhead it is totally dark. The Canal stretches away in both directions, an iridescent gray boulevard with gleams of silver. The tragheto is visible coming slowly back across the water.

Mark Anthony: "You see dat fellow behind?"

Malcolm: "H'mm."

Mark Anthony: "He dat same sbirro dey call Pipistrelo, one I previously trow in canal."

Malcolm: "Tarnish the pest."

Mark Anthony: "But dey no more Inquisitors. Who he working for now?"

Malcolm: "Whoever's running things, he's working for them."

The tragheto bumps in among the stakes, and they step into it. The gondolier says nothing. He resets the oar in the forcola and slides his craft swiftly out backwards with a single stroke. Behind, on the other side of the arbor, a squeaky voice rings out.

"Tragheto!"

The man is swinging the gondola around. It turns like a drifting black leaf on the water. But instead of stopping when it is pointed at the bank on the other side, it goes rotating until it is headed down the Canal to the right.

Gondolier: "A warm night, Paròn."

Malcolm: "Hey, we want to go across the Canal. Where are you taking us?"

Gondolier: "But there are clouds to the west."

Malcolm: "Huh. Looks like a thunderstorm."

Gondolier: "One can see that the Paròn is a sailor. Clouds to the west at sunset, and high clouds overhead. A thunderstorm."

Voice behind: "Tragheto!"

Gondolier: "A thunderstorm, that's good. It washes the air. After a time there are a lot of dirty things in the air, and the thunderstorm washes it clean."

Malcolm: "What kind of dirty things?"

Gondolier: "Nothing in particular. Smoke from chimneys. Bad smells."

Malcolm: "So the thunderstorm washes them away, eh?"

Gondolier: "Sometimes."

They go down the Canal for ten minutes or so, without very much more conversation. Somewhere in the neighborhood of San Marcuolo the gondola slides in to the bank and comes to a stop in front of a kind of shed. Malcolm recognizes it as the guild-house of the gondoliers, where they keep their costumes and special panoply for regattas, and where they hold their meetings. It is absolutely silent. The gondolier calls out softly.

"Ao. Anybody there?"

After a while figures appear and there is conversation. Malcolm and Mark Anthony, it seems, are to get out of the gondola. They climb out onto the rickety pier in front of the guild-house and are led around it and up the street.

"See, Captain," someone explains, "it isn't safe for you to go wandering around the city."

Malcolm: "Why?"

Voice in the darkness: "Because there's an order out for your arrest."

Malcolm: "I thought there were no more Inquisitors."

Voice: "Now it's the Provisional Government."

Malcolm: "What's that exactly?"

Voice: "It's an animal with no head and four front legs, all wanting to go in different directions."

Malcolm: "H'mm."

Voice: "But it bites."

Malcolm: "How can it bite with no head?"

Voice: "It bites with its rear end. Come on, Captain. Follow us and we'll take care of you. And the giant too. He's like a campanile, that fellow. Lucky it's dark so he can't be seen."

Malcolm: "How do you fellows know all this?"

Voice: "Gondoliers, Captain, know everything that's going on."

With some shadowy figures escorting them, they go up the street, around a corner, and along for a few hundred yards more. They pass the Israelite temple, then continue through an underpassage and out on the other side. The houses here are very high, five or six stories, since the Jews are confined to the Ghetto and yet go on reproducing, so that they have to build upward instead of sideways. There is a different stench in the streets; not worse, just different.

They stop before a house. It is a shop of some kind, or perhaps a tavern. Malcolm and Mark Anthony are introduced into the door. There are more whispers in the street behind them. Inside the house it is dark, but there is light from the room beyond.

The gondoliers leave, and Malcolm and Mark Anthony are taken into the lighted room. It is a kind of tavern or locanda, since many of the people crowded into the place seem to be travelers or refugees from the Terraferma. Some have children, others are sitting on bundles, and at least one is a Gypsy. It is a kind of warren, teeming with people, crawling over each other, giving suck to children, accommodating themselves to the situation as best they can. There are a number of old Sephardic Jews with beards, in black robes and yarmulkes. One of these, a venerable patriarch, serves as host. He rises shakily from the table.

"You are welcome, Captain. So is your friend, even though he is of the race of Ham. We are all sons of God. But afterward, tell no one you were here, otherwise these people will suffer."

Malcolm: "Don't worry."

Patriarch: "Will you take something? Food or drink. Anything you wish."

Malcolm: "No, nothing."

Nevertheless room is made for them at a table, and they are provided with a bottle of wine and a plate of lentils each. Everyone looks curiously at them. Evidently their fame has preceded them, or the gondolier has explained who they are. A boy with dark curly hair comes up and stares into Malcolm's face.

"Is it true you come from La Mèrega?"

Malcolm: "Yes, but a long time ago."

Boy: "Is it true that in La Mèrega the Jews are like everyone else?"

Malcolm: "They have Politicks there too."

Boy: "Is it true that a Jew could be king?"

Malcolm: "They don't have a king."

The Patriarch chases the boy away. "Let him eat his beans." But others come up and want to talk to him too. There is a great curiosity about Mark Anthony. Why is he so big, they want to know, and is he black all the way through or just on the outside? They feel his great knees, and would like to see whether he is circumcised, but the Patriarch forbids this. Che Moro! He's a giant! At least they have seen this before the end of their days.

An old man is led across the room to the table where Malcolm is sitting. Someone explains that this is the Algerino. He too wishes to inspect the new guests. The Algerino is short and fat, and limps horribly, so that he has to help himself along with a stick. His clothing is very dirty. His shirt hangs out, showing his hairy belly, and his breeches are stained from incontinence. He wears spectacles, one glass of which is white and opaque. There is a gleam of spittle at the corner of his mouth.

Algerino (after staring at Malcolm for some time): "Captain, give us a sip of that."

Malcolm: "You should be ashamed, old man."

Algerino: "Why?"

Malcolm: "For you wine is forbidden."

Algerino: "How can that be? Bismillah, a man must drink, otherwise he will despair."

Malcolm: "It's not lawful, because of your religion."

Cul shee halal, says the Algerino, everything is lawful. Of everything that God has given, it is lawful for the children of God to partake.

Malcolm: "What about your Koran?"

Algerino: "I can't read books because of my eye'

Patriarch: "Shut up, you old infidel. Keep your peace. The captain doesn't want to be bothered. You're drunk, it's a shame."

Algerino: "I an infidel? I wear out a rug praying. Bismillah, God is merciful."

Patriarch: "My son, this old person is not seemly, but we have to give him shelter, otherwise where would he go?"

Malcolm: "Leave him alone. He's doing no harm."

Algerino: "I have been in many places."

Patriarch: "So has the captain, old man. Shut up."

Algerino: "I have been to Constantinople, where is the great Mosque of Sancta Sophia, with its four minarets that reach the sky."

Malcolm: "So have I. Where else have you been?"

Algerino: "I have been to the sacred Mecca, where the Prophet himself is buried along with his forty-seven sons. No, that is a lie. I am not Haji. I have not been to Mecca. But I have been to many places."

Malcolm: "Where else have you been?"

Algerino: "I have been to Naples, in the kingdom of Sicily. And there I saw a burning mountain, and the tomb of a certain sorcerer called Virgilio, who made witch-rhymes, by which he could raise the dead."

Malcolm: "So could Odysseus. He went into Hell and saw Achilles. Achilles said that he would rather be a slave on earth than a king in the Land of the Dead. Where else have you been?"

Algerino: "I have been to many places in the world, and learned all the wisdom of the sons of men, and came out no wiser than I was before. But now I have a great desire to go piss." He gets up and staggers away in the direction of the door, supporting himself on the stick.

Patriarch: "My son, I beg your pardon for this Algerino. He is sunken in vice, but he too is a man." He notices with disapprobation that Malcolm has drunk most of his bottle of wine but has not touched his beans. "Will you not take something to eat?"

Malcolm: "Give it to somebody else."

Patriarch: "Times are hard. Food is precious. Is it true there is no more Doge?"

Malcolm: "So they tell me."

Patriarch: "And will Bonaparte come now?"

Malcolm: "That I can't say."

Patriarch: "Bonaparte is a Freemason, they say. He will make all the women naked, and then take his choice."

Malcolm: "I don't think so."

Patriarch: "Whichever it is, the Doge or Bonaparte, the Jews will weep."

Malcolm: "Why is that, old man?"

Patriarch: "Because they're God's chosen folk."

Malcolm: "How? I don't understand."

"God's chosen folk must weep, that's all," he insists.

Someone else comes to sit beside Malcolm. Everyone is interested in him and wants to talk to him. This person is a tall, strikingly handsome youth with a pale face and a beard. He wears a long black robe of some shiny stuff, not entirely clean.

Youth: "If I went to La Mèrega, Captain, would there be a place for such as me?"

Malcolm: "You can go to La Mèrega if you like. They threw me out, because I was on the side of the King."

Youth: "All men are free there."

Malcolm: "Free to think like the others."

Patriarch: "Don't bother the captain."

Youth: "You and I should go to La Mèrega together, Captain."

Malcolm: "Not likely."

Youth: "Tomorrow we can talk of this. Now it's late. Aren't you tired?"

Patriarch: "Stay, Captain. Don't go with this person."

But Malcolm is tired of talking, and allows himself to be led away. The youth takes him down a corridor. There is a smell of cooking mutton, and of rooms where too many people have lived. The youth, however, occupies a room to himself. It is very tiny, but there is a bed and an old iron-bound chest to keep things in.

The youth lights a candle and then undresses. The dirty satin robe comes off, and some underclothing. When everything is off he turns around, and there stands before Malcolm a girl with a beard. In some way or another, where the youth was handsome the girl is hideous. She is tall and raw-boned, as narrow as a board, and there is a yellowish cast to her skin. The lines of her ribs show on either side. On the chest are two buttons of black and dry flesh. No breasts, no belly—a boy with a hole.

The bearded girl: "Aren't you coming?"

Malcolm: "I don't want to."

The bearded girl: "You don't want to?"
Malcolm: "No, I don't want to."
The bearded girl: "Very well."

She puts on an old night-shirt, which comes to her knees. Malcolm takes off his breeches, leaving his own shirt on. And they sleep chastely together in the bed for the rest of the night, side by side.

IN THE MORNING WHEN A

In the morning when a kind of putrid light filters through the shutters—it is not clear what time it is—Malcolm is awakened by a loud racket from the street outside. There is the sound of splitting wood, and shouts. He springs out of bed and finds his breeches. There is no sign of the bearded girl. After a moment's hesitation he jams his boots on, then his coat and hat, flings open the shutters, and goes out the window carrying his saber and sling in his hand.

The room is on the ground floor. He drops to the pavement and looks around. Unfortunately he is in the small inner courtyard of the house, with walls all around him. The fracas from the street outside has now penetrated into the house itself. There are sharp feminine screams, the sound of a chair cracking, and orders bellowed in a peremptory voice. All this comes out the door of what appears to be a kind of scullery. At least there is a barrel of garbage outside it, leaking at the seams. There is no other way out of the courtyard. Malcolm skirts the barrel and goes in.

Beyond the scullery is the large main room of the house. This is where all the noise is coming from. Pipistrelo has penetrated into the room with four bravi behind him, and is piping at everyone in his reedy voice to render themselves. Mark Anthony is swinging a chair around in the air, holding it in one hand as though it were doll-furniture. Two of the bravi are attempting to get at him, and another is sitting on the floor disentangling rungs and chair-legs from his shoulders. The fourth is lying on the floor with all four limbs extended and a puddle of blood coming from him.

Pipistrelo (shrilly): "Captain, in the name of the Provisional Municipal Government, you are under arrest."

Mark Anthony upsets a table in his direction. Pipistrelo dodges this with a little squeal. There is a great deal of confusion. Malcolm gets his saber out but, since he has not had time to put on the sling, he is obliged to hold the scabbard rather awkwardly in his left hand. Pipistrelo comes at him with a dirk upraised, and Malcolm waits until exactly the right moment and then impales him. This is easily done, but the trouble comes in extricating the blade. Pipistrelo falls heavily to the floor with the saber under him, and manages to get his hand around the pommel. His eyes are glazed but his other arm is still swimming feebly back and forth. Malcolm turns him over with a push of his boot and tugs away at the saber. The Flaming thing is like a fishhook. It won't come out. Perhaps the point has turned on something hard inside. He wrestles with it, twisting the grip back and forth and swearing to himself.

It comes out finally, and as he thought the point is bent. The scene in the room resembles the climax of a bad opera. Bodies are lying on the floor in unlikely poses, one with a leg resting on a table-top. A good deal of this havoc has been wreaked by Mark Anthony with no other weapons than chairs. The Algerino totters around the room with a gleam of spittle on his mouth. From somewhere he has procured a rusty old Toledo, and he is whacking away with this without inflicting any noticeable harm. The refugees are huddled in the far corner of the room, hiding their children behind them. The old Patriarch floats about gesticulating, as though he hopes with motions of his hands to stop the fighting, moaning softly to himself. No one pays any attention to him.

There is only one more bravo still upright, and he is preoccupied with Mark Anthony, who is breaking up chairs in a methodical way and without anger, as though he is making kindling. Malcolm hesitates for a moment, then, still holding the saber in one hand and the scabbard in the other, he slips out through the smashed door and off down the street. When he looks back he sees someone coming out the door after him on his hands and knees. It is one of the bravi, oozing blood from his head but still functioning in his fashion. Malcolm breaks into a run.

There is nobody in sight. The threatening weather of the day before has not yet broken, and the sky is murky. An even, grayish, almost purple light filters down over the city, illuminating everything dimly. To the west, over the Terraferma, a great cloud with a shadowy underside advances on the centipede legs of a rainstorm.

After five minutes of loping along through the Ghetto—which is totally deserted and gives an eerie impression, like some city of the dead—he comes out onto the Grand Canal by the Scalzi. Here there is a tragheto waiting. He drops into it panting.

The gondolier pushes off without a word. He swings his craft around on the water, which in the curious light from the clouds resembles molten lead, and bends to the oar. Malcolm inserts the point of his saber between the planking of the gondola and one of its ribs, and bends it straight. He sloshes it off in the Canal, dries it on his breeches, and puts it into the scabbard. Then he takes off his coat, drapes the sling over his shoulder with the saber on the left, and puts the coat back on again. The gondolier, perched on the stern behind him, looks blandly over his head and goes on rowing.

On the other side, at Santa Croce, Malcolm gets out and sets off along the great curve of the Canal toward the Rialto, keeping to the smaller and more obscure streets. Still, he has not gone more than a mile before he is aware that there is somebody following him. If he looks around he glimpses a shape there like a spot at the corner of the eyeball, but it disappears if looked at directly. It is not clear how the fellow has got across the Canal, unless he crawled over it on his hands and knees in the same way that he came out of the doorway.

Increasing his pace a little, Malcolm crosses a bridge with a walled garden on the right. By now he is in Campo San Cassan, under the old church with its wall that seems to be made out of left-over bricks. He crosses the campo diagonally and slips into a street off to the right, which unfortunately turns out to be a cul-de-sac. He stops in a doorway and looks behind him. After a while the man appears in the campo and stops, with the dim purplish light shimmering around him. He puts his hand to his head, takes it away, and stares into his palm. He shakes the hand to dislodge the blood. Malcolm clearly sees the tiny spots dropping from it, like flies. The man looks around him, at one point staring directly up Malcolm's street. Then, as if by magic, he dissolves and is no longer visible. Evidently he has moved in under the deep shadow of the church. The campo is silent except for a very delicate noise like the chewing of insects, caused perhaps in some way by the action of this odd light on the stones. Working carefully, in order not to make a sound, Malcolm slips the saber out of the scabbard and holds it with the point resting on his boot.

He stands in this way for some minutes. Then there is the even tap-tap of footsteps somewhere beyond the campo. The sound grows louder, then a tall and slim figure appears at the end of the street, in a round hat with the brim turned up at one side. She turns the corner into the street and comes directly at him. When she is opposite him she gropes in the reticule and takes something in her hand. There is the metallic sound of the key being fitted into the lock.

The heavy door swings open, and she turns to look at him. In the dim purple light, which seems to buzz slightly, her face is calm and composed. At least the lower part of it; the upper part is hidden under the shadow of the hat.

"Why are you hiding in that doorway? Is somebody following you?"

Malcolm doesn't answer.

Winifred: "Why don't you stop being such a silly idiot and step into this door? I won't hurt you."

After another moment, and a glance down the street, he follows her through the door. It closes behind them with a prison-like sound. They are in a shadowy place of some sort and it is a time before his eyes adjust. After a while he makes out a square of light far overhead.

Winifred: "You're safe here. The door's heavy."

He realizes he is still holding the saber. Feeling for the tip with his left hand, he slips it into the scabbard.

Winifred: "Follow me on the stairway. It's dark. I know the way."

Her shape detaches itself and slips away upward and to the left. He follows her up, feeling with his fingers along the damp stone wall. They come to a landing, then a second flight. At the top she stops, still in almost total darkness. He can hear her fumbling in the reticule again for the key.

The heavy door creaks as it opens. They enter a kind of vestibule or hallway, and she leads the way into the room beyond. Here the shutters are open and the grayish light is filtering in. She goes directly to the windows and closes them. It is dark again for a few moments while she strikes a light. A sulphur-match flares; she carries it in her cupped hands to the table and lights a candle.

They are in a large room, rather untidily and shabbily decorated in the manner of the previous century. There is a bad painting in the style of Rubens, and a heavy table with a lace cloth. Across the room, between the two windows with their closed shutters, is a fireplace.

He is able to see her clearly for the first time. At least this time she is wearing a skirt. It is a long gown of stiff linen with brocade decorations, closely fitting her narrow body. Over it is a velours cloak that comes almost to her knees. The hat is the same: beige, a round crown, the brim turned up at one side, a yellow feather. Turning away from him almost absent-mindedly, as though he weren't there, she feels for a pin and removes the hat.

Winifred: "Won't you take something? Something to eat?"

He shakes his head.

Winifred: "You haven't spoken a word, do you know that? Perhaps there is something wrong with your vocal apparatus. Would you like some tea then?"

Her manner is grave but there is a slight fluster underneath which she is attempting to dominate. It seems to be important to her that he should take some tea. He makes a rustle in his throat, slightly embarrassed.

Malcolm: "If you like."

Winifred: "I'm afraid it's vile tea. It's *Chinese* tea."

He has the impulse to tell her that he really doesn't care for women who twitter on in this way, emphasizing some words as though they were underlined. But she has gone off somewhere to make the tea. He stands awkwardly for a moment, then he walks around the room inspecting things. The place has a gaunt and empty look. Its occupants have taken everything personal with them, leaving only the bare furniture. For some reason they haven't taken the lace tablecloth. It is an incongruous touch, fragile and feminine, in the male Venetian hardness of the room with its marble floor. There is a thin layer of dust on everything. He runs his hand over the mantel, looks at the fingers, and wipes them on his breeches.

She comes back through the door from a kind of pantry that serves as kitchen.

Winifred: "It'll be a little while, I'm afraid. Things aren't as they are with *us*. Not as *convenient*."

Malcolm: "It doesn't matter."

Winifred: "Won't you make yourself more comfortable? Perhaps you'd like to take off your—sword."

He makes no answer to this. He gives her a thoughtful stare and goes back to looking around the room.

Her long and slightly equine face is still thoughtful. She seems self-contained, but prim. She studies him for a moment before she speaks.

Winifred: "Perhaps you don't . . . trust me entirely."

Malcolm: "What d'you mean by that?"

Winifred: "I can assure you there's no one else here. I'm alone. Perhaps you thought that I . . ."

Evidently she is taking for caution, or suspicion, what is really only awkwardness on his part. He looks at her dubiously, then removes his hat and sets it on the table. The saber is a more complicated matter. To take it off properly he would have to remove his coat, and this doesn't seem appropriate under the circumstances. He unfastens the shackle, removes the scabbard with the sword, and sets in on a chair, leaving the sling on under his coat. He sits down, and they inspect each other rather gingerly over the lace on the table.

Winifred: "Who *was* following you?"

Malcolm: "A fellow."

Winifred: "Surely you have some idea."

Malcolm: "I have lots of ideas."

Winifred: "Are they expressible in words?"

Malcolm: "There's an order out for my arrest."

Winifred: "Because of me?"

Malcolm: "How, because of you?"

Winifred (a little flustered): "Because you—helped me when I landed at the Molo."

Malcolm: "No, it's not that. It's the French that want me arrested. Because of the affair at the Lido."

Winifred: "You mean—slaughtering poor Captain Laugier and all that?"

He nods.

Winifred: "But you were only following your orders."

Malcolm: "It's not a fair world."

She ponders over this for a moment, looking at him thoughtfully.

Winifred: "Then you've been going around all this time, hiding in doorways from people who were following you?"

Malcolm: "I've been out of the city."

Winifred: "Out of the city? Where?"

Malcolm: "On an island."

Winifred: "An island?"

Malcolm: "An island of monks."

Winifred: "I see." Then she adds, "Although I don't *really* see. Why?"

Malcolm: "It seemed like a good idea."

Winifred: "You aren't a . . . papist?"

Malcolm: "No."

They both smile.

After this things are easier. Presently, to his surprise—even to his mild alarm at his own indiscretion—he finds himself explaining the thing to her.

Malcolm: "They're Friars Minor. There's nothing much to do there. You just listen to the Brothers singing in the chapel. Other people there are mad. It's very restful. You go there a day or two, and you sort things out. You understand things."

Winifred: "What kind of things?"

Malcolm: "Anything that's bothering you."

Winifred: "The Brothers tell you?"

Malcolm: "No. It's just being there."

Winifred: "Can women go?"

Malcolm: "Of course not."

Winifred: "Still, I imagine they must have such places for women."

Malcolm: "I suppose so."

Winifred (subtly): "The Carmini."

Malcolm: "That may be. It's out in the lagoon, near San Servolo. They have madmen there too."

Winifred: "Why do you keep harping on about madmen?"

Malcolm: "I'm just telling you about these islands."

Winifred: "Oh! the tea."

She is flustered again. She gets up abruptly and disappears through the door. There is a considerable wait. It is very quiet. There are sounds of a culinary sort from behind the door. Malcolm becomes aware of two things. The first is that he is sexually aroused. He is unable to account for this, and decides it must be due to some sickness. Luckily he is sitting at the table where it won't be noticed, even in the tight-fitting breeches.

The other is a more abstract thing, a sense of peril or more precisely of uncertainty. He remembers that, when she came to his house in San Trovaso, something ambiguous in her manner made him wonder whether she were offering—something—in return for the packet. After he delivered her to the fine fiancé in Ca' Pogi, he dismissed this from his mind. Now the thought returns. Suppose she—did something or other. Under the impression that he still had the packet. Now that would really be dishonest. He is horrified that this infamy has even entered his mind. Still there is this infernal straining at his breeches.

She comes in through the door with the tea. It is on a tray, in a china pot with two fragile cups to match. It is far too fine for him. He has the impression that if he took one of the cups in his hand it might shatter.

She has taken off the velours cloak while she was out of the room. The gown has only short sleeves, and her long thin arms emerge from it. He notices for the first time how she has fixed her hair: drawn to one side and tied with a yellow ribbon, the soft mass of it falling to her shoulder. Her ears are bare. The earlobes are the only part of her that is a soft coral. Her face is pale. Her ears blush before the rest of her does. She sets the tray down, deftly but so abruptly that a little tea spills from the spout.

Winifred (for the second time): "It's *vile* tea."

Malcolm: "It doesn't matter."

They sip it, almost in silence. He is wary, alert, waiting to see what she will do. That clutch of blood, down there, is an enemy in the center of his body. It is as though an antagonist were plying him with drink or with drugs. But this drink, this drug, is a more subtle one. It permeates him from across the table, even through walls. This very warmth in him, this sense of flooding comfort and instinct to gentleness, is a danger.

Winifred: "There's a button loose on your coat. It's hanging by a thread."

Malcolm: "No doubt."

He gets up, pushing back the chair which makes an astonishingly loud noise against the marble.

Malcolm: "I thank you for the tea."

Winifred: "But you can't go out again—now."

Malcolm: "Why not?"

Winifred: "*He*—whatever—may still be waiting."

Malcolm: "Not likely."

Winifred: "In any case you can't go back to your house in San Trovaso."

He glances at her. She is regarding him fixedly, her upper lip pressed slightly against the teeth as though not to smile or—show some other expression. He turns away, reaches for the saber on the chair, and shackles it onto the sling under his coat.

Winifred: "You'd better stay here."

Malcolm: "How d'you mean, here?"

She bursts out, "You make everything so difficult! I mean—there are plenty of rooms. There's a room there"—she flings out her arm in an imperious gesture—"where you'll be comfortable enough. No one will disturb you."

What in blazes does she mean by that? He goes off down the corridor to look at the famous room. There is no bed, only a mattress on the floor and an assortment of blankets, not very clean. There are wood-shavings on the floor, and some tools. Evidently someone has been using it as a carpenter-shop.

"I imagine you're used to bedding down just anywhere," he hears her saying behind him.

It is not clear to him whether she is unfamiliar with the house and sees only now that there is no bed, or whether he is condemned to sleep on the floor because he has said—what the Devil has he said anyhow? He has said nothing. She goes away, and he closes the door.

But in only a few minutes she comes back, with a needle and thread.

Winifred: "Give me that disgrace of a coat."

She sews the button on for him, all the while pointing out his shortcomings.

Winifred: "Why can't you do this?"

Malcolm: "I can."

Winifred: "Then why don't you?"

Malcolm: "I don't know." (Helplessly) "Because you are."

Winifred: "There." (Handing it back to him) "Look at your boots. They're a disgrace."

Malcolm: "It's muddy on the island."

Winifred: "And your shirt. Don't you ever wash it?"

Malcolm: "I'm not one of your fine lords. Otherwise I wouldn't be sleeping in this room with the carpenter-tools."

Winifred: "If you don't like it you can—take my room, and I'll sleep here."

They are both frightened at this, as though they have skirted the edge of a chasm. She goes away again, and he shuts the door almost in her face.

But it is only a minute until she comes back once again, with her face set as though she has taken a sudden resolve.

Winifred: "Captain Langrish, where is my little packet?"

He stares at her. "It doesn't exist anymore, and you shouldn't play dangerous games."

Winifred: "Games? What games?"

Malcolm: "All this stealing into Venice carrying messages. You think it's a game, and you won't be punished if you're caught, because you're only playing. You sew packets into your drawers and pass them along to your lover. You dress up in clothes and pretend to be somebody else."

Winifred: "I'd rather you didn't refer to my underclothing."

Malcolm: "You know nothing about life. You think it's all some book by Rousseau. Have you ever known what it was to be hungry, or thirsty? Have you ever gone without sleep, or suffered pain, or seen your comrades killed before your eyes?"

"Well, yes, yes, yes, yes, and yes, for most of your questions," she replies, exasperated. Her earlobes have turned pink again. "Why are you directing this diatribe against me? What exactly is the terrible thing that I've done?"

Malcolm: "You haven't done anything. You're just a little fool. That's what you've done."

She goes off, slamming the door.

After nightfall it is too dark in the room with the shutters closed. Malcolm gets up, gropes his way to the window, and opens it. A faint light penetrates, barely enough to show the outlines of things in the room. He lies down again with his hands behind his head. He listens to the sounds. There is a faint but constant lapping in the rio below, and the knock of an oar as a gondola slips by. In the house across the rio somebody closes the shutter with a bang. Other sounds that he identifies one by one: a cat on the tiles overhead, a church bell in another part of the city, a grumble of thunder in the distance. Then there is a measured rustling on the tiles that gradually grows louder; it is starting to rain.

After he has listened to the rain for ten minutes or so he hears some sort of scraping on the stairway, scratchy and muffled through the walls. There are voices, and doors open and shut. A moment later there is a knock on his own door. It is she again, in night-dress with the velours cloak pulled on over it, holding a candle.

Winifred: "There is a person here to see you."

Malcolm: "What kind of a person?"

Winifred: "Well, you'll see. You know him."

Malcolm: "I don't know anybody."

She goes away, and after a while comes back leading Mark Anthony, in his old cloak but hatless. He has a purplish bruise on his cheek with a little dried blood on it. He crowds into the tiny room. There is no place for Winifred, and she stands behind in the doorway holding the candle.

Malcolm: "How in Thunder did you find me?"

He gazes at Malcolm with a dignified contempt. Even though he lowers his voice the rumbling basso fills the room.

Mark Anthony: "Copn, you are not one half part so invisible as you tink. I follow you all de way from de Ghetto, to be sure dat fellow wit de broken head not cotch up wit you. Den, when de English Leddy let you in, I have to wait for dark to come here, so de whole town will not know where you are putting up."

Malcolm: "Oh, Crucks."

Mark Anthony: "You may say dat, Copn."

Malcolm: "What are we going to do with this fellow?"

Winifred: "We can ask the Parona."

Malcolm: "Who?"

Winifred: "It's her house. Perhaps she has other apartments."

Malcolm: "It's not the King of Germany. He's just my bosun."

Winifred: "Still he has to sleep."

Mark Anthony: "I sleep standing up in de street, Copn. I sleep anywhere. I sleep in a spare gondola dat nobody is using."

Winifred: "I'll take him down if you like."

Malcolm: "No, I'll do it. Give me the candle."

The business is soon done. Marta, the old serving-woman, is aroused and a large nocturnal giant, with white eyes and an aloof manner, is confided to her. She is only half awake anyhow and has had other dreams like this. A pallet is made on the floor, behind the kitchen. There is some cold polenta and sausage. Marta goes back to sleep, where, she hopes, things will be a little more real.

In this way Mark Anthony passes, like a dark ship entering port, into the life of the Parona. It is not important that she has no name, because he can't speak to her anyhow. Everyone has forgotten her name long ago. She herself has forgotten it, almost; she has it written down somewhere. She was born a long time ago, almost in the previous century, in the time when Zovani Corner was Doge. Now there was a rascal. Her father often spoke of him. Although possibly her father was the Doge Zovani, or he was her uncle. It doesn't matter anymore, and somewhere or other she has a book dedicated to her and signed with some name.

She collects all kinds of things: antique marbles, some spurious and some genuine; indecent bronzes from Pompeii, incense-burners, scraps of Roman walls, mosaics from Aquileia, hookahs and camel-saddles, cowries from the South Sea arranged in a rosewood cabinet lined with felt. Also two lampadarii—black men dressed in the Turkish fashion, with turbans and loose trousers, and vests which leave their chests bare. They are trimmed in gilt, and they hold old-fashioned lamps with tow wicks. They have no names either; she calls them simply i do Mori.

When she acquires Mark Anthony she is unable, in her blurred but somehow tenacious mind, to form any important distinction between him and the other objects of her collection. He is large and has the quality of auto-gesticulating; this is distinctive. He becomes el Moro, the others remain i do Mori.

ZULIETTA COMES HOME AS USUAL IN

Zulietta comes home as usual in the indecent hours of the night. Her clothes are damp with rain. She enters by the heavy street-door, then pulls it shut behind her and locks it. It is not entirely dark in the atrium. There is a flicker of yellow up above, at the top of the stairs.

She goes up, running her hand lightly among the balustrade and humming. On the landing at the top of the stairs is a large squarely built person in a somewhat tarnished military coat—hatless—his hair tied in a piece of yarn.

She smiles at him. "What luck! You have a candle. I won't have to grope in the dark."

He only clears his throat. He is a queer bird, no doubt about that.

"I'm called Zulietta. What about you?"

"Noman."

He stares at her over the candle. There is no particular expression on his face, except that he doesn't seem to be the kind that warms to people easily. He seems to be examining her costume, although there is nothing extraordinary about it. She slips down the hood, uncovering her rich Titian hair. A few microscopic pearls of water glisten in the locks in front.

She smiles again. Everything is clear to her. She recognizes immediately the American captain that she has promised Zanetto—if it should ever happen, Heaven forbid—to keep away from the house. But this captain is a man! Not like the dandies and wan patricians who frequent places like Crespi's. He is as solid as a rock. In fact, he looks like the Colleoni monument in front of the Zanipolo, the condottiere with his chin stuck out. Zulietta finds unprofessional sentiments invading her person. Suppressing the smile, she raises her own chin as though he did not matter an iota.

Zulietta: "Well, aren't you going up? We live on the same floor."

Malcolm: "I don't think I've met you."

Zulietta: "I tried to introduce myself, but you weren't very sociable. There's the stairway. If you go first, then I can see where I'm going."

Malcolm: "I don't live here."

Zulietta: "Of course not. You're an angel, come to announce to the Inglesina that there's going to be a new Immaculate Conception. Very well, I'll go first."

She goes on up the stairway, and Malcolm is obliged to follow with the candle. On the landing above she waits, still with her chin raised and the ghost of a smile. She shakes her hair, and a few drops glitter away to spatter on the wall. Then, after pausing for exactly the right length of time, she turns and inserts the key in the lock. The door swings open.

Zulietta: "Won't you come in? Ordinarily I don't allow friends to visit me here, but I'll make an exception."

Malcolm: "Nope."

Zulietta: "Without anything derogatory toward the English race, you will find it more comfortable here."

Malcolm: "Mind your own damned business."

Well, that is just what she can not do. The captain makes her feel—not business-like at all—instead like a girl of seventeen, feeling the muscles of the Burano fishermen. If the rest of him is like that jutting chin! She smiles, at her own folly. But why not? Besides it would be doing Zanetto a favor, since it is not really the house that he wishes to keep the captain away from, only the Inglesina's apartments.

Zulietta: "Well, I don't engage in violence. Suit yourself. But people who know me are complimentary."

Malcolm: "You can go to the Devil."

Instead she slips in through the door, still smiling, and shuts it behind her. It would have been—but she does not waste her time in vain regrets. She goes quite blithely to her chamber, takes off her clothes, and falls asleep on the Moorish pallet under a shawl. A Titian lock, fallen over her mouth, rises slowly and falls with her breathing.

Malcolm, after letting himself into his room, goes to sleep too after not very long. The rain is still pattering on the tiles. Out on the lagoon if falls evenly, in widely spaced drops, making dimples on the black water. The wind comes up and begins to stir the cypresses.

But Winifred can not sleep. This spooky old house, full of shadows and secrets, fills her with odd stirrings of the womb. Turning in the bed, she wants, she wants. What does she want? To be away. No, to be here. To be someone different than she is. To be Nando, or someone who goes about the wide world in trousers, or—she wants to be with Jean-Marie, she tells herself, coming awake abruptly.

The wakefulness is violent as a shock; there is no question of going to sleep now. She gets up and floats into the salon, goes to the window in her night-dress, and draws open the shutter. The night comes in, along with a few drops of rain, which burn on her face like tiny points of ice. The air smells of something—it smells of Venice. The odor is thin and faintly corrupt, musky, like a perfume gone wrong. It reminds her of riding in Hyde Park, of riding in Kent, and she recognizes for the first time what it is: it is the odor of a male animal. Now the smell is cold, because the night is cold, and the rain is falling invisibly, with a rustling noise, onto the roof-tops opposite. On the Campanile, far away in the Piazza, it glistens on the great shape in the dark. Nando said, We call him El Paròn de Casa. As though evoked by this thought, something violet snaps far away to the south, illuminating the cupolas and roof-tops. A moment later there is a vast mumble which goes on for some time. Then darkness. Winifred feels strange. What is it? It is nothing, nothing. Only the storm. Still she is filled with this angelic flutter, as though warm honey were stirring in her. She can not admit to herself what she wants. Yet she knows.

As though sleepwalking she turns from the window and roams, or rather swims like a white phantom, through the other rooms. The pantry—the salon—her own chamber—the corridor. But there is something in the corridor. It is she who has provoked this, she knows in sudden alarm. She has wakened him with the keen gleamings of her thoughts, like a sun-flash through the walls. He comes down the corridor at her with his head lowered, in shirt-sleeves, his braces dangling from his breeches. He stops and menaces her with his head, pointing like a hunting-dog. Although this she really only imagines; all she can see is a blacker blur in the darkness.

Winifred (with a tremor): "What are you looking for?"

Malcolm: "Nothing."

There is only one thing she has neglected to tell him, and that is where the convenience is. However he would rather die than let a word of this pass through the bar of his teeth.

Winifred: "What—what—do you want . . ."

Malcolm: "What do I want? What the Devil do you want?"

Winifred hardly knows what she is saying. As in a dream she listens to her own voice. "Come to the window."

Malcolm: "Why?"

Winifred: "See. Clouds on fire."

And in fact there is, just at that instant, another indigo jagger. Malcolm hesitates; he does not understand what . . . she pushes him forward. They collide softly onto the window. There is no sound. Everything floats, as in cotton-wool, or in a dream. In the next lightning-flare her face floats toward his, their mouths bump clumsily together, her whole elongated body twines around him like a vine. He feels the sharp pressing fin of her hip, and, below, a knee. That witless demon has reared his head in Malcolm's breeches again—if she notices what will she think? As gently as Venice itself falling, without violence, hardly noticing what they are doing, they sink to the floor. In Malcolm's vision the white face blurs and swims. For a few seconds—perhaps it is only an instant—they are entwined like two octopi, neither knowing which limb belongs to either.

Just in time, Malcolm awakes from his dream. He lets go of her as though he has touched white-hot metal, and springs away like a cat. Crouched against the wall, he attempts to rearrange his thoughts into articulated speech.

Malcolm: "I beg your pardon. I must have gone mad. It was a mistake."

Winifred: "I, I."

But now the notion strikes him that—it was perhaps not a mistake. Or perhaps it was. He gropes clumsily through the blur of mistakes. He attempts to touch her. His hand stops and floats an inch or so from her elbow.

Malcolm: "You see, I didn't know whether—"

But no! She crawls away from him on her hands and knees, springs up, and bolts away like a small animal. Her face is pale as though she has been whipped. It is even visible in the darkness; it is phosphorescent. She whirls around, seeking to orient herself and find the door. He follows, bumping into the furniture after her. The door, the door! There it is; it leaps out at her in a violet flash. She pulls, fumbles at the latch, and is gone.

Malcolm: "Hold on a minute. I didn't mean . . ."

Winifred bumps her knees in several places in her precipitate rush down the staircase in the dark. She is careful not to sprawl, however, since a broken head would not do just now. With a broken head she could not flee from the house. Here she is in the atrium, where Nando sleeps on a pile of sacks. Dear Nando! She tiptoes, nothing breaking the silence but her short fox-like breathing. And the creak of the grille as it swings open and clangs against the wall. Quickly! Nando will wake. She steps over onto the black hull and gropes for the oar. No, the gondola is still tied. Her fingers fumble at the rope lashed around the palo. It makes tears come because she can not untie the knot. Cruel, stupid, and dumb knot! It comes loose at last, after some damage to her fingers.

She pushes against the oar, and the long black shadow slips out from the shelter of the porch. She feels the raindrops through her gown, which clings to her back as though some slimy thing were pressing her, caressing her. Never mind! She sets the oar into the forcola and pushes; it bites into the water. Premi! Out on the Canal there are more lightning-flashes, this time from the direction of San Marco. White dots of rain spring up all around her on the black water. Ahead is the bridge of the Rialto, like a house with a great hole in it. The gondola slips under it and emerges again into the rain. Now there is the long reach to Ca' Foscari. The oar digs, stinging at her hands. Premi, Winifred! The rain streams down her face and into her eyes. She shakes her head, as though she were trying to awake. The wind soughs over the roof-tops and a piece of laundry flops in the darkness.

The sharp halberd at the bow catches the light from a votive lamp, and gleams. Stali! The oar holds in the water, and the black shape curves slowly around to the right, into the rio. Specters of houses go by, the windows staring at her like eyes. The rio turns. Then the gondola bumps in among the pali. She scrambles out, holding her wet gown. The abandoned oar dangles from the forcola.

Massimo is difficult to awaken, but a determined banging on the wrought-iron grille will do it. Winifred is admitted into the atrium, where she stands with water dripping from her onto the marble floor. Massimo backs away with the lantern, as one will from an animal unexpectedly released from a cage, without taking his eyes from her. Then he turns and flees up the staircase. There is his voice from above, echoing through the rooms.

"Paròn, Paròn. Moussou."

What does Winifred do in these minutes while he is gone? No one knows. Certainly Winifred does not know. She comes to herself only when Jean-Marie appears at the head of the staircase, sleepy and uncomprehending but severe, in an embroidered dressing-gown and slippers. Perhaps the frown is only from sleep.

His hair is sticking up on one side; he pats it down with his hand. He comes halfway down the staircase, but doesn't seem inclined to descend any farther.

Jean-Marie: "Mais—ma chère Clélia."

Winifred: "I am yours. But quickly, quickly!"

He is appalled, most of all, not by this but by her dress. He stares at the sopping-wet gown clinging to her breasts, sticking to the knees, even outlining the small depression at the center of the abdomen. A lock of hair is plastered to her wet face.

Massimo is at the balustrade above with a lantern. Jean-Marie comes down the rest of the staircase and stops an arm's-length from her. He notices for the first time that her feet are bare, in the puddle of water gradually widening on the marble.

Jean-Marie: "But what has happened? Was it"—the idea occurs to him for the first time—"was it the captain?"

Winifred: "I want to . . . do that thing. Coucher ensemble."

Jean-Marie: "You must be out of your mind. The boy's listening."

He feels a cold horror. What she speaks of is not possible, if only because of the way he has earlier spent his evening. But even apart from this, the instinct is so connected with elegance in his mind, and with the proprieties of timing and fine ambience, that he is no more capable of feeling passion for this odd creature at the moment than he would be for a giraffe.

Winifred: "Then you . . ."

Jean-Marie: "Clélia—"

He retreats a little toward the staircase. They back away from each other with their glances locked, like two Gypsy dancers. Then she turns and flees, the damp hair swinging from her face.

Jean-Marie: "Clélia!"

The wind batters now. It is no longer soft; it has an edge that seizes fiercely onto the gondola and pushes it sideways. The rain whips into the water like flying gravel. She emerges from the rio into the Canal. Here large waves come up to race under the gondola, sending it swooping up and down. Stali! She manages to swing to the right, toward Santa Maria de la Salute and the open lagoon. Where is she going? Only a part of her knows; then she remembers and cries it out to herself. To the Carmini! Sweet Sisters sunk in sleep, wake and save me. At last the ghostly white shape of the Salute looms up on the right—O Lady, you too, ora pro nobis. However the gondola is becoming unmanageable; it is necessary to have Nando floating behind her, shy guardian angel, to tell her what to do. Turn the knuckles up, Siorina, and feather the blade as it returns through the water, then she will slip forward like an arrow. Here is the Customs-House, the last marble peninsula of the city. Fortuna is facing north. Her bronze garment is almost blown away. Now we are on the lagoon, Nando, what must I do? Premi, Siorina, premi! A great splash knocks at the bow, half-filling the gondola and tilting it over so that it rocks like a swing. Yet the wind is behind now and the black craft scuds through the tempest. Winifred has brought the storm with her. There is no fleeing this storm, because it is inside her. Which way I fly is Hell; myself am Hell. The youth at her elbow reassures her, his gentle touch consoles. It is only you that I love after all,

Nando, only you are faithful, it is to you that I must be True. He smiles, a little embarrassed. Ecco, Siorina. Something appears in the darkness ahead, a loom of buildings and a campanile. Is that it? No, that is San Servolo, the island of madmen.

THE STORM IS OVER. THE BRIGHT SUN

The storm is over. The bright sun bakes down on the Piazzetta, drying out the stones and sending up veils of steam to float around the market-stalls. Off to the west, over the Terraferma, there are still some grayish clouds lurking, but they don't seem to be a menace. The Ducal Palace is shut up tight. Even the guards are not in their usual places by the Porta de la Carta, and the great windows are blind. But in the rest of the Piazzetta, and in the broad Piazza beyond, things are going on much as usual. Florian's opens and a waiter sweeps the water out of the portico. There is a great cackle from the poultry-stalls, and an odor of droppings, enhanced by the morning sunshine. The Venetians have come out in throngs and are circulating around in the Piazzetta, doing their morning marketing, or just seeing what there is to see. A pack-peddler whips out a silky banner of crimson, then a sea-colored one, and begins exhibiting scarves. There is a good deal of fuss about something over by Todaro's column. People stand around and discuss it, some giving one opinion, some another. There is always something to do in the Piazzetta. A storm—and then the sunshine—and then some event or other to talk about. It passes the day. The hour clangs out from the Orologio, startling up the pigeons: nine o'clock.

This Orologio or clock-tower is a fine and curious structure. It is closely shut in by the buildings on either side, but it ignores them; it was there before them. It is all gilt, blue enamel, and white marble. In the center is a great wheel with the clock-hand going round on it. Above this is the Madonna with Bambino, and on either side are square holes in which Roman numbers appear and pass by, one after the other. A digital clock; and it was fabricated and put into place in 1499. Higher up still is the obligatory Lion of St. Mark, this one in gold, on a field of blue enamel with stars. And on top of the tower is a large bronze bell fixed on a vertical axis, with life-sized bronze Moors on either side. These Moors are older than the clock itself. No one knows who made them; some obscure artisan in the Middle Ages. At the appointed time, when the mechanism in the tower below stirs and grinds, they turn with dignity and clang the bell with their large bronze hammers. The Moors are unclothed except for bronze shirts that reach only a little below their waists. Their virile members have been well polished by the hands of visitors. This is a very old clock indeed. It was made in a time when there was a good deal less fuss about clothing.

It is a curious sort of tower too, because instead of being solid at the bottom it has a great hole cut in it, a portal that leads off to the Merceria and the Rialto beyond. Out of this portal Malcolm comes. He has a gaunt and sideways look, not because he has been up since the middle of the night—he is used to going without sleep—but because he has spent the hours wandering around the streets like a lost soul, saying nothing to anyone, and careless of whether French agents or anyone else might recognize him and interfere in some way with his liberty. Let them take him—but first he must find something. He comes out into the Piazza, hesitates, and stares around him as though the open air is a phenomenon he has not encountered before. No one pays any attention to him.

After some time—he has forgotten where he is, and perhaps he has been standing by the Orologio five minutes or more—he starts into motion again and crosses the Piazzetta, around the chicken-stalls and the vendor shaking out his scarves. Past the Basilica, past the great door of the Palace, along the Broglio—anyone can walk there, now that there are no more patricians. The sunlight wavers up into the arches of the portico. It shimmers and buzzes on the stones outside. Beyond is the open water of the lagoon. The sun glints on it too, and hurts the eyes. Pushing his hat down, he directs his glance out beyond the two columns, one with the lion on top and the other supporting Todaro with his crocodile.

He sees what he has expected, and what the pictures have whispered to him in the darkest and most pitiless corners of his mind. Beyond the columns is a rough trestle of boards. The stiffening of the body is that characteristic of the drowned: bent knees, arms bent at the elbow and reaching upward. For a body in the water drowns face down, and when turned over it seems to grope upward with its stiff arms, toward the sky. Someone has laid a rug over the lower part, since the flimsy soaked linen is not decent. But the upper part must be seen. The lock of damp hair, the open mouth, are there for all to witness. *Whoever has knowledge of the name and particulars of this person, let him communicate with the Signoria.*

Malcolm turns away. There is a black sensation before his eyes. As from a great distance he hears voices.

"She's only a young one, the poverina."

"Ma! xe l'Inglesina."

He has the sensation that there is a great deal of air around him. It seems curious to him that he is still upright, since there is so much air in the universe and only a little solid ground. Yet his feet stay on it somehow. The voices around him continue to babble and plash. Why should people talk? What can they find to say? he wonders. He is unable to grasp why all these buildings have been erected to stand about in the sunshine for some reason, or why people should calmly go about their affairs in the market, earning money and spending it. He is aware of the buzz of voices, but the sense of speech he can not understand.

"Captain, you shouldn't stay here. The Franzesi are all about, and also some other reptiles who have taken their money."

"Where do you want to go, Captain?"

Malcolm: "To Jamaica."

"Take him to the Arsenal. That's the best place."

"The old lady in San Trovaso can hide him."

"Testicle-head, that's the first place they'll look."

"To San Lazzaro then, to the monks."

"To the Mendicanti."

But the general agreement is to take him to the Arsenal. They set off, the wiry caulker holding him by one elbow and another

Arsenaloto on the other side. A small crowd follows along behind. They go up a bridge and down on the other side.

The caulker turns around. "What the hell! Do we need all this throng? Why doesn't somebody run for the purple umbrella and hold it over his head? That way nobody will miss him."

The Arsenaloto: "Everybody clear out. We two will take him. Beat it now!"

The crowd trails away. There is silence. The water laps at the stones. The sun glints, glints. It hurts even through the blackness.

BEFORE THE FAÇADE OF THE

Before the façade of the Basilica the French have erected a great scaffolding of wooden beams brought over especially from Istria. On this they are dismantling and lowering the four antique Bronze Horses from the balcony. Below in the Piazzetta the crates are ready to receive them, marked "Paris. Palais du Louvre." The business of lowering the horses is an impressive feat of military engineering. A good-sized crowd has collected to watch it. The horses are protected by straw matting around their bellies, and they are suspended from timbers sticking out into the air over the Piazzetta. They descend in little jerks, inch by inch, as the tackles are paid out with care.

A smaller scaffolding has been erected to bring down the twin matching statues of Adam and Eve, a pair of bronzes made in 1575 by Antonio Rizzo for the Foscari Arch of the Palace. A French captain of engineers is in charge of the whole thing. He watches the operation with his hands on his hips, chewing his lip and now and then shouting an order. He is in a black uniform with a bicorne and boots that seem too big for him. In addition to the engineers crawling over the two scaffoldings there are other French soldiers in the Piazzetta, leaning on their long muskets with their ankles crossed, seemingly more interested in the crowd of Venetians looking on than in what is happening in front of the

Basilica. Their uniforms are ragged and nondescript: dirty red coats, buff breeches, and powder-cases hanging from soiled white straps. They wear an odd kind of hat, not seen before, with the brim on both sides turned up to the crown. They have a grim and haggard look, as though they have been through much and are pretty cynical. These are troops of the Fifth and Sixth line regiments, the garrison force for the city.

Some red coats attempt to come out of the Basilica, directly under the descending horses. The captain of engineers shouts for them to go back. They disappear and come out again another way: a troop of soldiers carrying an alabaster statue, a silver ciborium, and an ancient icon known as the Virgin of Nicopeia, which for centuries has been the victory symbol of the Venetian armies. After them stagger four more soldiers carrying the massive gold altar-screen, a masterpiece of fourteenth-century craftsmanship. All these things are set down on the pavement in front of the scaffolding.

A similar activity is taking place before the great door of the Palace. Canvases of Veronese, Canaletto, Tiepolo, Tintoretto, Carpaccio, and Bellini are being carried out into the open, also destined for the Louvre. Some of the paintings are immense. They come down the stairway like great rafts set edgewise, the men laboring like ants beneath them. Among them is the *Juno Offering Venice the Ducal Cap* of Veronese, and there are also a number of paintings of the St. Ursula cycle of Carpaccio. Outside in the Piazzetta the engineers, under the supervision of a civilian curator, are hammering together crates to hold these canvases. The Carpaccios can be packed four to a crate. The Veronese is too large, and the French stand around making calculations on scraps of paper and accusing each other of having brought out the wrong painting. The four horses, now crated, look out from the timbers at the barges waiting to receive them at the Molo.

The crowd is very interested. Some of them—those who have never been inside the Palace—have never seen all these fine things. It is an opportunity not to be missed, for those interested in the arts. The Virgin of Nicopeia goes by, looking out of her box.

Someone yells, "Take the chickens too."

There are other voices from the crowd, some of them advice of this kind, and others grumbles of indignation—although these are in low tones. The infantrymen shift their ankles and lean on their muskets the other way. The captain of engineers is getting warm and flustered in the sunshine.

No one has bothered to crate the ciborium, and it sits glinting in the sun in front of the Basilica. It is solid silver and about the size of a small child. In shape it is an enormous goblet, with a round cover and a Greek cross on top. A boy comes up to it and looks at it, from a few feet away. The French are busy with other things. The boy is wearing an old sailor's coat, and a ragged cap hanging down on one side. His face is dirty. He runs up to the ciborium, snatches it from the pavement without breaking his stride, and races off with it past the Basilica and the Palace. It is so large that he has to embrace it with his arms rather than hold it in his hands.

"Halt!"

"After him!"

"Stop or one fires!"

The boy speeds away down the Broglio, his coat flapping and his heels flying. Several of the red-coated soldiers run after him. Others kneel down, cock their muskets, and level them. There are several flat bangs. The boy falls in a sprawl, then draws his legs up. A trickle of blood appears under him. The ciborium rolls over the stones and comes to a stop. An engineer in a black uniform runs to it, dusts it off, and turns it over in his hands looking for scratches.

Around the corner in the Piazza another sort of ceremony is taking place. The newly installed Provisional Government, in collaboration with the French authorities, is erecting a Tree of Liberty to commemorate the liberation of the city from tyranny. All the prominent Jacobins of the city are present, in a tribune inscribed with the words, "Liberty Is Preserved by Obeying the Laws." The Piazza is decorated with the new colors of the democracy, red, white, and green. The grocer Zorzi, who has been named Acting President, is installed in an armchair in the tribune. Next to him is General Louis Baraguey d'Hilliers, the commander of the garrison forces. The others on the platform were until a few days ago merchants, or minor clerks of the Signoria. There are no more nobles; now there are politicians. The Nineteenth Century has begun.

First the parade. A procession with banners and music marches twice around the Piazza. There are two children carrying lighted candles and a banner inscribed, "Grow up, hope of the Father-land"; then a young plighted pair with the motto, "Democratic fecundity"; then an aged couple bearing agricultural instruments and words alluding to their advanced age. These are followed by an escort of French and Venetian soldiers, minor officials of the government, representatives of guilds, and clergy (without the Patriarch, who has declined). The whole procession stops in the center of the Piazza, where the Tree is erected. It is nothing more than an immense pole, with tricolor ribbons braided onto it by children walking about it in a circle. At the top is a Phrygian cap, the symbol of popular liberty.

Next there is the sound of flutes, and some women come out and begin prancing around the Tree in a kind of Attic dithyramb. Their costumes are odd to say the least. They caper around in view of all wearing nothing but Greek tunics, which leave one breast bare. Zorzi chews his lip. Like most grocers he is somewhat puritan-ical. General Baraguey is looking the other way.

When these Maenads are removed, and the children have wound their ribbons onto the Tree, the Citizen-President makes a speech. He congratulates his fellow citizens that the dawn of freedom is protected by the force of arms, and reminds them that established liberty brings about universal peace. Not much more can be heard; Zorzi does not have a large voice. When he is finished, a salute is fired and the band breaks into a march that nobody recognizes. Perhaps it is the *Carmagnole;* perhaps it is the *Ode to Liberty* with words by Foscolo. Following this, a fire is kindled and various objects are thrown into it: the Ducal Corno, a straw man dressed in the insignia of the patricians, and a copy of the Golden Book. Zorzi leads the assemblage in a cheer for liberty.

A shout from the background: "Viva San Marco e viva la libertà."

The French authorities decide to leave it at this. Everyone forms up into a procession again, with Zorzi and General Baraguey in the lead. The idea now is to march to the Basilica for a solemn Te Deum. But this has not been very well planned; or, as is usual when things are entrusted to armies, the one outfit has not ex-plained to the other outfit what is supposed to happen. By this time the engineers have crated all the treasures from the Basilica and the Palace. They form up and prepare to carry everything to the barges, in a long line escorted by the red-coated soldiers. But this cortege, making its wide curve off toward the Molo, collides head-on with the solemn procession of dignitaries, little children, priests in purple, guildsmen in medieval costume, citizens with banners, and geriatrics with plowshares coming from the Tree of Liberty, where the ashes of the bonfire are still smoking. A French officer, exasperated, cries the halt.

Officer: "Who the hell planned this? Back off. You with the crates, go round the other way."

Baraguey: "What is your name and regiment, sir?"

Zorzi (reasonably): "It seems to me, gentlemen . . ."

Voice: "Assassini de San Marco!"

Others: "Viva la libertà. Death to tyranny. Polenta!"

The little children (breaking hysterically into song):

> "Viva Samarco e viva le Colone!
> Viva Santa Maria de la Salute!
> Viva i soldai che fa la sentinela!
> Viva Samarco e pò Venecia bela!"

Baraguey: "What's all this?"

Officer: "Just a bunch of little patriots."

Baraguey: "It's the wrong song. Get them to singing the *Carmagnole* again."

In the afternoon General Baraguey, accompanied by M. Fontenay from the French Legation (Villetard is still too unpopular to show his face), goes off to conduct an inspection of the Arsenal. They are followed by a corporal's guard with muskets, a naval attaché, and an aide-de-camp carrying a notebook. Louis Baraguey d'Hilliers is at this time a man of thirty-three and a most capable and experienced officer. Marmont, the memoirist of the Italian campaign, has a great admiration for this witty, educated, imposing, delicate, and honorable man, who has made the French name respected even in the occupied territories. His pace is brisk and he notices everything.

Baraguey: "Something must be done about these crowds, you know. They've burned Zorzi's house."

Jean-Marie: "Give him some palace or other."

Baraguey: "That's easy to say. Look at these inscriptions. Severe penalties must be prescribed for those writing on the walls."

Still the Venetians have always written on the walls. The one that has caught the General's particular attention is a couplet.

Liberté, Egalité, Fraternité
I franzesi in carrosa e noantri e pié

The French in carriage and we on foot. But this seems to be the work of foreign agitators; "we others" is spelled in the Roman way, and besides what Venetian would care to go in a carriage? Perhaps more typical of local sentiment are the shorter ones, which indicate pro or con by whether the viva is right side up or upside down.

W san Marco

W La Libertà

M i franzesi

W me

"An egotist," comments Baraguey. "This raggle-taggle is not really dangerous, but they could be a nuisance. The trouble is that you can't use artillery. The streets are too narrow. We should knock down these houses and build some broad avenues. Like the Champs-Elysées. Then you could set up a single battery and sweep the place clean."

Jean-Marie is not really paying attention. He has felt not quite himself for several days—queer and floaty—and in a part of his mind, in a shadow at the back, there is something he does not examine. All his thoughts, in fact, seem to involve a negative particle; he who before looked so sanguinely on the bright glitter of life. The General stops to look across the water at a French battery on the Isola San Giorgio, with its muzzles pointed toward the Piazza. As soon as they stop a few Venetians begin collecting and gaze at the foreign uniforms, with the mildest air in the world. A child stares straight at Jean-Marie, with his finger in his nose. Bland and brown-eyed, without removing the finger, he says, "Viva San Marco."

Baraguey: "Those guns over there are worthless. You'd only knock down the Palace. The thing to do is to find the ringleaders and lock them up. The rest will do what we tell them."

Attaché: "Popular sentiment is in our favor."

Baraguey: "That's merde, if you'll pardon my saying so, Lieutenant. There are a few hundred on each side who hold sentiments. The rest is a great bloody mass of indolence."

Attaché: "There's a lot of shouting in the streets."

Baraguey: "So was there in Paris. Then Bonaparte came in with his artillery and blasted away down the rue St.-Honoré. That's how he became a General in Chief."

General officers, perhaps, may be permitted these candors, but they make the attaché a little nervous. He makes no comment on the swift rise of the Corsican prodigy, although he has heard other versions. They go on down the Riva, and are met by an infantry troop coming the other way, with a sweating sergeant running up and down the bridge to steer them. There is a steady tramp-tramp of boots and a clank of weapons. For some reason this is a lively and clamorous bunch. They pass, under a cloud of French words like Peste and Sacre-Bleu.

Baraguey: "Fifth of the line. Those fellows are getting a little slack."

Attaché: "Fine-looking troops."

Baraguey: "I don't care how they look, Lieutenant. They shouldn't be allowed to talk in formation. M. Fontenay, how much farther is it to your precious Arsenal?"

Jean-Marie: "Two more bridges."

Baraguey: "You have to walk everywhere in this blessed town. It wears out your legs."

Jean-Marie: "You can go by gondola."

Baraguey: "That takes too long. We're not newlyweds. Let's get on with it, inspect this place and get it over with. I've got another appointment at five."

They come at last to Rio de l'Arsenale and turn down along the quay. There are more French troops here. The great gates across the canal are locked with chains, and there are sentries at the portal.

Baraguey notices the inscription. "Lepanto, eh?"

Attaché: "That was a long time ago. Galleys are no good in the open sea anymore. Not against a ship-of-the-line."

Baraguey: "Still, we're lucky they didn't come out and blast us as we were crossing the lagoon. That was a chancy thing. I don't know why they didn't."

Attaché: "Because they're a bunch of Macaronis, that's why."

Baraguey: "You're quite a nationalist, Lieutenant. Don't forget that our beloved General in Chief is also of Italian extraction. Fontenay, where are the ships-of-the-line?"

Jean Marie isn't sure. He comes to himself with a start, in fact; he was thinking about something else. They go on through the Arsenal and find the *Bellona,* which is half fitted-out, and the *Gran San Giorgio,* which is only a hulk without masts. Across the dock are two frigates, the *Oreste* and the *Rosa Mocenigo.*

Baraguey: "Well, there are a lot of ships in here. Make a note. No vessel to leave the Arsenal, and all vessels on duty in the lagoon to be returned inside the walls. The gates to be guarded. Fontenay, where is the *Vittoria?*"

Jean Marie: "I don't know where the *Vittoria* is."

Baraguey: "You listed her in your intelligence report as one of the ships still in the Arsenal."

Jean-Marie: "I'm sorry. I just don't know where she is."

The General sighs. "Gone to join the English by this time, I imagine."

Attaché: "The English, bah!"

Baraguey: "You may say so. They have a way of losing all the battles but winning the war. Do you know we have only two ships-of-the-line in the whole damn Med?"

Attaché: "How many guns has the *Vittoria,* M. Fontenay?"

Jean-Marie: "Twenty."

Attaché: "It's either sixty-four or seventy-two."

Baraguey: "And where is Pesaro? Eh? Since you're the one who knows where everything is."

Jean-Marie: "Who? Oh. Pesaro. He was still in the city, the last I heard."

Baraguey: "I know that. The question is, where the blazes is he? He's probably the one who is inciting all this riffraff to put up signs calling us pigs."

Jean-Marie: "Thieves."

Baraguey: "Which side are you on, anyhow, M. Fontenay?"

Jean-Marie: "I beg your pardon? I'm sorry. I wasn't quite following."

Baraguey: "What else is there that we're supposed to look at? These are all shallow-water craft. Our friend the Lieutenant doesn't think they're much good for anything."

Attaché: "A mortar-ketch. That's handy."

Baraguey: "Make a note. We'll take it. There's a lot of shot and shell lying around here too. Look at that, a whole magazine full of powder. And spars. Aren't those useful, Lieutenant?"

Attaché: "I've got them down."

Baraguey: "My God, these people could have fought a war for ten years with this stuff. We can thank our stars they never came out of those gates. When I think of us all crowded on those barges—"

Attaché: "We could have handled it."

Baraguey: "How?"

Attaché: "French pluck."

Baraguey: "Merde again. You're far too sentimental, Lieutenant, to go far in your profession. You should go back in the Piazza and sing songs with the little girls. Look at these sailors standing around. They're tough enough looking characters."

Attaché: "They're Arsenal-workers."

Baraguey: "Here's another one of your spit-kits."

They have stopped on the quay exactly opposite the *Pandora*. Her spars are down on deck with the sails lashed around them rather carelessly. There is a clutter all over her decks: broken keg-ends, rusty tools, a bottle or two left by the Schiavoni. Captain Langrish is standing in the main-deck, as though in a pit, staring out at them from under his hat.

Baraguey: "What's this?"

Jean-Marie: "A galeotta. An unimportant vessel."

They turn and go on down the quay.

Baraguey: "Who's that fellow?"

Jean-Marie: "Some Dalmatian or other. The captain."

Baraguey: "Insolent."

Jean-Marie: "They're like that."

In front of the door of the Ducal Prisons, on the Riva, a good-sized mob has gathered, shouting and brandishing slogans on sticks. Zorzi is along, and a number of other prominent Jacobins. They press up to the door and begin banging on it with bottles and other objects. Some of them go off to get a long timber balk from a ship moored at the Riva. A battering-ram, that's it!

Zorzi: "No violence, citizens. Let reason prevail."

Crowd: "Free the victims of tyranny. Viva la libertà! All political prisoners to be turned loose."

Finally the governor Musobelo, looking pale, comes out with a piece of paper in his hand.

Musobelo: "According to this, I'm supposed to turn everybody over to the Provisional Government."

Crowd: "We're it."

Objects sail up through the crowd, most of them fruit and vegetables, but one a bottle which smashes against the wall. Musobelo lifts his hands, and goes away behind the door which is shut again. There is a considerable wait. Zorzi exhorts everyone to patience. He is afraid they will wreck the Prisons which he may need later for other purposes. After some time the door opens again, and Musobelo appears with a half-blind and limping old man, in ragged clothes, who peers out uncertainly at the light.

Musobelo: "All right, you're free now. These people will take care of you."

Crowd: "Where the hell's the rest?"

Musobelo: "That's all. Sometimes there's a lot, sometimes only one."

Crowd: "You lie to us, you son of a bitch, you'll be fra Marco e Todaro."

Musobelo: "Cross my heart. Look through the place yourself."

Crowd: "How about that, Citizen Zorzi?"

Zorzi: "He's an honest man. If he says there's only one, there's probably only one."

Crowd: "Death to tyrants! Tear down the Prisons!"

Zorzi: "Don't bother Citizen Musobelo. He's only doing his duty. Instead, let us solace and honor this poor victim in a fitting manner."

The old man can barely support himself. They take him under the elbows. With shouts, and little children straggling behind, they lead him to the wine-shop down the way. There they all push their way in, with some damage to the doors. Wine is called for. And something to eat for the old man! Look at him, his ribs are showing, the poverino! The waiter comes running up with liver and polenta.

Old man: "What's this? I just had my dinner."

Crowd: "Eat! eat! it's all free."

They fill his wine-glass. All the other wine-glasses are filled too, and even small children manage to obtain possession of glasses and totter off carrying them in both hands. Their noses are soon stained with red Verona.

The old man is made to tell about his suffereings. Also, they urge him to drink more and more wine.

Crowd: "Was you in the Pozzi or in the Piombi?"

Old man: "I wasn't in neither. I was in the Quattro. That's the best rooms in the place. Light and airy. They treat you well there, that you can be sure."

Crowd: "Drink up! Look, his glass is empty! Bring another bottle!"

Host: "Who's going to pay for all this, I'd like to know?"

Crowd: "Shut up, you reactionary. Do you want us to smash the place proper?"

Old man: "Old Puzo, the turnkey, him and me was good friends."

Crowd: "What did they have you in for, Grandpa?"

Old man: "I disremember. It was for something or other. It was about Anzoleta."

Crowd: "Who?"

Old man: "My niece. I screwed Anzoleta, but I didn't mean to. I thought it was somebody else."

Crowd: "That's a political crime?"

Old man: "Maybe it wasn't that. I did something or other."

They ply him with more wine, although their enthusiasm is waning now. The little children are brought up to look at him, through the crowd, and then taken away again. The old man rests himself on his elbow, with his eyes watering, from too many different things happening at once, and also from the wine.

Old man (standing up unsteadily): "Well, I thank you folks for everything."

Crowd: "Where do you want to go now, Grandpa?"

Old man: "I better go home again."

Crowd: "What? What do you mean, home?"

Old man: "To the Prisons."

Crowd: "Oh, for God's sake! Senility! The testicle-head, he doesn't know what he's saying. Simpleton! His wits have been addled by his sufferings. Take him to the Palace, we'll put him on the throne. Dress him up in the Doge's robes!"

Others: "No, to the Piazza. We'll let him make a speech."

Old man (weeping frankly now): "Take me home. They all know me there. I feel like lying down. I'm not used to this."

Crowd: "Let Zorzi decide. Where's Citizen Zorzi?"

Host: "He left, before the bill was to be paid. I expected that."

After he has seen the General safely back to his quarters in the Palazzo Pisani, Jean-Marie makes his way on foot down the Calle Larga and through the Piazza, staying under the portico to avoid the crowds. He still feels odd; little spots dance before his eyes and there is a sensation as though his feet do not quite touch the ground. He fights against this lack of gravity, setting his teeth and keeping a firm grip on the pavement. On the Riva he passes the wine-shop where the old man is being fêted, with raucous sounds punctuated by the breaking of glass. He ignores this. He goes directly to Rio de l'Arsenale and down the quay. At the portal the sentries hardly pay attention. They have seen him before and know him to be French. In any case he goes through the door in a somnambulistic state, and it would be difficult to stop him without shooting him.

It is almost nightfall now. The docks are deserted, and the Arsenaloti for the most part have gone home. He passes a large cat, which arches its back and spits at him. An old man comes out and lights a lantern at the edge of the water.

The *Pandora* is still tied up in her stagnant corner of the Bacino Novo. Jean-Marie approaches slowly. There is no one in sight. It is very quiet, except for the lapping of water and the occasional cry of a swallow fleeting overhead in the twilight. The old stones smell of moss, and there is a faint odor of the things ships are made of: sawn wood, tar, and oakum.

He stops by the improvised gangway. He has not made a sound, but presently Malcolm appears out of the tweendecks and stands looking at him.

Jean-Marie remains motionless for a long time. The two men look at each other. The light fades gradually from the air, and to take its place there comes a very ancient darkness, Νεκύων ἀμενηνὰ κάρηνα, the fleeting shadows of the Dead. Jean-Marie's eyes slowly glisten and fill. He sees only through a blur. These two small windows of the soul, catching the gleam from the lantern down the quay, shine out like tiny pictures.

Malcolm: "Well, come on then."

Jean-Marie comes on board, floating along the narrow timber as though he is hardly paying attention to what he is doing. Malcolm starts to take him by the elbow, then drops his hand awkwardly. He turns away, and Jean-Marie follows him into the tweendecks.

Malcolm: "Would you like coffee? There's nothing to make coffee. What is there? Would you like a glass of wine?"

THE CAPUCHIN STEALING ALONG THE

The Capuchin stealing along the quay of the Bacino Novo, wrapped up in a cloak with a hood to go over his head, is actually Contìn, who is not under any order of arrest but believes in being prudent. When he reaches the *Pandora* he stops and looks around. It is very dark. A hundred yards behind him the old watchman has kindled a fire of sticks and is sitting cross-legged by it. Except for that nothing can be seen. Holding the cowl shut with his hand, Contìn, who is not under any order of arrest but believes in being

In the tweendecks there are two men waiting for him. A chart is spread out on the table, held down at the corners with four bottles. The only light comes from a lantern set on the cabin floor, the kind with a candle inside used by pedestrians to find their way through the unlighted streets. This lends a conspiratorial air to the proceedings; the darkness clings like a thick fluid to the arched ribs of the galeotta on either side and to the deck-beams overhead. Jean-Marie, who is standing back in the shadows, is visible only when the gilt facings of his coat catch a spark from the light. Contìn throws back the hood and frowns into the darkness. His ferret-like manner, as he grows older, is coming to resemble that of his uncle.

Contìn: "I don't understand about your friend. I think I recognize him. Who is he exactly?"

Malcolm: "He's all right."

Contìn: "Well, it'll be your funeral if he's not, Captain."

Jean-Marie comes forward out of the shadows until the pale oval of his face is visible, with a small nervous smile playing at the corner of his mouth.

Jean-Marie: "I have the honor to be in the service of Captain Langrish."

Contìn: "If you say so."

Jean-Marie: "You're saying I'm a turncoat. Is that it?"

Contìn: "I don't even know who you are, officially. You're very elegant for a conspirator."

Malcolm: "Handsome is as handsome does."

Contìn: "Let's hope so."

Malcolm (growling): "Let's get down to business."

Contìn: "Very well, Captain."

With reluctance he turns his attention away from Jean-Marie. He looks first at the chart—of which nothing can be seen, since the lantern is still on the floor and the table is a pool of darkness—and then at Malcolm.

Contìn: "Our man will enter the Arsenal by water. I won't tell you how that is to be done, because there is no need for you to know more than you need to know. At any rate he'll be here tomorrow night, with a small entourage and a secretary."

Malcolm: "Entourage?"

Contìn: "Some persons of his household. Two or three. I don't know."

Malcolm: "I agreed to take one man."

Contìn: "Well, you can't expect him to go stealing around alone, like a thief in the night. He owes something to the dignity of his name. I don't imagine you want to cook his meals and help him on with his breeches." He pauses, as if to reflect and judge his man. "The whole thing is a risky business. Do you think you can get him out of here?"

Malcolm: "I can get him out. Alive is another matter."

Contìn: "Alive would be better. How does the weather look?"

Malcolm: "The glass is falling. It's coming up a norther."

Contìn: "I'm sure your beautiful little *Pandora* can do it. Can you arrive in Pola by morning?"

Malcolm really doesn't care for the word little. Of course she is little. A jewel is little. If a jewel were as big as a house, it would not serve. He does not have to glance at the darkened table to answer Contìn's question. The chart of the northern Adriatic is precisely engraved in his mind: the Gulf of Venice, the great dangling peninsula of Istria like a bull's heart on the other side, and Cape Promentore at the end of it.

Malcolm: "If the wind holds. It's a hundred and ten miles."

Contìn: "As long as you're well offshore by daylight. That's the main thing. There's an English squadron off the cape. You'll see them as you make your landfall."

Malcolm: "What have the English got to do with it?"

Contìn: "Pola is still in Austrian hands. It's not certain whether they would receive a Venetian vessel. It would be better to deliver him to the English. They can turn him over to the Sausage-Eaters if they want. Besides you speak English."

Malcolm: "I also speak German."

Contìn: "I bow to your erudition, Captain. How do you plan to get the *Pandora* out of the Arsenal?"

Malcolm: "There is no need for you to know more than you need to know."

Contìn smiles faintly. "Touché, Captain. Very well. I leave it to you."

He puts the cowl up over his head, stares one last time at Jean-Marie, and leaves without another word. Malcolm and Jean-Marie are left in the shadowy tweendecks.

Malcolm: "You'll need lamp-oil."

Jean-Marie: "Very well."

Malcolm: "This woman you speak about. This female. Do you think she can do it?"

Jean-Marie: "She can do it if anybody can."

After that they are silent together for a long time, each keeping to himself. They never talk about that other invisible presence— the ghost that is strung between their two souls in the darkness like a fragile thread.

The Cat comes on board in some way with the Arsenaloti. All the cats of Venice are to be reckoned with, but this is the Cat of all cats. He is huge and brindle-colored, and he glares; he stalks about the tweendecks as though the vessel and everything on it belongs to him. He is more formidable even than the cat who attacked Malcolm in Campo San Fantìn. He is skinny but long and lithe. His pelt is thick and grows in stalks, almost like the feathers of some wild bird. Two extraordinary tufts of this stuff the size of a man's hand protrude from his shoulders, and there is a kind of tassel of it on the end of his tail.

The caulker Ballerìn, the chief of the Arsenaloti, seems to be on familiar terms with this beast, saying Ciao to him when they pass and addressing him as Marco. But Marco, if that is his name, does not respond to these overtures; he stalks haughtily around the deck getting in everybody's way, and goes aft to coil about the legs of Pesaro, which makes the Senator and Procurator rather nervous. Pesaro is concealed behind a hanging blanket at the after end of the tweendecks, where he sits stiffly on the only chair on board. His entourage—that is, a footman and a valet, two secretaries not one, and a young woman who is declared to be his niece—are obliged to arrange themselves as best they can, sitting around on various boxes and crates. The Senator himself is a small rotund gentleman in a full wig, with a receding chin and delicate little woman's fingers. He wears an ornate toga with an embroidered sash. The toga is dusty, and Pesaro himself has a sulphurous smell about him, since he has been smuggled into the Arsenal concealed under bags of gunpowder in a barge. This, along with lack of sleep, has somewhat shaken his physical well-being; he is querulous but still truculent and courageous, conscious of the burden laid upon him even in adversity by his celebrated name. There are three Doges and a number of Cardinals among his ancestors, and the Senator himself has a distinguished career as a statesman and a patron of learning. It was he who in 1784 caused a balloon of the Montgolfier design to ascend from the Grand Canal, the first such occasion in Italy. A medal was even struck to commemorate this event. Now he is banished, a fugitive, under order of arrest. He stares about him uneasily.

Pesaro: "What's this cat?"

The niece: "It belongs to the ship, Caro."

Pesaro: "It seems to want to twine itself into my soul. And who is this Meregano, this foreigner, to whom I am to confide my old bones? Where are our own admirals? Where is Condulmer?"

The niece: "Gone over to the Provisional Government, Caro."

Pesaro: "May he rot in Hell. Cast off the ropes! Let's get out of here."

The secretary: "The captain wants to wait until midnight. Anyhow the gates are locked."

Pesaro: "Then how can we get out? And this captain—a foreigner—a Meregano!"

A tattered shawl of clouds, at high altitude, begins creeping across the sky from the north. The ordinary night-wind, which sifts down from the mountains after dark, stiffens and blows the chimney-smoke out to sea. There is a cold and dry chill to it, a hard edge that cuts the face and presses the clothing against the body. By midnight, when the Marangona booms, it is blowing steadily. This is the Bora.

Before the portal at the entrance to the Arsenal is a baroque statue of Neptune by Giovanni Antonio Comino. The French sentries have hung a lantern on the god's trident, so that anyone approaching the portal on foot can be seen. In the light of this lantern a red-haired woman is talking to the soldiers. First they tell her to go away; then they exchange jokes; then one of them demands a kiss as a token of international amity.

Soldiers: "Un baiser!"

Red-haired woman: "Cossa?"

Soldiers: "Un bacio!"

Red-haired woman, laughing: "Ah, un baso!"

Diverted in this pleasant game, they do not notice Jean-Marie climbing up on the gates. In any case he stays on the inside where the lamplight does not penetrate, making his way up on the chains and on the holes in the fretwork. Even when he is up on top, straddling the left-hand gate, he is not visible to the sentries at the portal, who would have to crane their necks far out around the Norwegian lion to see him.

This feat of acrobatism is not easy, first of all because he is not an athletic person, and second because he is carrying under his arm a large demijohn of lamp-oil, the size of a horse's head, wrapped in straw. He pulls the cork out of this and begins splashing it down over the timbers. The noise is hidden by the hum of the wind, but it is still an untidy process, and a good deal of the oil gets onto his hands and clothing. The gold of his coat glints from the lamplight below in the campo. There is the sound of Jean-Marie striking a light with a tinder-box. This also is inaudible in the wind.

The soldier has his kiss but he gets no more. The red-haired woman pulls away, making little squeals but still laughing. It is some time before the flames are noticed, since they are chiefly on the inside of the gates and flare only fitfully now and then through the openings in the fretwork. Then, a few moments later, the wind catches them and they burst out over the top with a roar.

There are shouts in French. The soldiers run around the lion to the point where they can see the gates, then on their way back they collide with others who have also left their posts to look at the flames leaping into the air. They curse each other. The orange light flickers on the windows of the houses across the canal. There is an alarm-bell in the tower, but first the key to the tower is missing, then when the key is found there is no rope on the clapper of the bell, then when a piece of yarn is tied to it the fire from the gate is so hot that the soldiers are driven away. The Bora is dry and feeds the flames. A company sleeping in the barracks is aroused and comes out in a straggle, some trailing their muskets and some without. These soldiers run up and down the quay, perhaps looking for buckets, but in any case shouting at each other and exchanging blame a good deal too much. No officer has yet appeared. The officers are asleep in the quarters of the governor, at the other end of the Arsenal. The young French civilian on the quay does his best to offer good advice.

Jean-Marie: "Throw water on it."

Soldiers: "Who are you anyhow? You smell like oil. Somebody hold this civilian until we check him out."

Jean-Marie: "Take care it doesn't spread to the buildings."

It is at this moment that the *Pandora*'s bow appears slowly from the corner of the Bacino Novo. She is under jib and foresail, and two of the Arsenaloti are helping her along with the sweeps. Malcolm and the other two are attempting to swing up the big main-yard. It is eighty feet long, thick as a tree in the middle but tapering away gracefully at the end like a fishpole.

Malcolm: "Sway it, man. Put your back in it."

Arsenaloti: "Pacienza, Captain. A foot at a time."

Malcolm: "Avast heaving. Somebody get on the helm. Hard starboard."

The main-yard is still only halfway up. Under it the folds of the great canvas clutter the deck so that it is difficult to see anything. She comes around into the narrow channel, with the stones almost touching her on either side, and straightens out with the gates only a hundred yards ahead of her.

With a prolonged sound of crackling the gate on the left shudders and collapses. A burning timber swings like a pendulum, and sparks are borne away on the wind. The channel, the quay, and the buildings of the Arsenal are illuminated now in a light as bright as day. The French shout for the galeotta to go back. Being soldiers, they can't understand that it is impossible for a ship to go backward, neither do they have any idea why it is coming out. She comes on slowly, the two Arsenaloti still working on the sweeps.

But the other gate, the one on the right, has not fallen. It is held by the great chain that supports it on its pivot and is fastened at the other end to the tower. The chain comes down to the gate and ends in a staple, a stout piece of blacksmithing as thick as a man's wrist. One would think that this staple would pull out of the timber which is flaming brightly and almost turned to charcoal, but somehow it clings. Malcolm stares at it and clamps his teeth.

Malcolm: "Thunderation! Way enough. Let the wind take her."

The Arsenaloti rest on the sweeps, and the *Pandora* drifts. The gate is only a pistol-shot ahead now. A slim figure in a golden coat appears, mounting hand and foot up the still unburned part of the timbers. The French yell at him to come down. The figure reaches the top, straddles it, and begins inching out toward the flames. A yellow tongue appears at the skirt of his coat and licks upward. He gets out a short sword and begins prying at the staple. The sentries are beginning to come to their senses. Two of them, at least, kneel on the stone quay and level their muskets. One musket barks, then the other. Puffs of smoke spring from the barrels.

Malcolm: "Get off! Get off, you bloody fool! Give it up!"

More French are firing now. Jean-Marie's body contracts with a jerk—twice—and then slowly opens again, as a snail does when stepped on. The French raise a great huzzah, and four or five of them rush forward. Jean-Marie's head sinks as though he were looking down to contemplate something on the water below. Then, one knee raised and his hands in his lap, he turns and falls sideways, streaming sparks. At almost the same instant the staple pulls out of the flaming timber The gate crumples and falls, with a noise of crackling wood that goes on for some time. A few scraps float on the dark water with the flames crinkling on them.

Malcolm stares out from under his hat. For a moment he too is frozen in a spell, staring at the scraps of burning timber with the fixity of some optical instrument, a telescope examining Mars. There is a buzzing sound, and the air around him blackens. In the oddness he hears something like a clock-beat: once again the Old Women have cut the thread. Inside he rages: *You bitches. God damn you! I'll have your heart's blood for this!*

Then, wrenching himself violently out of this darkness, he comes to his senses and glares round for the Arsenaloti. They too are statues, crouched along the rail with their hands fixed on the halyard.

Malcolm: "Now, you apes! Now or never! Mainsail haul! Bend to it!"

The yard goes up inch by inch. It catches the wind, and the *Pandora* stirs forward as though wakening from a sleep. There is a fuss on the quay. Some of the soldiers are reloading, others are simply staring dumbfounded at the apparition of the tall lateens gliding by in the dark, the foresail pulling and the main still half-folded like a great limp glove. A pair of the French are grappling with the red-haired woman, who manages to elude their grasp several times and then is caught again by the arm. She breaks away finally and runs down the quay, losing one of her gold slippers in the process. The *Pandora* is coming along only four feet or so from the stones. She leaps over nimbly. A French soldier jumps after her, but an Arsenaloto catches him in midair with the end of a sweep. He falls like a rag into the water.

She throws away the other slipper too, and stands barefoot on the quarter-deck looking pleased with herself. She catches sight of Malcolm, who is still glaring straight ahead over the bow.

Zulietta: "I'm Zulietta. If you had come to my chamber, you would have had a better place to sleep."

Malcolm: "Damn your eyes. It isn't a question of sleeping now. See if you can do something useful. Grab that tiller."

She takes hold of this strange object as big as an ox-yoke, uncertain what she is supposed to do with it, and Malcolm and the others put their backs into the halyard. The yard goes up the last inches to the masthead, and the sail overhead curls out and gives a great snap.

Malcolm: "Belay that. To the sheets now. Trim all. Larboard helm, you're running into the Goddam quay," he shouts at Zulietta.

Zulietta: "Which way is larboard?"

Malcolm: "Larboard, larboard! Push it *that* way. For Thunder's sake, you up forward, what are you doing with that sheet? Trim, man, trim!"

The great towers float up slowly in the darkness. Only a few flames are licking now in the scraps of charred wood along the stones. Muskets are barking on the quay; little flashes spring out like orange dots. When the towers are exactly abeam Malcolm stares downward, through the deck, through the bottom-planks and the keel, as though all these were transparent, into the water below. There is nothing. Nothing, nothing. The waters are black and there is no Spirit either above or below, only emptiness. Malcolm knows all this in an instant. But the instant is infinitely prolonged; time is stuck and seems to have difficulty getting going. As though the ship were motionless and the towers themselves were moving, they slip by in an eerie way.

Then, when she comes out from the shelter of the walls, the wind catches her and she bends to it with a quiver of rigging. The canal-banks slip by more quickly; the water gurgles and mumbles under the rail. This increased motion of the galeotta seems to excite both the Arsenaloti and the French, and matters rise to a kind of fine frenzy.

A voice: "San Marco!"

The French: "Stop her!"

Arsenaloto: "Hey, Captain. The drawbridge."

Malcolm: "Steady helm. Trim that foresheet."

There is a medley of confused noises—shots, shouts, mysterious and unidentified bumps. The Arsenaloti throw things from the deck back at the French. Carpenter's tools and scraps of wood sail through the air. At just this moment the *Pandora* shoulders into the flimsy drawbridge, splitting it and sending the halves upward and to either side. The foremast takes the brunt of it; the noise of crackling and splitting wood goes on for some time. By some miracle none of the dangling cables snag on the vessel. She is free! Out on the bowsprit the Cat assumes a rampant position, raises a clawed hand, and spits.

The French run behind along the quay. But, after only a little way, they come up against some houses built out to the edge of the canal. They can only stop and fire, those who have had the presence of mind to reload.

They bang away; although it is a slow business with flintlocks. There is no damage, except that one of the Arsenaloti takes a ball in the fleshy part of his arm. He gives a leap and flings something, probably an iron belaying-pin, back into the darkness behind.

Arsenaloto: "Zingers! They sting, those French mosquitoes."

Malcolm: "Get down. You're not much of a fighting man, are you? You stand up like a banner at a fair."

They all sprawl down on the deck, hiding behind things, as though it is a children's game. The canal-banks dissolve as if by magic, and the *Pandora* slips out into the lagoon. There are a few more pops, and some flashes along the quay. Then everything is dark behind.

Once past San Nicolò the *Pandora* is in the open sea, and here with the wind on the beam she really begins to move. She bends down and digs in her rail, knocking up lumps of spray with her bow. With the grace of a dancer, the cunning of a wrestler, she plunges into the Adriatic swell; a bucketful or two of it sloshes onto the deck and streams away aft. Ballerìn stands like a statue at the great beam of the tiller.

Malcolm: "If the rail goes in the water, bear up, or you'll overset her."

Ballerìn: "Child's play."

Malcolm: "Throw all that junk from the land overboard."

The shipyard filth—all the bottles, scraps of wood, greasy rope-ends and carpenter's shavings—goes over the side. The tangled-up rigging is coiled and hung from the pins. She is clean and shipshape now. Venice is only a lumpy line on the horizon, under the stars that pierce fiercely in the clear air of the Bora. Ballerìn steers by Orion, which is wobbling rather crazily over the bow.

It is safe now for Pesaro to come out. He emerges from the tweendecks, followed by the two secretaries, one with a notebook; the niece is seasick. Gazing at the indistinct line on the horizon, in which the tiny upright finger of the Campanile can perhaps be made out, he announces in perfervid tones that the separation is only temporary and that he will return to Venice dead or alive: "O vivo o morto ritornerò!" The thin and dramatic voice, lingering on the vowel at the end, rings out over the crash of the waves. And the Cat too, twining between his legs, seems to glare at the city behind. "O vivo o morto ritornerò!" The secretary writes it down in his notebook.

Then the Senator and Procurator gazes about him and pereceives Zulietta for the first time. The sight pleases him so much that he lapses into Venetian.

Pesaro: "Ma ciao, Bela. Who are you, my dear?"

Zulietta: "I'm a friend of the captain."

Malcolm: "Is that so? First I've heard of it."

But she only says, "So che ora che xe," a mysterious Venetian expression that means more or less, I know what I'm about. The captain can go on looking stonily out over the bow, if he wishes. She has a way of getting what she wants. That chin like the Colleoni monument! She smiles. Still, it is hard to imagine her on a sugar-plantation in Jamaica.

Pesaro: "Friend? But we are all friends here!" He glances at the secretary, who lifts an eyebrow. He tweaks her chin. It pleases him!

And your niece, Senator? But the niece is seasick, dammit! He has an eye for a well-turned leg, for a pretty face. He is not made of stone, even if he is porcine in form and has a great belly so that the secretary has to help him with his waistcoat. He is a man! If he had been Doge, instead of that grandmother Manin—

The Bora lasts all night, blowing with the confidence of a wind that comes from afar, out of the Danube Valley, from the Germanic plains and farthest-off Bohemia. And at dawn the *Pandora* comes up to her landfall; there is Cape Promentore outlined in the dim gray to the east, and a mile or so off are the shapes of the two British men-of-war, the *Bellerophon* and the *Minotaur*. Pesaro is safe now. He looks back once more into the empty west. "O vivo o morto ritornerò!" And return he does, as an Imperial Commissioner of the government of Vienna, under the Austrian occupation. For the whispers are correct, and Bonaparte, by the Treaty of Campoformio in October, confirms the secret clauses of the Armistice of Leoben. In return for certain territories in the Lowlands, Venice is delivered over to her worst enemies, the Sausage-Eaters. The white uniforms of the Uhlans are soon to appear in the Piazza, and the ring of "Prosit!" is heard under the portico of Guardi's. The Serenissima—she who held back the Turk from Europe, and ruled over Cyprus, Candia, and the Morea—has come upon sad days. Her neck is to remain under the Austrian jack-boot until 1866, when she is liberated by the Italians under Victor Emmanuel. Meanwhile, pacienza! The Austrians take what ships the French have left in the Arsenal, and they also build the railway station in 1846, and connect it to the mainland with a causeway.

Except for that nothing much is changed today. There is no wheeled traffic, and the streets ring only to footfalls and the murmur of voices. The Arsenal is intact. I often walk over there to look at it, on a winter day when nobody is about. From Ca' Muti Baglioni you set off by way of Campo San Cassan and the Rialto bridge, then go along the Merceria to the Piazza, around the wall of the Palace with the Boca de Lion in it (you can still drop in denunciations if you like, even if there are no more Inquisitors) and on down the Riva to the Rio de l'Arsenale. There are the towers. The great wooden gates have never been replaced; a few traces of blackened wood cling here and there to the stones. Now and then there is a rumble, a flatulent burp of the twentieth century, and the waterbus called Cirolare Destra goes down the rio, between the towers and right on through the Arsenal, regardless of whatever old bones may be buried in the silt below. I stand and look for a while. And then I go home. What will Ann have for dinner? Perhaps she has been to the market for a Filetto di San Pietro—it is called a John Dory fish in English—and we will have it with rice and a lemon which I will buy from the old man at the Ponte de le Do Spade. The old palace has been modernized—we have gas now, at least in our apartment, and sometimes you can coax a little hot water out of the tiny tube in the kitchen. We might complain to the landlord, but we have never been able to find out who the landlord is. That is the way with Venice. Another thing that I find slightly enigmatic, or mysterious in the innocent and corrupt way of the place, is the matter of the kinky-haired children who play in the street in front of Ca' Muti Baglioni. Moroccan? Berber? Ethiopian? Perhaps they are diplomatic children. They are charming, even though in a grave and haughty way; they never reply when I say Ciao to them. They go on playing, after glancing at me disdainfully. They are the color of coffee with milk; their eyes, like tiny miniatures, reflect the crash of surf on a tropic beach. But, I tell myself, this is impossible, because it was I who invented Mark Anthony.